OF
SHADOW
AND
MOONLIGHT

LUNA LAURIER

Of Shadow and Moonlight
Book 1 of the Shadow and Moonlight Series

Story and Art Copyright © 2022 Luna Laurier
Cover Design by Luna Laurier
Editing by Natalie Cammaratta & The Fiction Fix
Illustrations by Huangja

IDENTIFIERS

ASIN B0BLWFL6SK (eBook) | ISBN 979-8-9859723-1-3 (Paperback) |
ISBN 979-8-9859723-0-6 (Hardcover)

For business inquiries email lunalaurierbooks@gmail.com

Revised Edition: August 2023

CONTENT WARNING

While these are not all the focus, please be aware that
this series contains scenes of the following

Alcohol,
Anxiety
Assault
Blood
Chronic Illness
Death
Depression
Death Of A Child
Discussion Of Child Loss
Death In Childbirth
Emotional Violence
Fire
Hospitalization
Kidnapping
Murder
Medical Content
Mention Of Self-Harm

Mention of Rape
Misogyny
Needles
Physical Violence
Panic Attacks
Profanity
Pregnancy
Poisoning
PTSD
Reincarnation
Sexual Assault
Sexually Explicit Scenes
Smoking
Suicidal Ideation (Implied)
Terminal Illness
Torture
Violence
War

If you or anyone you know is contemplating suicide, please call the
National Suicide Prevention Lifeline at 1-800-273-TALK (8255). Please
do not struggle in silence. Your friends and family care. I care.

For the most up to date list visit lunalaurier.com

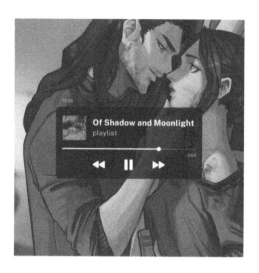

Check out the official OSAM Spotify Playlist

https://tinyurl.com/OSAM-spotify

Want to see a character sheet to see what the characters look like? Or view the pronunciation and up-to-date content warnings?

visit www.lunalaurier.com

Chat with other OSAM readers while you read.
Check out the official discord server!
General Chat, Chapter Checkpoint discussions, end of book discussions, unhinged theories, quizzes, and more!

https://discord.com/invite/9RvBn2cd3Y

To my love,
For showing me that soul mates do exist.

PROLOGUE

"What're you drawing, Cas?"

Her father peered through the doorway to find her sitting on her knees, tiny frame hunched over her art table. Papers, crayons, and pencils lay scattered across the surface in an artistically organized mess. Despite her mother having helped her clean her room only a few hours prior, her little art station looked as if it had been a mess all along. Her elbows rested on the paper she was currently fixated on, shoulders scrunched as she hovered over her work. She was focused in a way that made him question whether or not she'd heard him, which became clear with her lack of a response. When he rounded to face her, sneaking a glance, he laughed under his breath at the intense focus on her tiny, round face.

A mess of curly chestnut hair spilled over her shoulders, little eyebrows scrunched together, her tongue sticking out the side of her mouth as it did when she was wholly focused. She'd loved to draw from the moment she could grip a crayon in her hands. It wasn't long after, that, she began spending countless hours in her room, reading books with her mother at bedtime, then drawing and sketching the scenes of the pages, her dreams—anything she could imagine. At only five years of age, her drawings had grown from unrecognizable scribbles to clearer figures, and it had become easier to see what she was drawing.

She shifted, exposing her work just enough for him to catch a glimpse. His brows knitted, and he kneeled, scanning the other drawings she had. A number of sketches littered the table, of castles, large parties with lords and ladies, warriors fighting with swords. Peeking out from under her elbow, he caught sight of a drawing of a lonely woman sitting amidst the stars with long white hair, a sad expression on her face as she gazed into the dark loneliness around her.

The drawing she was currently focused on drew his attention. She wasn't finished with it, still scribbling away with her black crayon.

"It's me, Daddy."

He could almost see her in the mess of scribbles and lines. A little figure stood in the forefront, behind her stood a large, shadowed figure, the only recognizable feature, its face. The inky blackness spread out around her, nearly consuming her, and she'd worn down her black crayon until almost none remained.

"Who's that?"

"He's my dark knight," she said, adding more dark figures, ones that resembled crouched creatures on either side of them. "He protects me from the monsters."

"Monsters?"

"Yeah. We fight the monsters together to protect our kingdom." Her tiny voice was casual, as if she didn't harbor a care in the world as she spoke of this knight from her dreams. "They're scary, but he always watches my back."

He walked around the table, kneeling next to her. The face in the shadows had markings running up and down his cheeks. "What's wrong with his face?"

She sat up, her shoulders slumping. A sigh of clear annoyance escaped her lips, as if he were interrupting her creative process, and he chuckled.

"Those are tears."

His laughter faltered, brows pinching together. "Why is he crying?"

She didn't spare him a glance, and continued drawing. "He never says. Every time he appears, he gets rid of the monsters... but every time he sees me, he gets sad, because I can't stay with him."

Her hand halted against the paper for a moment, something strange settling over her, and she lifted her face to him. The look in her sweet hazel eyes made his heart clench; the pain residing within them reflecting how affected she was by this dream.

"And it makes me sad to say goodbye every time."

CHAPTER 1

Death eventually came for everyone, but it was coming for me sooner rather than later.

Doctor Robertson pushed his glasses back up his large nose as he rolled his swivel chair away from my bedside. In the years since I'd started seeing him, he'd gained weight, his hair growing more silver with each stressful year in the medical field. He stood, flipping through the pages of my extensive medical file. "All right, Cassie, that wraps it up for today. Go ahead and change, and we'll discuss it more when you're done."

I nodded, a numb sensation filling my chest at the routine that had somehow become my norm. The cold rooms of hospitals and medical offices were all too familiar now. Twenty years old, and yet his tone, the way he spoke to me during our check-ups, still somehow made me feel like a child. I parted my lips, wanting to correct his use of the full name I hated, but closed them, unable to bring myself to voice my frustrations.

My fingers tightening into fist atop the hard cushion of the medical bed I sat on, irritation flooding my chest at how much of a pushover I'd become. Why did I always bend to everyone else's wishes? Why couldn't I just speak up?

The warm smile Mom offered wasn't enough to light up her dulled hazel eyes. It was a near hollow smile, forced one too many times. Her smile was once genuine, so genuine that it had left crow's feet in the corners of her eyes, but years of stress and worry had etched themselves into her face in ways that were more prominent than those of happiness. I knew every wrinkle, knew the likely cause of it had been one health scare or another.

"I'll be right back, Cas. It's gonna be okay." Mom's voice was as soft and reassuring as she could muster, but it did little to fill the void in my chest. I'd almost gotten the courage to tell her I'd attend today's checkup on my own, but she'd been so eager for possible good news that I hadn't had the heart to turn her down.

So, once again, I'd bent.

How long before I broke, though?

The door clicked loudly as it closed behind them, echoing off the walls, and for a moment I couldn't seem to make my body move. Bland white walls surrounded me, decorated with diagrams of the heart and cardiovascular system. Various tools and odd gadgets sat on display along the counter of a nearby cabinet.

It felt... lifeless.

The things I'd experienced within the walls of a medical facility had never truly left me, and while I did my best to act like I was ok, I wasn't. I wasn't ok. I was tired. Tired of hospital trips, needles, IVs, tests. Tired of doctors' offices, the pitiful glances, the bad news, the dead ends. Tired of... the monotony of it all.

The tile was icy under my bare feet as I stood, untying the string holding the gown in place. The thin fabric slid off my shoulders and I crumpled it before tossing it back on the bed. If it were up to me, I'd never set foot in one of these places again, and live what little life I knew I had left.

Let death take me when it was ready. Nothing we tried to do would stop it. So, what was the point?

A chill ran through me, and I shivered. Warmth. I needed warmth. I grabbed my clothes from the nearby chair, and dressed myself. Hushed voices crept in from the hall, and I hurried over, pressing my ear to the faux wood door to listen in on their conversation. Doctor Robertson's reaction had already made it clear what the verdict of my checkup was, but I couldn't help but eavesdrop.

"...consulting with other physicians in our network, exploring other treatments available." He drew a breath, pausing a moment, and I could hear the faint flipping of pages. No doubt he was flipping through the pages in my thick medical file again. If only I could burn that heavy

reminder of the countless procedures and tests I'd undergone. If only burning it would erase the misery of it all.

"She's not responding favorably to the treatments we've tried so far. I'm sorry, Mrs. Hites, but we've run out of options at this point." Doctor Robertson's voice was apologetic as he spoke. I could almost imagine him rubbing the bridge of his nose between his thumb and index finger—the way he always did when he had to deliver more bad news of our failed attempts to save me. I knew he cared, yet I couldn't help but feel like a stain on his reputation.

The sadness in Mom's sigh rushed over me, leaving a tight feeling in my chest. "So, there's nothing more we can do at this point? No other therapy or treatment options?"

He didn't respond, and I knew his prolonged silence would only give Mom false hope.

"We're going to keep her on the medicine, and we'll just have to pray that it doesn't get worse. I'm going to continue looking into alternative treatments. There might be some new experimental options if you're willing." There was a moment of silence. "She probably has a few years at best. Last month's attack left more scar tissue—anymore, and she's likely to go into cardiac arrest again."

Mom's silence was painful to hear. He spoke again, discussing instructions to proceed, exercises I was allowed to continue, but my mind wouldn't latch onto the words as they blurred into ripples of an unrecognizable pool.

I turned to lean back against the door, my gaze lifting to the paneled ceiling. It felt like the walls were closing in on me, like the floor would fall out from under my feet at any moment. My knees weakened, and I slid to the floor.

No matter what we did, no matter how careful I tried to be, the damage had been done. I should probably cry at the news, but no matter what, the tears wouldn't fall. Perhaps they'd already been exhausted in my short life. The news didn't surprise me, though. No, I knew this day would come, and I cursed whatever cruel fate had sentenced me to this.

Displayed on the wall was the glowing MRI of my heart, a barely recognizable black and white mass of muscle and tissue. Next to it was an MRI of a normal heart, for reference—the two looked nothing alike. Cardiomyopathy. Whether caused by a genetic defect or by an outside source, there was something wrong with my heart. It was deteriorating, and I was dying.

After collapsing in gym class in grade school, tests had revealed scar tissue in the chambers of my heart, preventing it from functioning the way it should. They hadn't even seemed fully sure what it was exactly and had diagnosed it as a rare form of the disease. It made it more difficult to treat, let alone cure.

Curse whatever cruel fate had been placed on me. No matter how careful I was, it didn't seem to matter. Exercise didn't seem to help, diet and medical intervention seemed to have no effect, and the medications they put me on seemed to only delay the inevitable. I'd lost count of how many specialists I'd seen in my life, and every doctor I'd encountered failed to figure out why the treatments weren't working. They should have worked, should have at least bought me more time, but they never did. The only thing that was certain was my risk of heart failure had increased drastically in the last year, and none of the doctors could explain why.

It had only been a month since things took a turn for the worse. They still weren't entirely sure what it was that happened, their machines giving them strange readings, and they couldn't seem to settle on whether it was arrhythmia, a heart attack, or heart failure. By the time they got me to the hospital, though, I was already going into cardiac arrest, and in the end, I'd been left clinically dead for just over two minutes before they successfully resuscitated me. If Mom hadn't been downstairs putting groceries away when it happened, I wouldn't be here right now.

By some strange stroke of luck, I'd survived, but the damage had been done, leaving permanent scarring in my heart. That one attack had hammered the last nail into my coffin, sealing my fate once and for all.

After that, it wasn't if my heart was going to kill me.

It was *when*.

My weak heart danced beneath my skin. How I hated it. It was a curse, and I wondered what I'd done to deserve it.

The doctor's words stretched across my thoughts, winding and repeating, as if stuck in an endless loop. Maybe a few years, if I was lucky. I could almost hear Mom's heart breaking. The string of bad news and failed treatments must have been wearing her and Dad down to the bone. To know your twenty-year-old daughter would die before you... no parent should have to say goodbye to their child like that.

Peeking from beneath my sweater sleeve was a faint hairline scar across my wrist. It was a reminder of a time when I'd seen no way out, when I'd attempted to end it myself instead of letting the misery drag out. There must have been some small shred of hope for a chance at life still lingering within me, as I could never go through with it.

Who was I kidding? It was a lie that hope kept me from doing it. No, I'd been too cowardly to end it myself.

Still, the burden of my existence on my parents had weighed on my shoulders for a long while. Like every parent, they wanted to give me every opportunity they could for a long, happy life. Nothing they did, however, would change the truth.

I was going to die... before they could see me do anything with my life.

The air rushed out of me on a heavy sigh. There were so many things I'd never get the chance to experience, things most people took for granted. I thought about the possibilities, of what I could do with only a few years. A hollowness nipped at my chest. Was this the point where people started working on a bucket list? Bucket lists cost money, and I'd wasted enough of my parents' hard-earned savings as it was.

5

I pushed myself up from the tile floor as the hushed conversation in the hallway died out, and stepped back over to the bed. The cushions were uncomfortable, the paper crinkling beneath me as I sat, waiting for Mom and the doctor to return. While I knew this news was a long time coming and had expected it, it still didn't feel real.

The click of the handle turning broke my spiraling thoughts and Mom walked in with that same reassuring smile. I saw through it, but I still smiled back, feigning strength for her sake. I couldn't deny the truth staring me in the face, though.

My time was running out.

A thick blanket of darkness shrouded the sky outside my window, the orange pollution of city lights nearly blocking out the stars. I sat bundled up in my bed, but my warm blankets offered no solace. A strange restlessness had settled into my bones, and I found myself fidgeting far more than usual.

I'd somehow managed to avoid an awkward dinner with my parents. The look on Dad's face when Mom broke the news was something I'd rather not see. Did he cry? Had.. she cried?

I forced down the dread clawing its way up my throat, and focused on allowing my best friend's voice to drown out my grave reality. There wasn't much of a desire to contribute to our chat, but that never seemed to bother her, and listening to the one-sided conversation was a pleasant distraction from the weight of the afternoon.

"Oh! I got a call back from that job I applied for. They're having me start next week!" Kat chimed over the phone, and I smiled, pride swelling in my chest.

Kat, or Katarina, was my one true friend. She'd been the only one I'd stayed in touch with after switching to homeschooling, and we'd been inseparable ever since. The teachers used to call me a social butterfly when I was in grade school and losing touch with so many friends had been difficult for me, but Kat had been there, easing the transition.

"That's so cool! Maybe they'll move you up to full time once you have your nursing degree."

She hummed her excitement on the other end of the line. "That's the plan. Are you planning on getting a part-time job? I never hear you talk about it."

My mouth went dry, but I forced a smile, as if she would see through the bullshit excuse the moment it left my lips if I wasn't— regardless of the fact she couldn't even see me. "No. My parents are afraid work would distract me from my studies. They're taking care of the bills for me, so I can focus on school."

It was a lie. I'd begged to help with expenses countless times, but Dad refused every time, no matter how much I insisted. It had caused a few fights over the years. They feared it might be too much for me, but. I was so tired of being sheltered from life because of what-ifs. If I hadn't qualified for disability, I would've gone behind their backs to find some sort of way to help.

Years of near seclusion in my apartment had begun to wear on me, though, and I needed to get out somehow. Last semester, Kat gave me the idea of applying to take classes at the university she was attending. It had taken some convincing, but Mom had caved and worked her magic on Dad.

There was one little detail, though, one that left me sick to my stomach. Kat didn't know about my health condition, or that a prospective life-ending attack loomed over my shoulder at every turn—no one did, outside of my family, and my doctors.

I felt like the scum of the earth for not telling her. She, more than anyone, deserved to know, but my entire life had been filled with people treating me like a fragile piece of glass that might shatter at any moment, and I was tired of it. For once, I didn't want to be treated differently or pitied. Even if there was just one person in my life, one chance at normalcy, that was enough for me.

Despite that small reprieve, regret had crept its way into me over the years at the thought of going through my life missing out on something. What that something was, I wasn't sure, but I'd suffered enough run-ins with depression, and I refused to go down that road again. I couldn't shake the feeling, though, that there might be something waiting out there for me. At least something more than waking up another morning, wishing that I hadn't.

"You missed out on that party last night," Kat said, dragging me back to the conversation. "One guy got so wasted, he jumped off the second story into the swimming pool."

I rolled my eyes. "I'm surprised he didn't miss it."

"He almost did!"

Why would someone do that to themselves? It never made much sense to me, but then again, maybe it was truly funny in person. I was never really interested in going to the parties she did, had always avoided them. That was our relationship, though, Kat preferred parties and concerts, while I, on the other hand, preferred to be alone with a book or drawing. I'd never liked to "people".

"I met a guy," Kat said, as if she were dangling something juicy in front of me.

My chest swelled, curiosity piquing. "Well, don't leave me waiting. Tell me more."

She didn't turn down my invitation to share and proceeded with the utmost excitement.

Her stories left me curious, a part of me half-tempted to go out with her for curiosity's sake, but I always clammed up or got awkward around new people. Perhaps it was the years spent sheltered that gave me such anxiety. Kat always managed to somehow get me out of my shell, though, which probably was the best thing for me. Maybe I should try it, force myself to get out there and experience something else.

"I found out he goes to UPJ, too!"

Fall semester at the University of Pittsburgh at Johnstown started last month. While Kat was striving for a big fancy degree to go on in life and have a successful career, I didn't see the point in trying. I knew Mom still harbored hope the doctors would find some miracle treatment and I could go on to live a full life. Maybe it was this small semblance of hope that made this escape possible.

Kat continued in my ear, her excitement building. "We love the same bands, Cas. He's got tickets to see Paramore, and he offered to take me!"

Her happiness had me smiling before I realized it. Her life was on the up and up, and she didn't seem to have a single care in the world, like a bird free to sing and dance on the breeze. I didn't want to burden her with the knowledge that I may not be here with her in a few years. It was enough for me to deal with; she didn't need to suffer that heartache, too.

"Promise you'll take lots of pictures and videos," I said.

Subconsciously, I might have been a little afraid I'd lose her friendship if she learned of my situation, that she'd distance herself from me. Thinking rationally, I knew she'd never abandon me, but there was always that little flicker of fear that lingered. I didn't want to be alone in the end.

Given the sudden onset of my condition, though, the end could come without warning. No matter what I did, I'd likely die alone.

It was selfish of me to do this to her, and the guilt was a constant wound I nursed but never healed from. She was the distraction I needed, though. My parents were wonderful to me, but I wouldn't be able to keep going without Kat. Around her, I felt like a person, not a fragile piece of glass. She was the veil covering the truth I'd have to inevitably face.

Kat inhaled sharply on the other end of the phone. "We should go shopping! I need to get a new outfit for the concert."

"Didn't you just buy new clothes last month?"

"I only bought like two shirts and some jeans," she scoffed. "Besides, it's fall now! It's getting colder, and I need some cute fall clothes! Let's go to the mall tomorrow. I've got some things to do in the morning, but I can pick you up around three?"

I considered her offer, as I rolled over onto my stomach. I did have some extra money left over from this month's allowance. It wouldn't be a bad idea to get some new clothes for the semester. "I guess I don't have any plans. I can go, but only if you promise to let me go to sleep."

"Deal! I'll see you tomorrow!" The line clicked as she hung up. I couldn't help but chuckle at her and looked down at my phone to check the time.

Two in the morning. I couldn't entirely blame her, though. It wasn't like she was the one keeping me up this late. Mom always joked that I was her little night owl for as long as I could remember, but it had never been by choice. For as long as I could remember, sleep had always evaded me until the late-night hours.

Though it might have helped, I refused to take sleep aids. I never understood why, but the thought of being completely knocked out and unaware terrified me, there had been a few times when the doctors had tried to put me under for procedures... one of those times had resulted in a full blown panic attack in the office. With that option nixed, my nights were spent drawing, reading a book or staring up at the ceiling until I finally passed out in the early morning hours.

I reached up, gliding my fingers across the moon and star charms dangling above my bed like a dreamcatcher, the constellation presence somehow calming. It had always felt more natural to do things at night. Some of my best drawings and sketches had been completed in the late-night hours when I didn't have to be up the following morning. My mind just worked better under the moon's gaze.

If there was nothing to occupy my mind in the night hours, though, it tended to occupy itself. Without Kat's voice in my ear, my mind pooled with the thoughts that had fought for attention during our conversation. An unbridled drip feed of phrases and images poured into my mind—things I could have done well to forget. The doctor's voice as he discussed our dwindling options; Mom's painfully forced smile; the looks of the nurses and staff who watched me with knowing eyes as I left the office. Something twisted and coiled deep within me.

"Dammit, not now." My chest expanded as I inhaled in a desperate attempt to stave the tears that threatened to overflow, my eyes burning as I blinked. I shouldn't have gotten off the phone with Kat. I was still far too awake, and without her distraction, the day's news was smothering me.

I rolled over onto my side, looking out the window at the night sky. I tried to identify the few constellations I could see, and memories of Dad pointing them out when I was young flitted across my mind. I'd shown interest in the stars once, and Dad had latched onto it, learning everything he could about the stars and constellations, about the moon that glowed so beautifully. We used to go star gazing when I was little, used to spend weekends in the mountains identifying planets and distant galaxies. How I missed those days, when things were simpler, when I wasn't watching for death over my shoulder.

A heavy sigh of frustration left my lips, and I flicked my nails. Regret swelled in my chest. The lie that I was numb to it was beginning to fail me.

No, Cas. Don't let it get to you.

The shock seemed to be wearing off, and anxiety sparked to life in my chest, swelling and caving in all at once, building until it was a cup about to overflow. I blinked back tears of frustration, and inhaled deeply as my very soul cried out for something that wasn't there, that was missing. I recognized this feeling all too well.

Loneliness.

Why did I always feel as if a piece of me were missing, as if I were hollow and incomplete? How could I have my family, have Kat, and still feel so alone? The talk of Kat's potential new guy had my imagination running. Part of me, one I was ashamed to acknowledge, was a little jealous of her. What was it like to have that kind of relationship with someone, to feel loved in that way?

I feared I'd never have a chance to experience love.

While I'd never pursued a relationship, I'd be lying if I said I wasn't interested in one. My curiosity was very much alive, and yet my only real knowledge of men was in the books I read. Intimate, romantic, caring men who doted heavily and devotionally on their lover. The kind of love that was both emotional and physical. Passionate.

The kind of love I'd likely never experience in this brief lifetime.

Kat had tried to set me up on blind dates a few times, but I'd never gotten the courage to go through with them. Anytime a man showed interest in me there was just... something that didn't feel right, didn't belong. I could never understand it.

You're just avoiding heartbreak, Cas. Because that's all it could ever be.

My heart ached for that companionship, though. To feel loved by someone so unconditionally. To be embraced, to be touched like that. How nice it must be; maybe I could find someone who'd make me feel less alone. Someone to talk to me the way a lover would.

The hollowness in my chest only fueled the tears I held at bay, my eyes burning, and I pressed my hands to my face as if I could force them back down. It was wishful thinking to believe someone could love me.

Reality hit me like a boulder, and I cursed myself.

What was I even thinking? Regardless of whether I found someone who'd even look at me that way, would it be right of me to waste someone else's time like that? Was it fair to let them build feelings only to have them crushed? I wanted to experience love more than anything, but what would it cost them in the end?

"Shit," I sighed, realizing I'd nearly forgotten to take my nighttime dose of medicine, and I pushed myself up from my bed to head for the bathroom.

The house was quiet in the late-night hours, Mom and Dad likely already asleep next door with Dad's early morning shift at work. I reached into the medicine cabinet above my vanity to grab one of my prescription bottles. The pills rattled as I quickly dumped two of them into my palm, irritation burning in the pit of my stomach at the sight of them.

I hated being tied down to these tiny pills, left with no option but a medication that was more of a crutch than a fix. Regardless of my absolute disdain for them, they worked, relaxing my veins, thinning my blood, and helped my heart to work without too much strain. I popped them into my mouth, before downing them with a glass of water.

My eyes lifted to the mirror. I'd lost weight again; my face slender, cheeks shadowed in their faint hollowness. Some girls would probably be happy to have my thin jaw line, but it wasn't by choice. It wasn't that I was severely underweight, nevertheless; the doctors had been adamant I try to eat more. Contrary to their instruction, my medication often left me nauseous, and food was difficult to look at, let alone swallow.

Chestnut hair hung in a mess of loose curls and split ends around my face, spilling out from behind my ears and over my shoulders. I tucked it out of my face and rubbed my hazel eyes, shadowed with dark circles.

I slouched against the cabinet and slid down to my knees, trying to combat the panic creeping into me—the deafening silence dragging out the thoughts I dreaded being alone with.

I'm not ready to die.

CHAPTER 2

From the darkness, strong yet comforting arms wrapped around me pulling me back into a warm embrace. I should be terrified, and yet there was a resounding calm settling into my bones, as if my body, my very soul, knew who stood at my back. They felt like home, as if I'd belonged within them all along.

A calloused hand took my own. The gentle stroke of his thumb against my skin left an almost electric tingle in its wake, something deep within my chest stirring and tugging toward that connection. His chest pressed against my back, as if he might shield me from anything that meant to do me harm. Our bodies fit so perfectly together that I felt as if he were my other half.

I tried to speak, but my mouth wouldn't move. My thoughts echoed out into the endless abyss.

Who are you?
He didn't respond.

Do I know you?

His arms tightened, and I began to wonder if he could hear me or if the darkness had swallowed my words. I tried to turn, but my limbs wouldn't yield to my commands. His breath fell against my ear, his voice a pained whisper.

Why can't I find you, m—

The weight of my bed shifted, my world tilting off its axis, and I was ripped from the loving arms of whoever held me. Gravity pulled me into a free fall, plummeting to the earth, and I jolted awake with a gasp.

Kat's giggles snapped me out of my half-woken dream state as she bounced on the edge of my mattress. "You just gonna sleep the day away?"

"What time is it?" I groaned, rubbing my puffy eyes as sunlight leaked through my curtains. The light stung, and I winced, fighting back the urge to hiss and throw my blankets over my head.

"It's three already. I called, but you didn't answer, so I let myself in. It's a good thing you gave me a key to your house, or you'd never be on time to anything."

She wasn't wrong.

"Shit, where's my phone?" I searched through my blankets, only to realize I'd forgotten to plug it in last night. Of course, I hadn't woken to my alarm; it couldn't exactly alarm me if it was dead.

I tossed the useless phone to the side and stretched, tears kissing my lashes as I yawned. "I'm up, I'm up. Sorry. I didn't sleep well."

She took my hand before I could further protest, pulling me away from the comfortable clutches of my bed. Exhaustion clung to my bones, as if I'd tossed and turned all night, and the voice in my dream lingered in the back of my mind.

I'd had the dream before, but that's all it was. A dream. A painful reminder of the loneliness I struggled with.

Kat's coppery, curly hair bounced over her shoulders as she hopped into my swivel chair near my desk. She propped her chin on her hand as her deep-set green eyes peered through thick curled eyelashes at me. Freckles dotted her perfect nose and rosy cheeks, her lips curving into a mischievous grin as she waited for me to get ready. She was absolutely beautiful in every way.

I sifted through my closet in search of something that might at least scratch the surface of cute and stylish, so I didn't look like a cave goblin next to Kat. Eventually, I settled on a simple sweater and jeans, with my hair tied up in a messy bun, ears adorn with my favorite moon and star pendant earrings. It only took thirty minutes for me to throw on some makeup and take my medicine before I returned to my room, ready to go.

I tilted my head into my doorway to see Kat flipping through one of my books. "Come on, loser! Let's go shopping!"

She set the book aside, a coy grin curling the corners of her lips, before she jumped to her feet. I tossed my bag over my shoulder, and we headed downstairs to the living room.

My apartment wasn't anything particularly fancy. When I turned eighteen, my parents rented the other half of the two-story duplex we'd lived in since I was a child. I'd outgrown my room, and my parents felt it was only right I have my own space.

There wasn't much in terms of decoration as I lived on a limited budget. Shelves lined the walls around my couch, displaying my collection of books I'd built up over my lifetime. Books were the one thing I didn't fret about spending money on as they were one of my few outlets. Kat paused in the entryway near my art corner was.

"Oh my goodness, you made more progress on my portrait!" Kat exclaimed from where she stood before my easel.

A large pad of paper was displayed on the easel before her, donning an unfinished portrait of her I'd been working on for the last week. I'd spent countless hours in front of that old easel, sketching and drawing out intricate details of whatever I wished. It helped distract me from the thoughts plaguing my mind each night.

"There's still a lot of work left to be done before its finished," I said, heading for the door.

"It looks amazing already," she said before pulling herself away from it to follow me.

Cool October air kissed my skin as I opened the front door. Past the front porch, the street sloped downward along the mountainside. Cracked asphalt roads told the story of an old town, rich with history. Houses lined both sides of my street, squeezed tightly together with just enough room for the alleys running between them.

As I made my way down the porch steps, I looked out into the valley of the city. My home, Johnstown, was an old industrial town in Pennsylvania, famously known for a catastrophic dam failure that flooded the city, killing thousands in the late 1800s. History and age had carved its way into the very bones of the city, staining it in a way that wouldn't fade until long after I was gone.

I wished I could leave a mark like that.

Kat walked around the front of her little, green Volkswagen beetle and hopped in the driver's side as I situated myself in the passenger seat. The moment she turned the key, Paramore's "Ain't It Fun" filled the car, blaring from her radio. She reached across and turned the volume down just enough for us to hear each other.

"So, that guy Cody I was telling you about last night—"

I couldn't resist teasing her. "You mean the one you talked my ear off about for an hour?"

She brushed off my words. "Well, we were texting last night after we got off the phone, and he asked me out! Like *out*, out, not just on a date!"

"Are you really surprised? He obviously likes you enough to give you a ticket to a Paramore concert."

She went on, telling me more, and I happily listened. Hearing her talk about him on our drive fueled that selfish desire for my own relationship, but no matter how badly I wanted to, I couldn't allow myself to give into it. It would be cruel for me to want a relationship with someone, knowing how it would end, that it wouldn't just be the pain of a breakup they would endure.

Our favorite song came on the radio, and Kat perked up, her rant falling away as she reached over to turn the volume up, her voice filling the car.

I couldn't resist reflecting her wide grin as she sang, and I joined in, hoping the melody—the lyrics—might distract me from my lonely thoughts as the emptiness swelled in my chest, but it wasn't loud enough. Not enough to drown out these thoughts.

The automatic doors parted ways as we entered the mall, a blend of music and conversations echoing throughout the massive space. As we passed the security guard station, I noticed two women standing before a wall plastered with flyers of missing people. The posters filled a corkboard and spilled out along the surrounding wall until it formed a mural of faces. There were so many. Too many.

I couldn't help but overhear their conversation.

"–heard a girl went missing from our neighborhood last night."

"This city's really gone downhill," the other commented, her voice laced with disappointment. "How many have gone missing now? It feels like there's a new missing person report every week lately."

"Last I heard, it was getting closer to forty."

"Makes me terrified to live here. I heard the police still don't know what's happening, if it's human trafficking or a serial kil—"

"Cas?" Kat's voice cut across their conversation, and I blinked, realizing I'd stopped and was staring at the posters. I pulled myself away from the faces of so many lost men and women staring back at me.

I'd seen the articles in the paper, the broadcasts on the news. The victims always disappeared under mysterious circumstances, with barely any signs or evidence to get a lead. The investigators seemed to be struggling to decipher whether they were truly taken or had simply wandered off or OD'd somewhere in the woods. Often it seemed investigators didn't care to pursue it too deeply with the prevalent drug use in our city.

"Sorry, I'm coming." I hurried after her, and my eyes snagged on the nearby Starbucks booth. "Hey, I'm gonna get a chai. Do you want anything?"

"Sure!" Her eyes drifted across the open concourse, and her tone changed. "Actually, I need to go to the bathroom. Can you get me a caramel macchiato and I'll catch up with you?"

"Sounds good."

As she waltzed away, I turned to head to the booth to order our drinks, my thoughts still lingering on the disappearances as I placed our order and paid.

Could it be human trafficking? If so, how was it that the authorities could never find any evidence to give them so much as a direction to go in? How was it possible that nearly forty people had disappeared, and it not attract a higher branch of law enforcement?

"Is there a Cas, here?" I jumped when the barista called my name a second time and I hurried over to the pickup window, thanking them as I grabbed our drinks. I sipped my chai latte, feeling the warmth slip down my throat.

I turned and rounded the corner of the Starbucks booth to look for Kat. My mind wandered back to terrifying possibilities of the causes of the disappearances. A deep voice reached my ears, the smooth sound halting all thoughts, and I crashed into someone. The drinks fell from my hands, spilling all over the floor, and I collided with the tile.

Air hissed through my teeth as a splash of hot liquid burned my palm, my eyes falling to the mess before me.

"Shit, I'm so sorry," he apologized, kneeling beside me. "Are you ok?"

"Oh... I'm ok. It was an accident," I groaned as I pushed myself to my knees, shaking the drink from my hands, thankful I'd somehow managed not to get any on my clothes.

"I wasn't paying attention. I'm so sor—" My apology caught in my throat the moment I lifted my eyes to him.

His long dark hair spilled in gentle waves over his shoulders as he reached down, hand hovering as he moved to grab my spilled drink. He had the most dazzling eyes I'd ever seen, silvery gray with flecks of rich amber that burst from the center, popping against his deep olive skin. I could imagine myself drawing the lines of his face, his jawline, the dark stubble dusting his skin, bridging over his lips.

He sat frozen for a moment as our eyes met, a subtle look of shock on his face. "How—" He cleared his throat before he blinked and attempted to compose himself. "I'm so sorry, let me... Let me buy you new drinks."

There was something familiar about him, but I couldn't place it. It was then I realized he was waiting for my response. "Oh, n–no, you don't have to do that. It's ok, really. I'm... I'm a klutz. It was my fault. I should've been paying better attention."

Oh my God, why had my tongue and mouth suddenly forgotten how to string together a sentence?

The moment his hand touched mine to pull me to my feet, an electric shock shot through me, and I only became more awkward, words spilling from my lips. "Ouch! Sorry. Damn Static."

His shock melted into something humorous, and he stifled a soft laugh. Our eyes met again, and something stirred within me, my heart fluttering in my chest. It scared me at first, thinking it might be an

16

arrhythmia, but no pain came. It was so foreign, this rush of emotions and feelings.

A crooked grin tugged at his lips, amusement gleaming in those beautiful eyes as he looked down at me. "Please. It's the least I could do to make it up to you."

I hesitated but smiled. "Ok, if you insist."

His friends grabbed a bunch of napkins, and my body tensed as they knelt around us, helping to clean the mess.

"Here, let me help," I said, quickly taking some of the napkins before dropping to my knees to assist them.

A tawny hand swept in from the corner of my eye, wiping up some of the tea coating the floor. I didn't look up, but I just barely caught sight of him tilting his head to steal a glance at me. He briefly scanned my face, as if he were trying to figure out if he knew me, but I knew I'd never seen him before. Despite that, he almost seemed just as familiar.

His onyx brows furrowed, pale green eyes flickering between me and the floor when I lifted my face to look at him. I cracked an awkward half smile before my eyes fell to the damp napkin in my hand.

He lifted his head to the guy I'd bumped into. "Go ahead and get her a drink. We'll get the rest."

"Thanks, Zephyr," he responded, and I glanced between them before rising to my feet, allowing him to guide me back to the booth.

He greeted the barista with a nod of his head as she welcomed us and asked for our order. I couldn't help but watch the way he carried himself, listen to the way he spoke, the subtle accent painting his tongue.

I stiffened when he cleared his throat, and I blinked. "Sorry?"

He cracked a crooked grin. "What were your drinks?"

"Oh! Um. A venti hot chai latte with whole milk, and a venti hot caramel macchiato, extra caramel, please."

"A chai sounds good," he said, turning back to the barista. "I'll have the same thing she's getting."

My cheeks heated at the way he said it.

He paid the barista, and we stepped aside while they got to work preparing the order. Minutes ticked by in uncomfortable silence as we waited for the drinks to be remade, and I couldn't bring myself to look at him. What would I even say? My heart raced a mile a minute, and I was terrified that letting it get farther out of hand would cause problems.

"Here you go," the barista said. We stepped up to grab our drinks, and I awkwardly bumped into him as we reached for our drinks simultaneously, before we both let out a soft chuckle.

He smiled down at me. "I hope you can forgive me."

I bit back a grin. "I think I can just this once."

"Come on, man, we gotta go!" one of his friends called out to him, interrupting what I'd hoped might spark into a conversation.

He rolled his eyes and turned from me.

"Thank you," I said as he started off.

17

He glanced back at me, flashing a handsome smile. "You're very welcome. Maybe next time I buy you a tea, it'll be for us to enjoy together."

I watched from a distance as he walked away with his friends, shoving each other and laughing. The man with tawny skin, whom I'd briefly made eye contact with, gave me a hesitant glance before turning to follow after them.

The echoes of their conversation blended into the hum of the mall as I stood watching, lost in thought. I blinked, realizing I hadn't even thought to ask him his name, let alone his number.

Of course, I'd be so stupid as to space out at the first encounter with a guy I was actually interested in. I shook my head, internally scolding myself for the stupid thought. Why would I do that? Why would I start something with someone knowing how it would end?

Don't be stupid, Cas. Just forget it.

I met back up with Kat, but no matter what conversations sparked between us, I couldn't get him out of my head for the rest of the evening.

Was I crushing? No, of course not.

Maybe?

My bed creaked as I fell into it, my hair still wet from my shower, chilling my skin. Fall had arrived weeks ago, and with it came the cold temperatures signaling the swift approach of winter. I could feel the icy air seeping in through the walls, the old radiator already working to counteract it from the corner of my room.

My feet ached from the amount of walking we'd done, and by the end of the night, Kat had dragged me through almost every store, only leaving when the mall finally closed. It left me exhausted.

I let out a heavy sigh, my body drained, eyes heavy, and for the first time in a long while I thought I might actually be swept away in sleep's restful embrace. Perhaps it wouldn't be a bad idea if I started jogging again. Maybe that bit of exercise would be enough to help me sleep better. I'd enjoyed jogging, until last month's heart attack had taken me out of commission. The doctors always encouraged it, stating the exercise might help lower my blood pressure and reduce my heart rate. As long as I took it slow and built myself back up, it should be fine.

I sat up, rubbing a towel through my wet curls. Thirty Seconds to Mars lowly filled my room on from my nearby radio, but it slowly fell into a quiet hum. My thoughts drifted away, returning to the guy I'd run into at the mall. Literally. A smile crept curved my lips at the thought of it.

The details of his face, those intense eyes; they'd burned their way into my mind in a way that left me inspired. I wanted to draw him, to mark his features out in charcoal until my fingers and hands were stained with the blackness.

Was that weird?

Oh my God, what was going on with me? What was it about him that had me so hung up? He was just a guy—a beautiful guy—but just a guy! I let out a heavy sigh, my mind wandering again without my permission, but for some reason I allowed it to.

I wondered if he lived in Johnstown, or if he was from one of the surrounding cities. If only I'd gotten his name, exchanged phone numbers. Maybe I could've taken him up on his offer to go out for tea. Would that have been weird? I blinked, catching myself in the spiral before I could go further.

What are you thinking, Cas?

I groaned, eyes falling to the stars dusting the dark sky outside my window. I needed to drop the idea of a relationship. It was a cruel notion to even consider doing that to someone. Even if I didn't know his name, let alone what kind of person he was, he deserved someone who could walk through a full life at his side. That wasn't something I could offer anyone.

Even if I did meet him again, I couldn't let myself approach him.

My thoughts were interrupted as the news came across the radio station. "–for assistance in locating a twenty-two-year-old, Henry Thompson, last seen in downtown Johnstown." Panic crept over me at the mention of the name. I rose from my bed involuntarily, gravitating toward the radio as I listened, and I reached to turn the dial, raising the volume.

"Investigators are still unsure of the details surrounding his disappearance. However, the circumstances and evidence collected lead detectives to believe it may be linked to the string of missing persons cases they are investigating at this time. If anyone has any information, we ask that you please cal—" I turned the radio off, horror creeping farther into me. I knew Henry. I'd played with him in our neighborhood when we were in grade school. My skin crawled at the thought that something terrible could have happened to him—that my house was within walking distance of the very area he'd disappeared from.

What was going on in our city?

CHAPTER 3

Darkness danced around me, a hollow dark void of nothing holding onto me so tightly I feared it would never release me from its clutches. I was alone, trapped. This was where I belonged for what I allowed to happen. I would never be free of this darkness, never get to see...

I frowned at the thought. What had I done? Who was it I'd never get to see again? Who was it I longed for?

Something brushed my hand, but it was a whisper of a touch, as if the person reaching out to take my hand wasn't truly there but another world away. His voice was so soft, so warm.

Come back to me.

I lifted my gaze to the void around me. The darkness coiled around me tighter, wrapping around my feet, my hands, climbing up my legs. Claws raked at my flesh as if the darkness felt threatened that

20

someone had dared to reach out to me. My voice came out in a choked, painful whisper, the deepest sorrow welling in my chest.

I can't... I'm so sorry.

Please.

My eyes opened, pale rays of morning light spilling over me. I reached over and grabbed my phone, clicking off the obnoxious alarm I'd set for myself before tossing it back on the nightstand.

God, my dreams were getting weird.

I sat up, the cold air leaving me wanting to curl back under my warm blankets, but I resisted those urges. I had an early class, and I couldn't afford to be late.

A yawn crawled up my throat before I slugged out of bed and trudged down the hall to my bathroom to get ready. I groaned at the reflection in the mirror. At the sight of my curly hair laying in an unruly mess atop my head and around my face, showing just how badly I'd tossed and turned in my sleep. I splashed my face with cold water to wake myself up before I began my attempts to tame the near rat's nest. Ultimately, I gave up and climbed into the shower to condition it and get the knots out.

Last semester my classes were in the afternoon. I hoped all my classes would be in the afternoon again, but I'd been late to sign up and there were only morning classes available. Mornings had always been more difficult for me, what with my consistent inability to get to sleep at a decent hour. I just needed to suck it up and deal.

As I combed my fingers through my conditioned hair, I wondered the guy I met at the mall went to school here, if he was even in school to begin with. How old was he? Early twenties? He hadn't looked to be much older than me.

I blinked, snapping myself out of the spiral I'd somehow slipped into again, and I quickly finished washing my hair out.

An hour later, I grabbed my set of keys to Mom's car and hurried out the door, dressed, hair tamed and ready—peanut butter toast wedged between my lips as I slipped my coat on. Her car was old, beat up, and was probably on its last leg, but it did the job.

Should I get my own car? Probably, but with medical bills piling up, we couldn't exactly afford it, and I refused to let them buy me one. It wasn't like I went anywhere other than classes, and if I did, it was either within walking distance or with Kat.

I settled into the driver's seat and started the car, the engine shuddering to life after a few turns of the key and whines of the starter. For a moment I sat, hands on the vibrating steering wheel as I took a deep breath, and put the car in drive.

The parking lot was nearly full as I pulled in to park. Students were hurrying in every direction, and there was an energy that somehow left me uncomfortable. The air, crisp and dry, crawled over my skin as I climbed out of the car, the door creaking as I nudged it closed, and I shoved my hands into the pockets of my jacket.

Wet grass squelched under my boots as I made it to the main courtyard behind the admissions building.

"Cas!"

My head swiveled toward the musical voice, one that was all too bright and cheerful this early in the morning, and I wouldn't have expected any less of her.

Kat hurried over to me, her coppery hair bouncing with each perky step she took. It was a relief to see her face in the crowd of unfamiliar ones, but she wasn't alone.

"I've got someone I want you to meet," she said before glancing over her shoulder to the guy whose hand she held. "Cody, this is Cas."

My brows rose at the mention of the name. By the look of his palish complexion, it was clear he spent his days indoors. His eyes, so dark I thought they might be black, peered out from under his mop of dark hair. His shirt nearly hung off his lean frame, and he stood only a few inches taller than Kat and me. I could faintly hear the pump of rock music playing from an earbud stuck in one of his ears, the cord trailing down into his pocket.

"Hey," he said with a nod of his head.

"Wow, you're a real person," I said with a smile. "I was beginning to worry that she might have obsessive issues with an imaginary dream boy the way she talks about you."

Kat's cheeks flushed red at my statement, and she balked at me, to which I couldn't help but smile. Cody chuckled, glancing her way as she tried to hide her fluster. My smile almost faded at the sight of the warmth of his gaze, the subtle notion leaving some strange twisting feeling in my chest.

"Oh, Cas! I've got those notes from Environmental Sciences I forgot to give you the other day." Kat reached into her messenger bag.

All thoughts eddied from my mind as her lips parted, but no words reached my ears. Over her shoulder, I saw him, the guy from the mall, walking at the far end of the courtyard toward the library. A sense of panic and butterflies assaulted me as I tried to make it not so obvious that I was watching him. I couldn't help but stare in disbelief, though. Surely I wasn't this lucky.

Lucky? Surely you're not this cursed!

"Earth to Cas, did you hear me?" Kat waved the pieces of paper in front of my face, waking me from my daze.

I blinked, her words drawing me back to our conversation. "Sorry, what were you saying?"

Her coppery brows furrowed, and she looked back over her shoulder, Cody mimicking her as his curiosity got the better of him as well. "What are you looking at?"

"Oh, nothing important," I shrugged, taking the papers from her. "Just a guy I met at The Galleria yesterday."

She whipped back to face me, her eyes lighting up before she scanned the crowds again. "A guy? Who? I wanna see!"

I observed him as he greeted a group of students, smiling as he spoke with them, the group returning that smile before he continued past them. Kat knew a lot of people on campus, perhaps she might know him.

"The one with the long, dark hair."

Cody and Kat's gaze followed to where I pointed. When Kat's eyes found him, she frowned, and something heavy fell into the pit of my stomach. "You probably shouldn't get mixed up with them. I've heard... things."

Cody became preoccupied on his phone, chewing the inside of his lip, the conversation apparently too awkward for him,

I turned my gaze back to Kat, trying to keep myself from sounding too eager for an answer, but the words fell out of my mouth. "What things?"

I'll admit, I knew I was a little naïve, but he'd been so kind to me. He didn't seem like that bad of a person, but... maybe I was wrong. Maybe I'd avoided something by not getting his name and number.

"I've never had classes with any of them, but I've heard about them getting into fights with one of my classmates, Marcus. On campus, too. I don't think they're the kind of people you wanna get involved with."

I couldn't pull my attention away from them to spare her a glance, my mind not bothering to latch onto what she'd just shared. So, he did have classes here. Something built up in my chest, this strange tugging feeling. It was new to me, so foreign, like the gravity tethering me to the earth was instead puling me toward him. I mean, it wasn't like I was falling for the guy. He was just handsome, had a voice that was smooth as velvet, and...

Dammit, what was I doing?

No matter how much I wanted to deny it, something about him intrigued me, attracted me, and I didn't know what it was. From the way Kat described him and his friends, it was probably the same thing that should make me want to steer clear of them.

Perhaps I was the damned moth, and he was a beautiful flame that could burn me up. And perhaps that was what I was looking for— something that might drag me out of my seclusion and show me something I'd never experienced.

Kat's eyes narrowed, and I gave her a sheepish grin. "So, what were you saying about the notes?"

She didn't say anything more on the matter and snatched the notes from me before rattling off about the lesson. I didn't bother Kat about tall, dark, and handsome any further. She'd made her thoughts clear on the matter.

What if what she heard wasn't completely true, though? Rumors were rumors, and so what if he got into a fight?

I reined my thoughts back in, banishing the hope and curiosity. Kat was probably right. It would be for the best if I did as she suggested and avoided him.

For his sake.

"I didn't think I'd run into you here."

My body froze at the familiar purr of his voice from behind me. Conversations and voices flooded the dining hall as students grabbed lunch between classes, but his voice pierced through it all like a knife.

I cleared my throat, composing myself as best I could as I fumbled the aluminum foil wrapped burger I'd just grabbed from the buffet. "Oh! Hi."

He reached past me, grabbing a sandwich off the rack. "I didn't know you went here. I've never seen you around before."

There was a unique lull in his voice, like an accent different from our area, but it was subtle. It was beautiful, but I couldn't place exactly where it could be from. His words processed in my mind, and I pulled myself out of my trance, my response spilling out of my mouth. "This is actually my second semester here. You probably never saw me because I didn't have many classes, just a few afternoon classes. It's kind of complicated."

Oh, my God. Why was I rambling?

He smiled, seeming to notice my obvious fluster, and I averted my gaze, my face hot.

"Second semester," he echoed, as if he were letting that information absorb. "Have you settled on a major yet?"

That wasn't a strange question, but it was one I didn't really have an answer for. "Um. I haven't exactly settled on one yet." He moved along the buffet, and for some reason, I found myself gravitating alongside him. "Art probably."

He hummed in acknowledgement, and I wondered what he thought of that. Was he thinking it was unrealistic? Many people tended to think art could never lead to a successful—

"That's cool. I don't have an artistic bone in my body, couldn't draw to save my life," he said with a soft smile as he held the door open for me, guiding me out into the courtyard. "Maybe one day you'll be selling pieces for billions of dollars. You'll have to promise not to forget us little people when you take off, though."

I stepped through the threshold, feeling oddly warm at the way he said that, and I realized my lips had curved into a soft smile.

He's just sweet talking you, Cas. Don't let it go to your head.

"Shit, Damien, why you holdin' out on us? You gonna share or what?" My eyes shot up to find a tall blond guy calling out to us from where he sat on the lawn nearby. Others sat with him, all eyes on us—the same group of guys that had been with him at the mall.

He groaned, his hand coming over his eyes as he rubbed his temples. "Ignore them, they're a bunch of jerks."

I chuckled, my free hand fidgeting with the hem of my sleeve.

"You probably figured it out already, but I'm Damien." His eyes softened as he looked down at me, a charmingly crooked grin tugging at the corner of his lips. That feeling in my chest grew, rising until it pressed into the base of my throat, my heart fluttering in that way it had in his presence before.

"Damien. Oh, it's—uh, it's nice to meet you." I stumbled over my words, and he laughed softly again, a low smooth sound that sent my heart back into that chaotic, scary dance.

Just a guy, Cas, just a guy.

Just a guy or not, I mentally apologized to Kat, for I couldn't help but ignore her warning at this point.

My alarm went off on my phone, reminding me of my upcoming class starting in the next fifteen minutes. Dammit. I didn't want to go to class yet. My shoulders slumped I turned off the alarm, shoving my phone back into my pocket.

"You got somewhere to be?"

"Yeah, unfortunately. My next class starts in a bit," I groaned, unable to smother the sour expression on my face, and I turned to leave. "I've got to go, sorry."

"Wait, what's your name?" he asked, his hand taking hold of my wrist to stop me. My heart leapt at the contact, my thoughts scattering.

I drew a deep breath and turned back to him. "My name's Cassie. Most people call me Cas. You can call me whatever, though."

Real smooth.

My cheeks flared, and I prayed my embarrassment wasn't too obvious.

"Cas," he repeated with a smile on his face, almost as if he liked the sound of it. "Well then, it was nice to meet you, Cas."

"Cas! What are you doing? We're gonna be late, come on!" Kat's voice dragged me down out of the clouds, and I looked over to where she stood across the lawn, giving me an incredulous look. Shit, I needed to come back to reality, or I was going to be late.

"I won't make you late," Damien said, offering me a smile. "Maybe, if I'm lucky, I'll see you around campus?"

"Maybe," I replied, smiling over my shoulder before hurrying over to Kat.

I watched him retreat to his friends. A snicker bubbled up my throat and I had to stifle it as the blond said something, and Damien swiped at his head but missed when he ducked out of his reach. I took a hasty bite of my burger, which I'd barely touched, and fell into step with Kat, who gave me a disapproving look.

I shrugged my shoulders, throwing her an 'innocent' grin. "What? Don't look at me like that."

"Just... please try to be careful around those guys. You're too innocent to get tied up with bad boys."

I rolled my eyes at Kat. "Ok, Mom."

She'd been in my ear off and on over the last few hours, despite the fact we were in the library studying. Of course, barely any studying had occurred with her trying to talk me out of getting involved. She'd offered to introduce me to other "better" guys on campus if I wanted to go on a date, but I'd told her countless times that it wasn't like that.

Because it wasn't.

It couldn't be...

Kat gathered her books, as our study session came to a close. She turned to me suddenly, her books pressed against her chest. "If you're gonna talk to him, please Cas, just be careful. If you go somewhere with them, tell me where you're going."

I tilted my head to her, giving her a mischievous grin. "I promise."

She shook her head at me but smiled. "I've got to get to the store to get my scrubs before they close. I'll call you when I get home."

"Ok, talk to you then," I said, watching her hurry off toward the entrance of the library.

My smile faded as she disappeared, and a sense of insecurity crept over me in the absence of her presence as I sat there, alone. What was I even doing here anymore? Was there a point to all of this, forcing myself out of the house to mingle with people I didn't care to know? I sighed, gathering my books and returning any extras we'd used to where they belonged.

In the distant part of the valley, the sun was setting over the mountain ridges as I stepped out of the library and onto the balcony. Whoever was responsible for the disappearances was still on the loose, and I didn't want to risk lingering too long and being stuck out after dark where I might end up on that wall of missing faces. Clutching my bag, I headed down the stairs, eager to get home.

"Hey girly, where you off to?"

I froze, twisting around to find the tall blond friend of Damien's towering behind me a few steps up. I hadn't heard him approach, and nearly fell the rest of the way down the stairs at the power of his presence.

His sharp face tilted to the side as his steel eyes passed over me. His blond hair was cut tight along the sides of his skull fading into longer loose locks that were swept back out of his eyes. A smug grin curved his lips, but the tone in which he spoke left me uneasy.

Behind him appeared two more familiar faces. One of them lingered at the top of the stairs, his hands shoved into the pockets of his jacket. His pale green eyes almost glowed against his tawny skin. I recognized him immediately from the mall; Damien had called him Zephyr.

Our interaction had been brief, awkward, but brief, and I still couldn't quite figure out where I might have seen him before. While I didn't think I had, something gnawed in the back of my mind. Perhaps I'd seen him somewhere around campus and never paid any mind to it.

The other guy, shorter, with jaw length, dirty blond hair that was tied back in a half knot, walked up. He lowered himself to sit atop the ledge of the wall beside the stairs, his unreadable gaze settling on me in quiet observation.

"Hi," I said nervously.

The tall blond before me continued to stare down at me. "Seems you've taken a liking to our guy, Damien. You wanna talk about it?" The smug grin faded from his face, his tone intimidating, or maybe that was just how he sounded because everything about him was intimidating. The way his hooded eyes locked onto me nearly made me step back again, my eyes falling to the stairway behind me.

I whipped back to look up at him, and nearly missed Zephyr's body stiffen at the top of the stairs, as if he were ready to move. He remained in place, though, slipping his fist back into his pocket, and I frowned.

"Barrett, you know Damien's gonna be pissed that you're pickin' on her. You should stop." I lifted my eyes as I saw another member of their group appear. He pulled his hood down, his curly black hair falling free, his black eyes locked on Barrett. His face... I knew him from somewhere. Maybe from one of my classes?

Barrett glanced back over his shoulder, that smug grin returning to his face. "Oh, come on, Cole. It's just a little fun, no harm."

"Doesn't matter. You should leave her alone."

There was a moment of silence, but Barrett rolled his eyes and turned back to look down at me, opening his mouth again to speak, and I braced myself, ready to face whatever he had in store. My hands balled into fists at my side, something welling in my chest, something almost like... confidence?

"Knock it off, Barrett." Damien's voice, full of warning, came from the top of the stairs behind them. He stepped down toward us, eyes set on Barrett.

Cole shoved his hands in his pocket, a smug look on his face as he hummed. "Told ya so..."

Barrett clicked his teeth, and his entire demeanor changed, the intimidation and cruelty slipping away. "Awe, man, you know I'm just havin' some fun with her."

27

"Go have fun with someone else," Damien said, stepping between us. I swallowed, wondering if I should remain standing at Damien's back, or if I should take this chance to continue toward my car.

Barrett's eyes met mine over Damien's shoulder, and for a moment, I caught a hint of confliction within them. His brows furrowed, his tongue pressing into his cheek as he drew a deep almost frustrated breath.

"Back off, Barrett," Damien warned again. "Last warning."

"Whatever man, damn. You always gotta ruin the fun." Barrett huffed an annoyed breath and shoved past us and down the stairs.

The shorter blond on the ledge leapt down from the wall, with fluid grace. I inhaled sharply, but he landed smoothly on the sidewalk below. Zephyr's hesitant gaze briefly met mine as he followed. I watched as they disappeared down the sidewalk, muttering amongst themselves as they left Damien and I on the stairway. I let out a sigh of relief once they were gone, irritation rising in my chest. What the hell was that about?

Cole walked down the stairs past us, and Damien reached out to grab his arm to stop him. "Thanks for stepping in."

He shrugged casually as he continued walking, brushing it off. "Don't mention it."

Damien turned back to me. "Sorry about that. They're really not bad once you get to know them." He paused, a low laugh slipping from his throat. "Actually, I take that back. They're total menaces."

His smile quickly faded when he noticed I hadn't joined in his humor. "I'm sorry, I shouldn't be laughing."

"No, it's ok, really. It just caught me off guard is all," I said, trying to downplay just how much it had unnerved me. "I'm awkward around people, if that wasn't obvious already."

His warm eyes settled on me again, what almost looked like a soft smile tugging at one corner of his lips. I blinked, averting my gaze. Stop staring you idiot, geez.

"Did your friend leave already?" he asked, looking around for Kat in the clearing.

"Oh, yeah. Kat had to go get some new scrubs for work." I nodded toward the parking lot in the distance, and we began to walk that way. "So, his name's Barrett?"

Damien nodded. "Yeah. He's always enjoyed getting under people's skin. He can be a real fucking prick sometimes, but he's really better once you get to know him."

"I can see that," I said, huffing an uneasy laugh. "I'll bet you guys get into a lot of trouble."

A devious grin lifted the corner of his mouth. "What if we do?"

An odd thrill ran through me. Was I ok with that? Fuck, maybe I was. Maybe that was what was drawing me to him, the thrill of something exciting, something different. I shouldn't want this, should be avoiding him, and yet my soul seemed to come alive when I was around him. For years I'd lived my life just going through the motions... but was that truly living? I'd avoided trouble, and any signs of danger for fear of what it would cost me. There was no changing what was coming for me... so why avoid it any longer?

"There's no turning back now, I guess. Might as well join in, right?"

His crooked grin grew at that statement. "I have a feeling you could make even Barrett bite his tongue once you came out of that shell of yours."

Was he delusional? "I doubt that. Did you see the size difference? The guy's a freaking skyscraper compared to me. What is he, seven feet tall? He looks like he could throw me across the courtyard."

Damien scoffed. "Don't inflate his ego more than it already is. The man's maybe a few inches past six, but don't let that intimidate you. If he ever shows his ass to you again, just tell him there's a spider on his shoulder or something."

I tried to fight the smile creeping across my face. "You're kidding."

"Nope," Damien said with a huff of a laugh. "They make his skin crawl; he fucking hates them."

I bit my lip, trying to imagine someone as tall and intimidating as Barrett being afraid of something as small as a spider.

"One time, I swear I thought I heard him squeal when he ran into a mess of webs while we were out hunting dar—"

I glanced back at him as the words halted on his tongue, and he blinked, his brows furrowing as if he'd said too much. He cleared his throat, and I frowned, wondering what he was about to say. "Anyway, did you go to high school here in Johnstown? Or did you move here for the university?"

I hesitated at his question, at the avoidance, but I didn't pry, despite the questions welling in my throat.

Oh. well, I've been homeschooled most of my life because of a heart condition that I'm probably going to die from in the next few years, and I wanted to get some life experiences before I croaked. So, I decided to go to college.

Yeah, right. That would have been a really interesting conversation. I might as well pour my heart out about how lonely I've felt over the last several years. He'd probably even love hearing about the strange dreams I'd been having lately as well.

"I was actually homeschooled here most of my life, so I didn't go to any of the schools in town." Yeah, that sufficed.

"Ah, that's got to be cool," he said, gaze slipping from me as he surveyed the nearly empty courtyard around us. "You didn't miss out on anything, trust me."

That statement hurt more than he could have known. If only he knew how much I wished I could attend school with other kids my age. How badly I wanted to just be normal for once.

Despite the disappointment his words sparked, I couldn't deny the warmth spreading through my chest at how easy it felt to hold a conversation with him. Aside from Kat, I'd never felt so comfortable talking with someone, let alone someone I barely knew. Yet, here I was, longing for the conversation to never end.

He turned to me, something shifting in the air as a strange sensation skittered over my skin and I shivered. "Again, I'm sorry about Barrett and the guys. He just likes to push buttons, especially when it comes to women. You'll learn it the longer you know him. He's all talk. Don't let him scare you."

"I guess I can give him one more chance," I said with a smile.

Damien's mouth parted to respond, but his phone went off in his pocket. He grabbed it and lifted it to his ear. "What is it?"

The calm, soft expression on his face melted away, hardening in a way that knotted up my stomach. "All right... All right, yeah, I'm on my way." The phone beeped as he hung up. "I'm sorry, I've got to go. I'll see you tomorrow, though, right?"

"Yeah, I'll be here tomorrow. I've got a couple of classes. Not going anywhere, I promise."

"I look forward to it, then." He smiled and turned, leaving me alone on the sidewalk near the parking lot.

A rush of emotions hit me, and I had to remember exactly how to breathe. Had that just happened? What were the chances that I'd run into him again?

Surely, what Kat heard about Damien couldn't be true. He'd been so kind to me. There was no way he could be the person the rumors made him out to be. Just because he got into a few fights didn't make him a bad person. I'd have believed the rumors about Barrett, but Damien... there was something about him that was different. And fuck it if that made me naïve, I didn't care. There was something about his presence that brought something to life within me, and I was desperate for the thrill, for the change.

I couldn't explain it, but something within me kept drawing back to him, to them. There had been so many instances in the past where I'd met new people and struggled to connect with them, and yet for some reason I didn't struggle in that way with Damien. I couldn't understand why. Being around him felt almost as it did when I was with Kat. I wanted to get to know him, to laugh with him,. I should probably be scared of Barrett what the way he'd acted, and yet... I wasn't. I climbed into my car to head home, almost excited to return to campus for the first time in a long while.

Tomorrow couldn't come fast enough.

CHAPTER 4

Morning came too fast.

I trudged through the campus in a daze. My eyes were heavy, and I'd made a poor attempt to hide the dark circles with copious amounts of concealer and foundation.

It wasn't enough, though.

I'd lost track of time working on my drawing of Kat the night before. It hadn't been until close to four in the morning that I'd pulled away from my easel to stretch and seen the clock. To make matters worse, I slept through my alarm. Needless to say, this morning had been a rush out the door, only for me to have to go back inside because I'd nearly forgotten to take my medicine.

God, I couldn't believe I'd almost left without taking it. What was wrong with me? I didn't make these kinds of mistakes, didn't miss doses, and now I'd been late twice. I couldn't afford to make another mistake. Not again.

I cringed as I slowly cracked the door open to my first class, catching sight of Kat at the far end of the room, already working on today's project. She gave me a weak smile and waved.

"Ah, Miss Hites, glad you could finally join us," the professor said from his desk, and I offered him a guilty smile.

"Sorry, something came up," I said, and hurried to our table.

"Is everything ok?" Kat whispered as I slumped into my seat, letting out a sigh of relief.

"Everything's great, I just didn't wake up to my alarm," I said, forcing a smile. "Now, what exciting scientific discovery did I miss?"

Kat let out a huffed laugh as she rolled her eyes. "You didn't miss much. I don't understand why we're having to learn about how the mitochondria are the powerhouse of the cell. I already learned all this stuff back in high school."

"But that's what makes you such a great lab partner," I whispered as she passed over the microscope, which I wasted no time in lowering to inspect whatever slides we were looking at today. "If you weren't here to give me all the answers, I'd fail."

"Happy to help," she deadpanned, and I snickered.

Environmental Sciences crawled by at a snail's pace, dragging out for what felt like forever, until my stomach was howling. Sadly, there was no time in between classes to grab a bite to eat, so I had to suffer through the next hour and a half.

Normally I would be excited to be in art studies, but I felt uneasy, restless, my knee bouncing as I examined the pad of paper before me. I glanced over my shoulder for the third time, catching a glimpse of Cole—the one who'd stood up to Barrett in my defense the day before—sitting at the opposite end of the classroom, deep in his own work. I hadn't realize we shared a class together, didn't peg him for someone interested in art, but then again, maybe I shouldn't judge a book by its cover.

"Working with charcoal again, Cas?" Professor Ines asked as she leaned in to glimpse my work, and I stiffened as her words drew my attention from Cole.

"Y-yeah," I managed to get out, my skin crawling as she peered over my shoulder. I hated when people watched me draw. It always felt as if they were silently judging every move I made, and I couldn't help but feel like I needed to tread carefully, lest I make some wrong move for them to tear apart.

She inspected the drawing before me, lifting her hand to her chin. "Can you explain this piece to me? Is it inspired by anything?"

I bit my lip, hesitant to talk about it. My gaze drifted over the mass of black charcoal nearly engulfing the massive page in its entirety. A woman stood in the center, her body framed from the waist up, the angle at which she stood almost fully profile. Her hands were held out, palms up, but her eyes were downcast. Tears marking her cheeks, her dark hair dancing around her in the turbulent whirlwind of the dark shroud holding her within its clutches. I couldn't help but feel like I'd gotten the hair color wrong, that it should be far lighter, perhaps silver would have stood out better. Darkness curled and wrapped around her as it bound her to it, fighting to hold her prisoner, and long dark claws gripped her body, threatening to pull her under. From the depthless darkness behind her were a pair of strong arms made almost entire of shadows, reaching around from her back to cup the back of her outstretched hands. A subtle, reassuring comfort, an offer of solace in her imprisonment.

"It's a dream I've been having," I said, and wondered why I'd felt the need to mention it.

"I like the way you've used the charcoal to depict the shadows while not losing the subject within it, you can clearly see her hair. This portrait has an interesting story to tell. The way her body language reads, it almost seems like she's becoming one with the darkness surrounding her," she said, her soft blue eyes passing over the portrait. "Is this you?"

I inspected the features of the woman in the portrait more closely. It wasn't done intentionally, but it did resemble me in a way. "I'm not sure."

She leaned in over my shoulder to get a closer look. "I see there's another pair of hands, different from the claws."

"Yeah, in my dream it's as if there's someone there in the darkness, reaching out."

"Our dreams have a strange way of pulling things from our subconscious," she said, glancing at me. "Sometimes we find ourselves in dark places and need someone to offer a hand to pull us out. Perhaps these dreams are your mind's way of trying to tell you something."

I didn't respond, already regretting that I'd even mentioned the dream. Mentally, I prepared myself for her to offer counseling or an ear to listen. I'd ended up in the counselor's office a time or two in grade school for some of the drawings I'd done as a child; the school fearing some of them were too dark. That had been a fun time.

"I'll leave you to it then, Cas. I look forward to seeing it in its completed form."

"Thank you," I said with relief, and returned my focus to it as she strolled over to another student. My eyes drifted over the hands, and my mind wandered to Damien's hands, to that brief moment where we'd bumped into one another at the mall.

I shook my head, banishing the thought that I might be conjuring some stupid fantasy in my mind. Despite the urge to get my thoughts elsewhere, I couldn't help but linger on Professor Ines' words. Was that what these dreams were about? Was it not enough that I felt lonely when I was awake? Now my dreams had to remind me how utterly alone I was?

"Ok, everyone, that's it for today," Professor Ines said with a warm smile, and the sound of chairs sliding across the tile echoed throughout the room as everyone began packing up. She raised her voice, continuing to give instructions. "Don't forget, these pieces are due next week for the gallery competition. So, try to work on them in your own time if you feel like classroom sessions won't give you enough time."

I packed up my sticks of charcoal, placing them in my bag as I started breaking down my station. As I continued to pack my supplies, I glanced over my shoulder to see Cole shutting down his station, catching him looking my way as well. For a moment, something like guilt flitted across his face before he averted his gaze, continuing to pack his things in silence. Maybe he felt bad for what had happened the day before with Barrett. I absentmindedly reached for my pad of paper as a group of students passed by, so heavily focused on their conversation that one of them kicked the leg of my easel, tipping it over.

"Shit," I gasped as the drawing pad and easel fell into a mess of wooden limbs and folded papers.

I let out something of a growl of frustration as the group continued on, not taking the time to notice that they may have just ruined my work. I scrambled, reaching for the flipped pad of paper, but a tawny hand reached out first, turning it over carefully.

My eyes shot up, and I found myself face to face with Cole.

He didn't say anything at first as he focused on cautiously unfurling the folded pages of the pad, checking the drawing. "It doesn't look too bad."

I deflated at the sight of the crease marring the center of the portrait, the slight tear on the edge, and a groan of frustration slipped from my throat.

He glanced at me nervously. "Maybe if you lay it out with some books on top, it'll flatten out."

"Maybe," I said, taking the closed pad of paper as he offered it to me.

"It looks good so far, way better than mine."

I hesitated a moment, but ask, "Mind if I take a look?"

His eyes lifted to mine, and for the briefest moment I caught the hesitation in them, and... something else, but it disappeared too quickly for me to try to figure out what it was.

He reached into his backpack, pulling out a pad of paper that was far smaller than my own and flipped it open before offering it to me. I took it, my gaze passing over the sketch. His style was so different from my own, using graphite and colored pencil, but his skill with the color pencil was stunning. It was a portrait of an old woman, her warm face framed by silver curls, a few coppery strands catching the light. Deep-set wrinkles around her mouth and at the edges of her eyes told stories of years of laughter and warmth she'd experienced in her life. Happiness she likely gifted to those around her.

"Is this your grandma?" I asked, glancing at him. They didn't look like they were related, but you never knew, and it was obvious he knew the person for the smile she'd graced him with.

"Something like that," he hedged.

"It looks amazing," I said, losing myself in the detail of her green eyes, her spirit reflected in each facet of her iris'. "Her eyes are especially beautiful; you did a good job on the light and how it reflects on her soul. The saying that the eyes are a gateway to the soul really resonates in this piece."

His lip twitched into an almost smile, and I realized how weird that sounded.

I clamped my mouth shut and closed his notebook before hastily passing it back to him. "Sorry, here."

He offered me an apologetic smile. "Don't be. I'm glad you like it. I never thought about it like that. Maybe that's what I'll call it. 'Window to the Soul'."

My nerves eased, and I nodded to his drawing. "I think you've got a good shot in the competition."

"Thanks. I think you'll have me beat, though, your drawing looks intense and yet calming in a strange way. Way deeper than a simple portrait."

"If you're looking to outdo me in self-sabotage and degradation, I think I'll have you beat."

He laughed, and I couldn't fight the snicker bubbling in my throat.

I glanced back down at my drawing, eyes settling on the damage. "I'll see if I can fix this, but... I might just start it over."

"Don't—" he started, and my brows rose.

He let out a sigh, an awkward grin forming on his face as he ran his hand through his mess of black curls. "What I mean is... maybe the damage adds character. Maybe you could add more creases or wrinkles to represent the imperfections and damage she might be hiding in her darkness."

I lingered on that thought, and I had to admit I almost liked it. It wasn't something I'd normally think about, but maybe this once it would be fitting.

"It's just a thought. You don't have to do it, of course."

"That's actually not a bad idea," I said, smiling at him.

His brows rose, and a grin lit up his face, as if he'd been seeking my approval for some strange reason. My stomach growled and my cheeks heated.

He let out a huff of a laugh and slid his sketchbook into his bag. "I won't keep you from lunch. See you around."

I nodded sheepishly as he gave a dip of his head and rose to file out of the room among the other students. My eyes fell to the drawing in my lap, as I mulled over the idea he'd given me, and I decided to take a chance on it as I closed the pad of paper and slid it into my portfolio bag.

A little while later, I walked out of the student hall, half devoured cheeseburger in hand, and I caught myself scanning the courtyard for Damien. A war raged within me, my desire to see him colliding with the guilt of what it would mean for him in the end—the possibility of an attack this morning giving me a major dose of reality. I internally scolded myself for even considering talking to him again despite what I'd felt the day before. What was wrong with me? I shouldn't get involved with anyone, even as friends. It wasn't right. I was already lying to one friend, now two thanks to Cody. I didn't need another.

I shook my head, pulling myself from the thought, and made my way down the sidewalk toward my usual spot in the center of campus.

This is how it should be, Cas. It's better this way. This way, as few people get hurt as possible.

As I emerged from the tree-lined pathway, my ears perked up at the sound of Damien joking with his friends. My chest swelled at the chance to talk to him again, to see the smile of his that made me feel warm and alive. Fuck, why was I caving so easily? Why was it that I seemed to lose my conviction at the mere presence of him? Before I could turn and force myself to ignore them. I found their group hanging out along the wall in front of the library.

Everything in me wanted to join them, to ignore that voice telling me I shouldn't get involved. I hesitated, something in my chest tugging me toward them, but I shoved it down, continuing toward the place on the lawn where Kat and I sat between classes. My steps halted, though, as I found our spot empty, Kat and Cody nowhere to be seen.

I frowned. She'd mentioned nothing about having lunch elsewhere. I grabbed my phone to call her, only to see a text notification.

> Last class cancelled for the day. Cody and I are going to see a movie! Text me when your classes are over! Kisses!

My fingers tapped away at my screen as I responded to her text before I shoved my phone into my pocket. Should I go study in the student hall to kill some time before my next class? It would likely be the smarter option. Maybe I could get a jumpstart on tonight's assignments.

I took a bite of my burger, standing awkwardly in the open expanse of the campus courtyard. A sigh escaped my lips, and I slumped, turning to walk toward the study hall.

"Cas!"

I glanced over my shoulder to find Damien waving me down from where he sat with his friends.

Just pretend you don't see him. Walk away.

Before I could stop myself, I waved back, and internally cursed myself for not being strong enough to shut him out.

He had quite a few people sitting with him, four of which I'd met the day before on the stairs in front of the library. They all quieted their conversations the moment I drew near, and I resisted the urge to retreat. When some of their gazes settled on me, my stomach twisted as I wondered just what they might be thinking—what judgements they might have about me. One familiar face seemed welcoming, though, and I mirrored Cole's smile with one of my own.

My gaze snagged on Barrett, who was kicked back in the grass behind Damien. His steel eyes leveled on me. I found my smile fading, and I resisted the urge fidget with the hem of my sweater sleeve, if only to show I wasn't going to cower to him as I had yesterday.

Damien looked behind me to where I usually sat. "Your friend not here today? Her name was Kat, right?"

"Yeah, her last class cancelled for the day. She and her boyfriend left early to go see a movie," I explained, shrugging my shoulders. "I've still got one more class for the day, though, so I'm stuck here."

"That sucks. How much time until your next class?"

"Almost thirty minutes."

"Why don't you hang out with us?" Cole asked tentatively, and my gaze flickered to him.

"Yeah. We can keep you company," The shorter blond one from the day before, added from where he lounged nearby, kicked back against a tree as he bounced a rubber ball off the wall.

"I'm gonna tell Anna you offered to keep another female company," Barrett teased.

He fumbled his ball before sitting up to chuck it at Barrett. "You know it's not like that."

Barrett huffed a laugh as he caught it and tossed it back at him without missing a beat. My mind narrowed in on the word he used. Female? I shook it off as I realized they had offered for me to hang out with them.

Don't do it, just tell them you have plans, or need to study.

I couldn't, though, couldn't pull myself past the desires brimming inside me, threatening to burst.

"It'd definitely be more fun than doing schoolwork," I said as I eased my portfolio bag and books onto the grass.

"Since you assholes didn't bother introducing yourselves yesterday, this is Cas." My back stiffened as Damien started up introductions, which set my nerves on edge.

"That's Zephyr." Damien motioned to one of his friends sitting nearby. I already knew his face, had briefly met him twice now. He smiled, and the warmth of it stemmed to his strikingly pale green eyes that almost glowed against his tawny skin.

Despite his size and a build that looked like he could take a lion one on one in a fight, there was a strange sincerity to his face that eased my nerves somehow. He gave a light wave of his hand, and I couldn't help but return his warm smile as I dipped my head in response.

"Of course, you met Barrett." Damien glanced toward him, a hint of annoyance in his tone. Barrett barked a laugh without acknowledging me, and I couldn't help but feel he was enjoying the memory of how he'd scared me.

"Sorry about yesterday," Barrett said, holding his hands up in surrender. I narrowed my eyes briefly, questioning whether he truly meant it.

"Then you've got, Vincent." Damien pointed to the shorter blond one, who'd gotten flustered when Anna, who I assumed was his girlfriend, was mentioned. He acknowledged me with a soft smile. He'd been so reserved the day before, so cold and disconnected as he'd watched Barrett taunt me on the steps. The man sitting before me was so different now, bright and cheerful.

Damien nodded to Cole who sat near Vincent. "That's Cole."

"We've met," I said.

Damien's eyes shifted to me, his brows furrowing, before he glanced at Cole.

"We have art studies together," Cole explained.

"Ah," Damien said, and something flickered across his expression as his eyes lowered, a soft smile tugging at the corner of his lips, but it slipped away just as quickly as he turned to the others.

"This is Cole's girlfriend, Amara, and that's James." Amara spared me the briefest of glances from the corner of her eye before returning to checking potential split ends in her black hair. In that brief second our eyes met, her expression showed a sincere lack of interest in meeting me, and I immediately averted my gaze. She was beautiful, full lips painted in a deep red, smooth sun-kissed skin. Clearly, she was too good to associate with a wallflower like me.

Completely opposite from Amara's reaction, James' red beard stretched as he smiled, pausing whatever he was doing on the laptop resting atop his legs. His Scottish accent caught me off guard as he spoke. "Nice tae meet ye, Cas."

Damien leaned in, picking up on my curiosity. "James moved here from Scotland a few years ago to help his grandmother out."

"Oh, wow. A long way from home then," I said awkwardly.

He shrugged. "Eh. Ah miss home from time tae time, but ah love it 'ere."

"So, how long have you lived here?" Cole asked, leaning forward to see me around the others as Damien and I eased onto the grass. The question was a welcome distraction from my nerves.

I caught a momentary irritated glance from Amara directed at Cole, but I tried to ignore her, turning until I couldn't see her past the others. " When I was little, my dad got a job, and we moved here. So, pretty much my entire life."

Zephyr's eyes flicked to Damien for a half second, something passing between them, so fast that I almost didn't catch it. I glanced back and forth between them, a bit confused but too anxious to say anything.

Barrett sat up, propping his arms on his knees. He chimed in, as if to explain their subtle exchange. "Damien's just been wondering where you've been his entire life."

My cheeks heated, and Damien expelled a heavy of annoyance.

"Don't let him fool you. He hasn't shut up about you since the mall," Vincent whispered into my ear, and I bit my lip, stifling the urge to giggle with them. The group laughed as Damien cut Vincent a look of warning and Vincent threw his hands up.

I couldn't fight the smile that spread across my face. "He warned me you guys were menaces. He wasn't lying."

"Absolute scum of the earth," Damien added. He glared at them, but I could faintly see a smile looming behind his annoyed expression. A tiny feeling of satisfaction bloomed in me; and I found it oddly comforting to see something could embarrass even him. It was a relief to not be the only one.

"I'm going to get a drink. You want anything, Cas?" Damien asked as he stood.

"Sure, I forgot to grab a water. Can you get me one?"

"Not gonna offer to get me a drink?" Barrett asked, almost seeming hurt. "Thanks Cas. I thought we'd gotten past hiding our feelings for one another, but it looks like he's hiding our love now that you're here."

"Keep holding onto your delusions, Barrett. They suit you," Damien grumbled without looking his way, and headed off toward the vending machines against the student union building. Barrett's shit-eating grin widened before he turned his attention back to his phone.

I bit back my laughter turned my attention to Cole. "Do you have any other sketches you've been working on?"

His eyes shot to me, and for a moment that nervous hesitation flickered across his face before he nodded and reached into his back to pull his sketchbook out.

I scooted closer as he flipped through the pages, tilting my head to get a better view. He was talented, the similar style he'd used to draw his grandmother decorating each page in mixes of graphite and colored pencil. One page hosted a mix of the wild foxgloves that grew along some mountainsides in the valley, the colorful petals in various shades of soft pink, magenta, and lilac popping against the rocks and long, unkept grasses of the forest.

He flipped to the next page to reveal a portrait of a woman. She was stunning, her dark brown eyes were so full of life, and her tawny skin was rich and beautiful, nearly glowing as it caught the light. Her black hair was tied into a thick braid that hung over her shoulder, and the smile she wore was soft and welcoming, like she was home to someone.

"She's beautiful."

"She was my mother," he said, and my eyes lifted to him, catching the hint of a sad smile tugging at his lips as he gazed down at her.

My thoughts snagged on the one word in that sentence that dropped a weight into my stomach. Was. I didn't know how to respond to that.

"She died when I was younger, so I draw her from time to time to keep her memory alive. It helps me feel close to her."

"That's beautiful," I said, offering him a smile.

He nodded. "It took me a long time to draw again after losing her, but she ended up being the first thing I drew when I did. It was rough losing her and Dad, but Damien was there for me. Took me under his wing, let me live with him until I was old enough to move out on my own."

My heart squeezed at the thought of him losing his parents, and at the same time, something else tugged in my chest. That Damien had taken him in...

My thoughts slowed as I began to fully process that. Cole must have been younger for Damien to have taken on a role like that, and I wondered just how much younger he was, or how much older Damien might be. I figured Damien was likely in his early twenties. Maybe he was older. Perhaps Cole was still in his late teens? He couldn't be much younger if he was in college.

"I'm so sorry you went through that," I said, unsure of what else to say.

He shrugged. "It wasn't easy, but he was there for me when I needed him most."

I sat there a moment, fidgeting with my fingers, then lifted my eyes to him. "I wanted to thank you again, for yesterday."

He waved it off. "Anytime. I know Barrett can be a bit much for someone who doesn't know him."

"You talkin' about me, princess?" Barrett threw his arm over Cole's shoulder as he leaned in. "I knew you still loved me, Cole."

I stifled a laugh as Barrett made kissy faces at Cole over his shoulder. Cole growled and elbowed him off, the interaction turning into a tussle.

Damien returned, offering me a water bottle. "Here you go, Cas."

"Thank you. Cole was telling me what you did for him."

Damien glanced at him.

"I was just tellin' her how you helped me out when my parents died," Cole explained.

Damien eased into the grass beside me, resting his elbow atop his knee. "Someone had to toughen you up, show you how to watch out for yourself."

"Yeah, we watch out for baby Cole," Vincent said, as he roughed up Cole's hair, and Cole dropped his head in defeat. I couldn't resist joining in on their laughter, warmth filling my chest. Cole tilted his head to meet my gaze, and a sweet smile crept across his face.

Conversations blossomed, and I sat, quietly observing them, laughing along. Their jokes and laughter dragged on as they teased and poked fun of each other, and I even found times where I'd joined in. Barrett went on about plans for Halloween, and I couldn't help but feel

like those plans entailed getting into a lot of trouble, nor could I deny that I was enticed by what that trouble might be.

Watching them, how they treated each other, it felt like a family. I almost envied them for what they had, the carefree nature in which their relationships seemed to be formed upon. It was as if they could enjoy every moment to the fullest without care of the consequences or what awaited them the following day. I'd always been hesitant to fully commit to anything, wondering if it were the right decision, or if it would affect someone in the long run when things went south with my health.

Their laughter and conversations died out, and I stiffened. My brows furrowed as Vincent's gaze briefly flickered over my shoulder before shifting back to Barrett, and James closed his laptop. Cole's smile faded, and I glanced over my shoulder to find a guy walking past us on the sidewalk.

The others didn't acknowledge him, continuing their conversation, but all the cheeriness and jokes had seemed to vanish without a trace. I looked back at him, and I couldn't shake the uneasiness that overcame me in his presence. His pale blond hair was short, and his pewter eyes looked so cold and cruel that it sent a chill over me as his gaze swept over us.

Damien remained where he sat, his eyes following every movement the guy made as his steps slowed before us.

"Honored you could grace us with your presence today," the guy said to Damien, dipping his head as if he were bowing to him in mockery.

Damien's eyes narrowed, but he didn't respond, and from the corner of my eye, Cole glanced over his shoulder briefly. I turned my gaze back to find those cold pewter eyes had landed on me, and for a moment, it seemed as if he was confused to see me. There was something in those eyes, something that left me entirely too uneasy. I wanted to look elsewhere, wanted to avoid his gaze, but I couldn't seem to pull myself away.

"And who's this pretty little thing?" he asked

"No one important," Damien said coldly, and something in my chest twisted and shrank, the rejection tearing into me, somehow leaving me breathless.

His pewter eyes raked down my body, and I met his gaze, nervous, but shoving past it to glare at him. Unreasonable irritation clouded my thoughts at Damien's rejection, and while I tried to dismiss the deep ache in my chest, it hurt too much to ignore.

He opened his mouth to say something, but Damien cut him off. "Find somewhere else to be."

He huffed and worked his jaw as he gave Damien a once over. His eyes flitted between us one last time, and a grin slid across his face before he turned to leave us.

Something crawled over my skin, and my eyes fell to the ground as I drew a deep breath. The pain of Damien's words left me questioning every conversation we'd shared up to this point.

What am I even fucking doing? Questioning myself for why I'd bothered coming to sit with them, I grabbed my bag, and picked up my books, before standing.

"I'm gonna go ahead and head to class." I said awkwardly, trying not to let my irritation coat my tongue, but in that I failed.

Damien turned to me, hesitation painting his face, but he forced a weak smile that left me all the more confused and unsure. "We'll catch up after you get out of class."

"Ok. See ya around," I said, and the others waved as I turned to head down the pathway without another word. Thankfully, in a different direction from where the creep had disappeared to.

No one important.

My grip tightened on my books as his words flitted through my thoughts, over and over again, my mind latching onto each and every word until I couldn't take it anymore. He was right. I wasn't important. Maybe Kat was right, and I should just avoid him. He'd made it clear what he thought of me.

The walkway toward my class was clear of other students or faculty, the empty space suffocating in a strange way as my mind surged in the silence. My eyes burned as I continued to linger on the stupid thoughts clouding my mind. Why did he even bother coming to talk to me? Why show interest in me? Was it some sort of stupid game? Was it a prank? Were all of them in on this?

Clutching my books to my chest, I rounded the corner, and crashed into something solid. My books scattered on the ground as I fell back onto the sidewalk, my portfolio bag slipping off my shoulder.

"Dammit." I sucked air in through my teeth, and I groaned as my hands stung against the concrete. "I'm so sor–"

"*Shit.* The Fates seem to favor me today."

My spine stiffened at the sound of his voice, his tone neither warm nor apologetic.

"Damien's found himself a *lovely* little songbird."

My gaze drifted upward to find the last person I wanted to run into. Looming over me was the guy who'd crossed our path. The same one who'd exchanged heated looks with Damien just moments before.

And he'd seen me with them.

A strange weight seemed to descend over me, and his gaze left me feeling like a mouse caught in a cat's trap. I recovered cautiously, trying to get a grip on my thoughts. I wasn't safe here, the very air around him screaming predator, and I didn't want to stick around to find out why.

"I'm so sorry for bumping into you," I muttered, doing my best to ignore him as I gathered my books. Instead of taking the hint and leaving, he crouched at my side.

"That all you gonna say to me? Not even gonna introduce yourself or ask my name?" He tilted his head to force himself into my line of sight, his voice rough and callus as he spoke. "So rude."

He reached up and removed his black sunglasses from his face, revealing those sharp pewter eyes I'd seen earlier. They pierced straight through me, as if he could see through every layer of my soul, my thoughts—leaving me feeling exposed and defenseless.

"The name's Marcus. What's yours?"

I averted my gaze as reached to grab my portfolio bag, not wanting to give him my name or play this game of introductions. "I said I was sorry. Now, I need to get to class, so if you don't mind—"

He grabbed my wrist, forcing me to release my hold on my back before yanking me off the ground and throwing me up against the wall. My books scattered onto the ground again. The force of my back hitting the brick reverberated through my body, and a whimper escaped me.

My eyes popped open, the air rushing from my lungs. Our eyes met, and the sadistic look within them caused terror to pool in my gut.

"I can't wait to hear you sing for me. I wonder, have you sung for him yet?"

He took hold of my other wrist, plastering it against the wall, too. Shit. His hold on me tightened, his grip so strong it was as if I were shackled to the wall. I fought to free myself, but it did little, and he didn't falter in the slightest.

I grimaced, trying to gather my strength to fight him off, but my voice came out shaky and unsure. "It's not like that."

"He didn't fool me with that bullshit statement," he said with a cruel grin. "You've been hanging out quite a bit lately."

My body tensed, recoiling against the wall as his body pressed into mine. He buried his face in my neck, inhaling deeply.

"Mm, you smell good. I wonder if you'll taste good, too."

Panic flooded me, and my gut twisted into knots. Fight, Cassie! Get away from him!

I tried to pull away, my mind and body screaming at me to run, but I couldn't compel myself to physically move. My limbs remained frozen, and no matter how much I wanted to, I couldn't move an inch. His breath was hot against my neck, and I closed my eyes, screaming at myself to do anything.

Move, dammit!

He pressed his body against mine, knee pushing between my legs and tears dotted my eyes as the frustration, anger, and fear filled me. I was powerless against him. My lips parted to scream, but no sound came, as if my voice had abandoned me.

"Let her go, Marcus." My eyes shot open, head jerking to the side at the sound of Damien's voice from where he stood several feet away.

A sadistic grin spread across Marcus' face. "Oh? Why?" He gripped my wrists harder and I whimpered. "It's only fair if you let me have her. You know, so we're finally even? You're not seriously gonna try to stop me, are you?"

"Keep testing my patience, and you'll find out just what I'm going to do to you," he growled, and enunciated his last few words harshly. "Now. Let. Her. Go."

"Awe, what're you scared of? Showing her the monster you really are?"

"Who do you think you're foolin', Marcus? He ain't scared of that," Barrett called out from behind Damien as he approached. "But keep at it if you like. I'll enjoy watching him carve you up."

More of Damien's group appeared as well from around the corner as Barrett cracked his knuckles, seeming to enjoy the tension as he came to a stop at Damien's side.

My gaze locked with Damien's as he drew closer, a silent plea flooding my eyes, and he gave a slow nod. Marcus' palms grew sweaty against my skin, and the smile faltered for the briefest of moments, revealing the lies behind his once confident grin. He was outmatched, and he knew it. Still, he wore the mask, eyes locked on Damien as he continued to taunt him.

"What's this, Damien? You need your buddies to take me on?"

"I don't need anyone's help to beat the shit out of you." Damien inched closer, his pace steady and cautious. "I'd rather not in front of her, but I can jog your memory, if you insist."

The desperation began to show in Marcus' face, and his jaw tightened. His weight shifted as he started to move away, but he was unable to without releasing me.

"Last chance, Marcus. Let her go, before I make you." One of Damien's hands opened and flexed at his side like he was prepping to grab something.

Marcus's eyes fell to that very hand, his smile fading. "Fine."

He turned to me, his face inches from mine and I grimaced as he grabbed hold of my chin to force my gaze to his. "I'll see you later, little songbird. Maybe you'll sing for me next time."

He threw me into Damien and stormed off into the woods.

Damien caught me, his eyes focused on Marcus until he was out of sight. Barrett and the others moved to go after him, but Damien's hand flew up to stop them.

My knees buckled under me, and Damien eased me to the ground. He took hold of my hands, his eyes falling to them as if inspecting them, bu I pulled from from his hold, the sting of his words still burning in my chest. Guilt flashed across his face, and his lips parted as if he wanted to say something, but no words came.

My body began to shake, the adrenaline taking root as the shock wore off. No matter how much I tried to calm myself, I couldn't make it stop. My mind rushed through all the scenarios of what could've happened if Damien hadn't found us when he did. What would have happened.

The sickening feeling of Marcus' hands lingered on my skin, and my vision grew blurry as tears welled in my eyes. I furiously rubbed my face, trying to brush them away, but they kept coming.

"Easy, Cas, easy. You're safe now," Damien said, his voice soft, his hands hovering but not touching me.

45

"Why did you come?" I muttered, hurt coating my words. "I thought I was no one important."

Damien winced at my words, and he opened and closed his mouth as he tried to come up with a response. "I didn't mean that, Cas."

I turned my gaze to him, my brows furrowing as I glared at him, my vision blurred by the tears and it only left me angrier. Fuck, why couldn't I stop crying?

"I knew where Marcus' mind was going the moment he saw you. I was trying to avoid him putting a target on your back, but it looks like that only baited him more."

Could I trust him? Was this just part of a possible prank to get me to let my walls down? Or was he telling the truth? Marcus made it clear he didn't believe what Damien had said about me. Maybe...

"Does anything hurt?" he asked, holding out his hands in a quiet request to touch me again.

I hesitated a moment, but lifted my hands for him to take, and he gave me a weak smile before looking them over carefully. He turned my hands over, finding my scraped palms from where I'd fallen, pearls of blood beading along the cuts. My hands burned, studded with dirt and gravel. The pain in my chest eased at the sight of the concern on his face, but I remained hesitant.

"Did he do anything before I got here?"

Cold air flooded in and out of my lungs as I breathed deeply. The anger started to fade, but without it, I was left in the trembling wake of the panic that had taken hold of me moments ago. My eyes fell to my quivering hands in his.

"I... I think I'm ok. Just shaken up." It was a lie. I wasn't even remotely ok. My body was still panicking, but I couldn't bring myself to verbalize it.

"I'm so sorry. I was afraid you'd get hurt if I forced him off you." Damien's eyes romanced over my hands, and I stiffened the moment his thumb brushed over the hairline scar on my wrist. He remained silent a moment, and I almost pulled my hands from his but he spoke again. "Come on, let's get you out of here before anyone else comes along."

He helped me to my feet, and despite the fact I wanted to be angry with him for saying what he did, it felt oddly comforting. I allowed myself to lean into his support as he guided me toward the entrance to the building. From the corner of my eye, I found Vincent and Zephyr gathering my bag and books from the ground, before they followed us inside.

Damien hesitated once we passed through the doors. "I know you've got class, but... I can take you home if you want."

Everything in me wanted to say yes. I wanted nothing more than to just go home, to not be in this place any longer. For a moment, I began to have second thoughts about attending this school at all, but I refused to let someone like Marcus think he'd won, refused to let him take away the only normalcy I'd managed to find.

I couldn't meet his gaze, fearful that I'd give into his offer. "I really should get to class…"

"If that's what you want," Damien said, and he walked me down the hall to the bathroom.

Silence loomed in the air as I washed my hands, my pulse pounding in my ears as I tried to bring myself down from the panic. Damien leaned against the open doorway, his presence somehow comforting.

"Are you sure?" Damien's voice cut through the silence, and conflict tugged me in so many directions. "You don't have to put on a tough face for me, Cas. It's ok. Marcus is a piece of shit." I could almost feel the anger seething in him, his voice growing harsher with each word. "I should've seen you to your class. I didn't think he'd try anything with you."

"You couldn't have known." Was I making excuses for him? He seemed to know, and yet… he seemed to care, seemed to regret how he'd handled everything.

"If he ever so much as looks at you again, I fucking swear—" He cleared his throat. "Sorry."

My gaze fell to my hands as I tried not to think about how oddly comforting hearing him say that was. I frowned as my fingers continued to tremble under the water, and it frustrated me that I couldn't make them stop. God, I couldn't believe how helpless I'd been, how I couldn't even bring myself to try to fight back, try to escape.

Damien's presence fell over me as he drew closer, and he reached out to take hold of my hand. I hated that he could feel how much I still trembled, and I wanted to pull away, yet I couldn't bring myself to.

"It's ok, Cas. You're safe now." His voice was low, his words enveloping me in warmth like the soft caress of his fingers.

His hooded eyes remained fixated on my hand, his thumb brushing tender strokes against my skin. The delicate, affectionate touch left butterflies dancing in my stomach. Behind the soft expression masking his face, I could still feel his fury smoldering just beneath the surface. Though he tried his best to hide it, I could see through the facade. It eased my fears, in a strange way, and helped me settle.

"Thank you, Damien, but…" I drew a deep breath, summoning up the courage to force a smile as I pulled from his touch. "I really should get to class. I'm already late."

"I want you to have my number," Damien said, his hand reluctantly lowering to his side. "You can call if you ever need me. Anything at all. I'll be there."

I was a bit surprised by his offer. "Seriously?"

He nodded, giving me a smile that I wanted to believe was genuine.

"That would be nice, actually." I responded, handing him my phone.

"Seriously, don't hesitate to call me if you need anything." He quickly typed in his number and handed my phone back. "I'll be there, I promise. Doesn't matter when, even if you just need to talk."

I stepped out of the bathroom, saving his number before shoving my phone into my pocket. "Thank you… for everything."

His smile grew warmer, lighting his amber and ashen eyes. "Anytime, Cas."

Vincent handed me my bag and books and I thanked them all before turning to walk to my classroom just a few doors down the hall. Adrenaline remained heavy in my veins, and I tried to breathe steadily to calm myself before entering the classroom. It was no use, though; Marcus' voice would end up clouding my thoughts for the rest of the day.

CHAPTER 5

The edge of my charcoal ran against the grain of the paper, the gritty feeling vibrating softly into my fingertips. Lines of black ran downward along Kat's jawline, the shadows smudging under my fingertips as I blended them out under her chin, cascading into her long, delicate neck.

My curls dangled, untamed, against my face as usual. I sighed in annoyance as they got in the way of my view for the millionth time since I'd started a few hours ago, and I tied it back into a loose bun. The stool creaked under my weight as I leaned back, tilting my head to scrutinize the drawing before me.

The clock read 1:32 a.m., and I couldn't fall asleep to save my life, my knee bouncing. It would likely be hours before sleep finally welcomed me into its arms.

I pulled my foot up onto my stool, resting my elbow against my knee as I stared at the large pad of paper resting on my easel. My jaw rested against the palm of my hand, my thumb pressed to my cheek as I scrutinized the drawing.

In the portrait, Kat was sitting on a stool, her face tilted slightly as she looked out the window beside her. Streaks of light leaked in through the curtains, casting rays down over her to illuminate sections of her face amidst the darkness of her surroundings. After months of working on the details, it still felt like it lacked something, but I'd yet to figure out what that was. Was the shade of her hair wrong? Did it need to be darker?

It would probably be best if I tried to sleep again, but the thought of lying in bed alone with my thoughts left my heart racing. The moment I'd laid down a few hours ago, my mind had flooded with images of Marcus, of his body pressed against mine as he caged me. The last thing I needed was to have a panic attack. I needed to drown out those thoughts, and for once, the words in my books weren't enough to do it.

Focus on the drawing. Don't think about it.

I leaned forward, taking the stick of charcoal in my hands, adding more details to her hair. The moment the charcoal touched the paper a crash of trash cans rang outside the apartment, and I jumped, dropping it to the floor. My heart thumped wildly as I stared at the wall separating me from whatever was outside.

The walls were suddenly caving in around me, adrenaline-fed hallucinations dancing in the corners of my eyes in the dark places of my living room, and the weight of how alone I was in this apartment crawled over my skin. My gaze shot to my front door; it was locked.

Still, I felt the same. Unsafe.

My parents were asleep next door, but I couldn't bring myself to bother them, let alone set foot outside my front door by myself to go. Damn that bastard. Marcus didn't even know where I lived, and yet he'd somehow managed to make me feel unsafe in my own home.

I rubbed most of the charcoal from my hands onto my shirt and leggings and snatched my phone from my desk. Who was I even going to call, though? I couldn't call Kat at this hour. What would I say?

Hey, just calling at two in the morning to have a casual conversation. Nothing strange about that.

She'd see through it and ask questions. I'd have to tell her about Marcus, and I wasn't ready to talk about it. Not yet.

I didn't know if I would ever be ready to talk about it.

My thin contact list rolled over my screen as I ran my thumb down my screen. Damien's name caught my attention and I stopped, my finger hovering over his name.

Don't hesitate to call me if you need anything.

His words clung to my mind. I shouldn't call him this late. It wouldn't be right, especially if he was asleep.

He was just being nice. You're no one important, remember?

No. He hadn't truly meant that. He'd said that to try to keep me safe—had failed miserably at that, but it wasn't what I had thought. When I'd needed him the most, he came.

Maybe I could just text him, see if he's awake. That would be harmless enough, right? Just a text; he probably wouldn't even see it. His phone would likely be on silent at this hour.

My fingers tapped across my screen.

> Hey. Just wanted to see if you're awake. If you're not, don't worry. It's not urgent.

Sent.

I set the phone down on my desk, my heart falling into a heavy rhythm. Did I really just text him this late at night over a noise outside? Oh my God, I was such an idiot.

You're fine, Cas. It was probably just a raccoon or a stray cat. There are no monsters outside, you big baby.

I yelped when my phone suddenly vibrated on my desk, the ringtone piercing the quiet of the night. It hadn't rested there but for a few seconds, and I snatched it up desperate to silence the noise.

Damien's name flashed across my screen and my heart lurched. Holy hell, he was calling me, and for some reason I froze, unsure of what I was doing.

Dammit, Cas, answer the phone!

I pressed my finger to the screen and lifted it to my ear. My voice was hushed as I answered, wondering if it was a mistake that he'd called. "H-hello?"

"Is everything ok?"

I didn't answer at first. What should I say?

No, everything's not fine. I'm scared. I'm lonely. I'm on the edge of a breakdown. I don't want to be alone right now.

"Um..."

When I couldn't form a response, he spoke. "Where are you?"

"I'm home."

The line was quiet for a moment. "Are *you* ok?"

That question nearly broke the walls containing the overwhelming emotions I'd stifled up to this point, and my voice nearly cracked. "No..."

"Do you want me to come over?"

My heart leapt in my throat at the thought of it. Oh God, I couldn't believe I'd called him at this hour. He must have thought the worst. "Oh, you don't have to do that. I feel bad enough waking you."

"You didn't wake me, Cas. It's ok."

A heavy sigh escaped my lips, my shoulders sagging. "I'm just... I'm just a little spooked right now. I heard a noise outside. It's stupid; it's probably just an animal getting into the trash or someth—"

"Not stupid, Cas," he said, his tone so gentle and assuring. "It's ok, really. If you don't want to be alone, I can head over there right now. It's no trouble, honest."

"Actually… I'd—" It was difficult to get the words out, but I couldn't stifle the hope welling in my chest. "I'd like that."

"Send me your address. I'll head your way."

"Ok. Text me when you get here, my parents are asleep next door. And Damien..."

"Yeah?"

A smile tugged at my lips. "Thank you."

"Like I said, Cas. Anytime." The call ended, and I sat there in disbelief for a moment before I snapped out of it and sent him my address.

Damien was coming to my house. The reality of it made it difficult to breathe. This was fine, this was ok. He was just coming to be a good friend. That's all it was, nothing more.

For a moment, I couldn't move, couldn't do anything. My gaze lifted to the portrait of Kat I'd been working on. Kat's words flitted across my thoughts, leaving a touch of guilt in their wake.

If you're gonna talk to him, please Cas, just be careful. If you go somewhere with them, tell me where you're going.

Technically, I wasn't going anywhere with them, and it was just him. I mean, my parents were next door. I bit my lip, wondering if I should send Kat a text just in case. She would flip if I texted her that, probably come banging down my door. I set my phone back on my desk and sat back, looking over the progress again before continuing my work on her hair for a bit longer.

Eventually I set the charcoal down on the easel tray, hopefully for the last time tonight. The wood floor creaked as I stood, and a strange sense of excitement replaced the anxiety. My gaze drifted over the mess around me. Papers lay strewn in various places—sketches and practice works, crumbled failed attempts, and bits of charcoal littered the hard wood floors. I needed to clean. Badly.

While the rest of my house was neat and organized, my art corner had always been a bit chaotic. I knelt to gather the papers, stacking them loosely up on my messy desk, doing my best to organize the mess of graphite and chunks of used and new charcoal.

Unused and unopened acrylic and watercolor paint sets sat in the far corner of my desk. I didn't know why I bothered holding onto them. Perhaps it was the fact that my parents had gotten them for me, in the hopes I might add color to my work again. No matter how hard I tried, though, I never could. There was no color in my life—it was easier to look at things through a black and white lens. It somehow made it easier to cope.

I should just throw them away already. It made no sense to hold onto them. Instead, I pulled the desk drawer open, pushed the paints into it, and shut them away, likely forever.

My phone vibrated in the pocket of my leggings, and I pulled it out, seeing a text from Damien.

I'm outside. Which door is yours?

My heart leapt into my throat as I read his text. It had barely been thirty minutes since we'd spoken. I hadn't expected him to get here so fast. We didn't live far from downtown; maybe he'd been out with his friends.

I stopped what I was doing, leaving the partially cleaned mess behind, and headed for the entry. The wood was cold against my hands as I pushed myself up to my toes to look through the peephole. He was leaning against the railing of my porch, back turned to me as he looked out over the dark street. I unlatched the deadbolt and opened the door.

He turned to me, smoke slipping from his lips and he snickered as he swiped what looked like a thin cigar on the heel of his boot. He lowered his hood, his eyes landing on me.

God, he was beautiful, but his laugh clicked through me, and I cocked an eyebrow. "What's so funny?"

"What's all over your face?"

My brows knitted, hand raising to my cheek. Oh my God, what was wrong with my face? "What do you mean, *what's all over my face*?"

Before I could move to check, he pulled his phone from his pocket and snapped a picture of me. I flinched at the flash, blinking as he turned his phone to show me the screen.

Heat spread across my cheeks and over my ears as I looked at the picture. *Oh God.*

Black smudges of charcoal were smeared across my chin and cheeks, right where I always placed my hands when I was deep in thought. My eyes fell to my hands, my fingertips and palms still black from the charcoal I'd been using. I'd been so focused on cleaning my art space, I hadn't thought to clean—well... *me!*

I reached my hand out, my whispers a frantic mess. "Oh, my God! Delete that!"

Before I could grab his phone, he jerked it up and out of my reach as he slipped through the doorway past me. "Nah, I think I'll keep it. It's too cute to delete."

A slurry of unrecognizable words spilled out of my mouth, and I shut the door as I followed him back inside. I couldn't believe I didn't think to change.

He paused in the entryway, eyes surveying my humble apartment. I internally cringed, wishing I'd had more time to clean. I could only imagine what he thought of me. "Sorry about the mess."

"I didn't come here to tell you your house is messy, Cas, but it's not. You're fine." His smile eased my nerves, and somehow, I felt like I could relax a little.

"Can I get you a drink? I don't have much. I've got hot tea, raspberry iced tea, and water."

"I'll take a raspberry tea. No need to heat up a kettle on my account."

"It's no trouble, honestly," I said as I slipped into the hallway, leaving him in the living room.

The moment I entered the kitchen, I rushed to the sink, splashing water over my face to wash the charcoal markings away. I couldn't believe he'd seen me like this. My gaze fell to my clothes. Jesus, I was covered in charcoal. My heart hammered against my ribs, wondering if I should go upstairs and change.

You're fine, you're fine. But God I wasn't... Damien was here, in my house. And I was a nervous train-wreck.

As I opened the cabinets for cups, the glasses nearly slipped from my grasp as I fumbled them to the countertop. I needed to calm down before I broke something. The last thing I needed was for a glass to break. My cheeks heated as I imagined my parents rushing from their beds to find a guy in my house in the middle of the night. That would be awkward and humiliating.

When I returned with our drinks, Damien was standing in front of the drawing of Kat I'd been working on. I froze. What was he thinking? It wasn't finished, and there were still so many things to fix and add.

"Did you draw this?" He glanced back at me over his shoulder.

I handed him his drink, almost wishing I'd put the drawing up, that he hadn't seen it in its rough state. "It's not finished yet. I'm not quite happy with her hair, and the light isn't hitting her skin quite right—"

"It's beautiful," he said, his tone gentle as his eyes trailed over the paper. "It's Kat, right?"

I nodded, a smile fighting to spread across my face at his compliment.

"It's so realistic. You've got a gift, Cas."

"It's just something that helps pass the time." *Helps distract me.*

His gaze lingered on me a moment as if he were trying to read me, but he turned and walked over to the desk to set his glass down.

He paused, eyes locking on the stack of drawings. "What're these?"

When his hand reached for the stack of papers, I caught a glimpse of the rough sketch of him I'd jotted down after we first met. God, no, anything but that. It had only been from memory, and I wasn't happy with how it came out, not to mention the fact that it would be mortifying if he knew I was drawing him.

Before he could pick it up, I snatched it from the table, hiding it behind my back.

"It's horrible. I was gonna throw it away."

God, Cas, what are you doing? Could I be any more obvious?

His eyes narrowed, and he eased down onto my stool, as he propped his elbow on the desk and rested his head against his knuckles. A devilish grin formed on his face as those intense eyes lifted to mine. "Is that a sketch of me?"

My back straightened for a moment, but I sighed, slouching as I pulled it from my back. "I drew it after we met at the mall. It was from memory, and I didn't like how it came out. I planned on redoing it."

"Is this really how you see me?" he asked as he took the paper from my hand and his eyes trailed over the sketch. "Damn, I look hot."

I cupped my mouth with my hand as a laugh nearly exploded from my chest.

You have no idea…

He set the drawing down and leaned back against the desk, his dark curls sweeping across his broad chest. "Are you going to paint me like those French girls?"

I snickered at his reference, resisting the urge to let my imagination wander. "You're terrible."

His smile widened into a grin, and it warmed my heart as he gazed up at me. At that moment, I realized exactly what he was doing. I'd needed a distraction. He was seeing to that.

And he was succeeding.

"Seriously, though, if you ever want to draw me, all you have do is ask."

"That's tempting." *Hell yeah, it was tempting.*

A beat of silence stretched between us, and Damien cleared his through before gesturing to the bookshelves that filled my living room. "So, I see you read a lot."

"Yeah, that's another hobby of mine. I collect books and play-scripts. I haven't been able to see a play in a while, but I love theatre." My eyes drifted to the spines that housed countless means of escape for me.

He stood and walked over to look at my stockpile of books. I didn't even know how many I had at this point. My collection had grown over the years, some of the books nearly as old as I was, some far older from a time long since passed. It was never enough, though. Every time I finished one story, I needed more. The worlds within those pages were always vastly better than my own, and I so desperately needed the escape they offered me.

He reached out to pull one from the shelf, smiling to himself as he inspected the cover. "I can see you like vampires."

"Paranormal fantasy is definitely one of my favorites. Vampires, werewolves, dragons, fae, all that stuff." I approached him, hesitant to ask. "Do you ever read?"

He pushed the book back into place. "I used to. I used to read a lot, actually. Don't really get much time to lately, though."

I couldn't help but notice something in his eyes. Sadness?

"Well, you should make more time. Here." His brows rose as I stretched up on my toes, pulling down my copy of *Dark Lover* before turning back to him. "You can borrow this one. It's one of my favorite vampire stories. Ignore the lover part—I mean—there *is* romance, but the story is great, and I think you'll like the brotherhood. They almost remind me of you and the guys."

"Promise they don't glitter?" he said with a crooked grin.

I rolled my eyes. "It's not like *Twilight,* I promise. Don't hate on that series, though. The books are way better than the movies."

He smiled as he glanced down at the book in my hand, and I chewed the inside of my lip, hoping this wasn't a foolish offer, one that he might shoot down. Perhaps he needed the escape these pages offered just as much as I did. "Just promise you'll return it in one piece. Don't let Barrett draw in it or anything."

His gaze swept over my face, and he huffed a laugh. "You missed a spot."

His thumb brushed over my jaw, wiping away the remnants of charcoal I'd missed, and I scrunched my face as he wiped it away. The strange sensation I'd felt the first time we touched seeped into me where his fingers met my skin, something deep in my chest reaching out to him in response. My heart raced at the feel of it, and he inched closer, so close, until our breaths mingled.

"You're always smiling, but I can't help but feel like there's something else behind those eyes. I can't figure it out, but it almost seems... sad." His voice was low, and I struggled to focus on his words as his body pressed against mine, my back meeting the shelves.

"No matter what I do, though, no matter how much I try to stay away. I can't stop myself. You're too irresistible..." His hand lingered against my skin, and it slid along my chin, tilting my face up. His voice dropped to a low whisper as he leaned into me, his lashes lowering as his eyes fell to my lips. "*So, fuckin' irresistible.*"

His lips brushed against mine, like a whisper. For a moment I was so lost in the sensation that my hand fell to my side, the book slipping from my grasp and narrowly missing my foot as it clunked to the floor.

I gasped, breaking the kiss, afraid it had hit his foot instead. "Oh my God! I'm so sorry."

A low, deep laugh rumbled from his chest, and he ducked to grab the book from the floor. "I promise not to let Barrett ruin your book."

I smiled, my cheeks and ears hot as I tried to remember how to breathe. "Cross your heart?"

"Cross my heart."

CHAPTER 6

The grass was soft under me as I laid on my stomach, my legs folded behind me as I ran my charcoal over the pad of paper laid out before me. Students passed our usual spot in the courtyard, taking no notice of my presence as they talked in their groups.

A week had passed since my run in with Marcus, and while time helped, what little sleep I'd gotten had been filled with nightmares of him. Thankfully, it no longer felt as fresh, but I never knew when the memory would randomly arise again, triggering a panic attack. I couldn't bring myself to tell anyone about it, outside of Damien and his friends who already knew.

Would my parents flip out and push me to drop out if they found out? This was the only place I could feel some sense of normalcy, the only place that gave me an excuse to see Damien.

We'd made no other moves toward each other, past the kiss we shared at my house that night. I wasn't sure if the kiss was part of the distraction, or something else. While I knew his rejection of me in front of Marcus was for my safety, it did little to clarify just how he saw me and what kind of relationship we might have. We hadn't had a chance to be alone since that night, and there was no way I was having that conversation around the others. It would just give Barrett more things to tease me about.

I chewed on my lip as I scrutinized the last details of my drawing for the competition, smoothing out rough edges, and marking out highlights with a white gel pen. It was due today and, as usual I was second guessing every single detail up until the last minute. I hadn't been able to get the crease out of it and had proceeded to fold and crumple more of it, tearing edges here and there to leave the paper imperfect and damaged.

As I was.

"I know the semester only just started, but I'm already ready for it to be over," Cody whined, and I lifted my gaze from my work.

Kat closed her laptop and set it aside before climbing into his lap. "Speak for yourself. My professors this semester are actually really cool!"

Cody snorted in disagreement. "Of course, *you* would think your professors are cool, Kat. You make this shit look easy, and you seem to be the teacher's pet in every class."

Kat rolled her eyes and changed the subject. "I heard they finally caught one of the people involved in the disappearances. Maybe they'll finally get it under control and we can start our pizza dates back up."

Cody cocked a brow. "Pizza dates?"

I nodded. "We used to go out every Friday night for pizza at Gallina's."

The old pizza shop had been our favorite for years, but when the disappearances started happening, we decided to avoid going out at night. I hated that we couldn't feel safe in our own city. I used to feel safe enough to walk the streets of downtown Johnstown whenever I felt like it. Now, I was afraid of sounds outside of my own home.

"If I join you guys for a date can I get a slice of that ass afterward?" Cody whispered, just loud enough for me to hear as he pull her closer to nuzzle against her neck.

Kat's cheeks turned a bright red. "Cody!"

He huffed a laugh, and I chuckled, shaking my head as I turned my attention back to my drawing. They seemed to constantly flirt, and it was growing more difficult to watch them together lately. It was selfish and stupid of me, and I was furious with myself for feeling like that. Kat was happy, and I was happy for her, but I couldn't shake the selfish desires that rose to the surface at the sight of them like this.

"I'm gonna go see Damien. I'll see you in class," I said, packing up my things.

"Alright, love, I'll see you there," Kat said with a smile and proceeded to wrestle with Cody.

I'd somehow managed to convince Kat to accept my friendship with Damien. After what I'd told her about him, how our conversations had been, how he treated me, her suspicions seemed to settle. I hadn't been able to bring myself to tell her about Marcus. It would only give her a reason to worry. I was ok, though, so there was no reason to tell her. It wasn't as if anything had happened in the end.

At least, that's what I kept telling myself.

Damien's eyes lifted to me, as if sensing my approach, and a smile lit his face. "Hey."

He stood, taking my hand and guiding me away from Barrett and the others. "Come here for a second. There's something I've been meaning to ask you."

"Give Damien a kiss for me, Cas!" Barrett called, and the rest of the group whistled and laughed as Damien lead me away. My cheeks and ears grew warm, and for once, I wanted to smack him myself. I looked over my shoulder, throwing Barrett the middle finger, to which he only responded with more taunting and kissy faces.

"I swear, they only get away with it because you're here," Damien groaned, and as soon as we were out of earshot, he turned to me. "I was wondering if you'd like to go out this weekend."

Though I tried to hide my surprise, my heartbeat quickened and any words I might have said lodged in my throat. Was he asking me to go out as friends? Or go out. I was still unsure of where we stood, the kiss we'd shared only making it more confusing.

"W—well, I'm spending the night at Kat's tonight." I paused, my mind running in every direction. "I'm free the rest of the weekend, though."

"How about tomorrow afternoon, then? We could go to Stackhouse to start and go from there?" He seemed anxious, nervous even.

I lit up at the mention of Stackhouse. It was a large, wooded park, one of my favorite places to go when I was younger, and it had been years since I'd visited. The thought of us getting time alone after everything that had happened left butterflies fluttering in my stomach, my lips tingling as the memories of the all to brief kiss we'd shared.

You're getting ahead of yourself, Cas. You're just friends. It was all out of pity. He was just being a good friend. He was the reason it happened in the first place. He felt guilty. Why would he want you? What do you have to offer? Nothing.

I halted the spiraling thoughts, the doubt and uneasiness leaving nausea in my gut.

He waited in baited silence, a hopeful smile curving his lips, and the sight of it helped drown out the doubtful thoughts. A grin crept across my face as I focused on the possibilities. "Sounds like fun."

Something came to life in his eyes. "Pick you up from your house at two?"

"I'd love that."

"You're going on a date with Damien?"

"I mean, I wouldn't call it a date. I think he likes me, but I don't think he likes me that much," I murmured. "We're just friends."

I hadn't been able to shake the fear that he was simply trying to make up for what happened with Marcus. Was he doing this because he felt guilty? It hurt to think that everything he'd done might be out of pity.

"Oh, shut it. You told me he said—" She lowered the tone of her voice, trying to imitate Damien. "*I was wondering if you'd like to go out sometime.* That's asking you out on a date!"

I could barely stifle my laugh. "First off, that was a terrible impression. Second, I just find it hard to believe someone like him would even be interested in me."

A devilish grin spread across her face, and my heart fluttered in my chest as she spoke. "Yeah, except friends don't just kiss the way he kissed you."

She wasn't entirely wrong, but she also didn't have all the details of why the kiss happened in the first place.

Kat put her car in park in front of her cozy, tan house. We'd spent the evening studying and doing homework at the campus library, and it was already a few hours past nightfall. I'd been nervous about being out late, but Cody had stayed with us and seen us to our car before heading home himself.

I climbed out of the passenger seat of her little green beetle, taking my bags with me as we walked inside. Kat's house was far cuter than my own, neatly decorated and full of the nicest furniture. She lived alone; her parents having gone on the road in their retirement as soon as she'd graduated high school. It felt like it had been forever since I'd seen or talked to them, and I didn't think Kat really talked to them much, having practically cut ties. I'd never gotten particularly close to them, myself, as they'd always been a bit odd, and always seemed to be in fowl moods, especially her father. I remembered her stories of how they would fight when she was younger, her dad going on drunken tirades, and she'd sneak out and hide in my room to escape it. I didn't blame her for not keeping them in her life.

Kat headed up the stairs to her bedroom and I followed, hurrying down the hall and into her room before tossing my bags on the floor and falling back onto her bed.

She walked over to her entertainment center, rummaging through her shelf of DVDs. "What's Damien like, anyway? Besides those dreamy eyes and that cool demeanor."

"Despite the rumors you warned me about, he's been nothing but kind to me."

Kat glanced back at me over her shoulder. "I see the way he looks at you."

A smile spread across my face, and my eyes fell as I tried to hide it. "I won't deny that Damien looks like a hard ass and his friends enjoy causing trouble. I could see where rumors would come from. Still, he's helped me out a couple times since I've met him. I know he's not a bad person." Marcus' face flashed across my mind, and my smile faded as the fear churned in my gut, the panic resurfacing. I drew a deep breath, trying to calm it before it became something I couldn't stifle. Anything but that right now.

"Helped you how?" Kat asked, interrupting my train of thought.

I scrambled for a second, remembering I'd yet to tell her about Marcus, and now was definitely not the time to bring it up. "You remember when we went to the mall the week classes started? When I went to get us drinks, we bumped into each other, and our drinks got spilled. He felt so bad and insisted on buying us new ones. It was pure coincidence that I bumped into him again on campus."

A coy grin spread across her face as she drifted closer to her bed. "So that's how you two met. I was wondering why you kept spacing out after we met back up."

My cheeks heated. "Yeah, I kind of hoped I'd get to see him again, so when I did, I had to know who he was."

She lifted the back of her hand to her forehead as she fell back onto the bed in a false faint. "It's like The Fates brought you together."

I rolled my eyes and laughed. "You've been reading too many Greek tragedies."

"I can't get enough of them!"

Though, I feared a Greek tragedy might not be too far off the mark of where this situation was headed, I always failed to keep him at arm's length, rational crumbling in his presence. I shouldn't be giving into these feelings, should be cutting him out and distancing myself.

So why wasn't I?

"I'm gonna go downstairs to get a drink and make some pizza. You want anything?" Kat asked, pushing herself up to rest on her elbows.

"I'll be down in a minute. I'm gonna get changed."

"Kay," she said and jump off the bed before waltzing out of her door. The thumps of her footsteps rang through the walls as she jogged down the stairs, and I smiled when her melodic voice echoed as she started singing.

I quickly changed into my night clothes, and my gaze wandered over to the window next to me. It was getting late. The streets below were just barely lit by the old street lamps, and the alleys between the houses were blanketed in shadow.

The street light outside of Kat's house flickered off and on before going out entirely, leaving the street in inky darkness, and it almost felt as if the room grew colder. I shivered, rubbing my arms, and I wondered if there might be something wrong with the radiator or if Kat had forgotten to set the heat.

Movement caught my attention, a shadow darting across the dark street so fast I couldn't catch what it was, and I drew closer to the window, tugging back the curtain. I scrunched my eyes, but it did little. I shook my head, but as I started to turn away, more movement stopped me. My eyes struggled to adjust to the dark streets, but my brows furrowed as a man stumbled out of the alley, followed quickly by two others.

They came to a stop in the back street, their heads whipping to the alley they had emerged from. Their pursuer came into view, stepping from the shadow-cloaked alley. By their stature I assumed it was a man, accompanied by two others who followed close behind. I drew closer to the window, my lungs freezing as I watched in nervous silence.

It was too dark to really make out any features, and the pursuers all wore hoods cloaking their faces in darkness. The tallest of the pursuers walked up beside the one who seemed to lead them, flipping a long knife in his hand, and the others began to fan out their potential victims.

One of the fleeing men threw their arms up, shouting something, and my hand clasped over my mouth, my heart shuddering in my chest. *Oh God.*

There was no way this was happening. I couldn't move, could only watch in frozen horror, as the pursuer standing in the forefront took a step closer. He extended his hand out to the side, and I blinked, as black mist formed around his palm, building and building before it faded into nothing to reveal a long knife, almost like a dagger in his grip. Holy shit, was I hallucinating?

Air rushed into my lungs when one of the fleeing men lunged at him, fist raised as he attacked, but the hooded man shifted, clothes-lining the attacker. The guy crashed onto his back, and the shortest of the hooded pursuers surged forward, pinning him down. The pursuer who'd knocked him down jerked the blade over his head.

My heart sank as he plunged the blade into the guy's chest. I recoiled as the most horrendous screech assaulted my ears, my knees buckling beneath me as I clamped my hands over my ears. It did nothing; the sound clawing its way into my mind, rattling me down to my bones. As it faded, I shoved to my feet and raced downstairs, nearly falling down the stairwell.

"Kat!"

Kat's eyes widened as I stumbled into the kitchen.

"Where's the fire?" she asked, blinking at me as I gripped her arms.

"Call the cops!" I gasped, my hands shaking, and her face paled. "Someone was just murdered outside!"

Roughly a half an hour later, Kat and I sat on her front porch, wrapped together in a large blanket, her arm over my shoulder as she held me. The neighborhood was alight with the flashing red and blue lights cast from the cop cars parked in front of her house, and the neighbors had wandered onto their porches to see what the commotion was about. K9 units searched through the alleys between every house. Unfortunately, by the time the police arrived, there was no one in sight, no body, nothing.

I'd explained to the officers what I'd seen. However, when they searched the area, all they found was what looked like a large oil stain on the pavement, no blood or weapons. They must have thought I was insane, but the officers assured us they would keep looking, have an officer patrol the neighborhood tonight to ensure we were safe.

Had I lost my mind? Had it all been a hallucination?

Or had I just seen who was responsible for the disappearances? Who were they? How did they hide a body that quickly without leaving a single trace? Even the dogs didn't seem to pick up anything outside of them seeming all too eager to leave the alley where they'd found the oil stains with their tails tucked between their legs. It had seemed odd to me, but the officers didn't seem to be phased by it for some reason.

"Thank you, officer," Kat said.

"If you remember anything, here's my card," she said, handing us the slip of paper. "Any description of the victim or the attacker. We'll check missing persons reports and see if anyone meets the descriptions you gave."

I nodded, my mind barely grabbing onto what she was saying as we turned and headed back inside, terror still rippling through me. The horrifying scream from the person they stabbed echoed through my mind. It hadn't been a normal scream, though, the way it pierced my mind didn't sound like anything humanly possible. What could even make that sound?

I twisted to look at Kat as she closed the door. "That scream I heard. I forgot to tell the cops about it. You heard it too, right? You had to. It was so loud."

Kat blinked at me, a concerned look in her eyes. She rubbed my shoulders, trying to calm me. "Cas, I didn't hear anything."

CHAPTER 7

I gasped as the touch of icy asphalt against my feet jolted me to my senses, and I found myself standing in a dark, narrow street. Familiar buildings surrounded me, as if I'd seen this street somewhere before, but my mind was trapped in a fog of uncertainty, unable to pinpoint where I was exactly.

Puffs of white mist broke free of my lips with each shaky breath. Every part of my body shook, and I wasn't sure if it was due to the cold night air nipping at my exposed limbs or the terror holding me captive.

I turned, catching sight of the old church clock tower glowing dimly against the foggy night sky as it peaked above the buildings, and relief washed through me at the knowledge I wasn't far from my house. Just a few blocks and I would be safe and home. I could make it.

My gaze darted around the dark corners of the alley surrounding me. How had I gotten here? Was I dreaming? I could have sworn I'd just been with someone... but who? Had I been with Kat? Or had I been home? I drew a deep breath as I racked my brain, but it was no use, my memories locked away in a haze.

A street lamp shined dimly in the distance, flickering, and I feared it might go out on me, leaving me to the face darkness alone. There wasn't even the sound of approaching vehicles, the city left in a silent dream. My teeth chattered as I started toward the barely illuminated road, desperate to get out of this place.

A scuff of movement echoed from behind me, and I whipped around, my pulse pounding in my ears as I scanned the area, but I was alone. Air flooded my lungs, but oxygen seemed to evade me as I paced backward, my heart pumping panic to every inch of my body.

"H–hello?" My words barely made it out of my throat. "Who's there?"

No response came, and no movements followed. I turned back, praying my mind was playing tricks on me, and I choked on air as I found my path blocked by Damien.

"Oh my God!" My hands clamped over my mouth as I stumbled back. "Damien, don't scare me like that!"

I paused, brows knitting together. *Wait a minute*. What was he doing here?

Shock swept over his face as he snatched his hood down . "What are you doing here?" His words were clipped, voice laced with worry, his face a combination of near terror and confusion.

My lips parted to answer but the words caught in my throat, as I tried and failed to figure that out myself. "I... I don't know."

"You need to get out of here now. It's too dangerous." He grabbed my arm, pulling me along as he hurried down the road, and I couldn't understand his urgency.

"What's going on?" I demanded as we fell into a sprint. "Why are we running?"

He ducked sharply into an alley, and pushed me up against the brick wall, his hands plastered to the brick on either side of me. I stilled at the proximity of him, of the feel of his powerful body against mine, so close I swore I could have felt his heart pounding as fast as mine was.

My eyes lifted to him as he leaned over to peek around the corner, pure concentration painting his face. He was so big against me, his body like tightly wound cords, jaw clenched, and I felt my cheeks warm as my mind wandered to the kiss we'd shared. I blinked, pulling myself back, because now was not the fucking time to be feeling this way.

He turned back to me, his eyes a reflection of calculated thoughts as they fell to the ground, his brows furrowing. His throat bobbed, and he released me, looking down the alley now before us, as if looking for something. What had him so freaked out?

The temperature around us dropped, and a shiver ran through me as I wrapped my arms around myself. Then I looked down, realizing I was in my night shorts and T-shirt.

What the fuck?

Damien turned to press his back to the brick, cursing under his breath.

"You're freaking me out, Damien. What's going on?" I whispered nervously.

"Dammit, why are they acting different tonight?" he muttered to no one as his hands balled into fists, the black leather of his fingerless gloves groaning in his grip. He drew deep, steadying breaths, as if he'd been running long before he found me. His dark hair lay draped in a windblown mess over his shoulders, tied back in a half knot and out of his face, leaving the remaining free curls to spill over his shoulders.

"Damien!"

He looked down for a moment, as if he were considering what he might say before turning to me. "Weren't you supposed to be staying the night with Kat?"

I blinked. That's right, I had been staying the night at Kat's house. "Yeah, I was–"

"Then what are you doing out here?" He grabbed my shoulders, moving me further down the alley, amber and ashen eyes piercing mine.

"I told you. I don't know!" I bit back, wishing he would tell me what the hell was going on.

As the words left my lips, movement in the shadows behind him drew my attention. A slender black figure emerged from around the corner, just barely visible in the darkness. Its head hung low, back hunched to expose a jagged spine, its hair hanging in tendrils around its face as it prowled closer. Black smoke danced like steam off the creature's skin, which was so shallow and pale that I could see the black veins branching out in thin webs just beneath the surface. Its bones shone through its paper-like skin, its stomach hollowed out, ribs exposed, as if it were starved. Pale puffs of white mist billowed from the darkness under its black hair with each breath the creature let out.

It lifted its head, shadows falling away to reveal the creature's face. Every instinct to run came to life as I peered into its bottomless black eyes, hollow to the edges of its eyelids and void of any soul. Its lips parted, the skin tearing along a deadly grin that stretched from ear to ear.

I gasped, stumbling away as its lips peeled back, exposing rows of jagged, razor-sharp teeth and screamed, "Behind you!"

Damien whipped around, knocking the creature to the side with his leg. It crashed into the brick wall we'd been leaning against just moments before. I swallowed, my stomach churning as the creature sank to the ground, its side caved in. Its body started to almost vibrate, hisses and growls breaking free from its mouth as it writhed.

My chest heaved as terror clawed its way through me. "What the fuck is that?"

The sickening sound of popping and snapping bones had me nearly vomiting, and the side that was once caved in popped itself back out. The demon growled and hissed wildly as it folded forward, its massive black tipped claws slamming into the asphalt. Its head jerked to

Damien, eyes wild and crazed, and he widened his stance. There was no way he was planning on fighting this thing.

"You need to go," Damien ordered, pulling a long dagger from his side as it launched for him, and I stumbled back as he caught it by the throat and sank the blade deep into the creature's chest. A high-pitched shriek tore from it as it flailed, disintegrating into dust. The sound tore into the furthest depths of my mind, the same one I'd heard earlier that same night. I froze in terror, unable to move my feet, unable to run, unable to do anything.

Damien's eyes flashed back to me, and he roared. "Now!"

I clasped my hand over my mouth, keeping myself from screaming at what I just witnessed, and the world spun around me as I stumbled back.

Two more creatures came barreling around the corner, grabbing hold of Damien's shoulders and jerking him back from me. A feral curse slipped from Damien's lips as their long black claws tore the shoulder of his jacket.

"Damien!" I screamed as I watched him wrestle to get free of them, elbowing one to give him time to recover. I looked around for something, anything, to help him, but there was nothing I could use as a weapon, not even a broken bottle or glass. I was helpless.

I turned back in time to see him rip his dagger from the chest of one of the creatures. Before he could prepare, the other sprang back in, tackling him to the ground, grabbing hold of his left arm, its claws tearing into his jacket and ripping his arm open.

A growl ripped from Damien's throat as he rolled over atop the creature. He slammed his fist into the creature's face, a black oily substance splattering across his fist. Its body went limp, twitching faintly, face smashed and covered in the substance now covering Damien.

Blood. God, it was the creature's blood that painted his skin. My mind fell back to the strange oil stain the police had found in the alley. There was no way it had been from one of these creatures... could it have?

Damien sank his dagger into the creature's chest, and it crumbled into dust beneath him, just as the first had. My eyes fell to his shredded arm, the severity of the wound hidden by the torn sleeve. Fresh blood seeped from beneath the fabric, dripping onto the ground.

"Oh my God, Damien!" I hurried to his side, dropping to my knees to look over his torn arm.

"Get out of here, Cas. I'll be fine," he said through gritted teeth as he reached for his knife laying on the ground a few feet from him.

"But your arm—"

His eyes flashed to me. "Go!"

Something within me screamed to not abandon him, to find something I could use as a weapon. I couldn't leave him here, not like this. Still, I heeded his demands and stood. There was no way I could face those creatures. I didn't even know how to fight, let alone help him. I'd just be in the way if I stayed.

Damien's eyes shifted behind me, widening, and his yell became a demand, an order. "Move! Now!"

He shoved me out of the way as another creature lunged at him, taking him to the ground. It fought to get to him as he braced it with his forearm, serrated jaws snapping at the air within inches of his face.

I jumped to my feet, needing to get out of here, to get out of his way. I was a distraction to him, and I hated that I couldn't do anything to help. Fear coiled in my gut as I turned, every fiber of my being recoiling at the thought of leaving him.

Air halted in my lungs as I came to a halt, finding myself face to face with another of the creatures. I froze. This one somehow felt different.

Its face changed, shifting until it more closely resembled a human face. Her black hair flowed around her like shafts of pure darkness, fading into smoke that danced and writhed at her back. A disturbing clicking sound slipped from her lips, and other clicks echoed in the darkness around us in response.

Something about the sight of her aroused a strange sensation within me that I didn't quite understand, as if my body were trying to communicate something to me. Her lips parted as she breathed, her razor-sharp teeth glistening from behind them. Her hollow black eyes moved over me, as if she were inspecting me. I should be running, but I couldn't pull myself away from her gaze, and I took in the details of her face, the pale gray skin, so shallow that I could see the black web of veins, stretching out from around her eyes, under her neck. Her hand shot out, black-tipped, clawed fingers wrapping around my throat. I gasped, trying to move, trying to fight her off, but I found my limbs unresponsive.

Her breath, like ice, flowed over me, into me. She pulled me closer, our faces inches apart. Those hollow black eyes stared into mine, drawing me into their abyss, and the world spun around us. I couldn't pull away, couldn't fight it...

Did I want to, though?

Whispered voices echoed in my mind, speaking in a language I'd never heard before, and my eyes fluttered, my mind buckling under the press of this creature's will.

The distant sound of voices shouting Damien's name echoed through the alley as black dots blotted across my vision. I could almost hear Damien barking orders, his voice slurring too much for me to understand, but I heard one thing.

My name.

He called my name, and something tugged in my chest, crying out to him as I found myself plummeting into the abyss of those black eyes. They were beautiful... so beautiful. Why did I not want to succumb to them? They offered something.... more.

Freedom.

The creature jerked back, hissing at someone behind me as her face melted back to the horror of the others, like a mask.

My knees shook beneath me, and her clawed grip loosened around my throat before she slipped back into the shadows. I teetered for a moment and the world tilted as my legs gave out, my vision darkening.

"Cassie!"

I shot up in a panic, my skin and clothes drenched in cold sweat. My gaze darted around, mouth bone dry, chest heaving as I gasped for air. The morning light spilling in through the windows burned my eyes and I blinked as they adjusted.

Where was I? I was in a bed. Whose bed? Whose room was this?

I rubbed my eyes furiously, and the sound of Kat singing to her music echoed from downstairs. I was in Kat's room. Safe. I pushed myself to the edge of the bed, my mind swimming in a haze. I'd been in the alleys, or... was I?

Had it all been a dream? I'd had my share of lucid dreams, but this... I lifted my hand to my throat, skin still tingling from the icy touch of that monster's claws, and I shivered thinking about it.

The pounding of feet echoed up the stairs, interrupting my thoughts, and the door swung open to reveal Kat. "Ah, you're awake."

"Yeah, I'm up," I yawned, pushing back the fear lingering in the back of my mind, and stretched.

She was already dressed, her coppery hair pulled back into a ponytail. "Good morning, sleepyhead. I was wondering when you were finally gonna wake up."

"Good morning," I groaned, combing my fingers through my hair. "What happened last night?"

She frowned. "What do you mean?"

"Did I go for a walk or something?"

"No. After the cops left, we went upstairs and passed out. You were so freaked out that I didn't argue when you said you were turning in. Figured you were exhausted."

I racked my brain, trying to remember what happened after the cops left, but once again, I was met with a haze. "I must have been. I don't even remember doing that."

My gaze shifted to the clock on her wall. It was already eleven. Of course, I overslept this morning. "Shit, I've gotta get home to get ready for my—"

"Date?" she finished, using the word I couldn't bring myself to say as she looked at me with knowing eyes.

"Y–yeah. That." It still felt too good to be true, and I was reluctant to get my hopes up that it was anything more than two friends hanging out.

I jumped out of her bed, the old wood floor groaning under my feet, and I grabbed my bag before packing the few things I brought with me before I changed and hurried down the stairs.

Kat called to me as I walked down the road toward my house. "I'll see you Monday! Call me later or tomorrow and tell me how the date goes!"

"I will," I yelled back and turned to continue down the side street. The morning air was refreshing and cool, and the wonderful smell of aspen and birch drifted on the breeze from the nearby woods. I lifted my gaze to the forest standing at the edges of the neighborhood, the beautiful tones of orange and red painting the mountainsides surrounding the valley. My mind wandered as I rounded the corner, back to the dream.

Every muscle was stiff and sore, as if I'd run a mile. However, I didn't have any marks or anything that could prove it really happened. The notion of it was nonsense, though. How could any of that have been real? Monsters weren't real. It was just another stupid dream.

A dream about Damien.

I ran my hand over my face, frustrated at what I was feeling, and that it was now spilling into my dreams. Had it been Damien's hands reaching out to me from the shadows of my dreams all this time?

I blinked. No, those dreams started before we met... or had they?

A sigh slipped from my lips. Why was I thinking so deeply into this?

They're just dreams, not reality. Get over it.

Besides, I couldn't even remember walking out of Kat's house, and I wasn't a sleepwalker. I couldn't have just appeared out on the streets.

The deep thoughts made the walk home go by quickly and before I realized it, I was unlocking my front door. As I passed my bookshelf, I paused, remembering the too-brief kiss Damien and I had shared. My heart fluttered, and before I realized what I was doing, my lips were curving into a grin. I cursed internally before pulling my gaze away and hurrying up the stairs.

As two o'clock drew closer, I'd caught myself fidgeting more and more, chewing my nails, rolling my ring around my finger. Kat kept insisting this was a date, but I was skeptical to call it that. I was afraid to think it, and then be disappointed. Surely, there were other beautiful, more interesting women Damien would find more appealing. Still, I couldn't deny the way he looked at me. It was warm, like sunshine on my skin in the summer, and though I shouldn't give into it, shouldn't crave that warmth... I couldn't stop myself from seeking it out. He was the first person who'd ever made me feel this way, so nervous and yet so excited.

And for once, I was finding bits of color in my world of black and white.

I stood next to my bed, chewing the inside of my lip as I looked back and forth between outfits. God, I was overthinking this. We were just going for a walk in the woods. It wasn't like we were going anywhere fancy. We were just friends, there was no world in which I could allow myself to become more than that. If we never became more, he would be safe from the hurt...

So, why did I struggle so hard to fight the feelings stirring within me? Why was it so difficult to keep him at a safe distance?

A sigh slipped from my lips, the guilt curdling in my stomach, but I couldn't seem to be rational when it came to him, couldn't fight the selfish desires to get closer to him. I headed for the shower. There was no need to stress, he didn't like me that way, couldn't like me that way. I had to take a deep breath and calm myself down. I was getting worked up and probably for nothing. It should remain nothing, because my heart was already damaged. A relationship may only break it further. No amount of his love could heal my faulty heart—

But my love could destroy his.

My hand hovered over the spigot, doubt and something cold settling into my bones. That kiss could have meant nothing, could have just been his way of distracting me. I blinked, turning on the shower, desperate to drown out the thoughts, but it was no use.

He was just doing what you asked him to do. It was just a kiss. He could have anyone he wanted.

My eyes fell to my feet, the water pooling in the tub as it drained.

He could have someone who could give him a chance at a future. All you can give him is heartbreak. You'd be better to just—

No. If he wanted someone else he wouldn't be spending the day with you.

I blinked, feeling a strange stir of comfort in my chest, but I shook it away. He wasn't choosing me for anything, we were just friends.

The hot water rolled down my back as I washed myself, and I sighed in relief as the tension and aches ebbed from every muscle. I quickly finished washing the conditioner out and twisted the knob, the water trickling to a stop.

My phone rang as I finished blow drying my hair, and my nerves were so on edge that, I nearly dropped it before I reached for my phone to see if it was Damien.

I'll be there in 15. See you soon.

A surge of excitement rushed through me as I read his text, and I hurried to finish getting ready. We were going for a hike, no need to get all dressed up for that, so I threw on a sweater, a pair of cargo joggers, and boots. I checked myself in the mirror one more time, falling back into overthinking it, but I shook my head and forced myself to head down the stairs. As I reached the base of the stairwell, a knock rung at the door and my heart leapt into my throat.

Those beautiful amber and ashen eyes gazed down on me as I opened the door, a smile lighting his face.

I beamed at the sight of him. "Hey."

"Hey, Cas." He paused a moment in the doorway. "Are your parents home? I should probably meet them. Don't want them to think I'm a kidnapper."

I swallowed. He wanted to meet my parents.

Of course, why not? That's normal, right? Nothing to be weird over.

"Um, yeah, they're next door. Let me introduce you to them."

The front door creaked as I peered into my parents' side of the house. "Mom?"

"I'm in the kitchen, Cas. What's up?" Mom called.

"I've got a guy I wanted you to meet, but if you're busy—"

Mom suddenly leaned into the hallway at the mention of a guy, her brows furrowing. "What guy?"

Damien leaned into the doorway next to me. "Hi, Mrs. Hites, I'm Damien."

I don't think I'd ever seen Mom move so fast. Before I could brush it off as unimportant and close the door, she was pulling me inside.

"You didn't tell me you were seeing someone, Cas!"

I gaped. Well, if that didn't just make it awkward. "I mean… It's—it's nothing—"

"I was taking her out to Stackhouse and maybe to dinner after, and I wanted to meet you before we left."

While I was a flustered mess, Damien was cool and collected; and I couldn't help but feel like he'd dialed his charm up to its highest level. His gaze slid to me, and he gave me a quick wink, before he looked back to my mom.

"Well, thank you for that. It's nice to see her getting out of the house for something other than school."

"Mom," I groaned.

"What? You're always cooped up in your room reading or drawing." She smiled, turning back to Damien. "It's time you got out there and met someone."

An awkward silence fell, and I glanced back at the door.

Mom caught the hint, perking up. "Well, I won't keep you two. Be safe!"

I turned, eager to get out the door before she could embarrass me anymore. "Bye, Mom."

"Make good choices!" she called as I shoved Damien out the door before shutting it quickly.

I stood there a moment, heart racing. Damien's low laugh made me aware of just how heated my cheeks and ears felt.

He parted his lips to comment, and I shot him a look. "Don't you even..."

His only response was a devious grin and a look in his eyes that made my heart race faster, and I shouldn't have liked the feeling of that as much as I did.

Damien held the door to his car open for me and I lowered myself into the passenger's seat, the leather interior smooth under my hands. He lowered himself into the driver's side and I buckled up as he pulled out onto the road. My lips curved into a smile as I gazed out the window.

"I won't lie. I was a little nervous about meeting your parents," he admitted.

I looked back at him incredulously. "You? Nervous? I thought you had nerves of steel."

He gave me a sideways glance before looking back at the road.

I continued. "They're not that bad. Besides, I think my mom took a real liking to you."

"I'm glad about that. I wasn't looking forward to having to sneak you out without them knowing."

My cheeks heated and my heart thrummed as I imagined it. Curiosity sent ideas flying into my head that made me blush farther. "What? Would you have come tossing rocks at my window? Shared romantic conversations in the moonlight, like Romeo and Juliet in the late-night hours?"

His head turned just enough to glance at me out of the corner of his eye, and a mischievous grin tugged at the corner of his lips. "Amongst other things."

CHAPTER 8

I inhaled the crisp air, filled with the scents of the trees—the grass, the nearby creek—as Damien closed the passenger door behind me. The dense expanse of trees stretched out before us, and the sun's rays warmed me through my coat.

He took the lead down the path, seeming to have a course in mind. I tossed my small bag over my shoulder, which contained my sketchbook, along with some charcoal and graphite, and followed after him. It would likely remain untouched, but I couldn't shake the urge to have it handy in the off chance I found something out here that sparked the need to draw.

"You come here often?" I asked as we made our way into the trees.

"I do, actually," he said, glancing over his shoulder, and his brows rose before he slowed his pace. "Sorry."

I chuckled as I jogged to his side. "It's ok, I'm used to it. Short legs, ya know?"

That charming, crooked grin curved one corner of his lips and I turned my gaze to the forest, trying not to let my heart fall into the dangerous frantic pace it wanted to.

"Did you have a good time at Kat's last night?" he asked.

I bit my lip, my mind quick to dredge up the terrible dream I had, and the murder I'd witness. Or had any of it really happened? I frowned, questioning everything and the fact that the cops hadn't found any evidence of what I'd seen.

"You, ok?" he asked, and I blinked.

"Oh yeah, it was um... we had a good time, studied late at the campus, Cody saw us to our car, we ate pizza, and I passed out."

His brows pinched together. "You guys didn't go out and do anything?"

"Why would we? I don't want to end up missing or murdered," I said, and my tone turned grave. "I'd love to, in all honesty. We used to go on pizza dates every Friday, but I'm too afraid to now with whoever is out there taking people."

He seemed to misstep, and his gaze slipped from me for a moment before he blinked and offered a smile. "Maybe we can all go out sometime together. You, me, Kat, Cody—the guys. I doubt whoever's behind it could take out all of us at once."

All of us? I considered that thought, and I couldn't deny he had a point. Surely, we would be safer in a large group like that. "Maybe."

The warmth of sunlight faded above the trees, dwindling into small shafts of light that cascaded on us the further into the forest we went. Damien pulled something from his pocket, and I realized it was a black pocketknife as he proceeded to flip it open before closing it once more and doing the action over again.

"So, Cole told me you entered something in the art competition. He said the winning piece will be featured in a local art gallery."

"I did," I hedged, and despite the fact there was no way to tell the piece was about my dreams—those very dreams that may or may not subconsciously be headed toward including his hands and not those of a stranger's—I couldn't help but suddenly feel embarrassed.

He glanced at me sidelong when I didn't elaborate further, and I chewed the inside of my lip before caving into his inquiry. "I'm nervous about how the judges will perceive it."

"Why do you say that? I've seen your work. It's stunning."

My cheeks heated at his compliment, and I couldn't lift my gaze to him as I fidgeted with my fingers. "It's a little different from my normal work. It's dark, which isn't something new, but after it was damaged by someone, Cole talked me into trying to further damage the paper to reflect the internal flaws of the subject instead of starting the piece over."

"Someone damaged your work?" Damien asked, seeming to narrow in on that fact above all else, and for a moment he almost seemed angry.

"Yeah, but it's ok, I'm sure they didn't mean to." I didn't know why I was defending them in that moment, but the frustration in his expression left me wondering if he might hunt down the person and do something to them. "Besides, the new direction for the piece grew on me."

He didn't speak, but the question lingered in his gaze.

I carefully stepped over a large stone in our path, and gave into his unspoken request. "No one is perfect. Everyone has their flaws, their own darkness, but we never truly see those hidden pieces of us. So, I brought those imperfections to the surface, showing every tear and rip and wrinkle painting the soul of the subject."

"That's awfully poetic of you," he said, his expression soft as he processed what I'd said, and I blinked, suddenly feeling foolish for verbalizing it.

"It's sappy and foolish, but it seemed like a good idea," I said, not wanting him to think too deeply into the weird thoughts in my head.

"I like it," he said simply, and I lifted my gaze to him, taken back by the lack of judgement in his eyes. I couldn't help but smile, my eyes falling to the stony dirt pathway at our feet.

"Um... I've been wanting to ask," he said awkwardly, and I tilted my head as he seemed to consider his words. "How have you been? After everything that happened with... Marcus."

I swallowed as the inkling of dread curdling in my stomach at the memory.

Concern flitted across his face. "If you're not ready to talk about it, you don't have to. I just—" He groaned, running his hand through his hair. "I just wanted to make sure you were doing ok, and if not, I wanted you to know I'm here if you ever need to get it off your chest."

"Thanks," I said, a little touched at the notion. "It's been... difficult at times. I haven't had any nightmares about it recently, but I'm afraid of running into him again."

"I haven't seen him around campus lately," he said, his eyes darkening as he turned his focus on the path before us. "But if I do, he'll regret it."

Something rushed over me, something hot and I rubbed my forearms as goosebumps pebbled my skin.

"I don't mean to pry," I started, and I caught sight of his brows furrowing, but he withheld his gaze from me.

"If you don't want to talk about it, it's totally fine." I paused, trying to gather my thoughts. "I've just been wondering, ever since Marcus attacked me..."

His knife clicked open, but he didn't flick it closed again.

"Do you guys get into fights with Marcus often?" I asked hesitantly.

He drew a deep breath, and for a moment I wondered if he would open up to me about it or shut me out. "I guess you could say we don't get along well."

The looks Marcus had given Damien told me it was more than just not getting along. And the way he seemed to target me over the possibility I might be someone important to him... I wasn't, but he seemed keen to do what he did simply on the off chance I was.

"I was just curious. I didn't mean to pry," I said as we turned and stepped down the bank of the creek to cross.

"You're not prying," he said, a muscle feathering in his jaw, and guilt flitted across his eyes. "I hate that you got caught in the middle of it all."

He sighed, folding his knife closed before sliding it into his pocket. His brows narrowed, as if he were frustrated, but relaxed them quickly, as if to hide it. "Marcus tends to cross boundaries, and never learns when to back off."

"Why does he have such a problem with you?" His gaze shifted to me, and there was such a turbulent whirlpool of emotions, I feared I may have pried too far. "Sorry, forget I asked."

"No, you're fine. It's just—" He blinked and swallowed. "Complicated. There's a lot of bad blood between us. Has been for years."

"I don't want you to think that I feel any differently about you or anything." The words spilled out of my mouth, fearful that he might have misunderstood. "I was just curious. I know you're not a bad person, Damien. You helped me when he attacked me. You didn't have to do that, but you did. I really appreciate it."

"I would do it again in a heartbeat, if necessary."

A massive raven landed atop a branch before us, tilting its head to gaze down at us before letting out a loud caw, and Damien lifted his gaze to it, his eyes narrowing.

I gasped, my eyes lighting up as I gazed up at it. "Oh my God, he's huge."

The raven tilted its head to watch us as we passed below its branch, its black iridescent feathers catching the light, and I was almost tempted to stop and sketch the beautiful creature. It hopped around to watch us and as from the corner of my eye I found Damien watching it over his shoulder, as if he half expected the creature to swoop down at us.

"I've never seen one that big. He's so pretty," I said, turning to walk backward, returning my gaze to it as it seemed to preen at my statement, before turning around to walk forward. "Did you know you can befriend ravens?"

He blinked, looking back at me, with a humored look on his face. "Why would you want to befriend a raven?"

"My dad taught me growing up that they're extremely intelligent creatures. They remember their interactions with people. If you show them you're a friend, either with gifts or food, over time they'll remember that and may watch out for you, alert you if something is wrong, or even bring you gifts. They especially love shiny objects."

"Really, now?" Damien said, his tone full of something like humor as he gave the crow one final glance. "This one seems like a particularly nosey creature."

I frowned, opening my mouth to question him as the raven's shrill cry echoed through the forest. It filled my ears, and I squeaked, my hands flying over my head as it flew a few feet over us before continuing through the trees until it disappeared out of sight. Damien burst into a fit of laughter and I elbowed him.

"Did you do something bad to a raven?" I asked him accusatorially.

"Of course not. Why?"

"Just making sure," I said, continuing down the path. "Because if you do something bad to them—they would tell the other ravens in their... I think it's called an unkindness—"

"Unkindness?" Damien asked, cocking a brow.

"That's what you call a flock of ravens," I said with a smile, drawing a calming breath as I found myself growing winded as we started up another hill. "Anyway, they communicate with each other, and just as they would tell others that you're a friend, they'll tell others if you do something bad to them. They'll attack you and never forget what you did. So don't get on a raven's bad side."

He let out a huff of a laugh. "I'll be sure to be kind to the unkindness, then."

I shook my head, but a grin spread across my face as his cheesy humor got to me. My gaze snagged on his arm as he stretched it and flexed his hand before slipping it into his coat pocket—the same arm that had been hurt in my dream the night before. He was wearing a heavy canvas jacket, so I couldn't see if he had any wounds there. It wasn't like it was strange for him to be wearing a jacket in this weather, nothing to fret over.

It was just a dream. Why are you still hung up about it? Before I could say anything about it, we came upon a clearing, and my eyes lit up.

Branches stretched out to one another, forming a sparse canopy, and shafts of light leaked through the branches onto us. A deep creek ran through the middle, filled with river rock and boulders, the water flowing just high enough to cover most of the smaller pebbles on the creek bed. Dilapidated remnants of old houses were nestled in the trees nearby, having been reclaimed by nature over the years. The birdsong echoed through the forest, the sound of trees swaying in the breeze and other wildlife mixing and melding with their sweet music.

It was so peaceful.

Damien stopped at the edge of the clearing. "I come here when I just need to be alone—had a feeling you might enjoy it as much as I do."

I couldn't shake the feeling of familiarity this place held, but I knew I'd never been here.

"It's beautiful."

Damien smiled, taking my hand as he led me toward the creek, where we settled down onto the soft grass. A cool breeze danced through the trees, running over my skin, and I inhaled the fresh fragrance of the forest.

He laid back onto the grass, closing his eyes as he tucked his arms behind his head. "It's a little secret of mine. I come here when I need to get away. Now you can come here whenever you like."

His words touched me in a way I couldn't understand, and I had to pause for a moment. This place seemed special to him, and yet, he was sharing it with me. I frowned as his statement settled into my mind, something within me swelling with warmth at his words, and yet at the same time, doubts surfaced.

"Why would you share this with me?" I asked, my gaze lingering on the shimmering water rolling over the river rocks of the creek before me as I fidgeted with my fingers.

His gaze snapped to me, and he sat up, seeming shocked I'd asked. "It's..." He frowned, his eyes slipping from mine before he continued. "I thought it was the least I could do."

He's just doing this to be a good friend. He's just making up for what happened. This isn't anything special. You're not anything special.

Disappointment sank into my chest, and it frustrated me at how deeply it hurt, and how badly it affected me. I should be happy. It would be better if this was all we would be. Friends.

"What I mean is..." he amended, running his hand over his face, and I arched a brow.

"I've hated seeing you hurt. I've hated seeing how you've struggled after what happened." His eyes drifted to me once more, but this time there was something akin to hope within them. "I want you to be happy, and this just seemed like something you'd enjoy."

I turned to look across the clearing, bringing my knees up under my chin. He was right. There was something about this place that gave me a strange peace.

"Thank you," I finally managed to say, wrapping my arms around my knees. "I didn't think I let on what's been going on that much."

"You don't, but I see it," he said, and I looked back at him as he lowered himself to lay in the grass, folding his arms behind his head as he gazed up at the branches dancing in the wind. "You try to hide it, but I see it. I see how you look over your shoulder when you walk anywhere now. I can tell when you've had a nightmare by the look in your eyes in the morning, the weight of it dulling the beautiful hazel."

I blinked, taken back by his words, and my cheeks heated at the thought that he considered my eyes beautiful.

"And." his gaze shifted to my fingers wrapped around my knees before they rose back to the sky. "I've seen how badly you've been chewing your nails."

My eyes fell to my fingernails at his comment, frowning at how short they were. I hadn't realized he paid such close attention to me, and I wasn't quite sure how to feel about that.

I shoved down the thoughts of Marcus and how rough the last week had been as I reached into my bag to pull my sketchbook and graphite pencil free. My gaze flitted to him as his eyes slid closed, seeming to bask in the streaks of sunshine. I propped the sketchbook up on my lap and leaned over it, running my pencil across the paper. I snuck a peek at him again, and drew down the angles of his face, the lines overlapping as they took shape to define his features. When I glanced up again, I nearly dropped the pad of paper, yelping as I met his eyes.

At some point, he'd turned to face me, propping himself up on his elbow with his chin rested atop his knuckle as he watched me with a knowing smile. "Are you drawing me again?"

I pressed the sketchbook to my chest as I hid the drawing, wanting to deny it, but I knew he'd caught a glimpse. "Yes, but you can't see it yet."

A low laugh slipped out under his breath, and my heart soared at the sound of it. He sat up. "How do you want me, then?"

My mind fell into a frenzy of thoughts. This wasn't a difficult question. I just had to set him up how I wanted him... to be drawn, to be drawn.

It's just a drawing, Cas, calm down.

"Um. Sit up... Turn to me..." I set the pad of paper down, scooting closer to him. "Now turn your head just like..." I reached out, turning his face to angle it how I wanted. We were so close, and I could almost feel his eyes on me, feel the warmth of his breath against my hand. I tried to maintain my composure and act professional as an artist, but it was hopeless, and I knew he was seeing through me by his coy grin.

His eyes tracked my every movement, drifting over me as I positioned him. When I lifted my eyes to meet his, they almost glowed in the rays of light falling through the trees. They were dazzling, a mix of silver rims with a burst of amber in the center—like embers in ashes, so intense I was falling into the depths of them.

I cleared my throat, dragging myself back down to reality, and scooted back to lean against the nearest rock as I continued to draw. My eyes flitted back and forth between him and my sketch, my heart fluttering at the soft expression on his face, the warmth filling his eyes as he watched me work. I didn't know how much time passed as I jotted down the details of his face, but I started to lose myself in them. His neck. His shoulders. His chest.

After a moment, I realized that this was my first time working with a male model. His features were so different, the coiled muscles lying beneath the surface of his skin, the veins of his hands. I wondered what he looked like under that shirt. My ears grew hot, and he chuckled.

He sees you, dummy. Stop thinking like that.

I finally got the details down and closed my sketchbook.

He frowned. "Awe, don't I get to see it?"

"No, not yet. These are just notes."

"Notes? You take notes for drawing?"

I nodded as I grabbed my bag, shoving my book and pencil back inside before turning to him. "Yeah. This'll be my reference for the real drawing. I'll let you see it when I finish it."

"Well, I look forward to seeing it then, but only if you promise to make me as hot as you did in the first drawing."

I couldn't fight the laughter bubbling up my throat as he pushed himself up and extended his hand to me. I took it, feeling the roughness of his calloused palms as he gripped my hand and pulled me to my feet.

He took lead, stepping out onto one of the boulders before jumping down onto the bed of river rocks near the flowing water. The word to describe the way he moved across the broken stone path across the flowing water escaped me. It wasn't so much grace as it was watching a predator move lithely across the surface, each step natural yet calculated and perfectly balanced.

"So, did you ever figure out what Barrett's been up to with this plan for Halloween that he won't shut up about?" I asked as I hopped down from the ledge and cautiously stepped across the slick rock surface after him.

"Nope, him and Vincent are the only ones in on whatever they've got up their sleeves. And their lips are sealed," Damien said, and while there was a hint of annoyance, his lips quirked into a half smile. "It probably has to do with scaring people shitless. I can almost guarantee that."

I snickered as I hopped onto a boulder, my arms shooting out as I teetered and nearly fell. "He jump scares me and he's gonna get a fist to the face."

His eyes seemed to light up as he glanced back at me briefly. "I would love to see you lay him out. Promise you won't do it without me around."

"I guess you'd better stick close to me then. Be warned, though, I might just throw you in the way to escape."

"Throw me to the wolves, if you must, but I think it would be better to hear him squeal when you throw a fake spider in his face when he tries."

I barked out a laugh and gasped as my foot slipped. Damien twisted around as I fell back, and he lurched toward me, his hand stretching out to mine, but he narrowly missed my fingers.

Icy water raked over my skin like claws, soaking into my clothes, my hair, every inch of my body, and the rocks scraped and bruised my back and arms as I made a poor attempt to catch myself. I choked on my breath, the air rushing from my lungs at the shock of the cold.

"Shit, Cassie, are you ok?" I could barely hear him over the sound of water flooding my ears as I sat up, gasping for air. Damien grabbed me, pulling me to my feet as I groaned.

"Y–yeah… I–I think s–so. *Dammit*," I groaned through chattering teeth as I hugged myself. "I–I'm s–s–sorry. I'm s–such a fucking k–klutz."

He guided me back to the edge of the rock bed, steadying me as I stumbled and slipped over uneven rocks. Shivers rattled my body as he eased me down to sit atop one of the boulders. He cursed and quickly removed my wet coat, tossing it up near my bag before hastily peeling his jacket off. I focused on rubbing my arms, trying to warm up. The sound of movement reached my ears, and I looked over my shoulder, just as he pulled his sweater over his head.

My throat tightened, and for a moment I couldn't breathe, let alone keep myself from admiring his beautifully carved muscles as they flexed beneath the surface of his tanned, olive skin. His sleeve slipped from his right arm, revealing a tattoo of intricate patterns, strange markings or writing, and black smoke stretched out from a crescent moon on the corner of his chest before stretching and spiraling from his shoulder down to his elbow.

My heart lurched as his other sleeve slipped free, revealing his left forearm, wrapped in bandages. I whipped around, my heart hammering.

It's a coincidence, Cas. Just a coincidence.

"Do you have a tank top or anything under that shirt?" he asked urgently, the sound of him gathering his shirt and jacket reaching my ears, and his words clicked through me, my thoughts falling into a frenzy.

If I wasn't blushing then, I was now. "N–no…"

"We need to get you into some dry clothes. Here, you can change into my sweater until we can get you back to the car to warm up." He handed it to me and immediately turned to step away, gathering my bag and jacket as he gave me room to change.

Embarrassed, my heart pounding in my ears, I crouched behind the rock as I quickly removed my shirt and bra and slid his on. It hung loosely around me, but I wrapped myself into the remnants of his warmth in the fibers. I bundled my bra into my shirt, squeezing out some of the excess water.

"I'm done," I called, my hands shaking as I wrung my hair out over my shoulder and proceeded to try to press the water out of my pants, but it only succeeded in trapping the water in my boots.

"Here, put this on, too." Damien threw his jacket over my back, catching me off guard as the hood fell over my head, and he turned his back to me. "Get on, I'll carry you back."

I hesitated. "Oh no, I'm ok. I can walk."

"Do it. I don't want you to get sick on our first date. Your dad would kill me."

I bit back the smile at his joke. "O–okay."

"Did you hurt anything?" he asked, glancing over his shoulder with a worried expression as he knelt next to me.

I smiled, hoping to ease his worry. "I'm f-fine. I already feel a bit warmer. T-the jacket is helping a lot. Thank you."

He smiled back, and the butterflies continued their little dance in my stomach. There was something about his smile that had a way of getting to me. He helped me onto his back, and I prayed he wouldn't feel how fast my heart raced. I hadn't been able to get that brief kiss out of my head, my heart launching into a sprint every time I remembered how it felt to have him so close to me. I never thought we would get that close again, and yet here I was, chest pressed against his back, feeling every firm part of him shift and flex against me. I inhaled the lingering scent of him from his jacket, his hair. Cedarwood. Cedarwood and... leather?

My eyes closed as I focused on the gentle sway as he carried me, the heat of his skin warring with the icy air threatening to tunnel into my core. For a moment, despite the rush of emotions I was swimming in, I was sad our time here had ended so abruptly.

"Why am I such a klutz?" I muttered.

He chuckled. "Don't blame yourself. It could happen to anyone."

"Yeah, except it always happens to me, and I ruined your plans..."

"No, you didn't, Cas. Give yourself a break. Hey, you got to draw me at least."

I smiled and rested back against him, letting his body heat warm envelope me.

By the time we neared his car, my jeans had soaked through onto his. "I'm s–so sorry, I got y–you wet too."

"Don't worry about me." He lowered me down next to the car and helped me in, then closed the door and hurried around the front to start the engine.

Once the car warmed up enough, he reached over to turn up the heat, setting the vents on me. I stretched out my quivering hands, and I nearly moaned at the feel of the heavenly heat. As he reached for the shifter, my gaze snagged on the bandages wrapped around his forearm.

The terrifying thoughts resurfaced, and I tried to reason with myself that this was stupid to even consider the possibility of my dream being real.

"I live right around the corner from here. I could take you there to dry your clothes." He paused. "If you're comfortable with it, that is."

I glanced over at him, my mind struggling to latch onto what he said as I tried to force my gaze away from his wounded arm. "Are you sure? I—I don't want to impose."

"Cas, you're not imposing. I should've been more careful. It's my fault this happened. Let me make it up to you. Instead of going out, we can cook dinner and eat in. How does that sound?"

I smiled, the hope in his eyes too much to resist. "Only if you're okay with it."

His smile made it clear he was more than okay with it, and he started down the road.

"What happened?" I asked, nodding to his arm before looking back at him, my heart in my throat as I tried to stifle my fear. Last night's dream flooded my thoughts.

He was silent for a moment and then glanced down at his arm absentmindedly. "Oh, this?" He paused, and his eyes moved back to the road. "A dog attacked us."

I cocked an eyebrow. A dog bite? Really?

Dogs are real, monsters aren't, you scaredy cat.

I cocked an eyebrow at him. "So, a dog attacked you?"

"Yeah, not very exciting, huh?" he chuckled.

"What happened to the dog?"

"We managed to give it the slip over a fence, but Vincent won't leave me alone for not being fast enough to avoid getting bit."

"Oh my God, you guys are idiots." I sighed, rolling my eyes, dropping my head back against the headrest. Damien laughed, knowing he couldn't deny it.

I cocked my head to the side, smiling at him before joining in his laughter as he proceeded to make jokes which turned into our own scheming to try to scare Barrett on Halloween.

We never had the chance to hang out together like this, just the two of us. It had always been with the others.

For some reason, it felt… right.

CHAPTER 9

It wasn't long after we left Stackhouse Park that we pulled into the driveway of an old Tudor-style house with a beautiful bay window in the front. I frowned, wondering why we'd parked in front of this massive house. There was no way this could be his house. Could it?

My gaze drifted across the front yard, decorated with enormous maple trees that shaded the elegant white front porch. The historic architecture was detailed in a way that modern homes could only wish to emulate, and I wondered just how old it was. It wasn't like old houses were out of the norm in Johnstown, there were a lot, but the way this home had been cared for, it looked as if it hadn't aged despite the passage of time.

Damien got out and walked around to open my door before I had a chance to open it myself. "Come on, it'll be much warmer by the fireplace." He took my hand, lifting me out and onto my feet, and I lost myself in the gentle feel of his skin against mine.

"You still with me?"

I stumbled back into reality and looked up at him. "Yeah, sorry."

I turned to grab my soaked boots before he led me toward a path of stone steps carved into the hillside. "Your house is beautiful."

"It's... been in my family for a long time."

We continued up the stone steps before climbing the porch stairs. My heart raced as I came to terms with the fact that I was going into his house as he unlocked the door and led me in. My eyes popped as I took in the grand emerald-green foyer, lit by a large golden crystal chandelier hanging from the ceiling in front of the grand staircase.

It wasn't like I was wondering what his house might look like or anything, but this definitely wasn't it. It was so beautifully decorated, so clean, definitely not your typical college bachelor pad. Did he have roommates? He said it had been in his family for a long time, perhaps it was his parents' house, then.

Damien headed down the hall and disappeared into another room. The sound of logs clunking into a fireplace reached my ears not long after. "Bring your boots in here, Cas. We can set them by the fire to dry."

I tentatively stepped into the living room, admiring the combinations of dark grays, golds, and rich greens. My eyes passed over the intricately carved mantel above the fireplace. An array of pillar candles of varying heights, as well as a mix of potted ferns and vining plants, old books, and other bits and baubles decorated various shelves and other surfaces. So much character had been etched into every detail of his home, and it felt as if I were seeing a different part of him through the objects he surrounded himself with.

I came to a stop in front of the large sectional couch standing before the fireplace where he was knelt, tending to the fire. He rose, taking hold of my hands and rubbing them.

"Gods, you're so cold. Come on, I'm going to get you a towel and a change of clothes."

My thoughts lingered on that affectionate touch as he stroked the back of my hands, not fully latching onto what he was saying. He tugged me back toward the hall; the moment ending before I was ready, and I followed.

From the corner of my eye, I caught sight of a painting on the wall as he led me to the stairs. There was a man and a woman sitting with each other. The man looked a lot like Damien; and I wondered if it was a great-grandfather or something. The woman caught my eye—her dark hair hanging in stunning waves along her shoulders and her beautiful pale eyes that popped off her porcelain skin. There was something strikingly familiar about her, but I didn't get a chance to contemplate it further as he guided me into the hall.

He led me up the stairs and to his room, where he released my hand to head for his dresser. I watched him through the doorway anxiously, his back turned to me as he rummaged through the drawers.

He slid on a clean sweater and pulled out a pair of sweatpants before turning back to me.

"Here, you can wear these while I dry your clothes. I hope it's not too big." He handed me the sweatpants and headed for the hallway.

"Thank you," I said, though my voice barely made it out of my throat.

He flashed me a smile and closed the door.

I stood there for a moment, holding his sweatpants, feeling a little overwhelmed by the sudden turn of events. *Holy shit.* I was really standing here. How did a hike at Stackhouse end with me in Damien's room?

Just take a deep breath. This doesn't mean anything.

My eyes explored the bedroom, the large four post bed in the center, clad in a mess of deep gray sheets that sat unmade. I smiled when I found the book I'd loaned him resting on his nightstand, a bookmark jutting out from the pages, and my chest swelled.

He's... actually reading it?

The memory of his lips on mine resurfaced, and my heart picked up its pace. For a moment, I remembered the sensation of his skin, the hint of his taste...

I blinked. What the hell was I doing? I forced my gaze elsewhere.

Directly opposite the foot of the bed stood a rather large glass display case. It was hand carved and looked hundreds of years old. Behind the curved glass were beautifully displayed daggers and swords of different lengths and styles. I drifted toward them. There were so many, all so beautiful, with designs and patterns inlaid into the metal in a way that looked hand forged, but there was one in particular that held my gaze, displayed at the top of the case as if it were a crowned jewel in his collection.

Carvings of the most intricate designs were engrained in the ornate hilt, and as I reached onto my toes to get a better look, I realized that on one side of the cross guard was a warrior mounted on a horse, charging into battle, on the other side was a creature that I could only best describe as death itself riding atop its own horse. It was so beautiful, captivating even, and my eyes trailed down to the symbols, similar to the ones tattooed on Damien's arm, that extended down the blade in a beautiful gold pattern that popped off the black metal. In the center of the rune etched blade was a gold crescent moon that almost glowed. I blinked, snapping out of my trance, remembering why I was in here.

You can ask Damien about his fancy knife collection later, Cas.

I quickly changed into Damien's sweatpants, nearly laughing at how huge they were on me, and I had to tie the drawstring tight to keep them from falling off. My nerves continued to fray, my heart racing at the thought that I was in his room, at one point naked, and now wearing his clothes—and the brush of the fabric of his pants against the most sensitive bare areas of my flesh left my cheeks and ears hot.

Kat would freak out if she knew.

I turned to grab my bundle of wet jeans and underwear, desperate to get back to Damien, and I tiptoed downstairs. The combination of dry clothes and the warmth of the house left me near humming in ecstasy, and I pressed my nose into the sleeve of his sweater I wore, inhaling the lingering scent of him in it.

"Damien?" I called, when I didn't find him in the living room.

"In the kitchen," he called back, and I followed his voice down the hall to find him making drinks.

He tilted his head to glance at me before refocusing on the tea he was preparing. "Are they ok?"

I blinked. "Is what ok?"

He chuckled, and I shifted on my feet, wondering what he was talking about.

"The pants," he said as he pointed to them, a crooked grin on his face.

"Oh! They're perfect." I looked down awkwardly, wishing I could find a hole to fall into. "They're really comfy."

He handed me a teacup, and I closed my eyes as the heat of the ceramic seeped into my palms. I inhaled the steam that rose from it and frowned at the familiar scent of the blend. There was no way this could be my favorite tea blend. I'd never met anyone else who even knew what it was, let alone drank it. I lifted the porcelain cup to my lips, taking a sip, and moaned as the warmth slipped down my throat and settled into my stomach. Perfectly sweetened with just the right amount of cream.

I looked at him. "Is this Greek mountain tea?"

His brows rose, clearly surprised I knew what it was, and a soft smile curved his lips. "Yeah, my family's from Greece. It reminds me of home." He frowned then. "That's not a common tea here in the states, though. How do you know about it?"

Maybe that was where the subtle accent was from. "I used to buy all sorts of different loose teas to try. It came as a free sample one time and there was just something about it. I loved it, so I started ordering it."

"Well, we have something else in common then," he said with a smile, and he took my clothes to the laundry room down the hall.

"So, how long have you lived here?" I asked when he returned.

"A long while."

"Do your parents live here as well?"

He didn't answer at first. "No, they died when I was younger."

"Oh my God… I'm so sorry, I didn't know."

He shrugged. "It was so long ago. I barely remember them. Besides, how could you have known?"

It didn't make me feel any better. I didn't want to think what it would be like to lose my parents and could only imagine how devastating that might have been for him.

Damien took my hand and led me back to the living room to warm up in front of the fire.

"Apologies for the mess in my room." A certain kind of grin spread across his face as he glanced back at me. "If I'd have known I was going to have you in there, I would've cleaned up more."

His words left me flustered, and I nearly fumbled my own as we entered the living room. "No, no, it's ok. I don't mind."

He chuckled, and I eased down onto the carpet in front of the couch, stretching my hands out to feel the heat of the fire. The flames danced in the hearth, and I closed my eyes as it soothed my chilled bones. This place was so warm, and not just in front of the fireplace. There was an air of peace to this house that somehow made me feel safe and secure.

Damien eased onto the floor beside me, propping his knee up to rest his elbow against it. "Sorry our date went like this. This wasn't what I had planned. I was going to take you out to get dinner and—"

"Oh! Please don't apologize!" I said, and the moment the words left my lips, his words clicked. Date. Not day. Not time together...

Date.

"I've..." A smile curved my lips at his words repeated in my mind, his voice folding over and over itself until my smile widened into a grin. Warmth filled my chest, and I lifted my eyes to him again. "I've actually been having a wonderful time."

His eyes softened, and whatever emotions churned in their depths was enough to leave me breathless. I couldn't help but be drawn into them.

I wasn't sure how long we sat there like that. Seconds? Minutes? The only sounds I could hear, trapped in that moment, were the crackling and popping of the fire as it burned slowly through the wood.

Something flitted across his eyes as they passed back and forth between mine. Longing? Sorrow? Happiness? I couldn't make out what he was feeling, and I wondered what kind of thoughts might be swirling around in that head of his.

"You warm enough?" he asked, and I nodded.

"Yeah, the change of clothes helped."

His gaze drifted over me, and the certain look reflecting in his eyes left my skin tingling, my blood heating, my heart racing. "I think you look pretty damn good in my clothes."

"You think so?" I asked smartly as I inspected myself. "Maybe I'll keep them for myself."

The corner of his lips twitched, and a hint of a grin tugged at his lips. "Oh, really? And what if I say you can't?"

I don't know what came over me, but the words slipped from my lips before I could think better of it. "I guess you'll have to take them off me yourself, then."

My mouth clamped shut, and his brows rose, clearly just as taken back as I was at what I'd said.

Shit. Why would I say something like that? What was wrong with me?

His cocky grin melted away, his eyes darkening as they raked over my body once more, and I could have sworn my heart skipped a beat as he licked his lips. "That's quite tempting."

Damien grew closer, until I could almost feel the warmth of his skin, the power of his body. I didn't pull away, couldn't pull away... but did I even want to? I resisted the urge to reach out and run my fingers along every ripple of muscle lying just beneath the fabric of his sweater. The pounding of my pulse drowned out any rational thought, and anticipation tore through my system as his hand settled onto the floor beside me, drawing him closer still.

He hesitated as my eyes dipped to his lips, now within inches of my own. He was so close, his rich scent of cedarwood and leather filling my lungs, overwhelming and somehow settling me all at once. How the hell did that even make sense? His eyes flickered over my face, as if he were waiting to see how I would react to his proximity, if I'd accept him.

I shouldn't be playing this game with him, should push him away, and yet... I didn't want to. A part of me enjoyed the thrill I felt around him, and the ways I found happiness in how he made my heart race when it should terrify me, the way he made me laugh in ways I hadn't laughed in years, the way he made me rethink every decision to lock myself up and shut everyone out.

I swallowed as he moved to close the space between us, and my eyes slid closed before his lips brushed against mine. My heart leapt, and I fell into the motion as he tilted his head, his lips caressing mine with soft and gentle strokes, and he lifted his hand to cup my cheek. I failed to breathe as his tongue glided across the seam of my lips. He stiffened and pulled back suddenly, blinking as if he'd woken from some daze.

"Sorry, I—Uh... I got ahead of myself." He fumbled his words abruptly, as if he'd kissed me against my will, but he hadn't.

I'd fought it for a while, but I couldn't deny how much I'd wanted to feel him against me again, wanted to feel his lips against mine after I was robbed of that moment that night he came to lift my spirits. Had craved it in a way that had me questioning everything.

He raked his fingers through his hair, and a heavy breath of near frustration escaped him. A maelstrom of emotions warred with one another in his eyes, and a maelstrom just as intense raged within me. Something twisted in my chest at the confliction dancing across his face. He clearly wanted to continue, and yet he didn't. Did he think I didn't want this?

Words sat just out of my reach as I watched him, unsure what to do. What should I say? What *could* I say? Would it sound weird if I asked him not to stop? Would he think of me differently?

I sat there momentarily, lost, and my eyes fell as I tried to work through the chaos raging in my mind. My body begged for his touch, and my skin tingled where his finger—his lips—had been just moments before.

Was this what it felt like to be with someone? Were we even together like that? Or was this just something like the night of our first kiss? Did this mean anything to him, or was this more like a fling? Did it matter? Did I want more than a fling? Wouldn't it be better if he didn't develop any feelings for me? If he didn't get… attached?

My hand trembled as I reached out to him, and the fear of rejection left me questioning what I was doing. Before I could think better of it, I grasped the sleeve of his sweater, unable to find the words, but hoping I could convey my feelings in some way. I didn't want this to end, and for once, I didn't care to second guess what I was doing, didn't want to think too deeply into what would come tomorrow should I do something foolish today.

His gaze fell to where I clutched his sweater before his eyes found mine. We sat there for a moment, soaking up each other's presence, and I wished I could see the thoughts behind those eyes as they burned into me. A shiver ran through me as his hand rose to cup my face, and my eyes slid closed as I allowed myself to lean into his touch. I allowed myself to bask in the feel of his thumb grazing over my lower lip.

How could such a simple touch make someone feel this way? How could every brush of our skin be so electric? I stopped myself from thinking of it too deeply, wanting to relish in this moment if nothing else, regardless of what would come tomorrow.

Damien took my hand, lifting it to press his lips against my knuckles before trailing a line of kisses around to my palm. Something bloomed in my chest, my hand twitching delicately with each brush of his lips. The feeling took root in the very core of my being, stirring something to life. His other hand rose to my chin, tilting my face to his as his lips met mine again.

They were like velvet, and when they parted this time, I received him, desperate to taste him once more. I could feel his desire with each stroke of his tongue, and I gave into it, allowing myself to enjoy this moment wholly. His hand slid down along my neck, over my shoulder, and didn't stop, descending further and further.

He broke the kiss for a moment but didn't pull away, those fierce eyes reaching down to the depths of my soul. "We… We should probably stop. If we continue—I… I don't want to do anything you're not ready for."

We sat there a moment, and I tried to think rationally despite the cloud of need begging me not to. Was I ready if this went past just kissing? What was I hesitating for? It wasn't as if I was saving myself for marriage, but would I regret it if—

No. I was tired of not living because of what-ifs.

Tomorrow would come no matter what I did, and I was tired of living my life walking on eggshells. Without thinking, I pushed myself up to capture his lips with my own, meeting that desire of his with a need so intense I couldn't fight it, didn't want to. A groan ripped from his throat as he grabbed onto my waist and I gasped against his lips at the firmness of his callused palms as they molded against my skin.

His tongue passed through my lips, the kiss no longer soft or tender, but fierce and desperate. Something sparked to life as his grasp tightened on my waist and pulled me up against him, guiding me closer until I was straddling his lap, feeling every hard part of him against every soft part of me.

There was no one here to taunt and tease me. Damien and I were alone in this place, and I threw all hesitation to the wind as I gave into my desires and allowed myself to do something selfish for once. He groaned as my fingers found their way into his hair, tangling in the soft dark waves, and his lips trailed kisses over my jaw, down to my neck. I shuddered, my back arching into his touch. I needed more.

The sinful combination of his lips and tongue against my skin, left me teetering on some sort of edge. When the rush of his hot breath spilled over my skin, it sent a chill through my body, and my legs trembled, the heat coiling deep and low.

I wanted more, needed more, and I rocked my hips against him, feeling the brush of his arousal against me, the sensation dragging a breathing moan from my throat. His fingers ground into my hips in the most delicious way, holding me in place, and I shuddered.

He nipped at my ear before whispering, "Easy, *mea luna*. I want to savor you."

I frowned. What had he called me? I parted my lips to ask, but a heady sigh fell from my lips instead, my head falling back as his lips brushed against my neck, his fingers sliding under the thin cotton of his sweater I wore.

His hand trailed lazily over my waist, across my ribs, and farther up until he cupped my breast.

"Damien," I breathed, my body bucking against him, and his free hand tangled in my hair, tilting my head back to allow him room to savor my throat. The moment his name left my lips a deep sound rumbled from his chest, and almost heady groan of satisfaction.

God. This all-consuming feeling could only be described as pure need. I wanted him, more of him, all of him. As if on cue, his lips found their way back to mine, his tongue clashing with my own.

A low moan rippled from his throat as my nails bit into his back at his incessant, teasing touches. He gripped my hips, grinding me harder against him, and I gasped against his mouth, feeling the swollen bulge pressing into me through the thin cotton of the sweatpants.

My mind began to wander, wondering what it would be like, what it would feel like if we crossed that line. Was this too soon? Were we going to go that far? I could barely ignore the throbbing heat consuming me, the need to continue, but now that we were inching toward a cliff I could never turn away from... No. Why was I so nervous about this? Why was I thinking into this so deeply? It was just sex. It didn't have to mean anything.

He paused suddenly, as if he sensed my hesitation, breath erratic as he released my hips, and cupped my face to look me in the eye. "We don't have to do it," he assured me. "We can stop here."

I smiled, sighing heavily as I stared into those gorgeous eyes of his. "Maybe... that would be a good idea."

He smiled tenderly, kissing me once more before wrapping his arms around me in a tight embrace. I smiled at the way I fit against him perfectly, like a puzzle piece.

A missing puzzle piece I dreamed I might one day find but feared I never would.

CHAPTER 10

"What's your favorite food?"

I blinked as we entered the kitchen and pondered that thought. "Um... Chicken Parmesan?"

"Italian," he mused, as he washed his hands, as if that were humorous to him for some reason. "I think we can manage that."

I frowned and watched as he ducked into the fridge to grab some eggs, setting them on the counter before heading for the pantry and returning with flour.

"What're you doing?"

He glanced at me before returning to gathering ingredients. "Making chicken parmesan."

"Oh, we don't have to do that; we can have something else. I'm not picky."

"Nonsense, it's been a while since I've made pasta. It'll be fun to do together," he said with a smile as he retrieved some chicken from the fridge, before collecting a number of spices and herbs from a drawer.

"You know how to make pasta?" I asked, curiosity piquing as I inched around the island as he disappeared into what I assumed was a pantry. He returned with an armful of ingredients, laying them out on the counter before grabbing a pasta roller from the cabinet below. He stood back as he rolled his sleeves back, eyes passing over everything laid out before him.

He nodded. "I might be a bit rusty, but pasta's easy to make. Would you like to help?"

My gaze fell on the mess of ingredients before us. I'd never made pasta from scratch before, but I'd worked with dough. It couldn't be that hard. I shrugged and rolled my sleeves up as I headed to the sink to wash my hands. "Sure, how does it work?"

I caught sight of a warm smile tugging at his lips and he grabbed a measuring cup, proceeding to scoop flour onto the counter before sprinkling a pinch of salt over top it. "For pasta, all you need is eggs, flour, and salt."

"That's really all there is to it?" There was no way it was that simple.

He nodded as he worked his hands into the flour, forming a bowl in the middle of the pile. I inched closer, watching as he opened the egg carton and handed me one.

"Just crack the egg over the flour," he said, reaching for another.

I tapped the egg against the counter before cracking it open to deposit it into the flour bowl and discarded the shell into the trash. One by one Damien, and I dropped more in until there was a pool of buttery yolks amidst the white flour. He grabbed a fork and began breaking up the eggs.

"Now we start working it into a dough," he said as he stepped to the side, holding his hand out in a quiet gesture for me to try.

I glanced at him curiously before stepping closer the bed of flour and yolk. While I enjoyed baking from time to time, I wasn't much of a cook as far as regular meals went. This looked simple enough, though, like making pie dough, so surely, I couldn't mess this up.

"Just work it together slowly," he whispered. My heart leapt as his chest pressed against my back, and his arms came around to guide mine into the flour. In a steady rhythm, we began working the flour and eggs together, his hands guiding mine.

"See?" he whispered, and I struggled to focus on the dough coming together as we pressed it out before folding it together again and again. His hands were gentle and guiding, despite how much force we had to put into working the dough. The concoction started to meld together, the dough growing sticky.

"Go ahead and grab a bit more flour," he instructed.

I smiled, reaching out to grab a handful of flour from the spare bowl, and Damien paused to hold his hands out for me to drop some into his palm. He didn't speak as I ran my hand over his, the flour coating our fingers and palms, and he guided my hands back to the dough. The butterflies fell out of control as his presence grew closer at my back, his strong arms brushing against my own as we put our weight into kneading.

"That should do it. Now we let that rest for a bit while we prep the chicken," he said, and his hand shot up, dabbing flour over my nose in a flash before he backed away.

I gasped, twisting around to find a smug grin on his face. "You did not."

"Oh, I did," he taunted, stepping back.

I gaped at him before whipping around to drop my hand into the excess flour. He took off around the counter, and I chased after him. "Oh? Not willing to take what you dish out?"

He rounded the island, smiling over his shoulder at me. "You'll have to be faster than that, short stuff."

My jaw dropped, and I fought the laughter threatening to burst from my chest. "That's it!"

He managed to reach the opposite end of the island, and I huffed as he ducked and dodged in the opposite direction every time I started around it to get to him.

I panted, leaning against the counter to stare him down. "Cheater!"

"Sore loser," he countered, giving me a taunting smile.

Without thinking, I threw my hand out and peppered him with the handful of flour. He stood there a moment, hands hovering out at his sides, and he blinked in shock. My jaw dropped, and I couldn't believe I'd just done that. He looked over himself, at his sweater dusted in white. Oh, God, he was covered in the stuff, as was the counter, the floor.

His eyes lifted to me, and a wicked grin curved his lips before his hand shot into the bowl of flour. "Oh, you're getting it now."

I squeaked and took off as he ran for me. Shit, shit, shit!

"Where do you think you're going?" he taunted.

I squealed as his arm looped around my waist, pulling me back against him and his hand flew around to smear flour over my face, my neck, his sweater. I screamed as I pulled against his hold, kicking and fighting as he continued to cover me in flour.

"No!" I laughed, wriggling to get free of him.

"Where'd that fight go?"

Our laughter flooded the kitchen as he hoisted me against him, turning me until I was facing him. I gasped for air, my sides hurting as the laughter continued to poor from me, and he lifted me up and onto the counter. Tears dotted my lashes as I opened my eyes to gaze down at him and I bit my lip as he smiled up at me, situating himself between my thighs as he braced my hips, our chests heaving as we panted.

"You've got a little something…" I said, pointing to his face.

"Oh, do I?" he said, brows rising, and I giggled as he pointed to his face. "Is there a little something on my face?"

"A whole lot of something," I said, bursting into another fit of laughter as he leaned in, rubbing his cheek against mine, the stubble along his jaw tickling my skin. I pulled away, but his arms came around me, pulling me tighter against him.

97

He slowly stopped, our gazes meeting and our laughter faded. He was so big against me, the feel of his body between my thighs sending my heart into a frenzy, and I suddenly became very aware of how tightly we fit together.

"I guess we should clean this up and get back to cooking," he said through heavy breaths, his smile fading as his eyes dipped to my lips briefly.

"Y-yeah," I managed, and he released me, pulling away to move back around the counter to start cleaning up. I tracked his movements, turning in time to catch him sharing a glance with me, the mischievous grin tugging at his lips as he started washing the flour off.

"You've seriously never been on the incline plane?" he asked.

I shook my head, smiling as I speared another piece of chicken, which, by the way, was really fucking delicious. "Why is that so hard to believe?"

"Because you've lived here all your life," he said before taking a bite of his own food.

"I just haven't gotten a chance to." I eyed him a moment before continuing. "Ok, your turn. What's your guilty confession?"

He chewed his food, pondering his answer. "I've never tried a gob."

"You're joking," I said, hardly believing he'd never tried one of the most popular chocolate cake sandwiches in our area.

"Nope," he said, shaking his head before taking a bite.

I snickered, cutting into the chicken. "We'll have to fix that. I get them at least once a week. They're Kat's favorite."

"What's your favorite?" he asked, and my brows knitted together in confusion.

"Favorite what?"

"Sweet," he asked, watching me with curiosity.

I chewed the inside of my lip, my mind passing over all the various sweets I liked. "Cheesecake. Strawberry cheesecake, to be specific."

He nodded. "Is there anything you enjoy doing outside of drawing and reading?"

"Hey," I said, looking at him incredulously. "You can't ask two questions back-to-back."

"Indulge me," he said, leaving no room for objection, and I couldn't resist him.

"Well, I love hiking. I used to go to watch plays from time to time… um." What did I enjoy doing? I racked my brain, thinking of things I enjoyed doing other than drawing and reading. I didn't exactly get out much, so it was difficult to come up with things. "I play video games, but other than that, I don't really get out of the house much, so…"

His gaze lingered on the table before him, as if he were absorbing what I was saying and mulling it over in his mind. "You play video games?"

"Nope. It's my turn," I said before he could try to ask another question, and he huffed a laugh. "What's *your* favorite sweet?"

His brows rose, and his lips parted, but he seemed to retract what he was about to say, and I frowned. "You wouldn't have heard of my favorite sweet."

"*Indulge me,*" I said, giving him a teasing grin as I threw his words back at him.

His surprise melted into a huff of laughter. "When I was younger, my mother used to make these pastries with the berries that grew wild near our home."

Something twisted in my chest at the sight of his somber smile as he worked his fork into his pasta.

"I haven't had it in years."

"What kind of berries were they?" I asked, wondering if maybe I could somehow recreate it for him, or… would that be a bad idea? The dessert sounded special to him. Perhaps it might only make him miss his mother more if I made it for him.

"You can't find them around here sadly, but it's ok," he said, and I didn't miss the avoidance. "When's your birthday?"

"November 17th," I said wearily as I narrowed my eyes at him.

His gaze didn't lift from his food, but his brows rose, and he blinked absentmindedly as he continued to eat.

"When is yours?" I asked.

"June 29th."

"A cancer," I acknowledged with a smile.

He arched a brow, to which I shook my head.

"So, video games," he started, and I cracked a smile as he lifted his gaze to me and proceeded to ask another question, leading into more questions of my own. I didn't know how long we traded questions, how long we shared stories, but I couldn't help but lose myself in the conversation—

And wish tonight would never end.

My front door clicked shut behind me and leaned back against the frame as I sighed heavily. I twisted around, in time to see Damien through the window as he pulled out onto the road and disappear from view. The sun had set hours ago, and I wasn't entirely sure just how late it was. Time had gotten away from us, and I almost wished I could go back in time and do it all over again.

My phone rang, and I pulled it from my pocket to see a text from Damien.

> Thank you for indulging me tonight.

I smiled, remembering everything we'd done, from our flour fight to the millions of questions we'd asked each other, though, I hadn't exactly kept tally, it felt as if he'd snuck in more questions than I had. My phone rang again as he sent another text immediately.

> We're having a bonfire tomorrow at my house around eight if you'd like to come. You can bring Kat if you like.

I quickly typed my reply, excitement bubbling inside my chest.

> I'd love that.

My phone hummed as his response came through.

> I'll pick you up at 7:30. Sweet dreams.

My chest swelled reading his words, and I responded one last time.

> Sweet dreams.

I glided up to my room, floating on cloud nine up the stairs, and fell onto my bed. My mind relived all the moments we'd shared tonight, every side of him I'd never gotten to experience, every part of him I'd never felt. The thought of it left my cheeks heated and my heart racing. I longed to know him more, to see more of this intimate side of him.

My mind wandered, curious to know what it would have been like if we hadn't stopped where we had on his living room floor. It was for the best that we stopped when we did, though, I wasn't quite ready to take that leap, to be wholly exposed like that to someone.

My fingers brushed against my lips where I could still faintly feel him. I closed my eyes, remembering the feel of his hands gliding along my skin, the sound of his breathing, the heat of his mouth. My heart fluttered, and I stilled at the feel of it, realizing I'd gone nearly the entire afternoon without the cloud of its presence looming over me. I'd almost forgotten how it felt to just… live. I rolled onto my back, my eyes lifting to the dangling moon and star charms hanging from my ceiling as my lids grew heavy.

It wasn't long before sleep claimed me, and my dreams explored all the possibilities of what would have happened if we hadn't stopped.

CHAPTER 11

Kat had been trying to get me to go to one of her parties for years, so the moment I invited her to a bonfire with Damien and his group, she immediately said yes.

"How many people do you think are gonna be there?" Kat asked from where she sat perched on the counter of my vanity, already ready to go.

I leaned toward the mirror as I applied the last of my mascara. "It'll probably just be Damien and his friends. So, Barrett, Cole, Zephyr, Vincent, James, and probably Cole's girlfriend, Amara." I didn't say how much I hoped Amara wouldn't be there.

I couldn't figure out why Amara was so sour to be around. Maybe it was just that she was sour when I was around. She hardly interacted when she graced us with her presence on campus, save the random glances of what seemed to be jealousy or annoyance when I spoke to Cole—which was irritating given that I wasn't interested in him. We were just friends.

I shook off the irritation and continued getting ready. "Is Cody coming?"

"He's already got plans tonight, but it's ok," she said.

A knock at the door downstairs interrupted our conversation, and I glanced at my phone to realize it was already time for Damien to pick us up. I stepped back for a second to assess my hair and makeup before I turned to her. "How do I look?"

She gave me a coy grin. "I'd tap that."

I nudged her, and she let out a snicker before turning to head downstairs.

"So, are you ever gonna tell me about how your date went?"

My heart skipped a beat at the mention of it, and I chewed the inside of my lip as I tried to think of where I would even begin.

"We had a good time," I hedged, and her eyes narrowed. "I'll tell you later, I promise."

"I. Want. Every. Detail," she said, enunciating each word for emphasis.

"He's a good cook," I said before hurrying down the stairs.

She gasped and took off down the stairs after me. "You are not going to tell me that and leave me hanging!"

"I guess you'll just have to wait and find out!" I teased as I headed for the entry.

Damien greeted us with a smile as I opened the door, his eye settling on me. "You ready to get into trouble?"

I inhaled, the rush and excitement swelling in my chest. "You know it."

The moon hung in the sky as I climbed out of Damien's car. I could already hear the laughter and jokes echoing from the back of his house, see the glow of the fire illuminating the forest encroaching on Damien's backyard. He closed the car door as soon as Kat climbed out of the back seat, and she took my hand, dragging me toward the steps.

I pulled her to a stop when I noticed Damien lifting the trunk of his car. "Is there anything we can help with?"

He cracked a crooked grin. "I got it. You ladies go have fun."

I turned back to find Kat gaping at his beautiful home. "This is Damien's house?"

"Yeah, why?"

"Shit girl, he's got money," she whispered into my ear.

"Kat!" I whispered back. "You're terrible."

She snickered innocently. "I'm just saying. You'd be set if you could snag him!"

I rolled my eyes as we walked around toward the back of the house to find the guys all sitting around a sizable fire. Cole smiled, giving me a subtle wave. and I waved back in response.

"Hell yeah, the ladies are here," Barrett called, noticing our approach. "Now the real fun begins."

"Ignore him," I said to Kat.

Barrett clutched his chest as if I'd wounded him. "Ouch. That hurts, Cas."

"Play nice, Barrett," Damien said from behind us as he approached with a case of beer. He headed to a nearby cooler, unloading the bottles onto ice.

Barrett took a swig of whatever he was drinking before looking back at Damien. "You came too soon, Damien. I thought she might finally get the courage to lay one on me."

Zephyr leaned. in looking at Barrett. "You keep pushing buttons and I'll laugh my ass off when she finally snaps and rips you a new one."

"I'll enjoy that day," Barrett said, and cocked an eyebrow at me. "I know somewhere in there, there's a little spitfire waiting to bite."

"See? He lives for it," I said as Kat and I found a place to sit on one of the wooden benches near the fire pit. Kat laughed as Damien offered her a beer.

"You want one, Cas?" he asked, offering me a bottle as well.

I lifted my hand to decline. "No, thank you. I don't drink."

"Water?" he countered.

"I'd love one," I said, and he returned to the cooler.

Barrett hopped over to my side, opposite Kat, and leaned in closer to whisper in my ear. "So, I hear my boy got you wet."

The blood instantly rushed to my face, and in that moment, thoughts of Damien and I on his living room floor flashed across my mind. My eyes went wide, and I whipped around instinctually to smack him.

Before I could, Damien chucked a beer bottle at Barrett, who caught it without taking his eyes off me.

"Cut it out, Barrett. Next time, I'll aim that bottle for your head," Damien warned.

Barrett barked a laugh, popping the cap off the bottle. "I'm just playing, geez! I was talking about her falling in the river." His eyes shifted to me. "Where was your mind going little lady?" His smile turned wicked as I glanced at him. Asshole knew exactly what he was doing.

Kat turned to me. "You fell in the river yesterday?"

Shit. Here we go. I dropped my eyes to the bottle in my hands. "It wasn't a big deal. I'm okay."

She pressed. "Ok, you better get to talking. You promised you'd spill later. It's later, now."

"Not here." I said, flashing her a look. Her fern-green eyes lit up, and I immediately regretted what I said. She knew something happened between us. There was no hiding it; she knew me too well.

A sigh rushed out of my lungs, and I looked to Damien, who was taking a seat nearby. "Damien, do you mind if we use your bathroom?"

His brows rose. "Yeah, go through the back door. You remember where it is, right?"

Kat's eyes shifted to me the moment the words left his lips, a sly grin on her face. I suddenly wanted to bury myself on the spot. "Yeah. Thank you."

We rose, before Kat all but dragged me up the stairs of the back porch and through the back door. The moment the door closed behind us, she whirled around to face me. "What happened between you two?"

I tried not to be so obvious, running my fingers through my hair as my eyes drifted over the kitchen. My heart skipped a beat as I envisioned Damien between my thighs on the counter, our bodies so close that I'd almost given into picking back up where we'd left off on the living room floor. "Nothing happened."

Her eyes narrowed. "Cas. I've known you for fourteen years. Whatever happened, it wasn't just you two going for a walk in the park."

"I mean, technically we *did* go for a walk in the part."

She popped a hand on her hip as she arched an eyebrow, and I caved.

"We kissed."

"*Just* kissed?"

I couldn't answer, walking past her toward the hallway.

She gasped. "No judging if you did. But you didn't... you know."

"Oh my God, no!" I said, whipping around, mortified at the fact she even thought Damien and I had… sex. I mean, we could have, might have, almost did. My mind went into a frenzy as my thoughts imagined it and my cheeks and ears burned. "We didn't go that far…"

She snickered. "And here I was thinking my innocent little Cas had finally gotten out of her shell and done something bold."

"I've only known him for a few weeks. Geez, Kat."

"And I've had one-night stands with guys I met that night," she countered.

"It kind of just... happened. Neither of us intended it to."

"How?"

I sighed and told her about everything. About the date, how I'd fallen in the creek, how he'd carried me to his car, brought me here to get me dry clothes.

And how we'd ended up on his living room floor.

"—then he made me dinner, and we hung out talking for the rest of the night."

"Has money, good looks, chivalrous, and can cook?" She popped her hands on her hips. "You gotta lock this one down, Cas."

105

"It's not that simple," I said, my gut twisting at how easy she made it sound.

"Why not?"

Because it wasn't fair to him. Fuck. I shouldn't even be here tonight, but I couldn't resist it. Every part of me wanted to get closer to him, no matter how horrible I felt for it.

"It's... complicated."

"It doesn't have to be, Cas," she said, her face softening. "Look, I know you've never really been in a relationship. You've turned me down every time I've tried to set you up with a date. Maybe this is the universe telling you it's time."

It would be fate that would do this to me—do this to him. How cruel of the universe to wait until I was left with little time, only to allow me a taste of what could be something amazing.

"We're talking. Nothing is official right now, I don't think."

She took my hands, pulling me closer to her, her eyes full of endearment as her gaze locked with mine. "I love you, Cas. You've been on your own for so long. This is your chance. Don't let this one get away."

"I'll try not to," I said, smiling back, if only to make her feel better.

The wood cracked and popped as the fire worked through it in the pit, and embers danced in the dark night air.

"So how long have you guys known each other?" Cole asked.

"Almost as long as I can remember," I answered.

Kat leaned forward. "Since we were six."

"Wow, so pretty much all your life," Damien responded, and I nodded.

"I wanna know what spell you guys cast to convince her to get out of her house and socialize." Kat slid a glance at me. "I've tried all but dragging her out to go to parties, but she never budges."

I rolled my eyes. "I'm sorry, I don't like people."

Damien laughed. "It's ok, I don't like people either."

Barrett lifted his bottle to his lips , his tone sarcastic as he spoke before taking a sip. "I guess we aren't people."

"Nope, just a bunch of assholes," Damien responded without looking his way.

"It's our charming smiles," Vincent said.

Cole gave Vincent a sideways glance. "You wish."

"Don't worry, Vincent. I think your smile is charming." I laughed as he threw a cocky grin in Cole's direction, to which Cole rolled his eyes.

Damien pushed himself to his feet, walking over and leaning down to whisper in my ear. "Can I steal you for a second?"

I bit my lip but nodded and stood to follow him. "Sure."

Kat watched our interaction from the corner of her eye, a grin tugging at her lips. She didn't say anything, and instead started up a conversation with Barrett and the others.

Damien led me away from the fire, and toward his porch.

"How're you feeling today?" he asked as we entered the back door into the kitchen.

My brows furrowed. "What do you mean?"

"You took a hard fall yesterday. I didn't know if you got any bruising or anything."

I waved it off. "I'm tough. A fall won't keep me down."

"I didn't think it would. I was just worried," he said, smiling down at me warmly.

I hadn't realized that he still held my hand until I felt the sweeping motion of his thumb over my skin. My heart fluttered, and I took a deep breath.

"Kat seems to be getting along with everyone," I said, looking through the back window as I tried to ignore the flood of emotions leaving my lungs incapable of breathing.

He didn't respond at first, and for a moment I thought I saw a flicker of hurt in his eyes, but he glanced toward the back window to gaze out at the group around the fire. "She fits in. Hopefully, Barrett can stay on his best behavior."

Silence hung between us for a moment, and I was conflicted whether I should let him continue to hold my hand or if I should pull away.

"Look, Cas. If—" I looked up at him when the words halted on his lips. "If you regret yesterday... I'm sorry."

"Regret—" Shit, he'd completely misunderstood me. "No. I don't... I don't regret it at all."

His brows furrowed, those intense eyes full of a sort of sadness that sank into a deeper part of me. I hated this, hated that after something might be sparking to life between us, I was considering snuffing it out.

"If this is too much, I can back off."

I couldn't do it. Couldn't tell him what I needed to say. Do what I needed to do. Damn me—damn my selfishness and what it might cost him in the end.

"It's not that, it's just—" I tried to find the words, my eyes falling to our hands. "I'm awkward, and weird, and..."

"I like that about you," he said with a soft smile, and before I knew what I was doing, a soft smile curved my lips as well.

"I enjoyed it. Everything. Really," I finally said.

He lifted my hand, pressing it to his lips as he kissed it tenderly, and my chest swelled. "Then maybe we can do it more often." His expression changed suddenly, and he quickly spoke again. "The dates, I mean." He clarified, and laughter spilled from my lips.

"I'd like that."

CHAPTER 12

My bare feet smacked against the cracked pavement as I ran. I didn't know what I was running from, but the fear filling me was enough to question it. The cold air burned my lungs I gasped, and my heart pounded against my rib cage as I failed to pace myself.

No. No. No!

I couldn't pace myself; couldn't slow down. Something was chasing me. Trash cans and other rubble crashed against the asphalt and alley walls behind me as they were knocked over or sent flying by whatever pursued me. I choked on the air in a panic as I ran faster, the sounds inching closer and closer.

Street lamps glowed dimly in the distance, lighting a flickering hope that I might make it to safety. The dense shroud of darkness loomed around me as I ran, closing in as if it might devour me. I was too slow, too shaken, and I feared I wouldn't make it out.

A snarl pierced the air, and I gasped, my pace quickening. I didn't dare look over my shoulder to see what chased me. Tears welled in my eyes, my vision blurring.

Please, no!

I shook my head, trying to wake myself up, and I chanted under my breath. "It's just a dream. It's just a dream. Wake up, Cassie!"

It was no use, though. I was still on a seemingly endless stretch of street, still running for my life.

The sound of jaws snapping echoed off the alley walls behind me, growing louder by the moment, closer still. Little air remained in my lungs, and I feared my heart might burst.

A tall, hooded figure rounded the corner near the street light that seemed so far away.

He took a step forward, body tensing before he lunged into a sprint toward me. "Cassie!"

"Damien!" I cried out, but my knees buckled, and I crashed forward onto the asphalt. I grimaced as I slid to a stop. My knees burned where asphalt had shredded the skin, and I gasped for air, my heart hammering as if it were threatening to burst.

"Fuck, fuck!" I gasped through pants, wincing at the pain tearing through my body. I twisted around, freezing at the sudden silence looming around me. My eyes danced in every direction, searching the darkness.

An eerie clicking sound echoed around me from the shadows, the sound making my skin crawl. I could barely make out the figures looming in the inky blackness. They stalked closer, creeping up on me now that I was down, like wolves closing in on their kill—their long claws dragging along the ground. I looked up to where the shadows barely concealed more of them, climbing toward me along the brick walls of the buildings surrounding us.

Panic shot through me, and I pushed against the asphalt, desperate to get to my feet. My legs wouldn't obey me, though.

Damien slid to a stop in front of me, arms held out as he stood to defend me. Light barely reflected off the blade of the dagger he gripped tightly as he stared at the creatures.

"Are you ok? Can you stand?" he asked over his shoulder.

I couldn't answer him, couldn't peel my eyes from the demons surrounding us. Their features were the same as the ones I saw in my other dream: gray skin, so thin it revealed the black veins stretching out just under the surface, those hollow black eyes like bottomless abysses, waiting to suck you in with no way of returning. I pushed myself up to stand, but only made it to my knees.

One grew closer, crouching as it stalked us before letting out a snarl and lunged into the air. I gasped, clamping my eyes shut as I braced for its attack The creature let out a horrible screech, and I opened my eyes as it hit the ground next to me before disintegrating into dust, Damien still standing.

The group seemed to hesitate their advance as they eyed Damien, and the clicks spilled out from the creatures again. Were they afraid of him?

I forced myself to my feet and stumbled to the nearby wall to stabilize myself. My knees shook so badly that I could barely take another step. How long had I been running? My heart pounded, faint inklings of pain rippling through my chest.

God, no. Not now, I couldn't risk an attack now, but If I couldn't push through this to run, I was dead. I ground my teeth together. There was no time for exhaustion, no time for fear. I wasn't going to fucking die here. Not like this.

Damien glanced back at me for a split second before turning back as another grabbed a hold of his shoulder.

"Get your fucking claws off me!" he yelled through gritted teeth, punching the demon square in the face before throwing it back into the others, buying some time as they snapped at each other.

Damien rushed to my side, and I gasped as he scooped me in his arms before he took off, carrying me as if I weighed nothing.

"Are you all right?" he asked as he ran. The cold winds whipped through my hair as he turned into another alley suddenly before we could reach the lights. Our pace quickened.

Where was he going? Why did he turn? Why didn't he go into the street?

"I'm okay," I said as I clung to him, focused on breathing through the terror overtaking me, on slowing my heart rate. I peered over his shoulder as he ran. The horde of creatures spilled out onto the ground as they rounded the corner, and my heart plummeted. Like a pack of ravenous demons, they climbed over one another as the ones in front stumbled or fell, stopping at nothing to try to get to us.

Oh God. We were being hunted, like prey. I didn't want to imagine what might happen if they got a hold of us, what those terrible jaws could do. Would they rip us to shreds?

"What are those things?" I gasped.

"Don't look."

"Damien! What's chasing us?" I demanded.

"They're called darklings." A muscle ticked in Damien's jaw, his eyes stern as he avoided my gaze. "At night they look like this, but in the daylight, they take the form of humans. You'd be unable to tell them apart from any normal human."

"What're you saying? How is that even possible? They look like they're dead!"

"They aren't dead." He nearly spoke over me, gripping me tighter as we ducked around another corner. "They're cursed beings, and they're very much aliv–"

Damien cursed as one of the darklings grabbing onto his leg and he fell forward. He held me close as we fell, twisting, trying to brace us for the impact as best he could. We crashed onto the pavement, skin and bone smashing onto an unforgivable surface.

He pushed me away as the creatures crowded around him. White sparks of light exploded across my vision as my head smacked against the road, and I rolled to a stop, body aching from the impact.

I groaned as I blinked, the world churning around me. My eyes struggled to focus, and my mouth watered as nausea curdled my gut.

Get up. Get up, get up!

I turned my head to the side, barely able to make out Damien in the blur of movement, as he jumped to his feet to fight them off. One of the darklings plowed into him, knocking him into the wall, before its head jerked to me. Its black eyes met mine, and I snapped out my stupor, my eyes widening as I fought to move, but my arms and legs wouldn't respond.

"Cassie!" Damien pushed himself off the wall, but the others closed in on him, giving him no chance to come to my aid. One after another that attacked him while the one stalked toward me.

I rolled onto my stomach to crawl away, but icy claws wrapped around my calf. I cried out, grabbing for anything I could find, my fingers scraping along the asphalt as the creature dragged me back toward it.

"No! Let me go!"

It flipped me onto my back and wrapped its icy, clawed fingers around my throat, lifting me up off the ground to slam me up against the brick wall. Air rushed from my lungs and I gasped as I frantically grabbed onto its clammy arm, nails tearing through its paper-thin skin until black blood oozed. My feet slammed into its boney body as I kicked and fought, but nothing I did seemed to faze it.

It leaned in closer, and its soulless eyes locked with mine, tempting me into their depths, beckoning me to give in and let go. Its lips curled, revealing rows of sharp teeth as its jaws parted slowly. Putrid breath spilled out over my face as it hissed.

I became entrapped in its gaze, my limbs falling to my sides, useless as they hung from my body, and my eyes fluttered as I clung onto consciousness, my grip slipping.

No. I couldn't let myself pass out. I had to stay awake... had to stay...

"Get off her!" Damien yelled, his voice faint and fading further away.

The darkling's mouth stretched as it moved closer to me, the skin splitting, its jaws growing larger as its jaw snapped and spread further. Something large shifted in the darkness behind it and I watched as a completely different monster came into view. Clad in what I could best describe as black mist, its red eyes glowing in the dark as it grabbed the darkling's shoulder, and a terrifying snarl rippled from it. The darkling was ripped from me, its shriek tearing into my mind as the darkness swallowed it.

I hit the ground, my head smacking against the pavement.

"Are you fucking insane?"

The voice sounded so familiar, like words stuck on the tip of my tongue. Where was I?

"Maybe I am."

That voice caught my attention. Equally as furious, but brimming with agonized worry. What had I been doing before this? I tried to open my eyes, but my body wouldn't respond, trapping me in a state of half consciousness.

"What were you thinking bringing her here?"

"She was being hunted by darklings. She hit her head."

"Was she bitten?"

There was a different voice then, another guy, his voice softer, more concerned. Also weirdly familiar. How many people were there? The sound of footsteps approached, then went quiet at my side, and a presence weighed in over me.

"I don't think so. I searched her and didn't see any marks, and there's no sign of the change."

Something moved, and I realized it was part of my body. My head. I was being lifted, but I remained trapped in the state of endless floating, as if my body were drifting in a pool. The motion had taken me over entirely and I couldn't seem to find solid ground.

"How's her head?"

There was an odd sound, like a hiss and a groan. What was wrong with my head? What happened?

I was eased back down, and the conversation continued in a flurry of voices, speaking so fast I could barely keep up. I think there were four people talking now, each one of them just as tense as the other.

"Did Johnson look at her yet?"

"No, I didn't want her to wake up to some stranger. I'm about to take her down to better look at her head."

"We've gotta wake her up."

"You've gotta be kidding me. Here? You can't do that!"

"Cas, can you hear me?"

Something stroked my cheek gently, and a hand settled on my shoulder, nudging me softly. The delicate scent of cedar and leather filled my senses, the smell calming in a strange way. I struggled to open my eyes, fighting to climb out of the depths.

"Cas. Wake up… Come back to me. Please."

The sound of furious footsteps reached me. "Oh yeah. Real smooth. Let's wake the fucking human!"

"Shut up, Barrett. It's not as simple as you think."

Wait, Barrett? Oh my God, that was Damien's voice. How had I not realized that sooner? The other voice belonged to Vincent, and Cole was there as well. What were they doing here?

I fought against the heaviness holding me down, finding the strength to open my eyes. The room was dark, whatever light leaking from a lamp in the corner just dim enough to see. My eyelids felt so heavy, my vision so blurred I couldn't make anything out around me, but I couldn't bring myself to care as exhaustion tugged and beckoned me to slip back under.

God, I was so tired.

A large figure paced back and forth only a few feet away, and I couldn't tell if he was angry or not. He seemed to be shaking, though, arms folded over his broad chest. Two others sat in the corner of the low-lit room.

I tilted my head to look up at the one sitting beside me, hovering just above me. His body seemed to ease the moment our eyes met, and his hand gripped mine tighter, his thumb stroking my skin in a way that left my heart dancing. I liked that, liked the feel of his skin against mine.

He let out a heavy sigh of relief, as if he hadn't breathed the entire time I was unconscious. The fear and worry melted away almost instantaneously at the sight of his face, and I didn't know if I was smiling or not.

"Hey." Damien smiled tenderly down at me as he settled his arm above my head and leaned over me, brushing a tender kiss to my forehead.

"Hey." I rasped, my voice hoarse, throat sore. My face scrunched as I blinked through my blurred vision and attempted to sit up. Damien's body tensed, right before a sharp pain seared across the back of my head and I slumped back. My stomach twisted, and I sucked a breath in through my teeth, as I grimaced.

Damien's hand came up, urging me to stay lying down. "Easy, Cas. Stay down. Try not to move."

"What happened?" I groaned, raising my hand to rub my eyes. Damien hesitated, his eyes lingering on me for a moment, before falling away. "Damien?"

"Your hit your head when you fell."

I tilted my head, searching for Vincent when he spoke up. He sat in a chair nearby, Cole sitting adjacent to him. I remembered hearing him speak moments before. I looked back at Damien, but he couldn't bring himself to meet my gaze.

"Do you remember anything?" Vincent asked.

My brows furrowed. "What do you mean remem—"

Memories flooded my mind, unbridled as they tore through me. The dark alley, my feet pounding into asphalt as I ran for my life, the darklings, Damien fighting for our lives, claws around my throat,

115

terrifying jaws parting to tear me apart. My heart fell into panicked beats, my breaths quickening.

"Where am I?"

My eyes darted around the room, finding each of them watching me, each familiar face leaving me more confused than I was before, questions rising to the surface. How had I gotten here? Why were they here as well? My mind wandered back to those creatures. My gaze continued to flit around, as if searching for answers to questions I was almost too afraid to ask. This couldn't be happening. Those creatures weren't real. It was all my imagination. It was a dream; it wasn't real. This wasn't real, it couldn't be real.

But it was.

Barrett halted his pacing to level a glare on Damien, his voice laced with warning. "Damien—"

"Somewhere safe." Damien said, his voice soft and reassuring as he seemed to ignore Barrett.

Damien finally lifted his gaze to me, and I blinked as my eyes adjusted to the darkened room. My heart dipped at the sight of him. His skin had paled, eyes heavy and worn. Those beautiful amber and ashen eyes were more intense now, almost crystalline, like a silver tiger's eye gemstone. His pupils seemed to constantly shift, expanding and contracting with each movement, like a predator in the dark.

My eyes narrowed as I caught sight of something dark staining the torn fabric of his shoulder. I reached out to touch the soaked material, and I pulled my hand back to look at the rich red liquid on my fingertips.

"Oh my God! You're hurt," I gasped as I tried to push myself up, doing my best to ignore the pain.

"Oh, no. I'm fine, I'm okay," he assured me, as his hands landed on my shoulder, urging me to lie back down.

Was he insane? "What do you mean you're alright? You're bleeding badly!"

"Cas." His hand cupped my cheek, and my wide eyes locked with his. "I'm all right. I promise. Now, please, let me talk."

I took a deep, uneven breath before letting it out slowly, trying my best to ease back down onto the bed.

"I'm sorry I haven't been honest with you. The dreams you had of the darklings. They're—" He paused a moment, seeming to collect himself, and then after a few seconds continued. "Cas, I'm about to go against a major rule of our, uh, group, but I fear you're no longer safe if I continue to leave you in the dark."

My brows furrowed as I watched him, listening intently. Group? What was he talking about?

He chewed the inside of his lip as he calculated his next words. "It's difficult to explain right now. There's so much to tell you. I promise to explain it all, but you need to promise me you'll keep what I'm about to tell you a secret. You can't breathe a word of this to anyone."

His eyes burned like fire as he stared into mine, waiting for an answer, eager for it. What could he possibly have to tell me? Clearly, he knew something. I'd seen him fight those terrifying creatures twice now. My dizzy thoughts jumped around as I opened my mouth to speak.

"Damien, wipe her mind! She can't know!" Barrett yelled before I could say anything.

"You don't understand, Barrett!" Damien barked back, irritation burning in his eyes as he held my gaze, waiting for an answer.

"She's gonna tell someone. We can't trust humans. It's against our laws—"

"I promise," I cut in. Barrett stopped short and began to shake, his hands balling into fists at his sides. "I won't tell anyone your secret."

Damien's expression softened, and a smile lit up his beautiful face, his words so soft they were almost a whisper. "I can't believe you're really here..."

I frowned. What did he mean by that?

"You remember the dream you had before?" he asked, looking down at me, and I nodded, more desperate for answers than anything.

"Damien, erase her memory now or I'll do the job myself," Barrett threatened as he drew closer, and the way he said it made it clear it wasn't a threat, but a promise.

How could that be possible, though? How could he erase a memory?

Damien jumped to his feet, turning to stand against Barrett. "Touch her, Barrett, and I swear to the Gods, it'll be the last fucking thing you do."

Their eyes locked, a strange electric energy filling the air. When Vincent and Cole moved to intervene, Damien rose a hand, and they halted, obeying, but lingering on their feet all the same, seemingly ready to stop them. Barrett took a step back, as if some strange understanding passed between them.

"I believe they're luring her out somehow." Damien paused a moment, his eyes lowering as he sorted through his thoughts.

"How would that even be possible?" Cole asked.

Damien's gaze shifted to him. "I don't know,"

"They've never shown any ability to lure people," Vincent added.

"Regardless of what they've been able to do in the past, this is the second time they've hunted her. She didn't know how she got there, but she was there."

My eyes passed between them all as they spoke as if I wasn't sitting here. Who were they talking about? Those creatures? The... darklings? What did they know about them? I opened my mouth to speak.

Damien turned to glance back at me and I stiffened, the words falling short. "Cassie's no longer safe. They know about her. She's easy prey at this point."

My heart lurched at his words, and panic took hold of me.

"So? Who cares?" Barrett said with a shrug, but for a moment, a flicker of doubt danced across his face before it faded into one of indifference. "We kill them all the time. What's one more darkling?"

Damien's jaw tightened, his face contorting with rage, and I feared he might lash out. "It's *her*, Barrett. I know it now."

Barrett's gaze swept back to Vincent and Cole where they sat, something passing between them.

Damien's voice softened a touch as he continued. "I knew it from the moment I saw her. I was skeptical at first because she's human; this has never happened. I don't know why it happened this time, but it's her. I know it."

What was he talking about? *Who* was he talking about? My mind reeled, and realization dawned on me. If those creatures were coming after me would they go to my house? Oh my God, what would happen to my parents? They had no idea.

"Are those things coming after me? Is my family in danger?" I asked, my voice shaking as I looked at each of them.

Damien glanced at me. "Your family will be all right."

Barrett remained silent, his steel eyes remaining fixated on me, and he raked his fingers through his blond hair. Vincent blew out a long breath before he and Cole eased back into their seats once the danger of a fight passed. Cole's eyes met mine for a moment before they fell from my gaze, some unknown emotion stirring in those black eyes, something that left me uneasy.

"What if those things show up at my hou—"

Damien returned to my side, helping me sit up. "I promise, Cas. Your parents are safe. The darklings aren't smart enough to go searching homes, and they stick closer to the city for their prey, hunting the streets and alleys."

"Are they the reason people have been disappearing?" I asked.

"There's a lot to explain, Cas, but you're badly injured," he said without acknowledging my question, but I couldn't deny the throbbing headache piercing my skull and echoing through every joint in my body.

My lips parted to protest and demand answers, but Damien spoke before I could. "I promise I'll tell you everything, just... please let me make sure you're okay."

I searched his eyes for any sign he might cave, but the sincere desperation in them make me bite my tongue. My body tensed as his arms slid under me, lifting me with ease, and I settled against his chest, letting his warmth seep into me.

"Get in touch with Zephyr, tell him what happened and that she's all right. I'll be back," he said to the others, without looking over his shoulder as he carried me into the hall.

Nausea surfaced with each sway of movement, building something up in the back of my throat, and my eyes became leaden, begging to let me close them.

"You okay?"

I nodded softly. "Yeah, just a little queasy."

"Are you going to be sick? I can get you a trash bin."

"No, I think I'll be fine." I sighed, resting my eyes, my face tucked against his shoulder as he carried me. My mind swam with their conversation, trying to pick apart every hazy detail, my thoughts still struggling under... the weight of...

"I need you to stay awake, Cas," Damien said. "There's a chance you could've suffered a concussion."

I blinked, realizing I'd started to doze off. "Sorry."

The soft taps of his feet echoed through the empty hall, the sway of his movements like a wave, making it difficult to listen. If I stayed quiet much longer, I wouldn't be able to stay awake. "Where are we?"

Damien didn't reply for a moment. In fact, it felt like minutes passed before he did, and even still his words seemed to need coaxing from his lips. "It's the abandoned apartment complex on Short Street."

It took a few moments for the words to sink in, and I stiffened. Short Street was within walking distance of my house, literally a couple blocks from my road. Was it morning? Had my parents realized I wasn't home? Were they looking for me? "Shit, what time is it?"

"It's around two, I think. Why?"

"Dammit," I said, trying to climb out of Damien's arms, but he gripped me tighter, and my gaze snapped to hifI didm. My heart skipped a beat as his eyes pierced mine with such an intense look of concern that I froze.

"I'll get you back home before anyone notices you're gone. If that's what you're worried about," he promised. "I just want to make sure you're okay first."

My body eased as I gave into his request. He nudged open a set of double doors and carried me down a long set of spiraling stairs. I tried to focus on anything but the fear swelling in my chest and let my gaze wander.

He didn't need to elaborate for me to know which complex we stood in, I'd played hide and seek in the abandoned loading bays of Short Street as a child, new the exact building he spoke of. The neighborhood kids and I never dared venture into the abandoned complex for fear of the scary stories surrounding the abandoned building, stories of ghosts, of people disappearing to never be seen again. It had always looked ready to be torn down at any moment, but it was completely different on the inside, clean and well cared for.

After what felt like forever, or maybe it was only a few minutes, he pushed through a set of doors at the bottom, revealing a massive room. I tilted my head to look around. There were no windows, maybe we were in a basement level. There was a long row of cabinets with a sink, a desk, chairs, various medical equipment, and a small row of medical beds sitting side by side on the opposite wall. It was the most well-equipped medical facility I'd ever seen outside of a hospital, seemingly prepped and ready to treat any serious injury.

A lone man in a lab coat stood in the farthest corner, jotting down notes in a folder.

"Lord Dami—" His lips clamped shut the moment he noticed me, and I frowned.

Damien shook his head. "It's all right, Johnson. Could you give us some privacy?"

"Of course, sire," he responded, dipping his head. Was he bowing to him? "Is she ok?"

"I'm having a look at her," Damien assured him.

"If you need anything, just call," Johnson said before slipping out the double doors and closing them behind him.

I lifted my eyes to Damien, face scrunching as I tried to make sense of what had just happened. "Lord?"

"I don't want to talk about it," he said, without meeting my gaze. "I've got more important things to worry about right now."

He carried me over to a bed before I could protest, easing me down to sit on the edge and headed for the sink. Rushing water echoed through the room as he washed his hands, and I rubbed the sleep from my eyes.

I looked around nervously. Everything in this room was cold, and it left me unsettled, an all too familiar feeling of the hospitals I dreaded. Memories of all the terrible things that had happened to me in places like this crept into my mind, and I focused on calming breaths, focused on anything but the unease settling into the pit of my stomach.

Damien glanced over his shoulder briefly, his brows pinched, before he gathered an armful of supplies and returned to me, setting them down on a rolling tray.

He grabbed the small flashlight and lowered himself before me. "Just gonna check to see if you have a concussion, first."

I winced, but kept my eyes opened as he quickly flashed the light into each of them, and a wave of relief seemed to wash over him. "Looks like you didn't suffer a concussion, thankfully."

He set the flashlight down and eased onto the bed beside me, pulling gloves on, before turning my head.

I pulled away from his hand, looking back at him, desperate for answers. "Damien."

"Cassie," he urged, trying again.

"Damien, stop," I breathed, twisting to face him. "Please tell me what's going on. What were you talking about back there? What do you know about those creatures?"

"Look, I'm trying to get you patched up, ok? Please, let me tend to you first." I could hear the irritation in his voice, but he composed himself, his voice softening. "I promise, I'll tell you everything."

We held each other's gaze a moment but when he didn't back down, I let out a sigh of defeat, unable to deny the pain still pulsing in my head. I turned my back to him, and he got to work, cleaning and inspecting the wound on the back of my head. I winced at the stinging pain.

He let out a breath, and remorse painted his words. "I'm sorry. I didn't mean to snap at you. I'm just... a little worked up. A lot's happened recently."

"You've been hiding it pretty well. Had me fooled," I said bitterly.

Silence was his only response, and I almost regretted my words. Taking my frustration out on him wasn't going to solve anything. I could only imagine the look of guilt on his face. "Sorry, I shouldn't have said that."

"No, you don't need to apologize. You're right." Metal clinked on the rolling tray as he switched tools, and my eyes fell to my scraped palms, my knees equally torn up and dirty.

"I'm applying a topical anesthesia to numb the area. There's some shards of glass I need to remove. You're probably going to need a couple stitches, okay?"

My brows pinched together, and I looked over my shoulder. "You know how to do that?"

"It's a long story, but yes, I've had many years of medical training."

I hesitated but turned back to allow him to continue. There was clearly a lot going on that I didn't understand. If those demons in the streets were real, why couldn't he know how to stitch up a person? That was logical, right? I just needed to be logical about this...

He got to work, and the silence rang so loudly that I couldn't focus on my own thoughts. I was eager to hear him talk, explain, but a strange sensation had settled over my skin, and I wasn't sure what it was. It left my heart twisting, as if there were fear in the air, concern.

"What's wrong?" I asked, if only to break the deafening silence.

"You… You scared me out there," he said, his words so soft, so painful, as if the admission—the acknowledgement of what had nearly happened in those alleys broke something in him.

I sat silent for a moment, dreading hearing the answer and yet knowing what it would be all the same. "So, it was all real?"

He hesitated. "Yeah."

I felt him moving around behind me, heard clinks as he dropped shards of glass into the metal dish, and for a moment, I grew desperate for a distraction from the fear clawing its way into me at the thought that those creatures were truly real, that the dreams were real.

A nervous laugh escaped my lips. "Whatever you used it's working. I can't feel a thing."

He set the tweezers down on the tray, and he sprayed something into the wound before he exchanged the spray bottle for the needle and thread. "Thankfully, it doesn't look like there was much glass. I'm starting on the stitches now, so stay still for me."

"Okay," I said, my body tensing, bracing involuntarily for the pain, but it never came. There was an odd tugging sensation on the back of my head as he ran the needle and thread, stitching the wound closed. My shoulders sagged in relief.

"Sorry for leaving you in the dark this whole time. I didn't mean for this to happen."

I didn't respond at first, still irritated, but I didn't let it show as the stupidly rational side of me accepted why he'd likely kept it a secret. It didn't lessen the hurt, though. "I'm sure it was for my own good."

"I—" He struggled with the words. "I'd intended that originally. I didn't want to shatter the safe reality you knew as a human, not knowing the truth of the terrible creatures lurking in the shadows, but, then I found you in the streets, being hunted and I—"

He drew a deep breath and but didn't say anymore.

My mind pooled with thoughts of the creatures that would've likely torn me limb from limb if he hadn't saved me. I swallowed down the terror crawling up my throat as I imagined what an agonizing end it would've been like.

Damien's voice pulled me from the horrors coming to life in my head. "One more and you'll be good. You won't have any trouble hiding these with your hair. They'll either dissolve or fall out on their own in a week or two."

"Thanks," I said. "For everything, Damien, really. I'd be dead if it wasn't for you."

"I promised I'd always be there for you. And I always will."

I sat for a moment, allowing him to focus on what he was doing, and I wrapped my rms round myself, trying to block out the cold. "Is this place safe from them? Can they get to us here?"

"No, they won't get into this place. You're safe here," he assured me, and I tried to believe him.

"Ok, you're all patched up now," he said, dropping the needle onto the tray before he pulled the gloves from his hands and headed to the sink to wash up. "Are you thirsty?"

"Yeah, I could definitely use a drink right now."

Damien fished a couple of waters from a mini fridge under the desk and returned to me. My mouth was parched, throat bone dry, and I couldn't get the bottle cap off fast enough after he handed it to me. I chugged the water, feeling the coolness roll down my throat, and I groaned in relief.

"All right, shirt off."

He blinked at me, as if I'd just asked him to strip naked. My cheeks heated, and I fumbled to correct the misunderstanding. "N–No that's not what I... Damien, come on. I don't want to leave that wound untreated," I said as I motioned to the bloody wound on his shoulder.

A crooked grin crept across his face, and for a moment I thought he might deny care, but he slid his shirt over his head. I swallowed, trying not to stare at the smooth muscles of his body as they flexed and stretched beneath his olive skin... skin that looked paler than I remembered, and it left me all the more worried for him.

I grabbed a clean rag from the pile of things Damien had brought and walked over to wash my hands and soak it with warm water. I returned, settling down beside him, looking over his injury. It looked terrible, coated in dried blood, and I winced internally as I imagined how much it hurt.

I gently dabbed the rag against the wound, watching him for any wince or grimace. "Does that hurt?"

"Keep doing what you're doing. I'm fine." I could hear the smile in his voice.

"Is something funny?"

"It's just cute hearing you dote on me," he said, his voice low and calm, the sound of it like a caress of his skin. "This isn't anything serious for me, but I kind of like you tending to my wounds."

I bit my lip, trying to focus on what I was doing, but my heart raced at his words. "Stop talking. I'm trying to focus."

He laughed under his breath but didn't say more.

After several careful dabs of the wet rag, the wound cleared of blood, and I was relieved to find there wasn't any debris. The gashes were deep, though, the skin shredded from where the darkling had torn through his shoulder. My skin crawled at the memory of those horrible claws, and darkling's terrifying jaws. I didn't want to think about the pain he'd endured defending me.

He could have left me there, but he hadn't. He'd risked his life to save mine. My heart swelled at that thought as I sprayed the fully cleaned wound with antiseptic and secured a gauze over it.

My gaze lingered on the freshly dressed wound for a moment, but he didn't turn to me, and I wondered if he was just as eager to stall this conversation as I was becoming. I couldn't help but fear the information he was about to share, and how it would change everything for me.

I pushed myself off the bed and headed to wash my hands. No matter what he was going to tell me, the thought of him fighting those monsters left me reeling, fearing for his safety… for mine. How could he face those things?

The stream of water trickled to a stop as I switched the faucet off and turned back to him, bracing myself on the edge of the countertop. He stared at me from across the room for a long painful, moment before patting the bed beside him. I drew a deep breath, knowing the moment I sat down, my entire world was going to change. Nothing would be the same.

"I owe you an apology for keeping you in the dark," he said, as I approached, his guilt painting every word.

He gripped the edge of the bed, and a muscle feathered in his jaw. I resisted the almost involuntarily urge to take his hand and lace my fingers with his, and instead folded my hands together in my lap. The act only left the need writhing and surging within me, swelling to a point where my heart twisted in a near hollow agony, but I shoved it down.

"I understand your reasons for not telling me about whatever it is you're doing. That's not what hurt. We're only just getting to know each other. I'm no one special, and you don't owe me anything, but…"

Hurt flashed across his face briefly, and his eyes fell from me.

"I'm hurt that you hid what happened to us that first night I was hunted. All this time I thought it was a dream, that I was crazy. You knew, and you hid it from me."

"And I never should've done that. I'm so sorry," he said, meeting my gaze, and I couldn't read what emotions lingered in his eyes. There were too many to place. "I should've been honest with you, but I was terrified of how you'd react... How you'd take it."

"Well now you have a chance to make up for it," I said, trying to mask the fear in my demand.

He let out a heavy breath. "Are you sure about this? There'll be no turning back once I tell you everything." His eyes burned into me, the silence dragging on for a moment. "It becomes near impossible to erase every trace once the knowledge of everything becomes so entangled in your mind."

I pondered that thought, unsure of what exactly I was signing up for. Despite the fear welling in my chest from what I'd seen tonight, a part of me—the part that seemed to dismiss all rationale when it came to him—was desperate for it, no matter what he might tell me.

"Tell me to erase your memory, Cas," I lifted my gaze to him, and my heart sank at the intense look of fear and pain in his eyes. "Tell me you'd rather go back to your normal life." His voice was like gravel, the words clinging, begging not to leave his lips. "I'll take it all away. You won't remember anything of the darklings or meeting us. All of your original memories would remain intact, it would simply be as if we never met, as if none of this ever happened. You can go back to living a normal life, I'll pull some strings, move you and your family far away from this city where you'll be safe. I'll stay away, make sure you're safe from a distance."

Barrett had threatened to erase my memories just moments ago, and something fought from deep within the confines of my mind—my soul—to say no, but I found myself hooked on the thought that, that was something he could even do. How could he just erase my memories? And yet, as the skepticism filled me, an innate fear clawed its way into me at the thought of forgetting, of losing every memory we shared even if they only spanned the last few weeks.

My memories of everything. Of him. Of our time together. The times we shared on fooling around on campus, our time spent at Stackhouse, the moments we shared on his living room floor, cooking dinner together—memories that had become so precious to me. Barrett, Cole, Vincent... Zephyr. Would I forget them too?

For years, I'd longed to feel what I felt in their company, had only just found the chance and comfort to get a taste of what life should be like. How could I ever choose what I had before over safety? Would it ever truly be safety with those creatures out there? No. Regardless of whether I remembered or not, they would be there in the shadows, waiting, hunting.

I lifted my gaze to him. Agony filled his eyes, like a part of him wanted me to tell him yes, to tell him to erase my memory so that I might live a normal life. At the same time, there was hope, as if he might want me to tell him no. As if he hoped and prayed that I might say I was with

124

him, that I would accept everything he told me. I wanted it; wanted to remain at his side.

Hesitation crept into the back of my mind, and my lips parted but my response halted on my tongue as the opportunity presented itself. This was a chance for me to tell him to do it, to spare him from a relationship with me that would only end the way he feared. It would be the best thing for me to do.

No. I didn't want that.

How could I choose to go back to the life of loneliness I'd suffered before him? A life I no longer wanted to live. Now that I had gotten a taste of the joy I felt when he was around—when they were all around... I didn't know what to do.

His conflict seemed to mirror my own, the emotions nearly radiating off of him, and I drew a deep breath. I couldn't bring myself to douse the tiny flicker of hope in the back of my mind begging me to say no, begging me to tell him I would remain at his side.

No matter what...

If this was the world that I lived in for what remained of my life, I was ok with that.

"I don't want to forget," I finally decided, giving into that urge to reach out and touch him, and I laced my fingers through his. "I... I don't want to forget you, even if it means that I'll have to accept whatever you tell me."

I laughed at the words coming out of my mouth, eyes faltering as I questioned what I was saying. "You probably think I'm insane for saying it."

"Not at all." A warm smile curved the corners of his lips, and the glow of it reached his eyes, leaving them near glowing like embers in ashes. "I wouldn't expect anything less than a warrior willing to face the unknown darkness."

Any response I might have had halted on my tongue.

He reached out to run his finger over my cheek, the sensation leaving my heart fluttering. "I hate that I couldn't better protect you," he admitted, sorrow burning in his eyes. "You could've died."

My heart squeezed, and I gripped his hand tighter, drawing him back to me. "But I didn't. I'm alive, thanks to you. If you hadn't found me, I wouldn't be here right now. I couldn't ask for more, knowing what I know now." My gaze drifted, imagining the darklings. "It's still difficult to believe those creatures are out there. How you fight those things... I can't even imagine it."

He was quiet for a moment. "We're only able to fight them, because we're not exactly humans ourselves."

I lifted my gaze to him, blinking as I processed what he was trying to tell me. "I was a bit confused when Barrett called me a human."

"Sorry about him. He's been on edge lately, and when I brought you here—" He ran a hand through his hair, and for a moment it almost seemed as if he was still fighting with himself. "We aren't supposed to bring humans here. There are laws we must abide by—consequences for sharing our existence with your kind."

I didn't understand it, but his emotions rose off him, filling the room, the chaos whirling in his mind so palpable that I could quite literally feel it... but I wanted so desperately so ease whatever maelstrom had raged out of control in his head.

A morbid sense of humor laced my tongue as I spoke. It was all I could do to avoid the chaos raging in my head, all I could do to try and pull him back into the light. "So, if you're not human, what are you? Some sort of werewolf? An Atlantean God?"

He chuckled. "Neither. You're not far off the mark, though." It eased my heart to hear him relax, even a little. "I guess we'd be as close to what you humans call vampires as you can get."

Vampires?

"But." I frowned, blinking. "You can go out in the sun. Aren't vampires supposed to, you know, turn to dust in the sun or something?"

That I was making lighthearted jokes at this point had me questioning my sanity, but I'd seen enough by this point to know that the darklings, creatures I once believed to be a figment of my imagination, were very much real, I couldn't deny the fear that had taken root within me. The terrible thoughts and possibilities of what those creatures could do to me surged to life in the depths of my imagination, my mind latching onto what it might feel like for those claws to sink into my flesh, for those terrible teeth to tear me apart... I found myself spiraling again, my forced smile threatening to fade.

Don't Panic. This is fine. This is ok. Panicking won't make them disappear.

Damien practically snorted a laugh. "We prefer the term Immortals. The majority of things humans believe about us are just dusty myths. We can go out in the sun, I can see myself in the mirror, I appear in photos..." He sat there a moment, as if going through the list in his head. "Yeah, I think the only thing that humans got right is that we need blood to survive."

My skepticism spilled out of my mouth, and I leaned forward, eyes narrowing as they fell on his mouth. "You've smiled at me countless times and I've never seen fangs."

He fought back a smile before he opened his mouth, revealing his perfect white teeth, no fangs in sight. While his canines were slightly longer, they weren't, by any means, fangs. I gasped as his canines lengthened, as if they'd only been sheathed. They retracted again until they were perfectly hidden.

"Easier to stay hidden amongst humans if we don't have obvious fangs."

Shit. I could hardly believe what I was seeing. There was no way this was real... but it was.

He needed blood to survive. Did that mean... My heart fluttered at the thought of him biting someone, biting me, and for some strange reason, that felt almost thrilling. I swallowed, my cheeks warming as I remembered how his lips had felt against my neck, and my imagination got the better of me as it wandered to the possibilities of what it might have been like if he had bitten me.

What was wrong with me? That should be terrifying. And yet...

"Before you ask, no, I don't drink from humans. There are those of our kind that do, and while human blood can sustain us, it isn't as potent as the blood of our kind. Those of us who do feed off humans have to do it more frequently, and their magic tends to be affected by the lack of power present in human blood. I assure you, we aren't the bloodthirsty monsters Hollywood made us out to be. There's no murder involved." He offered me a smile. "We're actually more like protectors that predators."

They protected us from the darklings. I sat there a moment, trying to wrap my head around everything he was telling me, and I knew we'd only scratched the surface. So many questions swirled in my head. I needed to know everything. I shoved down the fear and lifted my gaze to Damien, ready to learn what he did. There was no turning back now. I wasn't afraid, though I probably should be.

Regardless of whether I gave into the fear or not, my world would never be the same after tonight.

CHAPTER 13

"So, Barrett and the others…"

"They're immortals as well," he said.

"Cole too?"

He nodded. "James is the only human in our group."

"And he knows?"

"There are very few humans who know our secrets, but yes, he does. To answer your question, though. Barrett, Vincent, Zephyr, and Cole, they're all like me. Immortals."

"So, when Cole told me you helped him when he lost his parents…" I hesitated but asked. "What happened to them?"

Damien's gentle smile faded, and something icy trailed over my skin. I shivered, wrapping my arms around myself.

"Cole's mother was human. It's extremely rare for our kind to reproduce with yours, but it's not impossible. His parents were both killed by darklings several years ago. He was only fourteen, no family to take him in. When I found out, I took him under my wing, sheltered him, taught him everything he knows and brought him into our ranks."

An odd sense of pride swelled in my chest. For him to do that, the selflessness of it; I could only imagine how difficult it must have been to take a child in like that. The way they acted, I knew that Damien saw Cole like a younger brother. The whole group did.

Still, the question lingering in the back of my mind began to gnaw at me. I chewed my lip, trying to figure out how best to ask him, but nothing sounded any gentler, so I just blurted out, "How did I end up out there? I don't remember leaving my house, and Kat didn't remember me leaving the first night either, so it must have happened after we fell asleep."

He leaned forward, elbows resting on his knees as he laced his fingers together to rest his forehead against them. "That, I don't know. I've been searching for answers since I first found you out there. Nothing adds up, and the number of darklings we encountered both nights I found you—we don't normally see that many together. If I hadn't found you when I did…"

I didn't want to think about what would have happened if he hadn't found me. I shuddered, remembering the feel of the darklings cold, slick claws around my throat.

He took a deep breath, calming himself before continuing. "For the last hundred years, the darklings have been nothing more than beasts. Uncoordinated, typically solitary. It's always been easy to keep them under control."

I stuttered at his casual statement. "H-hundred years?"

"Yeah," Damien chuckled. "My house's history dates back nearly two thousand years. I guess I neglected to mention that."

Two thousand years? Holy shit. How long had they been living among humans? Hidden from us. Or were there other humans who knew of their existence? How did they just exist the way they did?

"So…" My mind began to wander in every direction. "I have to ask, you don't have to answer, though, if you don't want to but... Exactly how old are you?"

A crooked grin spread across his face. "Are you sure you want to know?"

"Let me guess, you're like a hundred? Two hundred years old?" I smirked, lifting my water bottle to take a sip.

"Hate to break it to you, but I'm nine hundred and ninety-two years old now. At least, I think. It gets hard to keep track sometimes."

I choked on the water, spilling a bit of it on my shirt.

He belted out a laugh. "Yeah, I figured you'd react like that."

"You're joking right? This is a joke," I gasped, brushing the front of my shirt before grabbing a nearby hand towel to dab it dry.

"Nope, I've been around a while."

I couldn't wrap my mind around that. Almost a thousand years? What had he seen in his lifetime? Had he always been here in the states?

No. He told me his family was from Greece. Had he come from there? Or had he been born here?

The humor drained from his expression, and he continued before I could ask any more questions. "As I was saying, the darklings have always just been beasts. They don't typically hunt in groups of more than two or three. Even so, if they were together, they more likely to fight over prey. They're greedy and ravenous like that, quick to turn on each other for little more than scraps."

I thought back to the first night I'd encountered them; there had been several darklings. Tonight, there had been such a large group that I couldn't have counted them, and they weren't fighting amongst themselves as he claimed they normally did when it came to their prey. No, they were so focused on me that there was nothing else in their sights.

My mind revisited the sight, the towering dark creature made of black mist and shadow, the glowing red eyes. "Before I passed out, I saw a creature in the darkness, it wasn't a darkling, though. It was huge. I couldn't really make out what it was, but I remember it had red eyes."

Damien let out a low breath. "There are houses of power that have existed since the creation of our kind, long before my time, all harboring their own unique abilities and magics. There were once many houses of power, but many souls were lost in a battle we fought a little over a century ago." He shifted, turning toward me. "Each house of power has a blood trait or power passed down from generation to generation. I'm from the House of Skiá and we were gifted with the ability to use shadow magic."

My gaze snapped to him, my heart launching into an excited frenzy. "Shadow magic?"

A crooked grin formed on his face, and he held his hand out. My eyes widened as black mist fell from his palm, building until it swirled around his hand. "I can control shadows, small or large. I can travel through them, manifest weapons," I gasped as the shadowy mist condensed and disbursed, leaving a dagger in his palm, and as quickly as it appeared, the shadows swallowed it whole, erasing it from existence once more.

"I can even use it to summon shadow beasts like the one you saw tonight. Think of it as dark magic. The creature that stopped the darkling from biting you was one of my summoning."

"Wait," I said, frowning as the dagger he'd held just seconds before tugged forth a realization. "Were you hunting darklings near Kat's house the night before our date?"

His brows knitted.

"It was too dark to tell, but I think I saw you kill a darkling, or maybe it was someone else. I don't know. It didn't look like a darkling, but you said they can take the form of humans. The shriek I heard when it died was the same as the ones I heard tonight. I won't lie, it freaked me out, because I thought it was a person you killed." I paused, realizing I may have made things more difficult in calling the police. "Oh my God. I'm so sorry. I called the cops on you."

He lifted his head, cocking an eyebrow, a grin tugging at his lips. "So you're the one who called them." He paused, seeming to realize the weight of what I'd witnessed. "Sorry you had to see that. We try to keep them out of neighborhoods and away from humans if we can. It isn't like them to wander into quieter places, they aren't smart enough to enter homes to look for people. They tend to keep to more concentrated areas of human activity where they're more likely to encounter prey. That particular group was a pain in the ass to track down. They were the first we'd encountered acting in such a coordinated way. When they changed into their human form to escape, it was the strangest thing. It's not something they usually do. Typically, they save it for daybreak."

"When the darklings change into their human disguise—I know you said humans can't tell them apart, but can immortals?"

He shook his head. "No. It's a magic that's too powerful to see through, even for our kind. It would make things so much easier if we could search for them during the day as well."

It hit me then, and the realization left my gut twisting—mind reeling. Anyone could be a darkling, and there was no way to tell who was a friend and who was a monster. A lady at the grocery store. A teacher on campus. I shuddered at the thought. That someone I knew or attended classes with could easily be a darkling and I'd never know.

Damien wrapped his arms around me, pulling me against him. "I'm so glad I found you when I did."

I sat there a moment, melting into his embrace, his fear near palpable, and I didn't understand how I could almost feel it. My chest tightened, aching for him, and I wanted nothing more than to ease his hurt, to calm his worry.

I can't lose you... Not again.

I froze for a moment. "What did you say?"

He pulled back to look at me, his brows knitting in confusion. "I didn't say anything."

I blinked, pressing my hand to my forehead as the room seemed to sway. I could've sworn I'd heard Damien's voice, almost as if it was in my head. It echoed repeatedly as I processed it in my mind, but then it shifted, as if it were a distant memory. There were no words to describe the deep ache that spread through my chest. Like bidding a lifelong friend goodbye.

"Cas, are you ok?" Damien asked as his eyes, clouded with concern, passed over my face frantically.

I frowned, confused by his concern. "I'm fi—" My vision blurred, and I stiffened as a tear rolled down my face. Was I crying? My hand came up to my face, touching the tears that continued to fall, before rigorously rubbing them away.

What was wrong with me?

"Sorry, I... I think I'm just tired." My voice shook as I struggled to keep the tears at bay. "Maybe the shock is finally wearing off."

131

His mouth parted, as if he wanted to say something more, but seemed to reconsider his words. "We'll continue this conversation tomorrow. Let's get you home so you can rest. I've got to get back to figuring out how you ended up out in the alleys. Something about it doesn't sit right with me."

"No, I want to know more," I said in protest, but as I stood, a wave of dizziness rushed over me, and I grabbed hold of him to stabilize myself.

"Cas," he urged. "We have all the time in the world. I promise, I'll tell you everything, but you need rest."

He wasn't wrong. I was exhausted, my body sore and aching.

"Fine," I muttered, hating my own weakness.

He scooped me into his arms without another word, and I wrapped my arms around his neck as he cradled me. His scent filled my lungs, a mix of sweat and that calming scent of cedarwood and leather, and my body eased into his.

He walked toward the far side of the room where the single lamp didn't reach. "Do me a favor and close your eyes."

"Why?"

"Just do it. Trust me. You might get sick if you don't."

I sat there a moment, wondering why he wanted me to, but what could it hurt, right? I closed my eyes, obeying him.

"No peeking now," he added, and I could hear his grin painting his words.

I chuckled and pressed my face to his chest so I could better resist the urge.

Something cold brushed over my skin as he took a step forward. For a moment, it felt as if we were walking, then we were weightless, gravity shifting, and I stiffened, grabbing onto him tighter, as if I might fall into some abyss. It probably lasted a second or two, but it felt so much longer. Icy air enveloped us, wind whipping past me, through me, pressure building up against my body, and then all at once, it stopped.

I cracked my eyes open and nearly yelped, but Damien's hand came over my mouth before I could.

"Shhh. You're ok, I've got you," he whispered.

My chest heaved as my eyes darted around the room—my room—when we'd been standing in the basement of the apartment complex just moments before. It was dark, but I knew it well: my bed, barely illuminated under the moonlight leaking through my window, my desk in the far corner.

I opened my mouth to freak out, but Damien cut me off.

"Keep your voice low. Your parents are still asleep next door," he whispered, walking me to my bed and easing me down to sit. I stared at him wide-eyed, my breath uneven as I tried to come to terms with what had just happened.

"How did—what did you—How the fuck did you do that?" I managed to whisper.

He sat down beside me, biting back a laugh. "I told you; I can travel through shadows."

"You didn't say you could teleport!" I whispered loudly. "I could've better prepared myself for that."

A wicked grin pulled at the corners of his lips. "No amount of mental prep will ever have you ready for your first time."

Damien took my hand and kissed my forehead tenderly. "You should try to get some rest."

Fear crept back into my mind at the thought of being alone, of him leaving, and I clutched onto the sleeve of his shirt. "Please, don't go. Not yet."

His gaze fell to my hand before he took it into both of his and pressed a kiss my knuckles. "I'll stay for a bit longer, but I can't stay past that. Don't worry. We're keeping a close watch over your house now. Nothing will hurt you here."

He lowered himself onto the bed, wrapping his arms around me, and I nestled into his chest, losing myself in his presence—in his comforting scent.

Time passed slowly as we laid there, his heartbeat a steady, soothing rhythm in my ear, and I could almost feel myself starting to drift off to sleep. Goosebumps pebbled across my skin at the feel of his fingertips as he stroked my arm, and I couldn't resist the yawn.

"I have to report back to the guys. I won't be far, I promise. Cole's standing watch outside to make sure you're safe while you sleep. I'll see you tomorrow, though, and we can pick up where we left off after your classes get out."

I sighed in disappointment, but he was right. The sun would be rising soon, and I needed my sleep if I was going to function even the slightest bit tomorrow. "Okay."

I closed my eyes as he leaned over to press a kiss to my forehead. The sensation sent butterflies fluttering in my stomach. "Sleep well, *mea luna*."

"What does that mean?" I asked before he disappeared.

He smiled back at me. "It means 'my moon'."

My heart leapt in my chest, and I smiled at him as he disappeared into the dark corner of my room. I sat there a moment, waiting for him to step back out into view to say, 'just kidding', but he never returned.

I pushed myself up to look out my window just in time to see him emerge onto the street below. Cole was there with him, and they exchanged words for a moment before he disappeared into the shadows again. Cole glanced up at me, giving a light wave, and I smiled, returning the gesture.

My bed felt more comfortable than it had in a while, blankets welcoming me into their cushiony embrace. I'd get more answers tomorrow. I just needed to go to sleep, and for once I didn't think it would be hard to. My heavy eyes started to flutter as I lowered onto my pillow.

I was safe now. Nothing would harm me here.

CHAPTER 14

I ignored the hum of student voices around me, the sound not enough to pull my mind from the thoughts it so desperately clung to. Endless questions and possibilities had filled my head all morning. There was so much about his world he'd yet to tell me about, and I wanted to know everything.

My heart raced as I rounded the corner into the courtyard. The thought of seeing Damien brought me back to us laying in my bed together the night before. A smile curved my lips, but the moment I lifted my gaze to where Damien and the others usually were, he wasn't there. Something twisted in my chest, unease settling into the pit of my stomach, and I headed toward them.

"Hey, Cas," Cole said, offering me a smile.

"Hey. Where's Damien?" I asked.

Cole glanced nervously at Barrett, who gave me a sidelong glance, before returning his gaze to his phone and answered. "Not here yet."

For a moment I hesitated to respond to him, still stuck on the way he'd treated me the night before, but I pulled myself from the thought as I processed his words. Damien wasn't here yet? Had something happened to him? Did the darklings attack after he left?

Breathe, Cas. Damien had been fighting these creatures for God knows how long, long before he met me, and he'd fight them long after I was gone. I couldn't get worked up every time something out of the ordinary happened. He would be ok. He had to be.

I glanced over to where Kat and Cody usually sat. Kat was there, alone, working on her laptop.

"I'll be back," I sat my bag down, and hurried over to her.

The courtyard was hectic this morning, filled with students going in every direction. I worked my way through the crowd, narrowly avoiding bumping into them as I approached Kat. A strange sensation crawled across my skin, as if someone, or something, was watching me. I shoved it down, knowing it was pure paranoia, especially after what I'd learned the night before.

There was no way any darklings were here, where there were so many people around. I halted that train of thought as Damien's words from the night before resurfaced. At night, darklings took on their true, hideous appearance when they hunted, but come daybreak they disguised themselves as regular people, blending seamlessly into society.

My skin tingled and I looked over my shoulder at the passing faces. How could something so ravenous and savage at night act so normal during the day? The way they moved—still fresh in my mind— made me cringe. Their hollow bodies, hunched backs, and long black tipped claws. I stifled the shudder running through me at the memory and hugged myself as my hands began to shake.

Kat looked up, as if sensing my approach, and smiled. "Hey."

"Hey." I sat down beside her, rubbing the sleep from my eyes, and she started to speak, but I couldn't seem to focus as my eyes darted across the faces of the students that surrounded us. Were any of them darklings in disguise?

She did a double take, brows narrowing as she scrutinized me. "You ok?"

I blinked, trying to clear my head. "Sorry. Still waking up."

She gave me a weary look, but looked at where Barrett and the others were sitting. "Where's your cutie? Did he stay over at your house after the party last night?"

"No, Kat. Geez." I tried not to laugh and deny the fact that she wasn't far off the mark, as he'd been in my bed last night. "I don't know. Maybe he woke up late. We were out pretty late."

I glanced back toward the group, and a pang of guilt sank into my stomach for keeping him out all night. He'd been hunting because of

135

me, because he was worried for my safety. I could only imagine how exhausted he must be to function on such little sleep.

A sigh slipped from my lips, and I turned back to Kat, a hint of a strange expression on her face as she stared behind me. She immediately smiled as soon as she noticed I'd turned to her.

"What're you looking at?" I asked, glancing over my shoulder.

She shook her head before get gaze fell back to her laptop. "Oh, it's nothing."

I narrowed my eyes, my brows furrowing as I watched her. Was she hiding something from me? Had Barrett put his foot in his mouth at the bonfire last night? I'd left them alone when I spoke with Damien. It wouldn't take Barrett long to stir up trouble, and if he harassed her, we were going to have a problem.

"Where's Cody?" I asked.

"He's playing hooky this morning, something about a new game release today."

"Ah," I said, huffing a laugh. "Glad he's got his priorities straight. I was gonna go sit with the guys. You wanna join us?"

She glanced at me but shook her head before continuing to type away on her laptop. "Nah, I won't be much company. Cody came by last night after I got home from the bonfire. I got a bit distracted and forgot I had a paper due this morning."

I gave her a knowing look, and her cheeks turned a shade of pink. "What? He's distracting."

"Sure he is," I said, snickering.

"I'm sure he's just as distracting as Damien," she said, giving me a coy grin.

I elbowed her, unable to hold back a smile, and she let out a laugh.

"Well, I won't distract you anymore than your boyfriend already has," I said, as I stood. "I'll see you in class."

"See ya!"

I walked back toward Barrett and the others, eyes darting across faces as they passed. It wasn't the same as before, though, it wasn't unease from judgement, but fear—paranoia clouding my vision, and it was scary to think I didn't know who I could trust anymore. Were the people walking past me truly human? Were any of them one of the terrifying creatures that had hunted me just last night?

"Still not here?" I asked Vincent as I took a seat near my bag.

"Nope," Vincent replied, glancing back at me before returning to his game of wall ball, and I eyed him wearily. Were they going to just pretend last night didn't happen? Were things going to change between us now that I knew what they were? Or would they go back to normal?

My eyes drifted to Barrett, still a little fearful of how he would speak to me after how angry he'd been the night before. He wasn't acting out of the ordinary, though. Perhaps he was hoping Damien erased my memories like he wanted. The thought of that being possible still felt unreal. Maybe whatever strange understanding that passed between them had settled the concern he had about breaking their laws.

I was eager to know more about them, their race, what they could do, more about the darklings. Where did the immortals come from? How long have they been around, hiding amongst humans?

More importantly, where the hell was Damien?

"Is he ok? Did something happen last night?" I asked to no one in particular, flicking my fingernails in my impatience as I looked out toward the parking lot, seeking his face in the sea of them.

"He should be here soon," Barrett said, and I swore I heard a hint of confusion in his voice, like he himself didn't know why Damien wasn't there yet, which only worried me more. If Barrett was concerned, then something must be wrong, right?

Barrett's eyes briefly shifted to me, and I wondered if I'd imagined the tinge of guilt in those steel eyes. "Cas, I—"

I tilted my head to him, brows arched in question.

"I'm sorry about last night…"

My lips parted, but I wasn't sure what to say. "It's… I'm sure you were just protecting those you love."

He seemed to stiffen at that statement, his lips parting.

"Did I just hear right?" Vincent said before Barrett could say a word. "Did Barrett just apologize for something?"

"Oh, Gods. I think the world might be ending," Cole added, raising his hand to shield the sun from his eyes as he surveyed the horizon dramatically, as if he were looking for the impending doom.

Barrett groaned, rolling his eyes, and before I could say anything more, Vincent was wrapping his arm around Barrett's shoulder, cracking jokes.

"Donnae worry, Cas. He'll be here before yoo kno' it," James said, flashing me a reassuring smile as he placed a comforting hand on my shoulder.

"Thanks, James."

"So, you and Damien are a thing now?" Zephyr asked, and I could hear the humor in his tone. I rolled my eyes, knowing the teasing that would likely follow, but I smiled.

I shrugged. "I guess."

"That's cool. I haven't seen this side of Damien in a long time. He gets so uptight sometimes, it's about time a female made him lighten up."

I sat there a moment, still a little confused by his words—the use of the word female—but I shook them off. Now that I thought about it, Damien had used that term once before. Perhaps it was just how they spoke.

It was strange to think that the guys surrounding me were like Damien, immortals. Vampires. All except James, of course.

"So Damien told you everything last night?" Cole asked, his voice low as he scooted closer to me.

I nodded, the memory of being chased the night before sending my heart into a frenzy. I feared my heart might have given out on me last night. God, that would have been bad. I wouldn't be sitting here right now. "It's still weird to think about and difficult to believe, but after everything I've seen, I can't exactly deny it."

Zephyr rubbed my shoulder in comfort. "The darklings are terrible creatures, but we'll watch your back. All of us are here for you."

"Thanks, Zephyr."

Barrett, Zephyr, Vincent, James, and Cole's phones went off all at once. They retrieved their phones, eyes falling to their screens as they tapped it before the calm expression from their faces slipped. Barrett's brows furrowed as he read through the message, steel eyes sharpening. They remained silent for a moment, and I glanced between them, my heart launching into my throat.

"Is everything o—" My phone pinged, and I quickly pulled my phone from my pocket to find a text from Damien. I wasn't sure if I should feel relief of terror that he'd texted me instead of showing up.

I tapped the screen, hearing Zephyr rise to his feet, as the text message came up.

> Sorry, Cas. I won't be able to make it today. Something came up, and I have to deal with it. I'm so sorry. I promise we'll talk soon.

I quickly typed away, more movement sounding around me as the guys rose, muttering to each other.

> Is everything ok? Are you ok? What happened?

> I'm ok, just immortal business that I can't avoid. Hopefully, I'll be able to deal with it quickly and I can see you tomorrow.

I lifted my gaze to find Zephyr, Vincent, and Barrett grabbing their bags.

"Where are you guys going?"

"Work call," Barrett said. "Gotta go. It's important."

"All of you?" I asked, frowning as James folded his laptop and tucked it away in his bag.

138

Zephyr nodded to Cole, who remained sitting at my side. "Cole's staying here. He'll walk you to your classes, make sure no one bothers you."

I frowned at that statement. Who would bother me?

"We'll be back tomorrow, Cas. Donnae worry aboot us," James said with a smile as he slid his bag over his shoulder. "We'll look after Damien fer ye."

"Oh. Okay." I said reluctantly. "Be careful."

"Always are," Barrett said, giving me one final glance before turning away.

Zephyr pressed his index finger to my forehead, his lips quirking into a teasing smirk, and something warm filled my chest at the strange gesture. "You keep frowning like that and you'll get wrinkles on your forehead. It'll be fine, and we'll be back tomorrow."

I forced a smile as Zephyr waved and the guys headed off, leaving me and Cole alone in the grass.

"Do you know what's going on?" I asked Cole without looking his way as I wrapped my arms around my knees to rest my chin atop them.

He didn't answer at first, his eyes lingering on the guys as they disappeared into the crowds. His voice was full of remorse when he finally responded. "I can't really talk about it. Sorry."

My eyes fell to my phone, rereading Damien's last words before texting him back.

Be careful. I'll see you tomorrow.

CHAPTER 15

Nearly three days had passed since I'd last heard from Damien, since I'd seen any of the guys outside of Cole. I scrolled through our string of texts—er... my string of texts, it seemed.

October 28th 10:15am

So, Barrett apologized to me for last night. I'm shocked his ego allowed him to do that.

October 29th 11:38am

Submitted my art project, crossing my fingers. I'll freak out if my artwork gets featured in an art gallery.

October 30th 8:24pm

I hope everything's ok. Miss seeing you and the guys on campus.

My finger hovered over the unsent message typed out before me.

If I did something wrong, please tell me. Are you regretting telling me everything? Are you in trouble because of it? Please talk to me. I just want to know you're ok.

My finger hovered over the send button, my heart racing, mind falling into a spiral of doubt as I recounted every interaction, every word spoken between us. Barrett had flipped out over me knowing, had stressed the severity of it and how it broke their laws. Had something happened to Damien because I now knew of their existence?

Guilt twisted in my stomach at the thought of what he might be dealing with because of me. How severe was the punishment for breaking their laws? Was someone coming for me because I knew? Was that why Cole was sticking with me?

I sighed, hitting the delete button until each and every letter was gone, each and every doubt and fear coming into harsher clarity with each word's disappearance as I erased the chance to get them off my chest. I wasn't sure which I feared more, another text unanswered, or a rejection that might rip my heart out.

Cars passed me by as I walked down the sidewalk toward campus. I'd started working my stamina back up by walking to class the past few days so I could start jogging again. Cole had started joining me for my walks home after classes, we'd even managed to jog a few blocks before reaching my house the day before.

We'd grown closer, connecting over art and I found we actually had a lot in common. He enjoyed reading almost as much as I did, so we'd started reading together, him teasing me about my romance while I teased him about his real-world stories that held no fantasy. My phone vibrated in my pocket, and my heart leapt into my throat as I quickly grabbed it.

Disappointment pooled in my chest at the sight of Kat's name on the screen. God, I shouldn't be disappointed that it was her calling me and not Damien. What was wrong with me? I tapped the screen and lifted the phone to my ear.

"Hey, Kat."

"Happy Halloween! What time are we meeting tonight?" she asked without a moment's hesitation.

I hadn't paid much attention to the days as they came and went. My thoughts were so clouded with worry for Damien that I'd barely realized Halloween had already arrived. Yes, we'd spent countless Halloweens out together, but now that I knew what hid in the shadows, I was beginning to think better of it. What if we ran into a darkling? I couldn't imagine what I would do if she were attacked by one of those terrible creatures.

"Umm..."

"Don't you dare," Kat started, already picking up on the reluctance in my voice. "We are gonna go out and have fun, and you're not gonna stay cooped up in your room. This is the one night a year I actually get you to come out!"

I let out a breath. "I don't know if I'm feeling up to it today, honestly."

The line was silent for a moment.

"He still hasn't answered?" she asked tentatively.

"No," I said as I shoved my free hand into the pocket of my jacket and continued down the sidewalk.

"I'm gonna kick that asshole in the balls the next time I see him."

"It's not like that, Kat," I said, my voice rising. She didn't understand, but of course she wouldn't understand. She didn't know the truth—couldn't know the truth. "He had some personal stuff come up, sort of family emergency; you know that."

"I would understand not calling, but the least he could do is text you."

I hated that she was right, and yet, the fact that he wasn't texting me brought to life a number of fears I'd been trying to stifle the last few days. Had he gotten into trouble? Had he been attacked by the darklings? Had he been hurt? Was he in some sort of immortal prison for breaking their laws?

"I'm sure he'll get back to me when he's able."

"Mhmm," she hummed disapprovingly.

My phone vibrated against my ear, and I came to a halt on the sidewalk as I lowered it, putting Kat on speaker as I looked down at the notification on my screen.

Air halted in my lungs at the sight of Damien's name.

"Be at my house to get ready at six," I said quickly, fearing I might need her company after this phone call.

She squealed on the other end of the line. "Fuck yeah! Cody and I will be there!"

"I've gotta go. I'll talk to you later," I said, my hands shaking as my thumb hovered over the answer button.

"Later!"

I pressed my thumb to the screen, the call switching, and I lifted it hesitantly to my ear. "Damien?"

"I'm so sorry," he said, and the most profound relief washed over me, so much so that I thought my knees might give out.

"Are you okay?"

"I'm all right, it's just... A lot has happened, and I'm sorry I haven't responded sooner."

"You scared the shit out of me. I thought something happened to you. I thought you got in trouble or something for telling me what you are," I said, almost frustrated at how okay he sounded.

I frowned as I heard what almost sounded like a huffed laugh on the other end of the line. "I didn't get in trouble for telling you our secret, I promise."

"What happened then?"

The line was silent for a moment. "It's complicated. I had some business to attend to, then there was an incident with an immortal family—a murder that I had to handle, and..."

The walk indicator turned from red to green and I continued through the crosswalk toward campus, hanging onto the silence echoing down the line. "And what? What happened?"

"Just some shit with Marcus, but everyone's okay."

Marcus? I hadn't thought much about his ties to Marcus and whatever bad blood they had. Then my mind wandered to possibilities. Was Marcus immortal like him?

"Is everything okay?"

"It will be," he said, his voice low and laced with what almost felt like anger, as if he were making a vow to himself. "I don't want to talk about Marcus, though. What are your plans tonight?"

Plans? He said that so casually, like it was just some other day. We needed to talk, there was so much to discuss still. "I was gonna go out with Kat for Halloween, but I can figure something out."

"No, I don't want you to change your plans with her."

"We never got to talk, though. I feel like there's more you're not telling me."

"I know, I just—"

"Damien, I've been going insane the last few days, thinking the worst, questioning everything—"

"Cas, please. I just..." I slowed my steps at the pain in his voice. "A lot has happened. I'd just like to have an evening to just... be. Can we

143

have a night where the world isn't ending around us? Can tonight just be a night where we're just a guy and girl living their lives?"

The utter defeat in his voice left me without words, my heart twisting. What exactly had he been through in the last few days?

"Only if you promise to talk to me afterward," I said, standing firm in a way I never had before. "Kat will wander off at some point to go with Cody to some party or something, she always does. When that happens, I want you to tell me everything."

"I promise," he said without missing a beat. "We'll go to Stackhouse after we split from Kat and the others."

I drew in a deep breath, trying to push all the questions back until we could sit down and properly discuss it. "Don't think this means I've forgotten about the last few days. I'm still mad at you for leaving me hanging and making me worry like that."

"I deserve every bit of your anger, and I'll make it up to you, I promise."

I shoved back my frustrations, eager to just be happy again, to see him smile and have a good time. The last few days had been so lonely despite Kat, Cody, and Cole's attempts to cheer me up when they were around, and I wondered how I'd dealt with that loneliness all this time. I didn't want to go back to that after having a taste of what I felt around Damien and the others.

"I'll make sure to stay away from the creek this time," I teased, smiling as I hurried through another crosswalk.

"That's a shame. I enjoyed seeing you wet," he said, his voice dripping with sin, and I swallowed as the images of us pressed together so tightly in his living room, flashed across my mind.

I licked my lips, trying to ignore the way his voice set my blood on fire. "Kat and I are going out this evening, but I'm trying to find a way to keep her off the streets after dark."

"It'll be safe for you to go out tonight, as long as you stay to the crowded areas."

I frowned as I turned the corner, the campus coming into view a block down the road. "How?"

"Halloween is always heavy with human activity, so we always have a large number of our kind working overtime patrolling the city to minimize any incidents. While darklings are attracted to more populated areas, they tend to shy away from large crowds. They won't wander into large groups of people, preferring to pick off lone targets they can easily take down in a dark alley without interruption. Sadly, there are often more attacks on Halloween night, but we work hard to keep it to a minimum."

Would it truly be safe?

"We'll keep you guarded," he said.

"We?"

"Barrett and Vincent always enjoy getting into trouble on Halloween. I still don't know what they've been plotting, but Zephyr, Cole, James, and I are free tonight. What are you guys planning to do?"

"We usually go walking around, Kat always tries to drag me to a party by the end of the night, but I never go."

"Maybe, I'll drag you somewhere else by the end of the night," he said, and my skin heated at the way his words slipped into my ear.

"Maybe, I'm tempted to give into your idea of fun over Kat's," I said, mind wandering to what he might do if he got me alone again. I couldn't help but reminisce on the way his hands felt against my skin.

He hummed on the other end. "You're a tempting creature, Cassie Hites, and damn me, but I might be willing to give into that temptation regardless of what it costs me."

My lips curved into a grin as my blood heated, humor lacing my voice as I spoke. "And what if I were a darkling in disguise?"

"Then I shall happily let you drag me into the abyss."

I snickered, catching sight of Cole, who smiled the moment he saw me. Kat didn't have any classes today, so she was taking the day off—likely spending it tangled up with Cody, the literal sense of that more likely than not with the way their relationship had been. I couldn't say I blamed them, though, having gotten a taste of it myself.

"Want to meet at my place around seven? We should be ready by then," I asked.

"Sounds good to me."

"I'll see you then," I said, unable to fight the smile on my face.

"See you then," he echoed, and I pulled the phone from my ear.

"Was that Damien?" Cole asked, falling into step at my side as I strolled through the courtyard.

"Yeah," I said, drawing a deep breath and shoving down the annoyance that he'd kept me in the dark as much as Damien had. "I guess we're hanging out tonight."

"Sorry, I couldn't talk to you about it. I don't have the leeway Damien has."

I frowned at that statement. "What do you mean?"

He bit his lip. "I can't really talk about it. He'll tell you more about it. It's not my place."

My eyes narrowed as I stared him down. "And here I thought we were becoming friends."

"Ah, don't try to guilt me like that," he said, rolling his eyes as we continued down the path toward my first class. Cole had walked me to and from all of my classes since the others had disappeared, somehow always there waiting for me when I got out of class. His presence had given me some comfort.

"Thank you for walking with me these last few days," I said, glancing at him nervously.

He shrugged. "It's no trouble. I'm happy to have your back when the others can't."

A part of me was still confused as to why he was doing it, why any of them would do it, and yet at the same time, it warmed my heart to know there were here for me. I knew they were likely only doing it for Damien, but it was still nice of them to do.

"So, are you guys gonna finally get to talk about everything?" he asked as we rounded the corner, nearing my class.

"Yeah, tonight. He's taking me to Stackhouse after we're done walking around."

He nodded. "I'll be glad when I don't have to keep secrets from you anymore."

"I mean, you could stop keeping secrets from me now if the guilt is too much for you to bear," I said, tilting my head to him, a coy grin tugging at my lips. "You can tell me what Damien was up to the last few days. Come on, get it off your chest. Confess your sins, child, I shall forgive you."

He huffed a laugh. "Nice try, but that's for Damien to share."

I sighed and turned to the door to class. "Fine traitor. I'll see you after class."

CHAPTER 16

"You have got to be kidding me," Damien said, arms crossed against his broad chest as he eyed me in my doorway, the sun setting behind the mountains surrounding the valley of the city.

"Oh, I'm a hundred percent *not* kidding right now," I said, popping my hip as I flash a bigger smile, and I couldn't miss the twitch at the corner of his lips as he fought a smile.

Cole snuck a glimpse of me from over Damien's shoulder, immediately barking a laugh, and Zephyr bit his lip, trying not to do the same.

"Doesn't she make a cute vampire?" Kat said as stepped past me onto the front porch, bumping my hip with hers as she passed.

My smile widened into a grin, showing off the pair of fangs that fit seamlessly among my natural teeth. I wasn't necessarily wearing a costume, per se, just a normal sweater and distressed jeans. The fangs just felt like the right touch, considering what I now knew about Damien and the others.

Damien's throat bobbed as he swallowed, his eyes raking down my body, and he pulled his lower lip between his teeth. Heat coiled low in my belly at the glimpse of his canine, and the molten glow lighting his eyes.

He leaned down to whisper in my ear. "Cute isn't quite the word I would choose."

My cheeks heated at the sinful tone in his voice, the way his breath caressed my skin.

"Aren't you a little old to be dressing up?" Zephyr asked Kat.

"If I want to be a cute witch for Halloween, I'm going as a cute witch. Fuck age restrictions!" she said proudly as she headed for the steps. Damien's gaze slipped briefly to Cody, his brows furrowing as Cody snuck up behind her, smacking her ass, and she squeaked, her cheeks turning a bright shade of crimson.

"Cody!" she gasped, turning on him as he guided her back toward the steps, a sinful smile on his face.

"You forgot to add sexy to that title," I yelled after her as she twisted back around to make it down the steps.

"Damn straight, I'm sexy!" Kat shouted, and I snickered.

I cracked open my parents' door. "Hey Mom! We're headed out. I might crash elsewhere tonight."

"Did you eat something?" she called back, I knew she was referencing eating for my evening dose, which I had my bottle of pills with me to take later when we ate.

"We're gonna get something downtown."

She leaned into the hallway. "Ok! Have fun and be safe! Your father and I are going out when he gets off work, if you need anything just give me a call."

"I'll make sure she stays safe, Mrs. Hites," Damien called over my shoulder, and I nudged him with my elbow.

She tilted her head into the hallway from the kitchen from where she was cooking to give him a smile. "Thank you, Damien!"

He nodded his head and took my hand, tugging me from the door and toward the steps. Butterflies fluttered in my stomach at the feel of his skin against mine for the first time in days. God, how I'd missed it. I couldn't wait to talk with him tonight, ask him the questions that had been burning in my mind, but I understood what he needed. A part of me needed it as well after everything that had happened. We could enjoy ourselves for tonight, let everything else just be in the background for a little bit longer.

The demons would be there when we returned to reality.

"So, you promise you're not in trouble because of me," I said lowly, ensuring Kat and Cody didn't hear us, though, I don't know how they could with all the chatter of the children running around trick-or-treating.

Damien took the last bite of his slice of pizza we'd snagged from Gallina's and smiled, and I couldn't help but feel as if he considered it funny that I'd stressed about it all this time. "No, Cas. I didn't get in trouble, I promise."

My shoulders sagged in relief, and my gaze slipped to Cole, Zephyr, and James, who were talking amongst themselves a few steps ahead of us. Cole had been texting on his phone, off and on all night, and the look on his face made me wonder if he was fighting with his girlfriend Amara. I hadn't seen much of her over the last week or two, and I wondered if she was angry with him for hanging out with me as much as he had been.

"Was that really what you've been worrying about all this time? That I'd gotten in trouble over you?"

I chewed the inside of my lip. "That and whether you'd gotten hurt hunting darklings… or worse."

His smile faded, and he laced his fingers with my own. "To be honest, I didn't even go on patrol in the time we've been apart."

I tilted my head to him. "Then what… Never mind."

His brows pinched together.

"We're supposed to be enjoying tonight, remember?" I said, smiling in a way that flashed my fangs.

The corner of his lips twitched, and he leaned down. "You keep tempting me with those little fangs, and I'll show you just how much we can enjoy tonight."

A coy grin tugged at my lips, as I nudged him. "Does that mean you think I look sexy with these?"

"I think you are a lot of things, and sexy doesn't even come close, *mea luna*."

The name left my heard flipping. "What language is that?"

He blinked for a moment, his lips parting, then closing before he said, "It's… like Latin."

Screams erupted from down the street in the darkness, and my heart lodged in my throat as children ran toward us. Zephyr and Cole stiffened, their gazes snapping in the direction of the fleeing trick-or-treaters. Damien's hand tightened on mine for a brief moment before the screams turned into laughter and giggles. I narrowed my eyes as the familiar laughter of Vincent reached my ears.

I let out a heavy breath, my heart racing, and I shoved down the terror as I stormed toward where he crouched at the mouth of an alley between two houses.

"What are you doing?" I asked him, propping a hand on my hip.

Hands grabbed me from the shadows and my heart stuttered as a scream peeled up my throat.

The guys busted out laughing, and I twisted around at the sound of Barrett's own laughter at my back. I elbowed him and he grunted before recoiling away from me, as he stumbled against the alley wall holding his sides.

"You asshole! That's not funny!" I looked back to Damien, who immediately quieted, biting his lip.

Kat wrapped her arms around her stomach as she joined in with them, and I grumbled at her. "Goodness, Cas. You look like you saw a ghost."

She didn't scare easily, and I almost envied her for it. In the past, she'd coaxed me into a few haunted houses to enjoy watching me get scared senseless, but never seemed to be affected no matter how terrifying they were. Cody tugged her toward him, and they started up the hill again.

I crossed my arms as I turned back to Barrett. "This is what you guys have been planning to do? Scaring kids?"

Barrett pushed off the wall as he regained his composure from his laughing fit. His hood left him cloaked in shadows, and I narrowed my eyes to make out the markings on his face. He lowered his hood, revealing the markings of a skull painted over his face, his steel eyes staring back at me from the dark depths of the black paint coating the rest of his skin.

"What? The kids love it," he said incredulously, feigning innocence as Vincent climbed back into his perch, likely to wait for the next unsuspecting victim. "And this is by no means the only thing we have planned tonight."

"I swear, Barrett you better not scare *Mitera* again. She's getting too old for that shit," Damien warned.

"Calm your tits, Damien. I'm not gonna scare her. I've got bigger prey in my sights tonight," he said with a cocky grin, and Damien rolled his eyes as Barrett shifted his gaze to me. "And I just knocked one of them off my list."

I opened my mouth to retort, but Vincent launched off the roof, landing on the sidewalk next to us and scaring a group of kids with a roar. Squeals and laughter spilled from their lips as they ran up the sloped sidewalk and away from Vincent.

Zephyr crossed his arms, cocking a brow. "When are you guys going to start acting your age?"

"When I'm dead," Barrett said, pulling his hood back up before slipping into the shadows once more, followed closely by Vincent as they took off to get into what I assumed was more trouble.

I shook my head, glancing toward Kat who had wandered far enough away that she wouldn't be able to hear, before turning to Zephyr. "Zeph, I don't think act your age is the proper term. How old are they, exactly? If you say anything more than eighty years, then they should be sitting on a rocking chair watching cars pass by."

His pale green eyes seemed to brighten for a moment, before softening, and I tilted my head in confusion. He shook his head and continued up the sloped sidewalk. "I guess I'd better get myself a rocking chair, then."

I rolled my eyes, turning back to Damien. His gaze followed Barrett and Vincent, a hint of a smile tugging at his lips. I cocked a brow in question.

He cleared his throat before shoving his hands in his pockets and nodding for me to join him as he followed after Zephyr, Cole and James. "Barrett acts like a hard ass, but both of them are really just big softies. He and Vincent have been doing this for years. Usually, they target neighborhoods where there are immortal children—especially those who've lost family to the darklings."

My heart twisted at that thought.

"Immortal children don't get the luxury of being told the monster in their closet is just a sweater. They know the monsters are real and many have felt the cost of their existence. Barrett and Vincent get them out of their homes when they're too frightened to leave, paint their faces, and get them in on scaring other kids. They bring some positivity to the dark corners around us, make it a little less scary for the young."

My chest swelled at the thought of what they were doing under the guise of just being a pair of troublemakers. I hadn't even stopped to consider that what Barrett and Vincent were doing amounted to anything more than their childish antics. My lips curved into a smile at the thought of Barrett painting a skull on a child and encouraging them to jump out and scare others at their side.

"Are there immortal families in this neighborhood, then?"

"They're integrated all over the city. I don't think there's a neighborhood that doesn't have an immortal family living amongst the humans, sadly few are lucky to have children."

His eyes slipped from mine for a moment, lifting to the path ahead of us, and for a moment his eye seemed to dull at that statement, his smile fading. I shivered, rubbing my arms as something icy crawled over my skin.

I hadn't stopped to consider it, but I wondered if in the near thousand years of life he'd led, if he'd at one point had a special someone. Surely at some point he'd loved someone, and the thought of that twisted my gut.

"Are you okay?" I asked, and Damien glanced at me all too briefly. My heart squeezed at the sadness in his eyes.

"Cas!" I jumped as Kat's voice cut through any response Damien might have given me, and I'd never felt more eager for the two of us to be alone so we wouldn't get interrupted again.

151

She came to a stop in front of me, grabbing hold of my hands. "I just got a text. Melissa from Environmental Sciences is throwing a party not far from here! You remember her right?"

"Oh, my goodness, Kat. That sounds like so much fun," I deadpanned.

She pouted. "Awe, come on!"

"No. Thank you," I said, huffing a laugh. "Melissa is nice, but I'm really not interested. You can tell me all about how someone got drunk and jumped off a roof tomorrow morning, though."

She turned her gaze to Damien. "She'd go if you did."

Damien seemed amused by that statement. "Normally I might have said yes, but I'd rather keep Cas to myself this evening."

She clamped her mouth shut before opening and closing it again. Her eyes turned to me, and a coy grin tugged at her lips.

I glanced between them, my cheeks heating, and I looked at Kat. "Hey, it's not what you think."

"Mhmmm," she hummed knowingly, and leaned in to whisper. "I'll tell you all about the drunken idiots in the morning, and you can tell me how wild he is in bed."

"Kat!" I gasped as she grabbed Cody's hand and hurried back down the hill, her giggles echoing off the alleys.

"Have fun! Don't do anything I wouldn't do!" she called over her shoulder.

"There's not much you wouldn't do!" I called back.

She waved a dismissive hand. "Exactly!"

"You'll have quite the story to share with her in the morning then," Damien said with a smug grin, and I turned back to him, frowning in confusion. Had he just heard what Kat had whispered to me?

My heart lodged itself in my throat as he leaned in, and I stumbled back at the power of his presence pressing into me until my back met the wall. His hands planted against the wall on either side of me, caging me. He leaned in closer, brushing a kiss to the corner of my lips, then another along my jaw, and when he reached my throat, I gasped at the brush of his lips against my skin.

"Why is that?" I managed to say, though it barely made it past my lips on a panted breath.

His voice fell into a whisper then. "Because I'm pretty... how did she put it? Wild in bed."

I bit my lip, my skin tingling as my mind wandered to the possibilities. "I guess you'll just have to prove that, won't you?"

"I shall enjoy every moment of proving myself to you." His eyes darkened, his smile turning sinful. "But, first..."

I blinked as he pushed off the wall.

"I do believe I owe you some answers," he said, offering his hand to me.

"You do," I said with a smile, before drawing a deep breath to calm my racing heart. Barely a month ago, it would have terrified me to feel my heart take off as it did around him, but now, it felt normal, natural even, and I wondered when I'd fallen into a place of peace where every waking moment wasn't spent thinking about my condition and instead spent... living.

"We'll catch up with you guys later," Damien called to the remaining trio.

Zephyr's brows rose, and Cole's gaze lifted from his phone, halting whatever text he was typing.

"We'll see ye on campus tomorrow, then," James said, giving a wave.

"That'll depend on how late Damien keeps me out, tonight," I said, and Damien's lip twitched with a faint smug grin.

"Talking," I added to clarify, and Damien huffed a laugh before the guys said their goodbyes and we split off to head toward my house, where his car was parked.

CHAPTER 17

We came to a stop on the side of the road on the outer portions of the park, the moon hanging full in the sky. I'd been hesitant to go to the forest, fearful of the demons that had hunted me down just a few nights ago, but Damien had stressed they rarely ventured into the forests.

The smell of the aspen and birch trees filled my lungs as I stepped out of Damien's car, and he took hold of my hand before guiding me into the woods.

For a moment we walked in silence, and I just took in the sights of the surrounding forest, illuminated by the moonlight.

"I can't believe you convinced me to come into the forest at night," I said, watching the path beneath my feet, trying not to let my gaze stray for fear I might hallucinate and see monsters lurking in the darkness around us.

"You scared?" he asked, humor lacing his tone.

"No," I lied, shoving my trembling hands into my pockets. "Ok, maybe a little."

"I'll protect you, don't worry. Besides, I've got the others patrolling the edges of the park to ensure no one comes to bother us."

"Really?" I asked, turning to him.

"I'm trying to be cautious," Damien said, and something about the way he said it left me wondering if it was more than darklings he was concerned about. 'If I took you to my house, though, I might find myself... distracted."

I snickered, and shook my head, but I couldn't deny the temptation I felt for him as well. No, we wouldn't get distracted with each other in that way... maybe later.

We continued down the path toward the clearing he'd taken me to before, and silence stretched out between us as I tried to pull my thoughts together, tried think of where to even begin.

After a while, Damien spoke up. "Go ahead and ask. I'm sure you've got countless questions."

"I do, I just... I don't know where to even begin. Like, where did your kind come from? How long have you been here? What about the darklings? How do humans not know about them?"

He huffed a laugh. "Well, our kind were created millennia ago by the gods to serve them."

I wondered what gods they believed in, but I remained silent, listening as he continued.

"We weren't originally created to fight the darklings, but when they appeared, it became our primary focus."

"So, they've been around for a long time?" I asked.

He nodded. "Centuries."

It was terrifying to think that those creatures had been lurking in the shadows of our city my entire life and I hadn't known.

"What exactly happened over the last few days?" I asked.

His eyes dipped a moment, and his grip on my hand tightened. "A lot."

I lifted my gaze to him.

"Our... group doesn't just fight darklings, we also act as a sort of... law enforcement, I guess you could say, for the immortal society."

"You'd mentioned there was a murder."

He nodded, his jaw tightening. "They don't happen very often, and this one was bad. Had to clean it up before the police got involved as it not only included two immortals, but a few humans as well."

"You said something happened with Marcus..." I started, and fear crept over my skin at the sound of his name on my lips. "Is he immortal, too? Was he involved?"

"He is, and we think he was involved somehow, if not responsible," he admitted.

As the fear continued to pump its way through my veins at the memory of him, I found myself almost desperate to change the subject.

155

"What were you and Barrett talking about when he wanted to erase my memories the other night?"

Damien stopped, turning to look back at me, and he hesitated. "It's a long story, and I'm not sure you're ready for it yet."

Irritation burned in my chest. It had been days since everything had happened, and I'd been desperate for answers. "When will I be ready, then? There's so much happening, and it sounds like you know why."

"I'd like to know, too. Care to share?" My heart stuttered at the familiar voice, and Damien tensed, his gaze snapping behind me.

I twisted around to find Marcus emerging from the trees. The sight of that obnoxious grin on his face made my skin tighten.

"What are you doing here, Marcus?" Damien said, shock filling his eyes. "How did you get past the others?"

"Who says I got past them?" he said, darkly.

I turned to run back to him, but Damien's hand shot out, stopping me before I could take another step. "Stay where you are, Cas. Don't move."

Marcus laughed. "Sharp as ever, I see."

"Walk away, Marcus, and I won't have to put him down," Damien warned, and I stiffened. Was someone else here?

Something whipped through the air past my face, and a thin knife sank into the ground at Damien's feet. I gasped, my hand rising to the fresh sting in my cheek where the blade had nicked me. Damien tensed, his eyes falling to the cut, and I pulled my hand away to find blood smeared across my palm.

"I'd like to see you try to put me down."

I stiffened at the male voice and looked over my shoulder to find a man crouched in a nearby tree, flipping another knife in his hand before pointing the blade at us.

"That was just a warning. Next one lands a hit. Can you guess which one of you it'll be?"

Damien ground his teeth together, his hands clenching into fists, as he took a step toward him.

"Ah ah ah," the guy tutted, his lips curving into a sickening grin. "I'd think better of that if I were you. I do love a good gamble, though, so let's place a wager. Will you get to me first? Or will I land a knife between those pretty little eyes of hers?"

Damien remained still as his gaze drifted around the forest. My blood turned icy as I realized that Marcus hadn't only brought this one friend along. How many more were there? How had they snuck up on us so easily?

What did Marcus want? Damien said Barret and the others were patrolling the outskirts of the forest to ensure we were left alone. Had they been waiting for us here? How did they know we were coming to Stackhouse? We hadn't been followed from the city… had we? Oh God… had something happened to Barrett or any of the others?

"Did you tell her your little secret, Damien?" Marcus said, his voice like venom.

Damien remained silent for a moment, then his eyes met mine before he whispered, so low I barely heard him. "Run. Call Barrett and the others."

I gasped as Damien launched forward, sliding between me and Marcus, and he grunted as a knife lodged in his shoulder.

My hands clasped over my mouth. "Damien!"

"That's cheating," the guy from the tree called as Damien pulled the blade from his shoulder before sending it flying back at him. He jerked back against the trunk of the tree, and my eyes widened at the sight of the knife protruding from between his eyes. He slumped, and his body tumbled from the branch, crashing into the ground behind Marcus.

Marcus didn't even seem to flinch, and I stumbled back at the sight of his limp body in the grass.

Leaves and grass rustled as Marcus lunged into a run for us. Damien intercepted him, his fist colliding with Marcus' face before he could get to me. I stumbled back, my heart racing as my eyes darted around, wondering if more of Marcus' men lingered in the darkness. My back met something hard, and I gasped, whipping around to find it was just a tree. I turned back to them, watching the powerful blows they exchanged.

"What do you want with us?" Damien growled, teeth gritted, fangs bared. His muscles twitched as he braced Marcus' forearms.

"Oh, you, I don't want anything with," Marcus said back, his voice all too even and calm.

Damien's gaze flashed to me briefly, fear lighting his eyes. "You're after her?"

A devilish grin spread across Marcus' face. "Wouldn't you like to know?"

Damien hesitated before shoving Marcus away, but Marcus quickly steadied himself, straightening as he pulled a blade from his jacket.

Damien held his hand out to his side, and black mist billowed out from his sleeve. It dispersed, revealing a long, black dagger in his palm.

"Not gonna summon your Lupai?" Marcus taunted.

"Don't think too highly of yourself now, Marcus," Damien said, widening his stance.

Marcus's smile slid from his face, but after a moment it returned, as if he'd realized something. "Is that because you don't want to? Or because you can't?"

Damien didn't respond, his throat bobbing.

"Awe, Damien. Are you wearing yourself out in the chase?" Marcus asked. "I gotta say, this little game of ours has been fun. What did you think of my handy work the other night?"

Damien's eyes flashed at Marcus' words, a muscle feathering in his jaw as he gripped his dagger.

"You should've heard them beg for the end," he said before launching for Damien again.

Marcus swung his knife through the air at Damien, but Damien dropped low, avoiding Marcus' blade as he slid past him. I could barely keep up as Marcus whipped around to face him. Marcus threw a punch, but Damien evaded it again smoothly, swinging his fist into Marcus' gut.

What was I doing? I didn't have time to freeze. My heart raced as I grabbed my phone, fumbling as I quickly searched for Barrett's number. I hit the call button and pressed it to my ear. It rang and rang, my breathes coming in short pants, the ringing fading to the roaring in my ears.

"Dammit, Barrett, pick up."

Barrett's voice was laced with confusion as he answered. "Cas?"

"Barre—" Hands grabbed me from behind, and a palm slapped over my mouth. My heart stuttered as I was yanked off my feet, my phone falling onto the ground.

His hand muffled my scream, and I kicked at the air, desperate to get free. I jerked my face forward, breaking free for a split second to scream. "Help us!"

I slammed my head back into the guy's face. He recoiled and his hold on me slipped. My body hit the ground, pain searing in the back of my head where my healing stitches burned. My stomach twisted, saliva flooding my mouth, and I crawled along the grass, desperate to get back to my phone and try to get help.

"Cassie!" Damien yelled, and Marcus used that opportunity to slam him in the gut, and Damien fell to his knees.

Hands grabbed my ankle, dragging me back along the ground. I screamed, my fingers narrowly missing my phone as I tried to grab it. My nails dug into the dirt as I grabbed at anything I could to try to get free of his grasp. He wrapped his arms around my waist and yanked me into the air as I flailed.

"No!"

Damien's head whipped around, his eyes finding me, and the color drained from his face. He pulled away from Marcus, but before he could come for me, four of Marcus' men surrounded him, blocking his way. Marcus slammed his elbow into the back of Damien's head before the others stepped in.

I screamed as he hit the ground. Heat flooded me, but no matter how hard I fought, my captor wouldn't release me. I ground my teeth together, refusing to make this easy for them. I'd fight with everything I had.

Splashing water drowned out all other sounds as I was carried across the creek bed. With each splash, we grew further and further from Damien, and the fear overtook me at the thought of where he was taking me.

"Let me go!" I kicked back, slamming my foot into my captor's groin. He dropped me, and stumbled back, clutching himself as he crumpled to his knees.

I hit the creek bed, the rocks hard and slick against my hands and knees, freezing water drenching my clothes. Tears dotted my lashes, my head throbbing, heart racing painfully as adrenaline tore its way through my system. I crawled forward, grabbing onto a downed tree branch, gasping for air as the shock of the icy waters overtook me.

Everything in me screamed to get to my feet, to run, and I struggled to push myself up against the broken tree limb. I looked over my shoulder as he recovered, and I climbed up the bank.

"Damien!" I cried out as Damien fought back against Marcus and his group. One of the men looked my way, seeming to realize I'd gotten free and turned to me, but Damien body slammed him before he could come after me.

"Get to Barrett and the others!" he shouted before shoving himself upright to slam his fist into the gut of one guy, only to have the fist of another crash into his face.

"I'm not leaving you!"

"Now!" he demanded, wrestling to get himself back on his feet.

"You're gonna pay for that, you little bitch," the man growled as he staggered his way toward me, clutching his crotch.

I stumbled before turning to race into the woods toward the car, swiping my phone from the grass as I went. The call had ended, and there were two missed calls from Barrett. I quickly hit Barrett's name. It barely made it to a first ring before he picked up.

"Cassie, what the fuck's going on?" Barrett demanded, panic in his voice, and the way he spoke through panted breaths, it sounded as if he were running. "We're on our way. Zephyr flew ahead of us, he'll be there any minute now."

"Marcus—" I panted, my heart pounding, and I stumbled over rocks jutting from the forest floor as I glanced over my shoulder. A panicked cry burst from my throat at the sight of my pursuer racing after me.

Barrett cursed under his breath on the other end of the line. "Marcus is there? Where's Damien?"

I managed to get out what I could through gulps of air as I tried to focus on my breathing, but I failed, my heart pounding painfully against my ribs. "We're near the clearing! Marcus… he's here. There're others—they attacked us! Plea—"

A body crashed into me, knocking the air from my lungs, and I slammed into the dirt, crying out at the bite of the rocks against my skin. My phone flew from my hand, sliding to a stop in the grass.

"No! Stop! Barrett!" I cried as he hoisted me into the air and headed for the trees.

I screamed out in frustration, slamming my fists into his back as I kicked my feet, but my strength was waning, my heart pounding painfully. The distant call of a raven cut across the forest as I screamed again.

"Let me go!"

"Shut it, girl." My abductor threw me to the ground, and I grunted as I lifted my head to look up at him. His boot slammed into my face.

A gentle lull washed over me, as if I were floating on waves, and my mind fought to keep me there. I almost wanted to give in, wanted to let it wash me away until I was worn down into nothing, but something in the back of my mind tugged me back, a tiny voice screaming that something was wrong. My eyes flickered open, and I could barely make out dirt and vegetation on the forest floor passing below me.

My nose burned, and my head throbbed as my eyes threatened to close again in desperation to escape back into that weightless, painless abyss. A metallic scent filled my nose, and I realized blood had caked my face from my nostrils to my chin. Blood pooled in my mouth, dripping from my lips onto the ground and leaving a broken trail on the forest floor. My body shivered in the cold; my clothes soaked through.

Eyes fluttering, and barely holding onto consciousness, I muttered. "Damien?"

"You gonna cooperate now, little songbird?" I stiffened at the sound of Marcus' voice.

I swallowed, everything coming back to me in a flood of panic and terror. If Marcus had me, what had happened to Damien? Did the others get to him? Was he ok? How long had I been out? Where was I?

The guy carrying me stood me up on my feet. My legs bent and quivered under my weight, the forest tilting and shifting around me as I tried to regain my bearings. I groaned, biting back the pain echoing to every inch of my body.

"I had hoped we could've kept that pretty face untouched, but you left us with no choice. Be a good girl now and come quietly," Marcus reiterated.

I'd rather die than let you have your way with me.

Anger flared deep in my chest, and I spit blood onto his jeans in defiance. "I won't be your victim, Marcus." I fought the urge to collapse, to hide my weakness. "Where's Damien? What did you do to him?"

He stopped, eyes falling to the blood to his jeans. He worked his jaw, and his tongue slid over his teeth as he lifted his eyes to me, a cruel smile creeping across his face. I struggled to maintain my composure as I swayed, blinking to stay aware of my surroundings, but I didn't know how much longer I could cling to consciousness. He drew closer, lowering his face to my ear.

160

"Oh, I'm going to have fun breaking you until you sing for me," he said through his teeth before stepping back.

His eyes locked with mine, and I blinked. Our surroundings melted away, reality dripping into oblivion like trickling paint. Only he and I remained, the others fading into nothing, and the blurred figures around me began to contort and twitch.

I needed to get away, to get to... Wait... what was happening again? Where was I? Who was I with?

Nausea swept over me and I panted, swallowing as I tried to get a hold of myself. Icy, phantom fingers crawled over my skin, wrapping me in a frozen grip until my lungs constricted, air becoming difficult to breathe. Faint voices crept into my mind, speaking unrecognizable whispers of some unknown language. I blinked, fighting to stay conscious, my hands shaking and twitching as I panted for what little air I could get. The light around me faded, darker and darker, until I was swallowed whole.

And something stirred in the dark depths.

The void clung to me, and for a moment I didn't feel alone, as if someone were watching me, beckoning to me... but who?

Their presence faded, receding like the tide, and I found myself alone in the endless abyss once more. I drifted through the nothing, with no beginning and no end. Damien's voice called to me from the darkness, weak and barely audible. I tried to understand what he was saying, but his words were a like a rippling image in a pond, there but unclear.

The pitch receded in a rush, the earth rising to meet me, and I slammed into the ground. I found myself standing in an open field. A sliver of moon glinted in the sky, barely lighting my surroundings. My lungs burned as my chest heaved, pulling in any air I could get. The weight of cold steel hung heavy in my hand, and I looked down to find an ornate short sword gripped in my palm. Black blood dripped from the edge of the blade, and my hand quivered as I gripped the hilt.

Freshly spilled blood and cries of agony and despair floated on the air, the foul smell of burning flesh filling my senses mixed with the putrid smell of darklings. I looked out across the clearing, chest tight with sorrow... and fear.

Oh, Gods... What had I done?

Smoke and bits of fire rose from embers and ashes on the ground, remnants of a great battle surrounding me. The taste of blood filled my mouth and my eyes fell on the men and women littering the ground, dead or dying, some trying to resuscitate fallen comrades.

"Lucia!"

I turned to find Damien running toward me, and I frowned as relief and regret washed over me. He was dressed in strange black leather armor, his hair half pulled back out of his face. He was as much a mess as I was, covered in dirt and blood, both darkling and immortal.

He rushed to my side, cupping my face as he looked me over for any injuries. "I couldn't find you. I thought I'd lost you." He kissed me deeply, the feeling of his hands against my skin easing my own worry for him.

He was safe. He was alive. I couldn't form words as he released me, his hand falling to my stomach, swollen under my leather armor, before he dropped to his knees to press a kiss to it.

"Thank the Gods you're both all right."

CHAPTER 18

The faintest sound of metal dancing against metal echoed in the darkness. I groaned at the ache in my wrists, something hard cutting into my skin, and my shoulders threatened to pop out of place. As the numbness in my body receded, I realized my knees were pressed into a cold, hard surface.

Where was I?

I tugged at my arms to find my wrists bound in metal shackles, my arms suspended away from me by chains, preventing me from so much as lying down. My eyes stung when I opened them, and I blinked, trying to see, but the inky darkness left me blind. My nose burned. Was it broken?

"About time you woke up." Marcus' voice echoed off the empty walls.

Air sucked in through my teeth, and my body reacted involuntarily, shifting as I pulled back to get away, but the chains grew taut, preventing me from moving so much as an inch. The chains rattled, the sound ringing in my ears in a way that left me unable to hear where he was. My eyes darted around in the dark, but it was useless; I couldn't see anything. I wrapped my hands around the chains tethering me, grunting as I hopelessly jerked and pulled to get free.

"Where are you?" I snapped, heart pounding, unable to run, unable to see, completely defenseless in my inability to defend myself against him in any way.

"I always forget you useless humans can't see in the dark." His voice moved around me in the darkness, and each spoken word coming from a different direction. "I can't understand how your kind have survived in this world for so long."

I couldn't keep my mouth shut, the words spilling from my lips before I could think better of it. "You just don't want me to see what Damien did to you. How badly did he beat your ass?

Shit. I was going to get myself killed. *Stupid! Fucking stupid!*

A low growl ripped from Marcus' throat, but he didn't respond.

His fist rammed into my stomach, and I lurched, coughing and gagging. The chains went slack, and I fell to the floor before his hands wrapped around my neck, pulling me back up. I panicked, grabbing onto his arm as I tried to swallow air, but his grip only tightened. He forced me to the floor, the concrete cold against my back, his weight crushing me. His grip on my throat loosened but remained, and I coughed.

"Don't test my patience," he said through gritted teeth.

I bared my teeth as I stared forward, chest heaving as I panted. Even if I couldn't see him, it was worth it for him to see me meet his gaze.

"I'm not scared of death." I gasped for air once more. "It wouldn't be my first time. Just get it over with, already."

"Oh, I'm not gonna kill you." His voice was venomous. "She may want you, but she only needs you alive, and there's a lot I can do to you without killing you. No, I'm gonna have my fun with you first, then leave you in the woods for them to find you."

She? Who was he talking about?

I stifled the fear threatening to consume me as I tried to piece together what had happened before this moment. My head throbbed, remnants of a strange sensation lingering deep within the recesses of my mind. What exactly had Marcus done to me in the woods? I couldn't explain or understand what he did specifically, but it was almost as if he'd gotten into my head, into my thoughts, as if he'd touched a part of me that should have never been touched.

My voice was hoarse as his grip closed around my windpipe again. "What the fuck did you do to me in the woods?"

"Oh, did you not like me in your head?" I could almost hear the sadistic grin in his voice. "That's too bad. You'd better get used to it, because I'm gonna enjoy every minute of doing it time and time again until you're begging me for mercy."

"I'll never beg you for anything," I growled.

He huffed a laugh. "We'll see about that."

Air flooded my lungs as he released me, and I curled into myself, coughing and gasping. His footsteps faded, followed by the sound of a door opening and slamming shut, the lock clicking, then, silence.

I was alone... for now.

Groaning, I pushed myself up to sit, rubbing the skin on my neck where his hands had been. Darkness cloaked the room so thickly that I couldn't so much as see my hands in front of my face. My clothes were dry now, my shoes gone, but it was cold and given how his voice had echoed, I knew that the room was empty. Where had he taken me? And why had he gone to such lengths to get me? What did he want with me?

I shivered, terror sinking its claws into me as my mind ran through every possibility of what had happened after I was taken, and I prayed Damien was ok. Had Barrett and the others gotten to him in time? My stomach twisted at the mere thought of him lying dead in the woods.

No, don't think like that. If Marcus had killed him, he would've made sure to rub it in my face. He wasn't dead. I couldn't let myself give into that fear.

Bruised skin ached under the irons shackling my wrists. My shoulders screamed as I moved them, trying to ease the soreness. How long had I been hanging?

I dragged my hands across the floor around me, feeling for anything in my surroundings, only to find nothing but cold concrete a dirt. I didn't get far, the chains growing taut the moment I strayed a couple feet from where I sat. I hugged myself tightly, trying to find some semblance of warmth, but there was none.

What was going to happen to me now?

Was anyone coming for me? Did anyone know where I was? Marcus made it clear that he wasn't going to kill me, but the thought of dying didn't scare me. It was something I dealt with every day.

The possibility of the things that Marcus could do to me without killing me—that terrified me.

I drew a deep breath, stilling the rising panic. I had to stay strong. He relished in my reactions when he hurt me. I'd suffer, yes, but I'd be damned if I gave him the satisfaction of knowing how badly I suffered. Maybe he would get bored with me if he didn't get the reactions he desired.

A shiver ran through me, and I curled into myself, my chest tightening. Tears welled in my eyes, and it pissed me off that I couldn't hold them at bay. I fought them back, but I couldn't restrain them any longer. Letting go, I gave into the sobs, letting the darkness claim me.

And I dreaded what awaited me when I woke.

The loud rattling of chains rang through the room, ripping me from my restless sleep. I squeezed my eyes shut, desperate for even a moment more of sleep, but my wrists were jerked upward, yanking me from the ground and onto my knees.

I groaned as my head hung forward, my bones aching from sleeping on the concrete all... night? Was it day? Was it still night? I didn't know how long I'd slept, but it didn't feel like long with the level of exhaustion still clinging to me.

Lights pierced the darkness, bright and blinding, and I closed my eyes, turning my face down to try to escape the burning sensation. I cracked my eyelids, trying to get a view of my surroundings, my vision so blurred all I could make out were shapes and movement.

The room was barren, surrounded by what looked like unfinished concrete walls. Was I in a basement? There were four people in the room that I could make out. Someone crouched before me, and as my eyes adjusted and focused, I could see it was Marcus.

He was shirtless, loose cargo pants hanging around his hips, his bare muscular chest covered in a tattoo that reached over to his arm. Faintly beneath it, though, I could see that it covered an older tattoo, and I couldn't help but think it was similar to Damien's.

"I found this in your jacket." Marcus pulled a little orange prescription bottle from his pocket.

I clamped my lips shut, averting my gaze from him.

His eyes passed over the label. "I googled the name to find out what it is. What would you be taking blood pressure medication for?"

I remained silent, eyes glued to the floor. My heart condition was information I couldn't afford for him to know. It would only be another weapon he could use against me.

Marcus grinned. "Oh? Shit. I didn't know you had something like that." He barked a laugh under his breath, leaning closer to me, his voice low. "Have you told Damien yet? Or is this *your* little secret?"

I froze. Had he read my thoughts? My gaze snapped to him, my eyes widening in terror.

His eyes met mine, his face inches from my own, and the sadistic grin curved his lips. "You can't hide anything from me. There's no safe place for you here. Not even in your own mind."

"Damien will come for me." I said through my teeth, steeling my nerves as best I could, but I couldn't deny how my courage waned in his presence. "When he does, you'll regret this."

With a flash of movement faster than I could follow, he pulled a knife from his pocket, flipping it open next to my face. "Oh, I'm countin' on it, but not before I have my fun with you."

He slid the blade flat against my cheek, the tip of it like a needle dragging along the surface. My breath caught in my throat as he glided down over my chin, along my throat to my collarbone. I sucked in air as the sharp blade drew blood with the slightest pressure. My chest heaved irregularly as my body gave into the panic, the pain heightening my senses, but I fought to hide the tremors echoing throughout my body. He licked his lips, a satisfied grin tugging at the corner of his mouth, and I gripped the chains, closing my eyes as I focused on anything but what he was doing.

Marcus drew back, fingers grazing his jaw. "I will say. That heart condition's gonna make things a bit trickier. No worries, though, I might have a way we can work around this little issue of yours."

The door opened behind Marcus, and a spark of hope lit in my chest at the sight of Cole.

"Cole?" I gasped. "Thank God! Where are the others? Is Damien..." My voice dropped, the words falling before they could leave my lips as I took in his face.

His eyes held no emotion as he entered the room, and I frowned as my mind latched onto his presence. Wait.. what was he doing here? I tilted my head, desperate for him to look at me, but he didn't seem to care to, and the sweet boy I'd grown to know to know as a friend seemed as cold and distant as a stranger.

"W-what are you... what are you doing here?"

Marcus looked over his shoulder at him. "Ah, perfect timing, Cole. I was just about to call you."

Cole's eyes fell on me, and I suddenly couldn't breathe, couldn't think.

"You... You're with Marcus?" I said, though the words barely made it out of my throat.

No. This couldn't be real. How long had he been planning this? Had he been with Marcus all along?

Something clicked in my head, something that hadn't made any sense up until this moment, and my words left my lips in a whisper. "You're the one who told him we were going to Stackhouse..."

He didn't respond, and the betrayal shot through me, so painful I could barely breathe. Anger burned in my chest to the point that tears dotted my eyes, and I jerked forward against the chains, trying to get to him.

"You were my friend..." I couldn't breathe, couldn't think straight. "How could you fucking do this to me? Why?"

He remained silent, which only sent me into a spiral of rage and sorrow, and I yelled again. "Was that why you were so quick to talk to me—hang out with me? So you could do this? Why? Why would you do this?"

Still silence. Still no answers. Only that cold, distant stare.

"Cole was perfect, kept us updated on what you were doing all night so we could get into position and wait for your arrival," Marcus let out a laugh. "Gods, the look on Damien's face was priceless!"

My mind revisited that night, and I realized Cole hadn't been fighting with Amara, but feeding our location and actions to Marcus. The room spun, something cold settling over me.

"Cole, good news, you get to join in on the fun," Marcus said, and it snapped me from my daze, my heart lurching. I lifted my eyes in time to see Cole let out an annoyed sigh.

Marcus returned to me. "Damien and the others don't know it, but Cole here is one of the last with the ability to use Aíma." He cocked his head, eyes alight with something that drained the blood from my face. "That's blood magic, but they can do more to a body than I think any of us truly understood. Terrifying gift, really. I bet he could even use it to make sure your heart doesn't give out on me." He turned his gaze back to Cole. "Right, Cole?"

The world shifted beneath me, my lips parting as the reality that I might very well be on my own crashed down on me.

Marcus laughed. "This couldn't have worked out more perfectly!"

My pulse hammered in my ear as Cole watched me, nodding for the other guy to leave the room. He lowered himself into the now-vacant chair, propping his foot on his knee as he sat back, seemingly content to watch whatever was about to play out.

Fear clouded my vision, air suddenly becoming too thin, my lungs failing to work. What were they going to do to me? Did Damien and the others know yet that Cole was working against them? Was he still involved with them, leading them on that he was still their friend? Oh, God. He could very well make it so they never found me.

"Your nose looks a little rough. I should fix that for you." Marcus reached up, grabbing my nose before I could react, and cracked it as he readjusted it. I cried out, my body locking up as the burning pain radiated across my face. Sobs clawing their way up my throat as I collapsed, falling against the chains. I tried to breathe through it, tried to fight it.

Don't react. Don't react. Don't react. Don't—

Marcus rose to his feet, and my eyes darted around, searching for anything to use to get free, any sign of weakness in the chains. His knife clicked as he folded it closed and the sound of his footsteps was the only sound I could hear over the roaring in my ears as he paced around behind me.

His footsteps halted at my back, and his hands glided up my spine, over to the front of my shoulders. As his hands slid over my neck, I fought the urge to pull away from him. I just had to wait until he got close enough and catch him off guard. Even if I managed that, though, where would that leave me? I was still chained down.

Fucking think, Cas! You need to get away from him!

My thoughts halted as he closed his fingers around my throat, anchoring me in place, and his other hand crept over my face. I closed my eyes, turning my head to try to escape his grasp as his fingertips brushed the cut on my lip before covering my eyes. He yanked me back against him and I gasped as he lowered his face beside mine.

No. Don't touch me.

His whisper poured into my ear. "Let's see that pretty little mind shatter."

Blinding light consumed me, and it felt as if something were clawing its way into my head. My cries echoed off the walls as pain shot out to every corner of my mind—my body, like needles prickling every inch of my being, tearing into the depth of my existence. My body bucked, fighting to pull away of its own volition, but he held me firmly in place.

Time fell away, the pain going on and on until I thought it would never end before he released me. I collapsed forward against the chains, suspended just above the concrete, panting. Saliva dripped from my lips as my stomach turned, leaving me on the edge of throwing up. My body shook and pain pierced through my chest as my heart hammered against my ribcage.

He grabbed a fistful of my hair, yanking my head back to him. "Who said you could pull away? I'm not done with you yet."

"Let me go!" I screamed, thrashing against him.

His head dipped back, a sickening ecstasy painting his words. "Yes. That's what I was waiting for. I wanna hear you beg me."

He released me and the chains tightened, hoisting me up until my toes could barely reach the ground. I grunted, my shoulders threatening to pop out of their sockets under my weight as my feet scraped at the floor. He strolled around to my side, and I tracked his movements, unable to do anything as I hung from the ceiling. Fuck, I was defenseless.

His hand grasped the sleeve of my sweater, ripping the fabric to expose my arm. He grabbed my wrist, pulling it back, and I heard his knife click open before the sharp pain of his blade carved a path along my skin, cutting me down the length of my forearm. I hissed, fighting to pull away from him. His tongue trailed up my arm, catching the blood dripping down. The sound that left his lips as he swallowed disgusted me, fueling my need to fight.

I jerked my face to Cole, tears welling in my eyes. "Please! Stop this! I've done nothing to you!"

Cole stared flatly back at me as I fought against the chains, his dark eyes remaining firm on me as he watched.

"I can hear your heart pounding, little songbird. Let's see how hard we can get it working before we have to bring you back down."

"What do you want with me?" I demanded, as I slipped into the panic I wanted to deny.

"Oh, it's not you I want." His free hand grabbed my shoulder, steadying me, and his knife scored the skin over my collarbone. I whimpered, clenching my teeth to try to hide it, my body tensing as it tried to flee. "I want to see the look on Damien's face when he sees what I've done to you."

His free hand grabbed my shoulder, holding me in place as he continued to work his knife over me, nicking my flesh without warning. I began to feel faint, my breathing erratic, the chains biting into my hands as I gripped them tightly, fighting back the pain. My chest throbbed, and I tried to breathe through it. The familiar stabbing sensation penetrated my ribs, my heart ready to burst, and I winced.

Cole spoke up then. "That's enough, she's at her limit.

Marcus gave him a sidelong glance before he sighed, his shoulders sagging. Disappointment washed over his face as he stepped back. "She really can't handle any more?"

"No," Cole said, groaning as he rose, as if this whole thing were a chore to him.

Marcus stepped back, wiping the blade of his knife on his pants. "I guess we'll stop here for now and pick it back up in a few hours."

Cole approached us, and I jerked away from him—my legs kicking out, my toes uselessly grazing the floor as the chains prevented any further retreat. Cole stalked closer, extending his hand to me, and I froze.

I clamped my eyes shut, my heart threatening to burst, and the room spun. The moment his fingertips brushed my neck, it was as if I could feel my pulse where he touched, hear my own blood pumping through my veins. An odd sinking sensation overcame me, as if the blood was pooling at my feet, and I slumped, darkness rising to welcome me once more.

171

CHAPTER 19

Fight him.

My own voice echoed in the darkness of my mind, bitter and venomous. Only... I hadn't thought it, hadn't thought anything much over the last few... days? Weeks?

I didn't respond, couldn't respond. My skin tingled, as if someone were watching me. Was I not alone? Hands slid over my shoulders as a presence pressed into my back, the voice slithering into my ear. I couldn't turn to whoever spoke, could do nothing but stare forward into the inky, endless void.

He'll return.

The presence faded at my back, and as if I were looking in a mirror, my reflection rippled into view before me. The form solidified, my features becoming clearer, but something was wrong, there was a darkness that touched at my features. My skin was palish, dark veins stretching out from my eyes—up my neck, branching out down my arms. My reflection leaned in toward me, lips curving into a grin that was all too dark, and she lifted her hand to tilt my chin up, forcing my gaze to meet hers.

When he does, bite back.

Cold water splashed over me, and I gasped, icy water biting my skin as I jolted awake.

Fresh cigarette smoke filled my lungs as I gasped for air, the smoke burning my raw throat. I twisted away from him, my body weak as I curled into myself, craving sleep in a way I never had in my life.

How many times had he woken me like this now?

Thirty times? Forty? I remembered reaching thirty at one point... or had I counted fifty?

When I failed to keep count, failed to track how much time had passed, I tried to note when his clothes changed between visits, in hopes that signaled a different day. With each time his clothes changed, though, I found myself failing to keep track of them, questioning whether he'd changed clothes, or if he'd worn those distressed jeans the last time. Or were they cargo pants? Did he have that shirt on before?

How many days had it been now? Or... had it been weeks? In the darkness of my unknown periods of sleep, with no window to see the sun rise or fall, I had no way of knowing.

I groaned, my head throbbing, and I struggled to remember what it felt like to not feel this pain. How many times had he invaded my mind? How many times had I felt the sting of his blade, the burn of his cigarettes?

"Wake up, little songbird. That's enough sleep for you." He tossed the bucket to the side, the metal clanking off the concrete, the chains ringing out as they were pulled taut, lifting me swiftly to my feet. My body shook as the water dripped off me, my head hanging forward, eyelids heavy as I groaned in exhaustion. A mess of tangled curls fell in curtains around my face, and it was a relief to see he hadn't cut it as he'd threatened on a few occasions. I'd called him on his bluff a time or two, only to feel the cold bite of his blade against my skin. He never went through with his threat, though—he liked using it to tether me to him.

"Stop calling me that," I muttered, my voice barely audible as I shivered.

"Have a nice nap?" Marcus said, clearly ignoring me as he lowered his face to mine, a cigarette tucked loosely between his lips.

I lifted my eyes to him as he inhaled the smoke before letting it fall from his lips in a cloud that burned my lungs. Anger clouded my judgement, and I spit in his face as my only response. He jerked back, and his lips curled, jaw tightening as he wiped it from his face.

A low growl slipped from his throat before he backhanded me across the face. My head knocked to the side, and I swayed in the chains, feeling the sting of my busted lip.

Five busted lips... no... Six? I licked the blood from my mouth, spitting it onto the floor.

He jerked my chin up to him, pulling the cigarette from between his lips, and my body tensed, bracing for the feel of its burn. "Now, let's try this again. Did you have a nice nap?"

My eyes snapped back to his, holding his stare as I breathed through the pain. "I'm not gonna play this game, Marcus." He dropped my chin, and I let my head hang forward a moment, my eyes heavy with exhaustion. How I wished he would just end it. "Just get on with it."

"Giving up on me already, songbird? Oh, but that would just break Damien's heart." He lowered himself to whisper in my ear. "And after he's been working so hard to find you."

I tried to hide the overwhelming emotions welling in me at the thought of Damien looking for me. That meant he was ok. He was out there, still. The hope was dangerous to cling to, but still, I hoped, let that be the one thing I held onto tightly to keep myself from slipping into insanity. Damien. Zephyr. Barrett. Vincent. James. Mom. Dad.

Kat...

Just hold on a bit longer... Damien will come. He will come.

"He got so close too," he whispered, and my body tensed, the traitorous chains rattling faintly in response. "Took out one of my guys, but Cole managed to get him off our trail."

I bit my tongue, not giving him the satisfaction of the hope blossoming in my chest. Damien came close to finding me? Did that mean I wasn't as far from Johnstown as I feared? My eyes shifted to Cole, who was sitting idly by in the chair he usually resided in during our sessions, waiting and ready to work whatever twisted magic he possessed to prevent my heart from stopping. I ground my teeth together as I stared him down, fury flooding me at the fact that they had nearly found me only to have him lead them away.

"What are you to him?" Marcus demanded, grabbing a hand full of my hair and lifting my face to force my gaze back to him.

"I don't know what you're talking about," I groaned, not having the strength to fight as I closed my eyes.

God, it felt so good to just close my eyes.

"Oh? There's gotta be something special about you. For Damien to be so interested in a human after all these years, I find it odd. You don't just fall in love again after losing your mate."

My eyes shot opened, the words clicking through me. "Damien... lost his mate?"

"Oh, he didn't tell you?" Marcus asked, smiling now that he'd gotten my attention. "Lost his love over a hundred years ago. It destroyed him. Whatever you think you are to him, you're wrong. He's just using you for a good time."

"You don't know a thing about Damien," I groaned, letting my eyes slide shut, savoring the only relief I could find.

"Oh, believe me, love." He said with a cruel smile. "I know him better than you could ever imagine."

I lifted my face to glare at him, every ounce of my anger and hatred filling my eyes as I stared him down. Oh, how I wanted to hurt

174

him, to chain him where I stood and beat him as badly as he had me. If only I could get a hold of that knife of his, I'd run it into him again and again until the breath left his body—until it was his blood covering my body and not my own.

"Oh, those are some hateful thoughts." He leaned in, whispering into my ear. "But if I gave you this knife, could you do it?" Burning pain stretched across my shoulder as he pressed the cherry of his cigarette into my skin, and my body seized as a gasp ripped from my throat. Marcus released my head, letting me fall forward. As he did, the chains released, and I fell to the floor. I hit the concrete, stifling a whimper as my bones bruised beneath my skin. He rose, watching me with cruel calculation as I curled into myself.

I tried to push myself up, the burn searing my skin as I panted, and my arms quivered, unable to sustain my weight. His footsteps circled around behind me, and my spine stiffened as I remembered the pain of him forcing his way into my mind. He grabbed my arm before I could try to get away, jerking me up off the concrete and twisting it behind my back. Panic flooded me as his hand wrapped around my throat. I pulled and fought against him as he cupped his other hand over my eyes, pressing my back against him.

"No!" I shouted, fear tearing through my system.

"Keep screaming. No one is coming for you," Marcus breathed into my ear as he pulled me tighter against him, the chains growing taut as my handlers tugged them until I could hardly pull away from him.

"By the way." I froze, bracing myself for what I knew would come next as he whispered in my ear once more. "Haven't you been wondering how you ended up in the streets those nights you were attacked by the darklings?"

I stopped breathing, my pulse pounding in my ears not loud enough to drown out his words.

"You're beautiful when you sleep."

The blinding light ripped through me again, claws sinking into that intangible part of my head, shredding and tearing its way in. A scream ripped from my throat as he forced his way into each and every memory I held close to my heart.

And I prayed for the darkness to claim me once again.

CHAPTER 20

The muffled sound of voices echoed outside the door, drawing me from sleep. I was laying on something soft, and for the first time I couldn't feel the shackles on my wrists. Where were the shackles?

I groaned, rubbing my tender eyes and laid there a moment, my body too heavy to move. They must have moved me when I was unconscious, for I was in a bed. I allowed myself to melt into the blankets, relishing in the feel of it. It was the first time I'd gotten to sleep in a bed in God only knew how long.

You made it to seventy-four. No wait... seventy-five?

Had I counted seventy-five before? Shit.

My eyes drifted across the room. Just as it was in the other chamber, the walls were bare concrete with no windows. Adjacent to the bed sat the most basic set of furniture, a dresser with a mirror, a small table and chair, and a sink and toilet.

A deep ache lingered in my body, making it difficult to move, and I whimpered as I forced myself to sit up. My eyes fell to my hands, and my stomach twisted at the sight of the cuts and bruises marring my skin. They spanned from my wrists—bruised and chaffed from the shackles that had bound me—up until they disappeared beneath the tattered remains of my sleeves.

I winced as my hollow stomach growled, and I tried to remember how it had been since I'd last eaten something. Every so often I would awaken to food and water—nothing of any value, usually scraps, just barely enough to keep me going.

What had I eaten last? Had it been stale bread? Yeah, it was stale bread. That shit had been so dry it had hurt my teeth to chew, but I had devoured every last crumb.

Marcus was cruel and calculated, and nothing he did was by chance. There were many times where he would give me something to spark an emotion or reaction and then take it away, whether it was food when I was starved, or news of Damien. And, though, for the most part I'd managed to force myself to remain unresponsive, there were times where he'd managed to break through every wall I'd built. Those sessions where I'd slipped had been the worst.

He never provided enough information to give me any ideas of what was going on outside of the cell, just enough to spark hope. His games never ceased, turning into an endless charade of bait and switch that only drew my misery out.

My gaze drifted across the room to the dresser where a dim lamp stood. I groaned as I pushed myself up, every muscle and bone aching, and I winced at the pain as my tender feet met the cold concrete. It was a difficult walk across the room, but the glass of water resting atop the dresser was motivating enough. It was then that I noticed they had set my bottle of medicine next to the glass.

Oh? What? Is Cole growing tired of having to use his magic to keep my heart going?

Anger flared through me, and I grabbed the glass, desperate to ease the parch soreness in my throat, to wash the terrible dusty taste from my mouth. I drank it down ravenously, and the cool sensation left me desperate for more.

My eyes fell to the bottle, and I contemplated not taking my medicine, wondering how long I could go without it—allow myself to have an attack when they weren't around.

No, I couldn't give up that easily. Damien and the others were out there looking for me. I had to be strong, had to hold on.

Fight it. Don't let them see your weakness.

My shoulders slumped when I finished the glass. It wasn't enough; I wanted more. My gaze shifted to a note as I set the glass down.

I was half tempted to throw it away without reading it, but I grabbed it, giving into his stupid game.

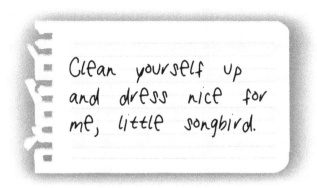

Clean yourself up and dress nice for me, little songbird.

My blood boiled, fury flooding me, and I crumpled it up before chucking it across the room, my throat raw as I screamed my frustrations. My fingers twitched at the thought of the things I wanted to do to him, of how I wanted to make him bleed.

God, I couldn't believe he was the reason I'd been waking in the alleyways at night, only to be hunted by darklings. Fucking bastard. He'd been in my room. My stomach churned, chest tightening as I imagined him there, in the darkness, watching me sleep. The sensation of his hands on me left my skin crawling, as if a part of me had been aware when he worked whatever manipulations he had into my mind, willing me to leave my house in the dead of night.

Because I was involved with Damien? Because I meant something to him? No. He had mentioned someone wanting me. The darklings had been hunting me, even Damien had noticed it. No, this wasn't Damien's fault... I couldn't think like that.

Fear pumped through my veins as my mind latched onto the fact that Marcus had known where I lived all this time. Did he know my parents lived next door? Would he do anything to them? I needed to get out of here. He hadn't mentioned them yet, hadn't used information about them to get under my skin.

Thoughts flooded my mind in a chaotic whirlwind, my imagination running wild with the worst possibilities of Marcus' plans. I'd been here so long, and the longer I was here, the more likely someone was giving up on looking for me.

I stopped breathing.

Would... would Damien give up on me? Would my parents and Kat give up thinking I was dead?

Terror swelled in my throat, and I braced myself against the dresser as the sobs built in my chest, threatening to overflow.

*No. Don't give into it, fight it. **Fight. It.***

Tears rolled down my cheeks without permission, the droplets falling onto my quivering hands. I was scared. No, I was terrified. I didn't know how much longer I could hold on, how much longer I could stand up against Marcus' torture. If I didn't get out of here soon, he may succeed in breaking me.

I lifted my gaze to the mirror atop the dresser, seeing just what had been done to me. Dark circles had formed under my eyes, my skin now pale, and sickly. Dried blood coated my mouth, streaking down from my nose to my chin, and staining my torn sweater. I could see the bruised outlines of his fingers around my neck from where he'd held me countless times as he entered my mind.

Marcus invaded countless private and intimate thoughts and memories I held close to my heart, taunting me about them afterwards. He knew exactly what he was doing, and I suspected he hoped to drive me insane before he handed me over to whoever had targeted me.

No matter what he did, no matter how much I baited him, he never let slip who it was that wanted me, and it left me wondering. Who would someone as twisted as Marcus answer to? And what could they possibly want with me?

I took a moment to inspect the clothes he'd so 'graciously' laid out for me. Perhaps I should've been thankful he wasn't trying to dress me in something revealing, though there had been countless chances for him to take advantage of me, I had no memory of him attempting anything. My brows furrowed as I inspected the outfit folded neatly before me, lifting the shirt as it unfolded in my hands, and the blood drained from my face. They were my clothes. I dropped the shirt and opened the drawers to find more of my clothes and personal things.

Knots twisted in my gut. Marcus had broken into my apartment again. He'd been in my room, touched my things. Did he hurt my parents? Did they notice the break-in and call the cops? I took a deep breath, gripping the edge of the dresser as the panic began to spiral. *No. Don't fall for it. Don't give into it.*

This was just another one of Marcus' mind games. There was nothing I could do here, and panicking wasn't going to help my parents or make the situation better. I could only hope and pray they were okay and focus on getting out of here to see them again.

I looked around the room, searching for any signs of a camera, but the room. Seemed clear. Camera or not, though, I had no choice if I wanted to clean myself and change.

The room began to spin as I pulled my sweater over my head, and I braced myself against the dresser before my knees could give out on me. God, I needed food. I dropped my dirt and blood-stained sweater to the floor, releasing the dresser the moment I felt I wouldn't collapse. Lifting my gaze, I winced at my reflection in the mirror. Bruises spread across my rib cage, and I lifted a hand to brush my fingers against the tender flesh.

Nothing felt broken, only sore, but that was no surprise. Marcus knew how far he could go before breaking anything—he would always stop just short of that. It wasn't worth it to risk breaking any bones—not like he had to break bones to cause the agony he had. No, he wanted me alive, and there had been a time or two where one of his 'helpers' had gone a bit too far. Marcus had lashed out at him, telling him how internal bleeding would overcomplicate things.

The water was icy as I turned on the faucet, and I shivered as I ran my hand under the stream. I grabbed the empty glass, filling it, and downed glass after glass to quench the thirst, to fill the raging hollowness in my gut until I nearly vomited. Then, I got to work cleaning the dried blood from my face. It stung faintly, but it felt so good to be free of the grime. I worried about the condition of the stitches in the back of my head, but I had no way of checking them. They didn't hurt any worse than the rest of my body, so I could only hope and pray they were healing ok.

I dropped the rag in the dish, my face and body as clean as I could get them, and I dressed—my clothes looser on me than I remember. I managed to find a brush and got to work detangling my hair. My eyes drifted around the empty room. The walls felt like they might close in on me. I wanted out, wanted to feel the breeze on my skin, smell fresh air again, see the moon shining in the sky, or the sun rise over the mountains. Even if only one more time.

The mattress sagged under my weight as I sat down, my hair finally detangled after what felt like forever, and I released a heavy sigh, containing my fear. He had control of my mind, Cole had control of my heart... but I'd be damned if I gave him the satisfaction of knowing he had control of me, that he'd broken me. Though, I was losing hold of myself, I refused to let myself bend to his will. If I could just hold out, take note of everything I saw outside of the cell, I may have a chance at escaping.

There was no denying it, though. The odds of escaping on my own were slim. I was human, they were immortals, skilled fighters. Maybe I should just end it before they come back... end the pain and suffering.

No. Don't give up. He would want you to keep fighting. He would want you to stay strong.

For a moment, I could almost hear Damien's voice, encouraging me, pushing me to keep fighting, to not give up. I wouldn't. I would fight every second.

I needed to try to come up with a plan. There was no telling where they were holding me, what lay outside these walls. For all I knew, I could be in a basement, underground and miles from town in the middle of nowhere. It would be pointless to escape if I was only going to get caught again.

Gravity shifted, and the room threatened to spin again as I imagined what Marcus would do to me if I failed an escape. No, I would only get one shot. If I failed, I'd do everything I could to make sure I wasn't brought back alive.

My eyes drifted over the place as I searched for any potential weapons. No matter how much I planned, I wouldn't stand a chance of escaping empty-handed, if I could even manage to escape at all. There weren't any objects that could readily be used as a weapon, only furniture.

I turned to the door, looking it over before grabbing the knob and turning it. Locked. It was worth a shot, at least. I grabbed the wooden chair sitting next to the dresser and swung it at the door. The steel hummed, but it remained firm. A cry of frustration peeled from my throat, and I threw the chair into the mirror on the dresser. It shattered into bits, shards of glass scattering atop the dresser and floor.

Great. Now there's glass everywhere.

Good. It was a mess Marcus could deal with. I'd ruin everything of his, everything he owned. Him.

I took a deep breath, my hands shaking, and I bent down to grab a shard of the broken glass. I turned it over in my hand, ensuring it wasn't too big to conceal in my clothes. I only hoped I would get the chance to run this shard across his throat.

My hateful gaze reflected in the shard, my eyes so dark that I hardly recognized them. I drew a deep breath, slipping the shard into my pocket and eased down to sit on the bed. Time passed as I stared up at the ceiling, and I didn't know how long I sat there pondering, how long I fought off the urge to close my eyes and let the darkness welcome me into its arms—accept the escape it offered. Was it morning outside? Nighttime?

There was a click as the deadbolt unlocked, and I shot up to find Cole opening the door, my hand freezing before I could grab the shard of glass in my pocket. No. I couldn't let him know I had it yet.

My blood boiled at the sight of him. His dark eyes passed over the mess of shattered glass littering the floor, and he frowned, as if it were a mere inconvenience to him.

"What do you want?" I said through gritted teeth.

No response.

My hands clenched at my sides. "So, how long have you been planning this with Marcus? Did he promise you something in exchange for selling us out like this? For making me his personal punching bag?"

Once again, he didn't answer, and he stalked toward me, grabbing my arm. I met his cold gaze, my hatred burning into him as I glared right back at him, but I stiffened as I took him in. He looked... tired, exhausted even, dark shadows hanging under his eyes. Gone was the sweet boy I'd met and left in its wake was a monster. A snake.

He jerked me to his side, and I stumbled forward before fighting against his hold as he dragged me through the door. "Fucking bastard. Let me go!"

He shoved me down the hall, and fear swelled in my chest as I stumbled to a stop, the pressure making me feel like my chest might

181

implode. I halted the deep rushes of breath, stifling my emotions, trying to hide any sign of weakness.

Was he going to put me in chains again? Had Marcus put me in that bedroom to give me a false sense of security? Was he luring me into a relaxed state just to plunge me into further misery when my defenses were down? It was something I could imagine him doing.

I took a tentative step forward, then another. I could feel Cole's eyes on my back as we walked. There was no way I could make any move to escape, not yet, but this was the opportunity I needed. I couldn't miss this chance to see what lay outside my room, this chance to survey my surroundings, find a way out if I managed to break free.

We came to a spiral stairway at the end of the hall, and Cole shoved me forward when I paused at the foot of them. Hesitantly, I inched up toward the door at the top.

Echoes of laughter and conversation reverberated through the door before me. Cole reached past me, turned the doorknob, and pushed it open to reveal a large room filled with people. They were... partying, as if they hadn't had a hand in torturing a defenseless woman, as if I weren't locked away beneath their feet. Cole and I stood in the doorway for a moment, my feet refusing to move.

Don't let them see your fear. Take this chance to look for an escape.

I doubted anyone would want to help me, but it wouldn't hurt to try to feel out Marcus' men, see if there were any that might not have realized what he was doing here.

My eyes drifted over the space, once again finding no windows. I hated this feeling of being trapped, of not knowing how to get out. I hated not knowing how much time had passed or what time of day it was. Had it been weeks? Or months? Was the time that had passed even real? Or had Marcus manipulated my mind? Was any of this real? Or had Marcus trapped me in some strange vision as he had before and I wasn't even truly standing here but unconscious, still bound in chains below?

The conversation piqued, shouts and laughter building from a group of people sitting nearby in the corner of the room around a huge indoor fire-pit. A beer pong table stood nearby where others gathered to play, and I halted as my eyes found a table full of food and drinks. My stomach growled, my mouth watering at the sight, but I did my best to fight the urge to run to the table, to eat anything I could get my hands on.

The foul stench of alcohol and cigarettes loomed in the air and my eyes found Marcus, a bottle of beer in his hand. Oddly enough, he didn't look even remotely affected by it, despite the mess of empty bottles littering the surrounding tables.

A woman sat in front of Marcus, her eyes glossy, cheeks and ears tinted red, and she seemed a little off balance with her own bottle in her hand. Unease settled into the pit of my stomach when I realized she was the only one who appeared that way.

I frowned as I got a good look at her. Wait... I knew her. We shared a class together. Melissa. She'd invited Kat and Cody to her party on Halloween night. She was well known around campus—a senior and exceptionally gifted, having assisted me a few times when I encountered problems. She'd always seemed genuinely kind.

What was she doing here with Marcus?

Marcus sat, grinning at her as they chatted and joked. That smile of his somehow made my insides turn. It was so well faked for the cruelty and hidden agendas I knew it hid. Melissa continued to flirt with him, seeming unaware of the monster lurking beneath that mask.

She wasn't safe here, but I was helpless to do anything about it. How would I escape with her? Why had Marcus decided to bring me out of the cell like this, especially with a witness? Would he kill her if I said anything? If I ran? Maybe he intended to use her to make me think twice about running, to keep me obedient. The glass in my pocket grew heavier, and I tried to shift my plans, tried to form any possible way we could both get out of here alive.

I flinched as Cole shoved past me to walk toward another woman sitting nearby. I recognized Amara immediately, and irritation built in my chest at the sight of that smug grin on her face. He hadn't been the only one to betray Damien and the others, though her betrayal wasn't as shocking to me as Cole's had been. Her gaze met mine, but I didn't back down from it. I didn't miss the lack of a beer bottle in her hand, which only left my all the more weary of what they were up to.

Marcus' brows rose as Cole passed him, and he turned to glance over his shoulder. His pewter eyes fell on me, and the cruel grin returned—the mask relaxed, revealing the malicious creature I knew him to be. My heart quickened, the feel of metal shackling my wrists weighed heavy on me, the burn of his cigarettes forcing air into my lungs in shorter bursts, the sting of his blade... My eyes fell as my skin started to burn and I realized that I'd unintentionally began rubbing my chafed wrists.

Marcus tilted his head, his eyes trailing over me. "Well, hello sleeping beauty, glad you finally decided to join us. I was about ready to come wake you up myself."

I internally winced at that thought.

The others glanced in my direction but didn't care to cease their conversations. I glanced around at them, counting the faces I knew, ones who'd stood by and watched as I was beaten within an inch of my life and done nothing, or worse, joined in. There were thirteen in the room outside of Melissa and me, a few women, but mostly men. I knew three of the men watching me from the corner of their eyes by name after they joined Marcus for several sessions, wanted to personally run this shard of glass into their chests until there was no life left in them.

Victor. Ethan. Joseph. Names I wanted to erase from existence.

The shard grew heavy in my pocket, and I forced my gaze away from them.

Not yet.

Melissa's brows furrowed when she caught sight of me, likely wondering where I came from. Did she recognize me? Remember me from class? The long sleeves of my fresh sweater hid most of the wounds left by Marcus' torture. Aside from my busted lip and the dark bags under my eyes, my face looked almost normal. I prayed she wouldn't question anything, feared what Marcus would do if she caught onto what had happened.

Ethan wrapped his arms around her waist, his brown curls tousled in a way that looked like he'd gotten busy with someone before I'd arrived, and he whispered something in her ear. She snickered flirtatiously, her attention straying from me.

"Why don't you come sit down?" Marcus asked, patting the cushion beside him.

My eyes dipped to the seat before lifting to him. Whatever he had planned, if he thought I was going to join them for a drink, he was in for a shock. I much preferred the idea of smashing a bottle over his head.

"That depends," I replied, eyeing him. "What are you planning?"

"Nothing, I swear." His tone was all too sarcastic.

My body tensed instinctively as I imagined the worst. Still, I had nowhere to run, hadn't been able to form a plan yet, and I knew what awaited if I tried something and failed—what he might do to Melissa. I walked over and cautiously eased onto the cushion next to him.

"There's no need to be so defensive. I promise I won't bite," he whispered, flashing me a pearly smile.

My eyes narrowed, and he barked a laugh, which made my insides boil. How he could just act as if he hadn't done what he had?

I tried to peer around without drawing too much attention to myself, studying the room as I looked for anything I might use as another weapon. I needed every option I could get. I was already at a disadvantage as a human. Even if they weren't immortals, they were clearly trained fighters.

My heart leapt and I stilled. Just on the other side of the fire pit were long iron tools used to tend to the fire.

I tucked the knowledge away for later before my gaze swept over the people in the room wondering who held the keys to my room, if I could possibly steal a set to get out. Cole had a set, that much had been revealed, I assume Marcus had one, or was there only one copy? I'd never picked a lock before, so I didn't have confidence to be able to manage that. Perhaps if I could get out of that room somehow I could get out when things were quiet, when less of Marcus' men were around.

Outside of the door we had entered through, there were two others The door we'd come from led down farther, so surely, that wasn't the way out. I didn't know which of the other two doors might lead out of here if I tried to make a run for it, though. That just left the issue of Melissa.

Damien had said Marcus was involved in the murder of a number of immortals and humans just a few nights before I was taken. There was no doubt in my mind that he held the same intentions for her.

I chewed the inside of my lip as I tried to work out a way I could save her from the fate I feared Marcus had in store.

My heart lurched as I glanced nervously in Marcus' direction. The lack of a reaction led me to believe he wasn't reading my mind for once. That, or he didn't let on that he was aware of my every thought and attempt at a plan of escape. If he tried anything, I didn't know what I 'd do. I couldn't go back to that cell, couldn't go back in those chains. I could have made a run for it by myself, but Melissa's presence made it difficult for me to try to escape. I couldn't leave her behind, and Marcus seemed to know that.

Bastard.

Melissa turned from the guy who'd been occupying her attention to share a smile with Marcus. "I'm gonna go get another drink." She stepped away, stumbling into the others only to murmur an apology.

"Food?" Marcus offered, setting his beer on the table behind him.

I didn't respond, watching as he pulled a platter from one of the side tables. A mix of sandwiches lay atop it, filled with meats, cheeses, tomatoes, pickles... my mouth watered.

"It's not poisoned, I promise."

"I have plenty of reasons to not trust any promises you make," I said under my breath, fighting the urge to look at the food.

He didn't move, testing my resolve. "Starve, then."

My eyes fell on the food, my stomach crying out for just a taste, and I caved.

A smile curved his lips as I snatched two sandwiches, one in each hand, and began devouring them. They tasted like heaven, and I couldn't get them down fast enough.

He returned the platter to its place. "So..."

"So?" I responded sharply through a mouthful, bracing myself for him to do something as I finished the first sandwich.

"I'm curious." He paused a moment. "Do you really know what we are?"

I swallowed. My breath quickened for a moment, fear taking hold of me. I'd known he was like Damien, an immortal, but to the reminder of it outside of his magical abilities brought forth a whole new level of fear. Would he try to bite me? My skin crawled at the thought of it, as if it were a violation beyond the things he'd already done to me.

He laughed under his breath when I didn't respond. "I am glad you decided to join us." Marcus grinned as he leaned into me. "Makes the party all the more fun."

My eyes fell from his, trying not to recoil from him as fear crawled its way into my chest at his proximity. "It's not like I had an choice to refuse."

He grabbed a beer bottle, twisted the top, and offered it to me.

I took one glanced at it and shook my head. "I can't drink."

His eyes darkened at my refusal, his voice slipping into a command. "Drink."

I drew a deep, shaky breath and took the bottle from him. The sour smell made my stomach twist, but his eyes lingered on me, and I reluctantly took a sip. My face scrunched at the terrible taste of it, but I forced it down.

"That's a good girl. You need to relax, enjoy yourself." He took a swig of his beer again. "While you can."

I nearly choked at his words, something deep within me tugging and twisting, screaming to run, but I forced my expression to remain the same.

"So, you didn't answer my question."

My eyes fell, as I avoided his gaze, and I winced as his hand clasped firmly around my forearm, squeezing tightly—the cut and bruised flesh under his grip, sore and tender.

His voice was venomous as he whispered in my ear, his true nature leaking through the veil. "Answer me."

"Yes," I whispered. I lifted my eyes as Melissa returned with her drink.

"Then you won't mind staying for dinner." His lips parted into a grin, flashing his teeth. I froze, unable to force my gaze from his canines as they lengthened into fangs.

I panicked, pulling away from him to run, but thick fingers knotted in my hair. The beer bottle fell from my hand, shattering on the floor, and I cried out as I was yanked back into place by my hair, Marcus' guy shoving me down to my knees.

Marcus' eyes shifted to Melissa.

"Melissa, run now!" I screamed, grabbing hold of my captor's hand as I fought to free myself.

She blinked in her drunkenness, eyes popping as the situation seemed to sober her. Marcus grabbed her by the shoulder and hair before she could react, jerking her against him as she struggled and fought. He yanked her head back, burying his face into her neck and bit down onto her jugular.

Her screams filled the room.

CHAPTER 21

The world stilled, air halting in my lungs, the world going quiet. No other sound broke the quiet hum except that of Melissa's neck snapping. Marcus tossed her aside, and her body fell into a heap on the floor. I froze, unable to take my eyes off her.

No. Please, don't let her be...

There was no movement, not even the subtlest hint of breathing. Her eyes stared up at the ceiling, unseeing, and I screamed.

Marcus stood over her, and I watched in horror as his eyes shifted in my direction, his hand rising to brush remnants of her blood from his lips. "I'm gonna enjoy taking you before Damien has a chance to."

I met his gaze, a combination of fear, anger, and hatred consuming me. I wasn't going to bend to him any longer, wasn't going to play his sick games, and I sure as hell wasn't going to sit and let him do what he wanted without a fight. Either I would get free or die trying. Both options were better than returning to that chamber.

The hand in my hair loosened, likely distracted by the pool of blood forming around Melissa's body. I didn't question it and pushed myself back and around him. Watching as his hungered gaze remained fixated on her, I scrambled and scuffed my way across the floor.

Marcus' eyes remained on me, something lighting them that promised something so much worse than death.

Shit. Shit! I pushed myself to my feet, my eyes darting around the room, looking for any means of escape. It was now or never. I reached into my pocket, grabbing the shard of glass, my bare feet pounding into the concrete as I ran.

"Get her!" Marcus roared behind me, and I bolted for the nearest door.

Please, let it be the way out.

I reached for the doorknob as I neared it, my heart in my throat. Someone tackled me hard from the side, knocking the air from my lungs as they pinned me against the wall. My eyes popped open, and didn't let the lack of oxygen stop me as I drove the shard of glass into Victor's neck, but he blocked me, the shard sinking into his arm instead. He cursed, pulling away just enough to examine it, and his murderous gaze settled back on me.

"Little bitch," he said through gritted teeth, and backhanded me.

I gasped, blood filling my mouth, and he jerked me back upright.

Marcus chuckled as he stalked toward us. "Ugh, you're a spicy one alright. I can't believe you still have this much fight left in you. It does make this more fun, though. Maybe I do need to bring you back downstairs. It's clear you haven't had enough."

My chest heaved as I panted, Victor pinning me in place.

"I'll enjoy breaking you, and when I'm done, I'll give Damien a chance to find you before the darklings do; let him see what remains of you."

The blood drained from my face at the thought of those chains on my skin again. No. I'd do everything I could to make sure I never went back to that room.

He slammed his hand against the wall beside my face, and Victor shifted out of his way. I steeled my nerves, refusing to flinch at his strike and Marcus' grin only seemed to widen at the sight of it.

"Ah, I love that defiance in those eyes. It'll make it all the more fun to watch when you fall apart. No sense in ending the fun so soon, though. We've got all the time in the world."

A familiar icy feeling crept up my spine. It was the same as I'd felt in the woods when he'd taken me, and no matter how much I tried, I couldn't seem to fight or resist it.

The room darkened, voices echoing around me, speaking to me in that strange language, yet I couldn't make out what they were saying. They were poetic, lulling, enchanting. Hands released me, but I had no control over my legs, over any part of my body, as I fell into the sea of voices, giving into whatever sweet things they promised.

"You wanna see your lover, don't you?" Marcus' voice grew closer as reality shifted, the walls melting around us, lights dimming. Fingertips trailed up my cheek, brushing my hair out of my face and behind my ear. "I'm sure you miss him dearly."

I did. I missed him more than anything.

"I'm right here, Cas." Damien's voice drifted into my thoughts. My vision returned to find him standing before me, just within reach. I blinked, my focus slipping in and out, his form rippling and solidifying. My heart swelled at the sight of him. How I'd longed to see that beautiful face again, even if it was just one last time. I wanted to touch him, to hold him, to know he was ok.

I reached for him, but my hands halted before I could touch him. My fingers trembled, something deep within me recoiling and screaming at me. I frowned, fighting through it, desperate to feel him against me. In the back of my mind, though, I couldn't shake the feeling that something was... wrong, unnatural.

His hand lifted to my chin before he glided his fingers down my neck, over my collarbone, farther still until he wrapped his arm around my waist, pulling me into him. My body slumped against him of its own volition, my mind buckling under the weight of the sweet voices as I gave in wholly to what stood before me.

Damien leaned in, whispering into my ear. "You are mine." His voice seemed muddled, overlapped with another. I didn't know whose it was, and the realities began to mix and melt together.

He jerked my face up before pressing his lips to mine, and I lost any sense of where I was or what was happening. I couldn't move, couldn't pull back from him... but why would I?

My eyes flickered as he kissed me, threatening to fall closed as I gave into the feel of him. For a moment, the image of Damien rippled, Marcus replacing him as he held me, his mouth moving against mine as I hung in his arms. His lips brushed over my check, drifting further down until he reached my neck. Then something sharp dragged across my skin.

His fangs.

"I. Will. Break. You. And you will know who it was that ruined you." It wasn't Damien's voice that spoke now, though he stood against me still.

It was Marcus' voice.

He pressed me against the wall with his body, pinning me in place as his hands moved up over me, around my neck, until he held my

189

head in his palms. "And he will know that it was I who tasted you first, who took you first."

I tried to brace myself for what I knew would come next, but he stopped short of invading my thoughts. His grip slackened, and I dropped to the ground.

My body shivered violently as my mind began to slip free of the spell he'd put me under, the room coming back into focus. I blinked, and my brows pinched together when I realized Marcus' attention had been drawn elsewhere. Victor stiffened beside me as Marcus turned, and the room quieted as a subtle whistle of wind emanated from the wall.

The room spun, and I blinked, trying to force my way past the nausea rolling through me. I didn't know what was happening, but I couldn't afford to linger on it. I pushed myself up, bracing myself against the wall as I struggled to stay on my feet.

I froze as I caught sight of the shadows on the wall growing and stretching out from under lamps and tables, reaching out to each other until they enveloped the far wall entirely.

My heart leapt Damien emerged from the darkness, his face marred with so much rage. Barrett, Vincent, and Zephyr, stepped out of the dark void behind him, fury painting each of their faces.

Marcus' men launched at them, and chaos erupted, magic exploding as they clashed. The room swayed and blurred as my mind fought to recover from Marcus' mental manipulation. They came for me. The found me. I drew slow, even breaths as I tried and failed to stabilize myself against the wall.

Fire exploded from Barrett as he slammed his flame engulfed fist into one of Marcus' men, and I couldn't believe what I was seeing as it crawled over his skin, ready to burn whoever rose against its wielder. Another man's roar shifted into a snarl as black mist enveloped his body before a coyote emerged, slamming into Zephyr, who threw his arm up. The coyote bit down on Zephyr's forearm before they slammed into the concrete. Vincent twisted around, evading Victor's fist, before he threw his hands out in a fluid motion, and I gasped, the air growing drier as water seemed to manifest and coil around him before slamming Victor into the wall.

I took a tentative step forward, eyes locking on Damien as he went for Marcus, and the mass of colliding bodies and explosion of magics became almost too much to track.

Amara stepped into my path, her narrowing gaze landing on me. "Going somewhere?"

I paced back when she advanced, my strength slowly returning to me, as she continued to back me toward the fire pit. My eyes darted to Damien and the others as they clashed with Marcus and his men before slipping back to Amara. I was on my own, and I needed something, anything, to fight her off. Amara took another step toward me, and I searched for anything I could use to defend myself, finding nothing but discarded beer bottles and plates. A beer bottle might not be enough. My mind flew through every detail I'd looked over when I first entered this room.

The irons by the fire.

Hope swelled in my chest, and I whipped around, searching for them. Amara's foot slammed into my back, knocking me into the pit. I gasped, narrowly avoiding the fire, and adrenaline clouded the pain in my palms and knees as I lifted my face. My blood iced over as my gaze met the unseeing eyes of Melissa's body laying before me.

Oh God…

I reached out to touch her, to shake her, but I knew it was no use. If only I could've saved her. She was gone. She was gone, and there was nothing I could do for her.

"I could send you where she went if you like," Amara sneered.

I twisted around to look back at her as she stalked toward me. Out of the corner of my eyes, I found the irons, leaning against one of the tables. I jumped to my feet and lunged to get a hold of one of the pokers, before turning on her, hands shaking as I gripped the metal firmly.

Her lips curled as she approached me. I drew a deep, even breath, focusing on stabilizing myself. I didn't know if I stood a chance in hell against her, but I wasn't going to go quietly.

"How pathetic. You really think you can take me on?" she snickered, placing her hand on her hip. "That's adorable."

I stumbled back as she stalked closer, the truth of her words casting doubt into my thoughts. She was right: a human didn't stand a fair chance against one of her kind. I ground my teeth together as a cocky grin spread across her face.

She lurched for me, and my feet slid in an oddly instinctual way as I stepped out of her path. I swung the iron down as hard as I could as she stumbled forward, the metal cracking against the back of her head, and she collapsed to the floor, unconscious.

The iron slipped from my hands, the metal ringing in my ears as it bounced on the concrete, and I stumbled back, heaving as bile rose in my throat at the feel of the metal connecting with her skull. A cold sweat broke out over my skin, my palms clammy, and I inhaled heavily through my teeth.

I'd contemplated killing each and every one of them, but now that there was the possibility of that truly happening...

She's not dead, Cas, just unconscious.

The concrete was icy against my palm as I planted my hand against the wall to support myself, and I turned to the chaos before me, magic surging all around as they fought. I pushed off the wall and stumbled forward as I searched frantically for Damien.

A guy crashed onto to the floor, unconscious, and I looked up to see Barrett brushing his blond hair out of his eyes, blood painting his knuckles before he turned his attention to his next target. Nearby, Zephyr slammed his head into Mike's face, busting his nose open before pulling his dagger from its sheath. My heart plummeted as he ran the blade into the guy's chest. He dropped him to the ground and looked to Barrett, saying something but I couldn't seem to hear them.

Hands grabbed hold of me in my daze, and I yelped as they twisted me arm behind my back. I looked back, glimpsing Cole's face, and his hand plastered over my mouth before I could scream. He dragged along the wall, and I fought against him.

Barrett went rigid as he found us, eyes locking on Cole at my back. Shock and confusion melted into sorrow, and his eyes wavered a moment before he looked away. He turned and shouted Damien's name into the chaos.

I followed his line of sight to find Damien. His fist was bloodied as he repeatedly slammed it into Marcus' face. Marcus slumped as Damien clenched the front of his t-shirt, his face a bloody mess. I didn't know if he was even conscious, but it didn't seem to stop Damien as he relented. Damien grabbed a handful of Marcus' hair, slamming Marcus' head into his knee, before yanking him back up, ripping a dagger from the sheath on his hip, and jerking it back to slam it into him.

"Damien!" Barrett yelled again, and his gaze snapped to him before Barrett nodded in our direction.

Damien's gaze shifted toward us, and when his eyes found us, a wave of shock washed over his face. He released Marcus, who collapsed to the floor. His eyes darted between Cole and me for a moment, his brows furrowing, and I watched as it all seemed to click into place, his shock and sorrow melting into rage.

"Cole!" Damien roared. Shadows quaked around the room, black mist billowing out from his coat, licking at his skin as it twisted and curled. The flames in the pit flickered and waned before dousing entirely, and the lights threatened to cas us until darkness.

Zephyr slammed the face of the last man onto the concrete floor before he joined Barrett and Vincent at Damien's side.

"Don't come any closer!" he snapped, backing us against the wall. I froze as the icy touch of his knife met the skin of my throat, and I stopped breathing.

Zephyr, Vincent, and Barrett all stopped short at his threat, halting their approach.

Damien stepped in front of them, his eyes locked on Cole. Cole's hand twitched suddenly at his advance, and I winced as the blade nicked my skin.

The icy sting of the blade vanished, and the black smoke billowing around Damien's hand dissipated, revealing Cole's knife. I gulped for air, as Cole's hand plastered against my neck, and adrenaline flooding me. His grip tightened, his heart pounding against my back as Damien's eyes remained on him, unmoving, deadly.

"Let her go, man." Barrett's tone was level, empty hands outstretched. "You know as well as I, the only way you leave alive is if she remains unharmed."

Cole didn't say anything, his breath uneven against the back of my neck. This could be the end. Every moment I'd held out, every moment I'd fought back. It was all for nothing in the end. It wouldn't take but a second and he could finish me right where I stood, weapon or not.

Please, not like this. Not when I was so close to freedom. Not when I was so close to being reunited with Damien—with my family.

In a flash of movement, Damien flipped the knife in his hand before slinging it forward. The blade sank into the wall next to Cole's face and we both flinched, his grip loosening for a split second, and I broke free the moment I could, running toward Damien as he ran for me.

Cole cursed, his hand narrowly brushing down my back in an attempt to grab me, his fingers catching a few strands of hair. I bit back the wince of pain as the strands were ripped free. It didn't matter, not when I was so close to freedom.

The knife as it reappeared in Damien's hand, shadows crawling over Damien's arm as he lifted his arm behind his head mid-step. His eyes met mine, and somehow something inside me knew what to do. I dropped to the ground as he threw the knife again, and I twisted around as the blade plunged into Cole's chest.

He fell back onto the floor, his agonized gasps filling my ears, and my heart sank as the blood seeped into his shirt around the knife. Damien launched himself in front of me, his eyes on Cole. My muscles twitched and shook, my chest heaving as I struggled to breathe.

When the others encircled Cole, Damien whipped around and fell to his knees before me. His hands settled on my shoulders as he searched me frantically, his eyes falling on the wounds peeking from beneath my clothes.

"Gods, what did they do to you?"

I sat there, unable to form words as I took in every detail of his face, the stubble along his jaw that was longer than I remember, the eyes that I had held onto so tightly in the darkness. My hands trembled as I grabbed onto him, feeling him, that he was real. "Is it really you? Are you really here?"

His face contorted into a painful expression and he pulled me close to him. "Yes, *mea luna*. I'm here. I'm real."

"How do I know?" I asked, tears welling in my eyes as I struggled to give into the hope that this was really happening. "How do I know you're not another trick?"

He winced at my words. "I don't know what he did to you, but it's really me, I promise. We're going to get you out of here."

Damien lifted his head to search the room behind me, and I turned follow his gaze. Marcus and the others had used Cole's distraction to flee, leaving a few of their dead behind.

A low growl slipped from Damien's throat, his jaw tightening. "Gods Dammit."

Instead of going after them, though, his eyes fell back to me. "Come on."

He wrapped his arms around me, helping me to my feet before guiding me into the shadows. I stiffened as I found my feet met moist soil and dead leaves. We were outside of the compound. My eyes darted around. There were no signs of the city's lights through the dense forests surrounding us. The moonlight cascaded onto me through the canopy of the trees, and the air was so refreshing, so crisp against my skin that I almost cried.

In the pitch shadows, I could hear the rustling of grass and foliage around us and I tensed. Something was moving in the darkness, surrounding us. As my eyes adjusted, I could faintly make out black figures emerging from the trees, and I grabbed onto Damien a what looked like massive wolves prowled toward us.

Glowing red eyes peered at me from the darkness of their being. Their bodies seemed distorted, forms made up entirely of black mist, almost resembling Damien's magic. Their jaws stretched back to their ears, almost reminding me of how the darkling's jaws were. Razor-sharp teeth lined their jaws as they growled, heads dipped low as they approached.

"Don't be afraid. They're with me," Damien spoke softly as he held me. "They were standing guard while we were inside in case any more of Marcus' men showed up."

As they drew closer, their red eyes faded to a beautiful ice blue, their bodies becoming less deformed and more like that of a real wolf. Their jaws retracted, closing until they stood before us, black and devastatingly beautiful.

One nudged my elbow affectionately, whimpering to be pet. I reached out, hesitating before I laid my hand atop its head. The beast bent into it, closing its eyes as it relished in my touch. I could feel its power radiating beneath my palm, a conflicting icy heat that gave me goosebumps.

Damien held his hand out, the largest of the beast's wagging its tail in response as it slid its head into his palm. "Thank you, my friends."

He ran his hand over the creature's head, and it whined affectionately to him. The pack dissolved into black dust, and the creature I was petting disappeared before my eyes.

Vincent and Zephyr appeared from the shadows behind us, startling me. Barrett emerged close behind them, dragging Cole along. He yanked the knife from Cole's chest before throwing him into the dirt. Cole cursed, his fangs bared as he hissed in pain. Without realizing it, I'd clutched onto Damien's hand, his skin whitening under my fingers.

"What the hell were you doing?" Damien demanded, glaring down at Cole.

Cole avoided Damien's gaze, his jaw clenched. Barrett grabbed Cole by the collar of his shirt, snatching him off the ground. I shut my eyes as Barrett punching him, knocking him back to the ground.

Barrett's voice was agonizing. "What the hell were you thinking? How could you fucking do this?"

Silence.

Damien turned, leading me over to a downed tree before easing me down to sit. He lowered to his knees before me, his hands rising to cup my face as he looked me over over me, checking my hands, my arms.

He returned to my face, and I flinched as his thumb grazed over my busted lip. The cords in his neck tightened, muscles quivering. I could almost feel the anger rising in him as he looked up at my forehead before gently brushing my hair from my face. I winced again at the sting of something over my brow.

My body tensed when he found the markings hidden under my sleeves, and my hands retracted from his hold. I hated him seeing the cuts Marcus left, the bruises, the burns. Every mark was a reminder of each hour of agony I'd endured.

"I'll rip his fucking throat out when I find him." His head hung forward a moment and he almost seemed unable to ask. "Did Cole have anything to do with these wounds?"

I couldn't find the words as my eyes flitted back and forth, looking up at him before glancing at the others. My gaze snagged on Barrett as he grabbed the collar of Cole's shirt, demanding answers. I flinched when he slammed his fist across Cole's face again, only to pull him back.

Damien stroked my arms, his voice low and gentle. "Cas... did he?"

My eyes fell from his. "He... helped."

The moment the words left my lips, Damien was on his feet, stalking toward Cole. The shadows of the forest came to life all around us, snaking from the darkness of the trees under my feet. "*You put your fucking hands on her?*"

Vincent and Zephyr rushed to intercept Damien, bracing him.

"Damien! Stop, man!" Vincent said through his teeth as fought to hold Damien back. His eyes fell back, widening as the shadows slithered along the dirt, coiling like snakes around Cole's legs and Cole struggled to back away, to get free.

195

Damien pressed against them, the ground beneath their feet offering no resistance.

Zephyr tried to reason with him. "Damien! We need him alive! He may have information on Marcus!"

My heart plummeted as the shadows seemed to reach for Barrett and he released Cole, stumbling back as they snaked up Cole's torso, reaching for his throat. Cole struggled against them, and I jumped to my feet, running over and stepping in front of him. "Damien! Please!"

The moment my hand pressed against him; he froze. His chest heaved against my palm, his heart racing beneath my touch. His eyes fell to me, and the fury faded. Vincent and Zephyr released him cautiously, preparing to intervene again.

I swayed. Something was wrong. Very wrong. A strange realization crossed Damien's face, his eyes flashing, and he grabbed hold of my arms to steady me.

"Easy, *mea luna*. Breathe."

Agonizing worry reflected in his eyes, and he seemed suddenly more concerned as his eyes danced between mine. My legs buckled under my weight, and he eased me to my knees. It was in that moment I realized my body was shaking uncontrollably. My eyes fell to my hands, quivering so badly I couldn't stop them.

Shit, I was going into shock.

"He... He did something to me, Damien. He g-got into my head..." I stuttered as I tried to speak. My grip on the world began to crumble around me as the weight of it all caved in.

Vincent knelt next to us. "It's ok, Cas. He's gone. You're safe now."

I stared blankly at him, and it took a moment for me to process his words. Damien's hand reached out, lifting my hair back, looking over my neck. I knew what he was checking for. He was checking to see if Marcus had bitten me. He hadn't... at least. I didn't think he had.

"Melissa... He... he killed Melissa." I looked up at Damien. "We can't leave her in there."

A growl slipped from Damien's throat. He wrapped his arms around me, trying to offer any comfort he could. All I could see was her lifeless body, her unseeing eyes, hear her screams still ringing in my ears.

"Don't worry. We won't leave her here. We'll give her a proper burial."

The touch of Marcus' hands... I could still feel it, the shackles he'd bound me in still stinging my wrists. I inhaled, breathes turning into shallow gasps, yet no oxygen found its way into my lungs.

Air. I needed air. I couldn't breathe. My lips started to tingle, a numbness branching out until all I could feel were pins and needles as they crawled out over my face. I panicked, grasping onto Damien.

"Cas? Cassie. Easy. Breathe slowly. In through your nose—" Damien's words were a flurry of panic as he braced me. "Shit, she's hyperventilating. Vincent, do you—"

Damien's voice became distant, and what little light the moon shined faded into darkness.

CHAPTER 22

Weightless, I drifted in the nothingness, darkness welcoming me into its embrace once more… as it always did. Images of what I'd seen in that strange dream of Damien and me on the battlefield flitted across my mind. The black blood painted sword, death filling the air, sorrow and fear holding me in its clutches. His voice called out to me, breaking the silence, piercing through the darkness holding onto me, clinging to me as if it never wanted to let me out of its clutches.

Lucia…

I clung to his voice, grounding myself to it if nothing else. My sense of self blurred into the void surrounding me. Images and thoughts continued to flash and overwhelm my mind, rushing over me like a heavy wind, and I couldn't help but be swept away in the current.

Agonizing pain ripped through my body, robbing me of my senses. A cry filled the room, echoing off the stone walls, and I realized it had been me who cried out.

Damien consoled me, gripping my hand tightly as I gasped. His free hand reached up to dab a cool, damp rag over my brow. I allowed myself to lean into it, giving in to the cool touch, sighing in relief at the momentary reprieve as I fell limp.

"You're doing amazing, *mea luna*. Hang in there, you're almost there," Damien coached, his voice gentle yet powerful, and it gave me strength to continue through the pain.

Sweat drenched my skin, soaking the fabric of my robes, and I couldn't so much as lift my head. A thin fog hung around us, leaving my view in a haze. Candles dimly lit the room, their warm glow dancing off the stone walls surrounding us. A woman draped in robes and cloth was crouched low, and bent over the foot of the bed, speaking commands to me. I strained to listen, but I couldn't make out what she was saying, her words somehow muffled.

"*Push*," Damien urged into my ear, holding me as I cried out, every muscle in my body contracting. My nails bit into his skin as I gripped his hand, clenching my teeth together before my lips parted to let out another cry of pain. The coiling in my muscles released, and I fell back on the bed, my limbs useless.

The softest cry reached my ears and a wave of emotions stretched out over me, consuming my heart and soul. My hair stuck to my skin, soaked and matted, and I tried to lift my head to look, desperate to see, but I didn't have the strength.

Gods, the room was cold. So cold...

The attendant spoke, but once again, her words were murky in my ears. Damien's forehead pressed gently to my cheek, the pride and love he felt thick in the air, and I breathed in the scent of his adoration, like the scent of sweet tobacco.

"She's beautiful," he breathed.

I couldn't respond, tears rolling down my cheeks as an unrelenting wave of joy, love, and adoration crashed through me.

Despite the sweat drenching my body, I continued to grow colder, my body shivering, teether chattering. I tried to reach for Damien, my hand quivering but unable to lift but a few inches from the blankets. Gods, I wanted him close to me, to feel his warmth. My lips had grown numb, and the sensation continued to spread through my body. My chest heaved as I breathed irregularly, and it grew harder to do so. I struggled to keep my focus, my eyelids flickering as they threatened to close without my permission.

I was so tired...

There was a flurry of movement as more people poured into the room, the attendant urgently calling for help.

Damien tensed at the words the attendant spoke. "What's wrong with her? *Mea luna*? Hey, stay with me, stay awake."

His hand patted against my cheek as my eyes fluttered, threatening to fall shut, and he gripped my hand desperately, gently shaking me.

I fought to keep my eyes open, and I managed to speak words, but they came on the voice of another. "*Mea sol*... Is she ok?"

"They're taking care of her. Stay with me, Lucia. I need you to keep your eyes open for me."

"I'm so... so tired..." I breathed.

"I know, I know," He moved suddenly, and the reflective glint of metal danced in the corner of my eye as he slit his wrist.

There was so much I wanted to tell him, but I could feel it creeping over me. My time was running out. That fear I'd felt on the battlefield crept into my chest, the dread at what I'd done.

Not yet... I wasn't ready. I wanted more time.

It took everything in me to speak the words I did, my voice breaking as I gasped for air. "Watch over her... please. Protect her. Protect... Emilia."

"Don't you dare talk like that. We're going to watch over her together." He pressed the wound to my lips. The sweet, metallic taste of his blood filled my mouth, overflowing and dripping down my chin. Gods, it tasted so good, but I... my fading strength wasn't enough to swallow, and the droplets trickled down my throat.

"Drink, Lucia, please!" Damien begged as I tried but failed to do so.

Shouts echoed in the room as people rushed around me, and the cries of the sweet babe faded into the next room. My eyes fell to the doorway.

No! Don't take her away. I want to see her... I want to hold her.

Damien wrapped his arms around me, lifting me from the bed, holding onto me tightly, as if his grip alone could tether me to this world. The life began to fade from my body, like a wave receding from the shore.

His agonized voice poured into my ear as he held me. "I can't lose you... not again."

"I love you... *mea sol*." The words floated on what little air I had left.

"Please, stay with me," he begged, holding me tightly. I wanted to stay, wanted to hold the sweet babe whose little face I hadn't even been able to see, but I couldn't hold on any longer.

He pressed his forehead against mine, as I gave into the exhaustion, my eyes fluttering closed.

The sounds of twigs and brush, bending and snapping, reached my ears, and the smell of stone and burning candles faded into that of

damp earth and trees. My eyes popped open, and I gasped for air. Panic shot through me at the feel of someone's arms around me. I was being carried. Where was I?

"Cassie? Cassie, you're ok! Easy!" The arms tightened around me as I fought against their hold, and they struggled to ease me to the ground.

"No! Let me go!"

I recoiled, but Damien planted his hands on my shoulders firmly, settling his face before me and I froze.

"They don't have you anymore. You're safe with us."

"Damien?" My voice shook as I dangled on the edge of an abyss. What was I safe from? Who didn't have me? I blinked, reality blurring, and I couldn't discern where I was or what was happening.

"Where—" I frantically looked around for the babe the attendants had taken from the room, tears now rolling down my cheeks, my voice shaken. "Where's Emilia?"

Damien froze at the name.

"*Mea luna...*" He paused, pain lacing his words, his eyes searching for strength as he began to waver. He took hold of my hands as he leaned into me. He didn't respond, couldn't seem to respond, for some reason.

Tears soaked my cheeks, and I realized I wasn't in the stone room anymore. I looked down at myself. Instead of robes I was dressed in a sweater and jeans. No longer was I in the bed where I'd laid in agony, bleeding out.

Dying...

We were surrounded by trees, by forest, the light of the full moon cascading down on us, and for some reason it felt as if it had been a lifetime since I'd seen it, since I'd smelled the grass and the trees, felt the breeze on my skin, hear the rustle and activity of the forest life.

My breath quickened as my mind seemed to rearrange itself, piecing everything back together until every detail of the present resurfaced.

What... who... I shook my head, blinking as I tried to reorientate myself, tried to ground myself as the effects of the vision began to ease, allowing reality back in. Yet the vision remained in the back of my mind, like a deep wound I might never heal from... but why? It had only been a dream. It wasn't real.

Had Marcus succeeded in driving me insane? What was real and what wasn't?

"What's happening to me, Damien?" I whispered.

I looked around when he didn't answer to see Barrett and Cole were nowhere to be found. Only Vincent and Zephyr stood nearby, seeming to give us space. Vincent's eyes lowered, unable to meet mine, but Zephyr watched me, the hurt in his eyes sinking into me.

"I'll explain, I promise, but I want to make sure you're all right first." Damien's words dripped with the same depth of pain that still clung to me.

It was a dream. Just a dream.

My hand slid down to my flat stomach where I'd carried a child just moments ago. To feel it that way was a painful reminder that I would never be able to bear a child myself, never get to have a family of my own.

Damien pressed his lips to my forehead and brought my face to his shoulder. "I was so scared I wouldn't find you in time."

We sat there like that for a moment, and he lifted his head, eyes passing over me in quiet assessment. "I know you're hurt, Cas. How bad is it?"

I smiled weakly. "I... Nothings broken. He always made sure not to break anything. Just cuts and burns mostly... some bruising."

My voice was even, too even, too numb. My eyes trailed over Damien. Sweat, dirt, and blood, marred his olive tone skin, which upon closer inspection appeared pale and duller than I remember. He looked exhausted. I noticed the rip in his shirt, a diagonal cut revealed a gash down his chest. Had Marcus pulled a knife on him during their fight?

"I should've fucking sank my blade between his eyes when I had the chance," he said through clenched teeth.

"How long did they have me for? What day is it?" I asked, guiding the conversation away from Marcus. Guilt replaced the worry, as his gaze slipped from mine. My heart crumbled at the sight of it.

He finally spoke. "We've been looking for you for nearly two weeks now."

Not even two weeks? Had it only been that long? It had felt like far longer... months, even. "Are my parents okay?" I asked.

"They're okay. They've been searching for you as well. I've had my teams combing the city for you at all hours. The last thing we wanted was for your parents or the police to find you. Gods forbid what could have happened."

My stomach flipped at the thought of it. It would have been a bloodbath if the cops had found us. Who knew how far Marcus would've gone? How many people would he have slaughtered? It was clear, he held no remorse, no morality, not with the things he did to me, the way he killed Melissa. Taking human life seemed no different to him than swatting away a fly.

"Come on, let's get you home," he said.

My hand involuntarily clutched his arm tightly, and I didn't move. My voice was weak, barely a whisper. "No."

He paused, brows furrowing as he looked back down at me. "No?"

"He was there," I said, struggling to get the words out of my mouth, my voice so low I didn't know if Damien could hear. "He was the reason I was waking up in the alleys those nights. He was in my room after they took me. My things were in my chambers. I don't want to go home. Please, Damien, don't make me go there."

His eyes widened, and the shadows around us seemed to twitch. "I knew he went to your house after you were taken, but that he was there before... Cole must have—"

He swallowed, remaining silent for a moment.

"You're not safe there then. If you want..." he hesitated. "You're welcome to stay at my place. I can set you up in a room. Or we can get you a room at The Complex, whichever you choose. We'll keep you safe, but your parents are terrified, and it'd be best if you at least saw them."

He was right. No matter how much I hated it, how much I dreaded the thought of them seeing me like this. I couldn't just avoid them. I missed them dearly, wondered how they were holding up, how Kat was doing.

I let loose a shaking sigh and nodded my head.

CHAPTER 23

The city blurred past us, my eyes unable to focus on the buildings, the lights, the few people. I slouched in the passenger seat of Damien's car as I watched them all, living their lives, completely unaware of the horrors that had just transpired. Damien drove in silence, and from the corner of my eye I'd caught him sliding worried glances my way every so often. My heart hammered in my chest as I chewed on my nail.

Returning home after everything that happened... what would I find there?

Damien had wanted to take me to Johnson, the doctor I briefly met at the apartment complex, to have me examined before we saw my parents. It was the last thing I wanted, though, to be inspected and exposed to more eyes. Instead, I'd allowed Damien to check me over in the forest to ensure nothing was broken or needed immediately attention, which seemed to satisfy his concern for now.

We managed to hide most of my wounds beneath my clothes—Damien adding his jacket as an additional layer, just in case. I couldn't bear for my parents to suffer the sight of the damage done to me, but it wasn't what caused dread to pool in my stomach. It was the images of Marcus standing in my room, touching my things, watching me sleep, that occupied my mind. Would he be there waiting for me when I opened my door?

Every instinct raged within me, begging me to stay away, but I had no other option. I had to return. I was desperate to see my parents, to know they were okay. I wondered how Kat was holding up. Had she been searching for me, too?

Damien's hand intercepted my fingers where my nails were near bleeding between my teeth.

"Your parents think we got separated in town on Halloween night," Damien explained, his eyes not leaving the road, his hand gripping mine reassuringly, and I nodded numbly. "The cops believe it was a trafficking ring that was responsible for your disappearance."

The car came to a stop in front of our house, but the little tan house no longer felt like home—like the place I could always find safety within no matter what. I sat there a moment, my eyes burning into the little porch, lit and waiting for me to come home, but I couldn't summon enough courage to do so much as move. The car door opened, and I lifted my gaze to find Damien extending his hand to me.

Hurt danced across his face as I hesitated to take it, nearly ready to sink back into the seat and never set foot on this sidewalk again.

"It's going to be ok, Cas," Damien said softly. "I'll be here. Every step of the way."

I swallowed, my eyes slipping past him, but nodded and took his hand. He helped me out of the car, and we headed up the stairs of the porch. From the outside it looked as if nothing had changed, as if nothing had happened... but so much had changed through the actions of one man, so much had happened—so much pain and fear seared into my mind, etched into my body.

My feet halted before my hand could take hold of the doorknob, trembles rattling down my fingertips as my mind spiraled with thoughts and images—images of me opening this door to find him waiting for me instead of my parents, images of my parents dead at his feet.

I took a step back.

No. No, it wasn't real. He couldn't be here.

Damien's hand brushed against my back, and I sucked in a breath before relaxing into his calming touch.

He leaned in to whisper. "I'm here. Every step of the way. You're free. You're safe. He can't touch you."

I nodded, steeling my nerves. He didn't have me anymore, I was free. And never again would he have his way with me.

He opened the door for me, and I peered inside hesitantly. "Mom? Dad?"

Chairs scraped against the floor in the kitchen in a flurry of movements the moment my voice breeched my lips.

"Cassie?" Mom peered from the kitchen, hesitating as if she thought she might be hallucinating. Our eyes met, and she cried out, "Oh my God!"

She rushed for me, followed closely by a distraught Kat, as if they'd been hoping with each passing minute that I might walk through that door. I stumbled as I stepped toward them, my knees nearly giving out as they threw their arms around me, pulling me tightly against them. Tears flowed down their cheeks, mixing with my own as we held each other closer.

Mom muttered unrecognizable words or relief, and she pulled back, her hands taking hold of my face as she looked me over.

"I'm okay, Mom. I promise." I forced a smile, my eyes burning as I tugged on my sleeve, fearing the bruises and marks might somehow be visible under Damien's jacket. There was something strange in the air, an almost balmy and icy feeling crawling over my skin, but as soon as the icky feeling of it set in, warmth washed over me, and I shivered. I blinked, questioning if I were imagining things.

"Oh my God, what did they do to your face?" Kat asked, nose puffy, eyes red.

"It's not as bad as it looks," I said, trying to calm her.

Mom released me, and I turned to watch her wrap her arms around Damien. "Thank you so much for finding her, Damien."

A big hand came to rest against my back, and my heart launched into my throat as I twisted around, grabbing hold of it. Dad hissed and I froze, realizing who it was. I hadn't seen him approach, too focused on Mom and Kat. His eyes widened, and I tensed as I realized how tightly I grasped his wrist. I recoiled, releasing my grip on him, and the hurt in his eyes as I shifted away twisted my heart.

"Sorry, I..." I hesitated but reached out for him, desperate to bridge the gap. "I didn't see you come up."

His eyes dipped hesitantly to my outstretched hands, before he pulled me into a tight hug and pressing a kiss to my forehead, silent tears rolling down his cheeks. "I didn't mean to scare you, baby girl. God, I'm glad you're home safe."

I wrapped my arms around him as he squeezed me. "I missed you so much."

"I missed you too," he breathed into my hair.

"Are you thirsty? Hungry? I'll make you some food." The words flew from my mother's mouth in a flurry as she looked from Damien to me. "You probably want a shower. Here, let me get your coat."

"No!" I stiffened, stepping out of her reach when she tried to remove it. "It's... It's ok. I'm actually a little cold. And I'm not hungry."

Her smile faltered, and her eyes flitted to Damien's before falling back to me, though I couldn't meet her gaze as I tugged the jacket around me tighter.

"Ok, sweetheart," she said, a hint of pain in her voice.

Kat's lips parted, but she seemed to halt whatever she was about to say, her eyes falling to the floor as she rubbed her arm. God, I hated to see her tiptoe around her words, as if I were the fragile piece of glass, something I never wanted to be to her.

"We. Uh... We put a kettle on the stove when we got the call from Damien. I... I could make tea," she said finally.

A weak smile spread across my face in response. "Thanks, Kat. Tea would be nice."

"I'll help you with that," Mom said, and Kat nodded before turning to return to the kitchen, Mom following after her.

We passed through the living room, and Dad groaned as he lowered himself onto the couch, seeming to return to the news as he worked on what I hoped would be his last cup of coffee so late in the night. Or, I guess, early in the morning...

Damien squeezed my hand. "I have to step out and make a few phone calls. Take all the time you need; visit with your mom and Kat."

I hesitated, my grip on his hand tightening, afraid to be separated from him again. He seemed to notice, for he didn't move, and instead leaned in. "I'm not going anywhere; I'll be just outside the front door. Zephyr and his team are standing guard nearby. He won't be getting anywhere near this street."

Zephyr's... team? I nodded, trusting his word, and my grip on his hand loosened.

He pressed a tender kiss to my forehead before he left me in the hallway.

I lingered there a moment, the walls too close, too narrow, and I hated how rattled I'd felt from the moment I set foot on the porch steps, the fear of rounding a corner to find Marcus waiting for my return. My hands balled into fists at my sides, anger simmering within me at the fear I couldn't seem to shake. I ground my teeth together, wishing it had been his head I'd slammed an iron into instead of Amara's.

The sound of glass clinking against the dining table drew me back to the present, and I peered into the kitchen. Mom and Kat sat at the table, Kat's hand running back and forth along Mom's back as she sipped from her tea. Mom looked as if she'd been dozing off, dark bags hanging under her eyes. Kat wore no makeup, her hair a mess tied in a bun, and I'd never seen her so ragged.

They perked up when I finally mustered the courage to enter the room.

"I'm so sorry," I whimpered at the exhausted sight of them, tears welling in my eyes.

My mom jumped up and rushed over to embrace me. "No, don't apologize. You did nothing wrong, sweetheart."

"I can't—" my voice broke as tears welled in my eyes, at a loss for words for how I would her that I couldn't stay here, that I couldn't handle being within these walls, so close to a place so tainted by Marcus.

She guided me over to the table, where Kat handed me a warm teacup, steam rising from the caramel-colored liquid. "I made it how you like."

"Thanks, Kat," I said, wiping the tears away before taking the cup. I inhaled a shaky, deep breath, my hands quivering.

"You can take a shower once you're done, I've cleaned up your old room upstairs, you can sleep there until we can figure things out..."

I stiffened at Mom's words, at the fact she intended for me to stay in my old room upstairs. "Sorry, but... I can't stay here. Not after everything."

Mom eased into the seat next to me, exchanging a look with Kat. While at first she appeared hesitant at my statement, her eyes softened. "I figured you could move back in with us until we get your apartment put back together."

My stomach flipped at the mention of my apartment, of it needing to be 'put back together'. What exactly had happened in there? Had Marcus done something to my apartment? My palms grew sweaty at the thought of it.

It didn't matter, either way. I couldn't live there anymore, couldn't live here. There would be no place within these walls that I would feel safe enough to be, let alone sleep. As long as Marcus walked freely, I knew he wasn't done with us—with me. He would be back.

"I'm sorry Mom, I just... it's too close, I'm barely handling being here right now."

"But maybe with time and some therapy—"

"Just stop," I bit out, my hands shaking under the table, and she blinked. "Please don't try to pressure me into this... I almost couldn't walk through that front door."

Hurt flashed across Mom's face and her and Kat exchanged nervous glances.

"I found out he somehow got into my apartment before he took me..." I admitted, and Mom stiffened. "That he..."

"Before?" she asked, eyes widening, and I nodded, my eyes falling to the table.

I blinked back tears, mustering every bit of courage to explain, to tell them, but the closer I coaxed the words to come out, the closer I came to breaking down, and my breathing became labored as the panic swelled in my chest. "Fuck. I can't talk about this right now."

"Cas, it's ok... you can talk to me."

"It's not ok, though. He's still out there. He knows my apartment. I can't..."

"You can move in with me," Kat offered, concern painting her face. "I have the spare room; I can clean my stuff out of it."

I lifted my gaze to her, and images of Marcus flashed through my mind. If there was one thing I knew about him, it was that he didn't quit until he had what he wanted. He would be back for me, and all I could imagine was him breaking into Kat's house to get me. What if she got hurt in the crossfire. She wouldn't stand a chance against him.

"Thanks, Kat, but..." I drew a shaky breath, blinking as I tried to shove back the tears. "I think I just need space right now."

My eyes fell to my teacup, and I chewed the inside of my lip as I prepared to lie if only to avoid the fight until I was in a better state of mind to discuss it with them. "Damien has some connections with some rentals in town, he's offered to get me into an apartment."

Kat's smile faded, and she slid a concerned glance to Mom. Something inside me hated the sight of it, that they felt they needed to make decisions for me, as if they understood what I'd been through.

Mom smiled softly, but she couldn't hide that motherly look in her hazel eyes. "That's very kind of him, but… are you sure? I don't know if you should be alone right now."

"I just need… I need space. I'm so messed up in my own head right now. I need to process everything that's happened. Please don't push me on this. I'll be ok. I just need time."

Mom sighed, and I internally cringed as what she might say. "You're an adult, Cas. I can't exactly tell you want to do, but… I just want you to be safe and happy. Maybe stay elsewhere for a few nights and we can revisit this conversation when you've had time to settle."

Kat stood, and I knew it was likely the awkward air that was pushing her to leave. "Um, it's getting late. I'm—" She slid an uncomfortable glance in Mom's direction before turning to me with an almost forced smile that hurt to look at. "I'm gonna head home. I just wanted to see you, to know you're safe."

"Thanks, Kat. Sorry you had to hear that," I said, offering her a smile. "And thanks for offering me a place to stay."

"It's no trouble, Cas, honest. The spare room's always open to you."

I nodded, and she drew closer.

"I'm so glad you're safe." She wrapped her arms around me, and I fought the urge to wince at the pain radiating from the sores and bruises as she hugged me tightly. "Text me tomorrow—wait… Shit, sorry. I guess you don't have your phone anymore…"

She continued to stumble over her words, and I squeezed her arm, her eyes snapping to me.

"It's ok. I'll get in touch with you as soon as I get a new phone."

A smile crept back across her face, and she nodded her head. "Okay. Let me know if I can do anything to help. I love you so much."

"I will. I love you so much, too. Thanks for being here for Mom."

She smiled, shrugging her shoulders. "Goodnight, Mrs. Hites. Let me know if there's anything I can do. I'll come by after work to help you with the clean—" She stopped herself, her eyes flitting to me, as if she realized her words, and I frowned, unease once again settling into the pit of my stomach.

"Thank you for everything, Kat," Mom said with a warm smile. "You drive safe going home, now."

"I will." Kat offered me one final smile before disappearing down the hall, and I couldn't help but feel as if something had just changed between us, as if she didn't know how to function around me.

Because to her, I was fragile now. Because to her, I might fall apart at any moment. Because I was broken... and would never be the same again.

"I'm happy you have Damien," Mom said, pulling me from my spiraling thoughts. "He never gave up on you, you know. I don't think he's slept much at all since you disappeared. Every morning I'd wake to find a text update from him, and he'd call throughout the day to see if we'd heard anything or had any new leads, sometimes he'd even stop in to check on us and make sure we were okay."

I smiled, warmth filling my chest at the thought of everything he'd done, how he'd not left them out and made sure they were safe and watched out for. "He's become special to me... I feel lighter when he's around, like I don't have to constantly think about my condition."

She reached out to run her hand along my shoulder.

"I've seen how you look when he's around, how you light up. I haven't seen you so carefree since before..." Her eyes dipped before she could say the words.

Before I was diagnosed. Before I knew that my life was coming to an end far earlier than it should. Before I started losing reason to look forward to each new day.

"Have you told him?" she asked.

I shook my head.

"You should tell him, sweetheart."

"I know," I said, my stomach twisting, and my fingers tightened around my teacup. "I've been trying to figure out how to tell him, then Halloween happened and I—" I drew a deep breath. "I don't want to talk about things, right now, Mom. I'm sorry, I'm just not in the right headspace to deal with this right now."

She gave an apologetic smile. "Sorry, sweetheart. I don't mean to stress you out; I just want to make sure you're going to be okay. I've respected your wishes to keep it a secret, but... it worries me sometimes. What if something happens and he doesn't know what to do?"

I didn't have a response for that, hadn't thought that far, I'd been so hung up on how much I feared he'd react to the news, whether he'd treat me differently, or... cut me out of his life.

Mom drew a deep breath, and I braced myself for what I knew she'd follow with. "I know you're going through a lot right now. I can only imagine what you've endured, but... I wish you'd take a bit more time to think this through, even if you just slept here until morning and we discussed it as a family when you've had rest."

My eyes fell to my teacup as I bit back my comment, fearful of what I might say under the haze of irritation and exhaustion.

"I just..."

I stiffened as her voice shook, my gaze snapping back to her. Tears welled in her eyes and the sight of it broke something within me. She lifted her hand to my face, and I flinched away from her touch on instinct. Her hand tensed, but before she could pull away, I took hold it, bringing her palm to my cheek.

"Sorry," I muttered.

A weak smile curved her lips as the tears rolled down her cheeks. "I thought I'd lost you. That you were never going to come home to me—to us. That you'd suffered alone, and I hadn't been able to be at your side in your final moments."

I wrapped my arms around her, and she held onto me, her body shaking as the sobs tore from her chest. There had been far too many times where I'd thought the very same thing, and though I wanted to comfort her, I couldn't even bring myself to think of anything to say.

She drew a deep breath after a while, and let out a shaky sigh as she wiped her face. "Sorry about that. I'm sure you're exhausted and want to get cleaned up. I have some things I'd like you to take. Some extra medicine as well."

"Thanks," I said as she rose from her chair, and I followed her into the living room.

"Damien still outside?" she asked, and I lifted my gaze to find Dad sitting alone on the couch.

He nodded, running his hand over his eyes as he yawned.

"Can you go get him? I have some things I'd like Cas to take with her. I could use some muscle."

My dad frowned, his attention drawing from the news as he looked up at us. "Take with her? Where's she going?"

I swallowed, opening my mouth to try to explain, but Mom spoke up for me. "Cas is going to go stay elsewhere, temporarily, to get her head straight."

"She's not going anywhere, she needs to be here with us," he said, rising from the couch.

"Dad, please, not now," I muttered as I took a step back. God, why was I flinching away from him? He wasn't going to hurt me. None of them were, and yet something within me had gone into a sense of high alert, my body prepared to defend itself or fight back.

"No, we're having this conversation right now. We just got you back. Look at you!" I stiffened as he gestured his hands to me, and I pulled Damien's jacket tighter around me. "You're traumatized, you look like you haven't eaten anything since you were taken. You need therapy, you need to get to a doctor and get checked ou—"

"Dad!" I shouted, and he halted. "I'm doing this. I can leave peacefully, or I can leave with a fight, but either way, I'm going to stay elsewhere."

He bristled, and something inside me coiled into itself, ready to strike, but I stifled the urge.

"He was here." The admission of it the first time had left me nauseous, but to do it a second time, it stoked the fire, the irritation and anger I felt for him.

Dad froze, his eyes slipping to Mom's who gave him a week nod before he looked back at me.

"He broke into my apartment before I was taken, was apparently stalking me for some time, had fucking watched me sleep a few times." Dad's hands curled into fists at his side. "I know he broke in again after I was taken, and from the way Mom and Kat were acting, I know it isn't pretty in there."

His jaw tightened, and he ran his hand over his face as he took a step back, and I hated that it gave me relief to feel the space. "Are you staying at Kat's?"

"It doesn't matter where I'm staying. You seem to forget I'm twenty. I can make my own decisions, and this is it. It's not up for discussion."

His mouth opened, but Mom stepped in, her hand lifting to his arm. She'd always been the peacekeeper when we argued, and I couldn't have felt more grateful for her than I did right then.

"Perhaps we should give her time to sort this out for herself," she said, the inner corners of her brows curving upward as she spoke. "Maybe we've kept her too close for too long."

His lips parted and closed as he "What about your cond—"

"Stop!" I bit out, my heart threatening to stop as the words almost left his lips, and he stiffened. My eyes flittered to the door, wondering if Damien could hear every word from where he stood outside.

I did my best to calm myself, not wanting to fight with them, not wanting any of this. "Thank you for everything, but this is what I need right now. You've done your best to give me room to breathe in the last few years, but after everything that's happened... I just need space right now. I need to work through this on my own. Please don't try to force me to stay. Don't make me go from one cage to another."

He flinched at my words, his mouth opening and shutting as he tried and failed to argue my wishes. "Fine. Just... promise me you'll check in."

"I will," I said, fidgeting with the sleeve of Damien's jacket. "Nothing's set in stone right now."

"I'll... get Damien, I guess," he said reluctantly, turning his back. "Dad?" I started.

He halted his steps, glancing over his shoulder. "Yeah?"

"Maybe," I hesitated, hoping this little bit might give him some comfort or reassurance that just because I was leaving, it didn't mean he was losing me. "When I've sorted through everything, and I figure out what I'm doing... maybe we can try to go stargazing again. Like we used to."

His eyes softened, and a gentle smile tugged at his lips. "I think that'd be a great idea, baby girl."

I smiled and watched as he headed for the door, guilt curdling my stomach at how I'd just handled that. Was this the right decision? Or was I hurting my parents more by doing this? My hands tightened into fists at my sides as I swallowed the guilt down before it could fester.

No. This was my life. From now on, I wouldn't let anyone else make decisions for me, wouldn't let other's feelings be the thing that dictated how I lived my life. I would decide what I did with my life moving forward. It was mine, and I only had so much of it left. They would have to accept that.

"I'll be right back," Mom said, and I nodded as she headed up the stairs.

Just as Dad and Damien returned, Mom came down the steps with a box in her hand. "This is a few of the things we managed to save. It's probably best you don't go in there."

Damien's eyes fell to the box, as he drew a deep breath, and from the corner of my eye, I noticed his hand form into a fist at his side before he stretched his fingers back out.

"I'll go ahead and take this to the car," he offered, taking it. He turned to head for the entry, the moment he was out the door she turned to me, pulling her hand from her pocket.

"Here are your spare bottles. Be sure to call the doctor so he can order you another prescription before you run out."

I nodded, taking the bottles, and pushing them into the pocket of Damien's jacket. "Thank you."

She let out a heavy sigh. "And please think about what I said."

"Okay."

"Damien's got my number stored in his phone, call me as soon as you're able," Mom said, her words a near plea.

"I will," I said, my eyes growing heavier.

"You ready?" Damien asked as he returned.

I nodded and wrapped my arms around mom as I hugged her goodbye.

"It'll be okay," Mom said, and I forced a smile for her sake.

"You'll get through this, baby girl," Dad added as he pulled me into a hug. "You're tough, but we're here for you, when you're ready. We'll take it one step at a time."

"I know, Dad," I said, my eyes burning as I pulled away.

I waved to them as I headed toward Damien, and the moment he closed the front door behind us, I couldn't help but feel like we were closing the door on a part of my life that would be forever changed. Would I ever be able to set foot within my apartment again without thinking of Marcus? My eyes slid to the door next to my parents', and while I was terrified to think of it, a part of me was curious at just what Marcus had done in there. I turned, walking for the door, but Damien's hand took mind before I could grab hold of the knob.

"Don't..." he breathed, and I looked up at him. "It's not... It's not something you need to see."

"What exactly did he do in there?" I asked, and something strange wound tighter in my chest until I thought it might combust—a burning hatred that had been festering ever since Marcus had first taken me. I was terrified, yes, but a part of me needed to know, needed to stoke the fire for that moment when I would get my revenge for everything he'd done to me.

"He..." A muscled feathered in Damien's jaw. "He destroyed everything. James got a hit on his computer, and we scrambled the cops' system so we could comb the place before they could."

"Everything?" I breathed.

He nodded, guilt marring his face.

I turned to him, my stomach sinking. "My art supplies? What about Kat's portrait? My books?"

His throat bobbed, and he shook his head. "Destroyed."

I couldn't form words, my fingers digging into Damien's sleeves as anger swelled in my chest, burning in a way that I wanted Marcus to. Damien pulled me into his arms as I stood, frozen on the porch, tears threatening to fall again. I hated them, hated that I couldn't do more than cry in my anger, in my frustrations at what Marcus had done to me, to what I once called home, to my life.

"Fuck," I breathed, the tears coming harder and the more they fell, the angrier I felt. "*Fuck!*"

Difficult wasn't enough to describe the pain I felt. I'd always known a day would come when I'd walk out that door, never to return. I just hadn't been ready for that moment. Not yet.

My parent's front door clicked, and I pulled away from Damien, quickly running my hands over my face to wipe away the tears as Mom stepped out.

"Sorry, I didn't mean to bother you, sweetheart," Mom said as she hesitated in the doorway. "But I forgot something and wanted to catch you before you left."

That strange balmy feeling coated my skin again, as if the air had become so humid and muggy that I felt sick, and I frowned at the way it left my stomach uneasy, like something was wrong.

"I'm sure you're tired, but the police are going to want to take a report. Damien told me the guy ran when they found you." She took my hand, my heart plummeting into my stomach at the thought of talking to the police when I just wanted to be left alone. "I figured it might be better, while any details are fresh in your mind. Do you think you can handle it?"

I glanced at Damien, who gave me a reassuring nod, and I drew a deep breath. It was just one more thing, one more thing and then I could leave.

"Okay..."

CHAPTER 24

It was around three in the morning when we finally made it back to Damien's house. My mind replayed everything I'd told the deputies, for fear that I might have slipped something inconsistent or risked exposing Damien's world. They'd been patient and accepting of the answers I'd given them, but the anxiety remained. I wasn't aware whether I'd breathed or not during our interaction with them, and it was a relief that they'd believed the lies I fed them.

I blinked, realizing that I'd walked in a daze all the way to the second floor, unaware of my own movements. Damien's room looked untouched, and by the shadows under his eyes and sluggish movements, I imagined he hadn't slept much since I'd been taken.

Silence filled the air as I watched him pull concealed knives from beneath his clothes and lay them out atop his dresser. I took a step toward him, wanting to say something, anything, but the words seemed to lie just outside my reach.

What could I say? That I missed him? That not a moment had gone by that I didn't think of him? How I'd wished every moment that I'd spent more time with him, thinking I may never see him again? That more than anything, I just wanted to hold him, to feel him? To know that he was real, not another dream.

He disappeared into his bathroom. The sound of water splashing off the tile echoed out into the room as he turned the faucet on, filling the tub. He returned, heading for his dresser before he rummaged through his drawers in silence.

"Sorry for the mess," he said, offering me a guilty grin before he pulled some clothes from his dresser and motioned me to follow him into the bathroom.

The bathroom was just as stunning as the rest of the house, draped in gray tones with rich brass accents. A large, gold, ornate mirror hung from the gray wall above the vanity, and just past it, against the far wall, stood a large shower, but it seemed like it was also a tub and my eyes passed over it, taking it all in. I'd never seen such an enormous tub. The shower head was accompanied by three faucets already working hard to fill it.

Damien reached into one of the cabinets as he fished out a towel for me to use and set it on the vanity. "That should do it. Go ahead and take a good soak. I'm going to prepare the spare room for you." He kissed my forehead tenderly before walking past me. My heart sank as he neared the door. What if he walked out that door and never returned? What if he left and Marcus returned in his place? What if—

"Wait," I said, twisting around to him.

He stopped in the doorway.

"Please don't go..."

He hesitated but looked back at me. "Are you sure?"

Was I? My hands trembled still, and I only grew more and more frustrated that I couldn't stop it. "Please, Stay... I don't want to be alone."

A sort of pain touched his eyes, and he nodded before he stepped back into the bathroom. "I'm not going anywhere. I'll turn around, let me know when you're in the bath."

A sense of relief washed over me at his reassurance, and I inhaled deeply, calming my nerves. He turned his back to me, allowing me privacy, an I started to undress. My muscles protested and my joints popped with each movement, but I managed.

The bath was already mostly full by this point. He must have added something to the water, for it was white and murky, and the soothing aroma of rosemary and lavender filled the room. I stepped in, warmth sweeping through me, and a sigh of relief escaped my lips as I lowered myself down into the bath.

The water met my wounds, and I winced at the sting. The pain of my bruises ebbed, but the cuts littering my skin stung deeply, and I forced myself to breathe through it. Once the pain subsided, the heat of the water began to soothe aches and soreness in my body. It burned away the horrible sensation lingering on my skin, and I didn't want it to stop. I wished it could erase every mark on my skin until nothing remained... until I was clear and new.

"I'm in," I said as I turned the faucets off.

He didn't turn around immediately, and I saw as he drew a deep breath before turning to face me. He seemed to hesitate before he approached the tub, settling down on the floor next to it. I drifted closer to him, raising my arms to rest atop the ledge. I laid my head against them, closing my eyes as I let the heat consume me. The moment I closed my eyes, my body started to give into its exhaustion, but before I could relax into it a flicker of fear prevented me from letting sleep claim me.

What if I woke up, and I was back in the cell?

Damien reached out to take my hand, holding it as he rested against the edge of the tub. The tender touch grounded me, proving that this wasn't a dream. I was safe... and it was all thanks to him.

I'd barely known him a month, but despite that, Damien had come for me. He never gave up on me when I'd nearly given up on myself. He'd faced so many dangers to ensure that I was brought home safely.

He traced his fingers along the back of my hand in gentle sweeps. I opened my eyes to look at him, to see his pained eyes moving over the markings on my wrists from the shackles. I could see his mind working through the possible causes of the wounds.

"About what the deputy said." His eyes slipped from mine, his words trailing off. "About the rape kit..."

My skin tightened as the memories resurfaced, when the deputy had tried to talk me into going to the hospital, my throat going dry at the thought.

"He didn't..." He couldn't finish the sentence.

My eyes fell to the tile floor, and I retracted my hands. I'd caused him so much pain when I'd been taken, and the sight of me only seemed to hurt him more.

"He never touched me like that."

This was exactly what Marcus had wanted. To get under Damien's skin, and he'd succeeded.

"I'm so sorry this happened," he said, voice faltering. "I should have been more careful, should have—"

"Damien, this wasn't your fault."

"It is my fault. Because I couldn't protect you. Because I was careless. I should've erased your memory that night, moved you and your family elsewhere far away from this city and Marcus, far away from this mess, where you could be safe. I should've seen the warning signs with Cole. I can't believe he—" His words faltered, and he let out a long breath.

A painful silence was left in the wake of his words, the only sound that of water droplets falling from the faucets to the pool below. I sat at the ledge of the tub; my chest pressed against the tile. Guilt and sorrow marred Damien's face as his eyes moved over me.

I pushed off the tub's ledge, turning to the back of the shower in the water. "Get undressed."

"What?"

"You're in just as rough of shape as I am, and I feel terrible being clean while you sit there like that." I mustered as much confidence as I could. "Now get undressed. This tub is plenty big enough for both of us to get cleaned."

I closed my eyes, tilting my head back into the water to wet my hair, losing myself in the sensation of being able to properly bath again.

As I lifted my head from the water, fabric shuffled behind me, and the unzipping of his pants reached my ears. I focused on my breathing, the sound sending my heart into a frenzy.

Oh my God, had I really just told him to get in the tub with me? This was fine. It wasn't right for me to be clean while he was still covered in sweat, dirt, and what blood he'd missed cleaning off before we got to my parents' house. I swallowed, my heart launching itself into my throat as I returned to the thought that he was just feet from me, fully undressed...

The water rose as he sank down into its depths. My heart thumped wildly, my senses heightening until I could almost feel the narrow distance between us.

"I don't blame you," I said, running the water over my arms.

The water rippled as he moved behind me, his hands coming to rest against both sides of my upper arms, and he tenderly kissed the top of my shoulder. "I still disagree that I wasn't responsible but thank you for that."

Damien reached over, grabbing a bottle of shampoo, and poured some into the palm of his hand before reaching up to massage it into my hair. God, he was so gentle, so tender and careful as he worked around the area where I was still healing as best as he could. I closed my eyes, the feel of his fingers against my skin relaxing me down to my bones. My shoulders went slack, and I hadn't realized how tense I'd been.

I can't lose you... not again.

The echo of Damien's voice danced again through my mind. Everything I'd seen in the dreams had felt so painfully real. The moments after I'd awoken were a bit of a blur, and I barely remembered what I'd said to him in the forest, but I remembered how fresh the terror felt, how death felt. I'd felt it once before... had happily forgotten it.

The question lingered on my lips, but I was too scared to ask, wasn't ready to talk about whatever it was that I saw. Not now. Too much had happened, and I just wanted to feel some semblance of normalcy. Even if just for tonight.

Tomorrow... Tomorrow, I would face my demons.

Tonight? Tonight, was for me to be with him, to live when I'd accepted that I'd die before I could again, to just be myself, to escape the reality of what I'd faced over the last two weeks. I wanted to gaze upon his face and know that if nothing else, he was my reality.

Warm water cascaded over me as he washed the shampoo from my hair, and he followed it with conditioner, combing his fingers through my curls. My heart swelled at the affection that poured into me with each touch.

"It's your turn." I turned around to him, staying low in the water so I remained hidden from his view, the murky water the only thing giving me confidence at this point. He sat unmoving, his eyes meeting mine for a moment, and he settled back against the wall of the tub, his arms lifting to rest on the ledge.

My eyes wandered across his face, down to the wound on his chest. I cupped my hands, lifting water to pour over it. He closed his eyes, breathing deeply.

I tensed, halting my movements. "Sorry, does it hurt?"

He gave a subtle shake of his head, his eyes remaining closed. "It's fine. This is nothing."

His words were almost too painful to absorb—the truth that they exposed. This likely wasn't the worst injury he'd sustained in his lifetime, and it likely wouldn't be the last.

I grabbed the soap, lathering it into a bath sponge. His eyes followed my movements as I returned to him, gently working it over his skin, washing away the dirt and sweat. I did my best to avoid the gash, washing around it. His skin was so soft, slick from the bath, his tight muscles shifting under my touch. My palm settled against his chest, his heart racing beneath the surface just as mine did, and it made me smile.

The raw power of him was electric under my fingertips, power that I still hadn't been able to fully comprehend, power I'd seen kill with my own eyes tonight. Yet, knowing what I did, it didn't scare me.

I knew this dangerous creature, more than I could explain. There wasn't a doubt in my mind that he would never hurt me. No matter what.

"Turn around," I said. He did, and I glided the sponge over his back, the suds slipping down his olive skin into the pool of water below. I hated how pale he looked. Had he not been taking care of himself all this time?

He tilted his head back as I reached my fingers into his hair. I pushed myself up and the cold air nipped at my exposed body. Hesitation coiled in my body, leaving me tense, but his back remained turned. I knew he couldn't see my nakedness, but I tried to focus on massaging the shampoo into his scalp as my heart continued to race. It was all too tempting to let my eyes wander over his exposed flesh, his broad shoulders. His lashes lowered against his cheeks as he closed his eyes. A heady sigh left him, his shoulders relaxing, and it gave me some relief that I could aid in easing his stress even if only just a little.

Once I was done, he washed his hair out and sat back up, running his fingers through his dark waves. It took everything in me to resist the urge to reach out and touch him.

I dipped my head back, washing the conditioner from my hair, and as I came back up, I became aware of his presence closing in on me.

Marred and naked before him, I fought the urge to sink into the water until I vanished from his sight. The water's surface rippled in his movement, the surface reaching just above my breasts.

His hands glided just beneath the water, reaching for my own. Before I could pull away, he took hold of my hands and lifted my arms up above the milky surface. I resisted, not wanting to see the reminders of what had been done to me, but it did little as he held them up between us. He dipped his head, his lips gently brushing over each bruise, cut, and scrape, attending to each lovingly.

"For each wound they left, *mea luna*." He kissed my wrist. "I swear I will give them tenfold."

My chest swelled, my heart fluttering at his words, at the feel of his lips against my skin. He lifted his gaze to me, and I wanted to lose myself in those eyes, let the embers in that ashen silver claim me in their heat. I didn't care if nothing of me remained.

He turned my hands over, lifting them up to press his lips to my knuckles as he breathed deeply. "Dammit, I can still smell him on you." He pressed his forehead against my hands as he tried to calm himself.

A part of me was nervous of the heat his words aroused in me. Though he struggled to contain the primal urges he was combatting, I could feel my own need just beneath the surface, my thoughts warring with one another as to whether this was right, whether I should be sitting here with him like this. The feel of Marcus' hands lingered on my skin, and though I was sore and tired, I didn't want to feel that anymore. I wanted to feel Damien's hands, his kisses, his skin against mine. I needed the distraction, needed something else to think about, something else to feel, if only to erase it.

I lifted my eyes to him, and my heart danced in my chest. Was it right of me to want this after everything? I'd accepted death, had accepted that I likely wouldn't make it out of that compound tonight...

Damien's eyes flitted to my lips, and he drew closer. When I didn't pull back, when I didn't resist his gaze, he leaned, brushing a kiss to my lips. Something possessive took hold of him as his tongue swept, the kiss deepening. My heart soared and I ensnared my fingers in his hair, pulling him against me. I wanted to feel him, to feel something, to erase the remnants that lingered on my skin.

I needed it more than I probably should.

He broke the kiss, but it was as if he couldn't pull himself away fully. "We should stop. I can't... I don't..."

I lifted my hand to his cheek as he seemed to war with himself. We sat there a moment, breathless as we stared into each other's eyes, standing at the end of the line that we would never come back from. Was I ready for that?

God, yes I was, but...

My eyes drifted from his, but he hooked my chin with his finger, lifting my gaze to him.

"When you're ready," he breathed, as if reassuring me. "Don't think I don't want you. Gods, I want you more than anything, but not like this..."

I nodded, warmth filling my chest at the tenderness in his voice. He wrapped his arms around me, and I leaned into his embrace, drowning myself in his scent and allowing it to settle me. My body began to sag against his, the exhaustion settling into my bones.

"Just a bit longer and you can rest. I'll step out and dress outside the door to give you privacy," he said, reluctantly pulling away. I didn't want him to leave, didn't want this moment to end, but I nodded and shifted back before my back to him.

The sound of the water rolling off his body and falling into the pool echoed off the tile as he rose, and I resisted the urge to look over my shoulder, my cheeks warming at the thought of what I would find. Just a short moment later I heard the door open, and I stiffened, the fear welling in my chest.

"I'm just outside the door. You're not alone," he said, and I smiled at his reassurance.

"Thank you," I breathed, and the door shut.

My body didn't want to obey my command, but I forced myself to rise to my feet and unstopped the drain. Just a bit longer and I could rest. I dried off and quickly dressed myself in the clothes Damien laid out for me, the familiar feel of his oversized sweatpants causing my heart to flutter and a smile to curve my lips.

The floor was icy beneath my feet as I stepped toward the door and knocked.

"I'm decent," he said, and I opened the door to find him waiting for me.

"I'm sure you're exhausted," he said, almost awkwardly, running his hand over the back of his neck. "Umm. I know you don't want to be alone, but..."

My stomach twisted at the thought of being alone right now, and I wrapped my arms around myself. "I don't want to make you uncomfortable."

His eyes flashed to me, and he stepped closer, his hands rising as if he wanted to console me. "That's not what I—"

I lifted my eyes to him as he struggled to find the right words.

"If you want, we can set you up in the guest bedroom, I can sleep on the floor in the hall to give you privacy until you feel well enough."

"Oh, no. I don't want you to sleep on the floor—"

"And I don't want you to suffer," he said, his hands coming to rest on either of my arms, his face grave as he stared down at me. Air rushed into my lungs, and I hesitated.

"Tell me what you need. Don't think you're inconveniencing me. Whatever you need of me, I will happily see it done. You want me on the floor next to your bed I will be there, you want me to sit outside your door all night, then I shall stand guard. If..."

222

His eyes slid from me as he hesitated, "If you want me to hold you until you fall asleep, I can do that. If you don't want me to leave your side, then at your side I shall remain, until you are ready to face your demons on your own."

A smile tugged at my lips, tears dotting my eyes as I wrapped my arms around him.

"Don't leave me tonight," I said, the admission somehow giving me a sense of relief. "Keep me company. I don't care where we sleep."

"Then this bed—" he smiled as he nodded to his bed beside us. "Would be the better option as I'd prefer not falling off the tiny twin in the guest bedroom in the middle of the night."

A snicked bubbled up my throat. "Awe. So chivalrous until faced with the possibility of falling out of the bed for me."

"You don't seem to realize that I've already fallen for you." He said, pinning me with his gaze and I stilled. "I fell so hard and fast, and I don't regret it one bit. I'll do it again and again if I had to. There is no reality, no realm that exists where I wouldn't fall for you."

I swallowed, the depth of his words washing over me. A smile tugged at my lips, and I lifted my hand to touch his face.

"I..." I didn't know how to respond to that, didn't know how to put words to the feelings churning inside me.

"You don't have to say anything," he said. "Don't think I said it expecting something in response. As I said before, when you're ready... If you're ever ready, then you can cross that bridge."

How could he be so patient? How could he do so much and expect so little? He pressed a kiss to my forehead, and I melted into the sensation, before he released me to head to the bed. Maybe one day I could give myself wholly to him. I wanted to. Wanted to give him everything, every piece of me.

My heart fell into a heavy rhythm as I turned to the bed, watching him pull back the comforter. I swallowed and headed for the other side, trying not to think too deeply into it. It was just sleep, it wasn't like anything was happening.

The mattress sagged under me as I climbed into the bed, and I nearly moaned at the feel of it. Damien watched me with a somber smile as I melted into the blankets, relishing in their warm embrace. God, it was so soft, and the moment I closed my eyes, it was almost difficult to open them again.

Damien scooted closer under the comforter, and I found myself gravitating to him, wanting to feel his warmth. I nestled against his chest, and he wrapped his arms around me, pulling my closer to him.

"Try to get some rest," he whispered, pressing a kiss to my forehead.

"I want to, but..." I swallowed, my thoughts threatening to drift from this safe haven I'd found myself in within his arms. A part of me was content, safe in his arms, while another part of me dreaded what always followed when I awoke from sleep. What if all this was a dream?

Damien pulled me close against him. "Would you like a distraction?"

A hint of a smile tugged at my lips, and I settled my palm against his chest. His heart raced beneath my touch, nearly as fast as mine was. "What sort of distraction did you have in mind?"

"A story," he said as he ran his fingers through my hair. I closed my eyes, melting into the sensation of his touch.

I hummed. "What kind of story?"

"An old legend that's been passed down from generation to generation by the immortals."

"Consider my interest piqued," I teased.

"Many centuries ago, there was a kingdom. A kingdom of beings born of powers that rivaled even the Gods. This kingdom was prosperous, powerful, and they thrived in a way that few could hope to. Many craved what they had, tried to bring them down, but failed."

My eyes fluttered, but I didn't allow myself to give into the exhaustion sinking into my bones, curious about this kingdom he spoke of.

"Within the kingdom lived a princess, and her people treasured her above all else. She was powerful, and kind, and would do anything for her people. She wasn't like the rest, though, for you see, she was a gift from the Gods, blessed with more than anyone could bear. The weight of it sometimes bore down on her, and at times it became too much, but she rarely let it show, always smiling, always shining for her people, giving them hope."

He ran his fingers through my hair, drawing out the strands of damp curls before letting them fall over my shoulder, and continued again.

"The Kingdom worshipped a Goddess, the very one who gifted them this special princess who would defend them from anything that would bring them any harm. The Ruler of the kingdom fell in love with The Princess, and when she returned his affection, they became one, forming a union more powerful than the foundations of their realm. Together they ruled as king and queen, bringing about an even greater strength to their kingdom. Though few tried to break them, they failed, and The King and Queen saw many years of prosperity."

"Sounds sweet," I muttered, realizing I'd let my eyes fall shut at some point, but I held out, waiting for him to continue.

"The Kingdom's happiness could only last so long, though. A great evil crept into their domain, and The King and Queen's bond and protection over their people was tested. Darkness swept across the kingdom, destroying everything in its path, and The King and Queen were torn apart, The Queen falling to that very darkness."

Something stirred in my chest, and I lifted my eyes to him. "What happened?"

"The Goddess passed down another blessing, but this blessing was so powerful, and balance had to be maintained, so a curse was laid

224

down as well. The King was bound to where he resided, waiting for the time when his queen would return to him."

"Did she ever return?" I asked.

He smiled, running his fingers through my hair once more, the sensation leaving goosebumps trailing over my skin. "She did, and they were happy, but there are many evil things in the world, and time and time again they were torn apart. And so The King was left to wait for his queen to return to him, cursed to live on without her."

"That's terrible."

"It is... but he never gave up hope that she would one day find him again. And he spent the rest of his days searching for her, until she would return to him, and he could feel whole again."

I laid there a moment, my heart heavy as I imagined being separated from someone I loved time and time again. "That's such a depressing story. Is this really what immortals tell their children at bedtime?"

He snickered. "It is one of many stories, but this particular story gives them hope."

I lifted my head to rest my chin atop his chest as I cocked an eyebrow at him. "How does it give them hope?"

"That, though dark times come, hope will always return."

CHAPTER 25

The sun's late morning rays leaked through the curtains onto me, and it was a relief to wake to sunlight for once, to the sound of birds chirping in the maple trees just outside the window. My eyes felt heavy as I opened them, and I was half tempted to just let them remain closed.

The night had been rough. My sleep wasn't as restful as I'd hoped, and true sleep had evaded me. The constant interruptions and irregular sleep patterns Marcus had subjected me to had thrown my internal clock out of balance.

I should have been able to sleep through the night for how exhausted I'd felt, but I'd only managed to sleep for an hour or two at a time before waking up, sometimes feeling startled and disoriented, forgetting that I was safe, that I was home. Damien had been there to comfort me every moment, somehow always knowing how to bring me back to him, but I couldn't help but feel guilty for interrupting the rest he needed.

Damien lay plastered against my back. My cheeks heated when I noticed his arm draped over my hip, his hand tucked between my legs, his fingers pressed into the space between my thighs. Heat coiled low, my heart leaping as I imagined what if would feel like if there were no clothes dividing us. He didn't move, and I realized he was fast asleep. Every muscle in my body was sore, every bone ached deeply, and I it took everything in me just to shift and turn to him.

His face looked more peaceful than I'd ever seen it, and I absorbed every perfect detail. I inhaled the rich scent of him, that warming hint of cedarwood and leather lingering in the air around us, in his shirt that I wore.

I lifted his arm, placing it on the pillow as I sat up. He groaned but didn't wake, and a lock of my hair slipped from behind my ear as I lowered myself to leave a soft kiss atop his brow. A lazy grin tugged at his lips as he shifted, and a soft, sweet sound left him, but he remained asleep.

This was likely the first time he'd gotten a proper rest in weeks, and I wanted to let him rest. I pushed myself to the edge of the bed, moving the blankets to cover him again. The cool air chilled my skin as I rose, needing to use the restroom.

As soon the door clicked behind me I found the coat Damien had loaned me laying on the floor with my discarded clothes. I grabbed it and fished my medicine from the pocket. For a moment I remained in place, my eyes glued to the orange bottles I hated so much. What was I going to do with these? I wasn't sure where my things might go while I lived here. I quickly downed the two pills and looked around for a place to hide them for now. Dammit, what was I doing? I needed to tell him, but there was so much to deal with right now… too much.

One bridge at a time.

Soon. I would get there, I just needed to get through this, figure out what was happening and where I was going. I just needed to find the right words when the time was right. When we weren't dealing with Marcus and the possibility of darklings attacking our city. My heart twisted with guilt as I opened the cabinet before stashing them back and out of view behind one of the drawers.

When I re-emerged from the bathroom, Damien was still resting easy in bed, the sound of his steady breathing the most reassuring sound. A strange urge came across me to cook him breakfast, to feed him in bed and tend to him. I wanted to do so much for him, anything I could to make him feel good, to show my appreciation, to express my feelings for him, though I wasn't entirely sure what those feelings were. They were a whirlpool, one so turbulent and chaotic that I couldn't seem to fully grasp each emotion that surged to the surface in his presence.

I headed for the doorway, fully intent on cooking him breakfast, but my feet slowed as I passed the glass display case full of daggers and swords, and I lifted my gaze to the short sword at the top. The beautiful gold and black design of the blade I'd seen the last time I was in his room drew me in, as if it called to me. The familiarity of it tugged at something in the back of my mind. I opened the glass door and reached up to it, running my fingers across the carvings in the metal, over the symbols cast in gold, and the metallic crescent moon shining in the center of the intricate patterns.

The image of the same sword, dripping blood in my hand, flashed in my mind from the vivid dream of standing on that desolate battlefield. Though I hadn't inspected it in the vision, there was no doubt this was the sword I'd held. Surely it had been a coincidence. I'd seen this sword before I had the dream, it was just my imagination, a result of the manipulations Marcus had started working into my mind that night.

It wasn't real.

I stretched to my toes, reaching up to take the sword in my hands, and brought it down to inspect it closer. Light shimmered across the metal as I turned it over, holding it level in front of me.

"Elena."

I turned to find Damien standing before me, his brow cocked as he looked at me expectantly. His hair was half pulled back, tied out of his face and he almost looked... different. Not younger, just different. A loose black tunic hung from his torso, the collar wide with the top few buttons undone. His long sleeves were rolled up to his elbows, so they were out of his way, and his shirt was tucked loosely into black pants that hugged his legs down to the black leather boots.

"You're daydreaming on me again. Come on. Let's get back to it now," he said, firming his grip on his short sword. He paced around me before stopping, waiting, as he widened his stance. The subtle accent I was used to was a bit stronger now.

Stone walls surrounded us, mountains barely peeking above them in the distance. The ground was barren dirt beneath our feet, having been stomped free of any vegetation from the endless traffic of people long ago. Old wooden houses stood nearby within the safety of the walls, nestled close together. The faint smell of smoke from nearby fire pits and torches reached my nose. People came into view in the distance, men and women walking together around the houses to where I couldn't see. The women wore the most beautiful gowns, their arms laced with the person they accompanied.

My eyes fell to my hands, my fair skin covered in dirt and sweat from hours of training. A thick, pale blonde braid hung over my shoulder, reaching down to my ribs, and I was clad in black attire similar to Damien's.

"Pay attention, Elena!" Damien demanded as he stepped forward, swinging the sword down on me.

Instinct took over, my body moving on its own, sword rising to meet his in the air to stop his blow. He shifted, sliding the blade down before turning it to move past my block. I dodged and stepped back as he advanced, moving the blade to deflect each blow he made. The sound of metal ringing with each swing echoed throughout the training yard as we stepped around each other, and our blades bounced off one another as we circled and evaded the blows we exchanged.

At the last step, as his blade hit mine once more, he stopped his advance. He lifted his blade from mine, lowering it to his side, and he smiled down at me. "Good, good. Your form is getting better. Let's see if your footwork's improved."

He advanced again before I could think, and I ground my teeth together as I braced myself. His sword spun lithely in his hand before he swung it from the right, and I parried swiftly, stepping back.

"Don't doubt yourself! Push me back, Elena!" Lucia! The two names overlapped in my mind, his voice blurring together, causing me to stumble, my hand rising to my head.

I bit my lip, shaking it off as I shifted my stance and listened to his words. My feet planted firmly in the dirt as I held my ground, absorbing the weight of his blade against my own as he swung once more. He'd taught me that while I was small, I could use my opponent's strength against them. I intended to do just that, moving my blade to the side each time I blocked him, and his weight behind it caused him to falter when I released him away from me.

I tilted my sword, swinging it around to the left. He met it easily. I swung it down. He blocked. I continued swinging and spinning in an attempt to catch him off guard, using everything he'd taught me, but, Gods, the lazy grin on his face as he blocked each and every move made my blood boil.

We'd fought side by side for years. He'd taught me everything I knew, and my mind flew through it all, using every last bit of it to try to beat him. I stepped to the side in a rush of a spin, and I ducked under his arm. The dirt kicked up as I spun around gracefully, feet falling perfectly into step beneath me, and I rose my blade to hold it at his throat. Without so much as turning to me, he flipped the sword in his hand.

Our blades met before I could reach him.

My jaw tightened, irritation clouding my head. Gods, he made it look so effortless to stave off my attacks. I panted, tired and worn, and my hands quivered as I gripped the hilt of my sword. No matter how hard I worked, I couldn't best him.

I yelled as I stepped to swing again.

"Cas?"

I whipped around at the voice behind me, the fresh adrenaline fueling me as I swung the sword into my new opponent.

Damien caught the blade in his hand before it could hit him. I froze, chest heaving as our eyes met. He braced the blade as I stood frozen, my eyes passing over him. He was shirtless before me, loose sweats hanging around his hips. My eyes darted over our surroundings, the smell of smoke and earth fading away, overtaken by the rich musk scent of Damien's room. I looked back over my shoulder to look for the Damien I'd been training with for the last few hours.

He was gone.

We were no longer surrounded by the stone walls, or the wooden carts, loaded with supplies for the battles to come. I was standing in Damien's room. My eyes fell, looking down at myself to see my small frame wrapped in his baggy clothes, the wounds peeking from beneath the fabric...

I lifted my eyes to him, struggling to think straight before I realized what was happening. Movement snagged my attention, and I gasped as blood rolled down the length of the blade from where he still held it. I shrunk back, the handle slipping from my hands.

"Oh my God! I'm so sorry. Damien, I don't—" I stuttered as he caught the sword before it hit the ground. "I don't know what happened. I—"

He was unflinching as he looked down at me. "What did you see?"

I couldn't answer, and I choked on air, still coming to grips with what had just happened as the room spun.

"Cas?" Elena. Lucia. Damien's voice was overshadowed with his other selves in my head, the three voices mixing and overlapping in my mind as they called me by different names. I blinked, shaking my head as I stumbled back, my hand coming to my face as my head throbbed.

"Easy." He set the sword down before grabbing my arms to steady me. "It's ok, *mea luna*. What did you see?"

I sat there a moment, the images fresh in my mind, like a memory. "We were... we were in a training yard. You and... me? I don't know. You... you looked different." I struggled to find words to describe the feeling, my hands trembling as I tried to hold on to him for support.

"You were training me, and—" His gaze was intense, and my eyes fell as I tried to recall what had happened as my mind fell into a whirlwind. "You... you called me, Elena."

He didn't speak, and when I lifted my face to him, his eyes were full of... sympathy? Pain? Sadness? I couldn't quite tell. Was he feeling bad because I was seeming to lose touch with reality? Was he upset because he hadn't gotten to me before Marcus was able to permanently scar my mind, leaving me to hallucinate and lose myself to the point where I couldn't tell what was real and what wasn't?

I took his hand, looking at the fresh wound as it bled. "I'm so sorry, Damien."

"It's ok, Cas." His other arm came around me, pulling me into him. For a moment he held me so tightly, as if he were afraid that if he let me go, I would disappear.

I stood there, trying to get a grip on myself. "What's happening to me, Damien?"

He didn't say anything at first.

"This is the second time I've had a strange vision of us... er, not us. Maybe it's just my mind playing tricks on me." A cold hollow laugh slipped up my throat. "Maybe Marcus really did break me..."

"I need to take you to Selene." He released me and reached into a nearby drawer, pulling some gauze and a roll of bandage for his wound.

I hurried after him. "Stop. Let me help, please." I took them from him and gently laid the gauze in his hand before carefully wrapping the bandage around it. "Who's Selene? Is she a doctor or something?"

"It's... complicated, but she can help explain what's happening to you."

The moment I finished wrapping his hand, he headed for the closet to get dressed. His clothes ruffled as he changed.

I sat there for a moment. The images of him from the vision and him here now blurred over each other and pain shot through my skull. I scrunched my forehead and rubbed my eyes.

He emerged from the closet, pulling a shirt over his head. "Just try to relax. I know it isn't easy."

That was an understatement. I could barely make sense of what was real and what wasn't.

"You need to eat before we see her, though."

"I'm not really hungry—"

He squeezed my hand. "Please, *mea luna*. Try. For me. You're so thin..."

I sighed. "Ok."

CHAPTER 26

As we reached the foot of the stairs, the sound of pots and pans and a woman humming echoed from the kitchen. Who was here other than us?

"Lord Damien!" exclaimed a voice as we entered the kitchen, and I remained hidden behind him, weary of whoever greeted him. The smell of bacon and freshly baked biscuits filled my nose, and my mouth watered.

The tiniest old woman stood in the kitchen, cooking breakfast, her silver hair flecked with strands of copper, and I halted the moment she glanced over her shoulder. She looked oddly familiar, and as she turned to face us fully, her eyes lighting up, I realized the portrait Cole had drawn was of her. I shoved down the memory, though, as the tainted presence of Cole relit the anger smoldering in my chest.

She paused her cooking to walk toward us, hands high as she came up to Damien. He lowered himself as she took his face in her hands, kissing both of his cheeks.

"Good morning, *Mitera*," he responded politely, kissing her cheek tenderly.

She cupped his face as if inspecting him closely. A thick Scottish accent painted her tongue as she spoke. "Are mah eyes deceivin' meh? Ye look like ye've finally gotten yerself a good night's rest fer once."

Her eyes caught sight of me, and she beamed. "O', whit a ray o' sunshine! She's beautiful, Lord Damien!" She paused before she hurried back to prepare our breakfast. "Ye sit yerself doon now, darlin', get comfortable. Ah hope yer ready fer a nice warm meal. I kno' ye've had yerself a rough time o' it, but ye can rest easy noo, darlin'."

I smiled, unable to resist her charm. The air around her was warm and inviting, and it felt as if she'd cast a spell on me, pulling me into whatever sunshine she radiated.

"Lord Damien?" I asked, cocking my head to look up at him. It was just like the doctor at the apartment complex. He'd called him that as well. "That's the second time someone's called you that."

"It's a long story." A crooked grin cracked across his face as his eyes avoided me. "This is Ethel. We call her *Mitera*. Her family has served and cared for mine for many generations. This is James' grandmother I told you about."

"She knows as well?" I whispered, looking up at him.

He smiled, giving a light nod.

"Poor child, do ye no' have any clothes of yer own here?" she asked, looking at me in Damien's shirt and sweatpants. "Lord Damien, she cannae walk around in yer clothes! Look at her, she's practically swimmin' in them."

I grunted a laugh under my breath as the little woman scolded him. It was so sweet how he acted with her—another side of him I'd yet to see.

He struggled to fight the smile hinting at his lips. "I'm ordering new clothes for her today, *Mitera*. Don't worry."

"Good!" she exclaimed before returning to the food she was cooking. "Donnae ye mind his poor manners, child. He's a good boy, I promise." She gave me a wink. "Smolder an' all."

He glanced at me, and I avoided his gaze as I fought to contain my smile. The chair groaned against the wood floor as he pulled it out for me to sit, and I took him up on the sweet gesture. He walked over to the stove to prepare drinks as Ethel carried over two plates loaded down with freshly cooked eggs, bacon, and biscuits.

It smelled delicious, and my mouth watered. "Thank you so much, Miss Ethel. It's delicious."

"O', please, child. Jus' call me *Mitera*. Any time ye need anythin', donnae hesitate tae ask."

Her warmth resonated in me, and I couldn't help but smile. "Thank you, *Mitera*."

Damien returned to the table, setting a teacup beside my plate. *"Mitera* has something for your wounds."

"That would be nice," I responded, as I lifted the teacup. The delicate aroma of my favorite tea blend and cream filled my lungs. "You made this for me before. How did you know I like my tea like this?"

He settled into his seat and sipped his coffee. "For the same reasons that you know Elena and Lucia."

I blinked at that statement, and for a moment something like unease churned in my gut at the acknowledgement of the two women that were starting to haunt me. The unease melted away, though, as he ran his fingers through a loose strand of hair, pushing it behind my ear. I caught a glimpse of Ethel smiling over her shoulder, watching him look at me. My chest swelled at the look of endearment on her face. How genuinely happy she seemed to see him like this. It warmed me even more.

He pressed his lips to my temple before setting back in his chair. "Now, eat."

"What happened between you and Marcus?" Damien gripped my hand the moment Marcus' name left my lips.

Ethel had left us moments ago to run some errands, and while our conversations over the last hour had been pleasant, they hadn't been enough to keep my mind from playing through every interaction I ever had with Marcus.

Why had he targeted me? Because I was with Damien? What did he have against Damien to begin with? So much that he would go as far as he had just to upset or hurt him? There had to be more to it than that. I remembered the venom in Marcus' words every time he mentioned Damien, how he'd somehow made me feel so unsafe in my own home, not to affect me, but to get under Damien's skin.

My hand curled into a fist as I lingered on how badly I wanted to get back at him. To hurt him in every way he'd hurt me... maybe more.

"He was once a very dear friend of mine."

My head jerked as my gaze snapped to him. "What?"

"It happened many years ago, long before your time." His voice wavered for a moment, but he continued. "He was as much a part of our inner circle as Zephyr, Barrett, and Vincent."

A friend? How had they gone from dear friends to... this?

"Our kind mate for life. It's a bond that goes beyond just basic attraction. It's difficult to put the feeling into words, but it's like..." He paused, eyes lowering as he thought. "When you find your mate, things change. Everything that is you, your very being, lives for your mate. Your world revolves around their very existence. You would do anything for them… You would die for them."

His gaze fell to where he held my hand, his thumb gliding back and forth against my skin in tender sweeps. "We are immortals. We don't die of old age, but that doesn't mean we can't be killed. When one of our kind loses their mate, it isn't enough to simply mourn their loss. It leaves you broken, lost in ways that words cannot describe, as if a part of your soul breaks away and leaves you permanently incomplete…"

Marcus' words flitted across my thoughts.

Lost his love over a hundred years ago. It destroyed him.

Had Marcus been telling the truth then as well? Had Damien been with someone at one point in his life and lost her?

"Many of our kind don't live long after losing their mate. Many either accept death in battle or take their own lives." A heavy sigh slipped from his lips.

"I made a mistake." He clenched his fist, trembling as he pressed it to his lips, his eyes falling closed. "Something happened, and I was summoned away to attend to it."

Images flitted across my vision, Damien's voice an echo in my mind as I found myself walking with Marcus. I wasn't in the kitchen with him anymore, but elsewhere, in a place far, far away, much like the place he and Elena had trained.

Damien's voice echoed through my mind as he spoke, breathing life into the world before me.

Marcus found evidence that there were darklings near our village.

For a moment I wanted to recoil in his presence, but for some reason there was no fear in my chest, just a feeling on content as. We walked through the encampment, and I realized I was… somehow reliving it through Damien's eyes. Marcus' hands moved frantically as he explained the situation to me—to Damien.

"It's not safe, Marcus. We'll arrange a party when I get back from the sister camp," Damien said.

"There were only a few tracks. It's likely only three or four darklings. The tracks ran right past camp, Damien. They're fresh; we can still catch them," Marcus urged. "It would be easy to take out that small of a number."

I… Damien stood there a moment beside him, our jaw working as we tried to decide the best course of action.

Marcus continued when Damien hesitated. "I'd sleep better knowing the village is safe. They could return in the night, catch us off guard."

Damien's body seemed to tense at that thought, some sort of strange fear surging through us at the thought of the darklings attacking our home in the middle of the night… again.

Again?

Damien's voice rippled across my mind, speaking the vision into reality as he continued.

I wanted him to wait until I got back, but he pressed, certain that they would be fine without me. I caved and allowed him to take on the mission, as long as he played it safe and took extra warriors with him.

"Thanks, Damien. I'll report back as soon as we're done," Marcus called over his shoulder, heading off to collect his group.

Her name was Vivienne.

The pain in his voice was raw at this point.

She was a special female, wild and untamed, born of the old bloodlines that had faded centuries ago. She was sharp as a knife, and that tongue of hers would put anyone in their place on the spot.

In that moment, when he spoke her name, I saw her, as if she stood before me now. Her long, curly, golden-brown hair framed her face, her tawny skin glowing in the sun, and her pale eyes were full of that untamed spirit he spoke of.

Marcus felt the bond the moment he saw her, and nothing made me happier than to see him bound to a female like her. They'd been together for close to two hundred years when it happened.

Marcus and Vivienne stood before me then—a perfect match in every way. He didn't look like the Marcus I knew. He was happy as he held her, and she him. No malice or hatred, no cruelty in his eyes. Just pure love and adoration.

"Marcus, Vivienne, and a group of ten other warriors found more than they expected that day. They stumbled upon a darkling nest. They're rare, and it had been the first we'd found in a long time. The sheer number of darklings was overwhelming. When I got word that they hadn't returned, I rushed to aid them with more warriors, but I was too late..."

The world shifted, emotions and images passing in a blur, and I was suddenly standing in dense, dark woods, heart racing. The foul smell of dead darklings and freshly spilled blood hung in the air. Fallen brothers, sisters, and darklings littered the ground, the warrior's bodies ravaged in ways that made my stomach twist into knots.

The most agonizing cry rang out behind me, and I turned to find Marcus on the ground. Blood covered him as he clutched Vivienne to his chest. Her beautiful face was bloodied, her body torn and broken, unseeing silver eyes lingering on the sky. Marcus' sobs tore through me, and a deep anguish sank into my chest, as if I were feeling his agony, his pain, his loss. It was too much, too painful.

Tears overflowed onto my cheeks as I listened, somehow reliving the agonizing memory he told me, as if I'd been there firsthand. My lips quivered as the deep sorrow grew more and more painful until the agony was more than I could bear.

"She was beautiful," I muttered weakly as my eyes wavered, the tears continuing to roll down my cheeks.

"Marcus was the only survivor. Something dark took hold of him after that, and he snapped. He was never the same, and he blamed me for her death. He blamed Selene, blamed anyone he could, except for the monsters who actually did it... He disappeared not long after that, collecting any immortals who didn't want to serve under Selene, and he's had it out for me ever since."

The pain in his expression rattled me as he reached his finger out to sweep the tears from my face. What was Selene's role in all this, that Marcus would feel she held some sort of responsibility for any of this?

"But that's... that's stupid! You didn't kill Vivienne, the darklings did. You didn't make the decision to go, Marcus di—"

"As I said, *mea luna*. When one of our kind loses their mate, it does something to them. They're never the same, while some take it quietly, some lose all sense or care of the world around them." He lifted his hand to wipe the tears from my cheeks. "I'm sorry. I didn't mean for you to experience that pain, but you deserved to know. Regardless of our past friendship, regardless of what happened to Vivienne, I can't forgive him for hurting you. He will regret the moment he laid a finger on you."

I sat there, reeling from the emotions and feelings that weren't my own. "Why is this happening to me, Damien?"

He hesitated, throat bobbing as he swallowed. "You were never meant to return as a human."

I blinked, brows furrowing. "Return? What're you talking about, Damien?"

"Lucia and Elena... Your visions of them. They aren't just some visions of the past or dreams, and you're not broken, this isn't damage from Marcus... The visions are memories of your past lives."

His words didn't sink in at first, and any thoughts I might have formed went still. This couldn't be—no. It didn't make sense, couldn't be real. That kind of stuff didn't happen, magic wasn't...

I stilled. Magic was real. I'd seen it with my own eyes numerous times now. Damien's shadows, Marcus' mental manipulations, the darklings.

Oh God...

The room began to spin, and I turned my gaze to Damien, half expecting him to tell me this was a joke, that it was all just a parlor trick or some other bullshit joke. Air halted in my lungs at the pain in his eyes as he gazed down at me.

His sorrow seeped into me as he reached out to cradle my face, as if my physical presence was still hard to believe. "I didn't think I'd ever see you again...."

My heart leapt at his words, as something deep within my chest seemed to reach out to him, echoing that same notion.

"Normally, it would only be fifteen to twenty years before your next reincarnation, but..." he let loose a breath. "It's been nearly a hundred and twenty-five years since I lost you." He sat there a moment in silence, collecting his thoughts.

Reincarnation. The word folded over itself in my thoughts over and over as I struggled to process it, as if it were just out of my grasp. Reincarnation. Reincarnation?

"How is this..." How was this even possible? Was this just something that happened? Was this normal? Of course, it wasn't normal.

"The first time we met at The Galleria, I knew the moment I saw you. I couldn't believe my eyes. I was skeptical, because you've never returned as a human before, but I could feel it." He squeezed my hand. "I'd know your face anywhere, even hidden beneath human skin."

"So, the dreams I had..."

He nodded. "They really happened. You've lived three lifetimes before this one. Each time you're reborn, the fates bring us together, drawn to each other by some strange force. It never fails. We always find each other."

I sat there for a moment, absorbing what he was telling me. I remembered the moment we met, the strange feeling I'd gotten. The odd familiarity, the pull.

"The vision you saw of us in the encampment when we were training: that was Elena. The village you saw was called Moonhaven. It was our home for many years. However, the darklings launched an assault, killing countless civilians and warriors. It was a bloodbath, and I lost you in the destruction."

Damien's fear I'd felt in his memory when Marcus had mentioned the possibility of the darklings attacking in the night. That must have been what I felt, what drove him to give into Marcus' request.

But the memory of Moonhaven wasn't the only one I'd seen...

"I saw a battlefield..." I started, and his eyes turned to me. "When Marcus... when Marcus first took me in the woods. He used his magic on me, and when I woke up, I was surrounded by death... by fire. I held the gold and black sword in your room." My hand drifted to my stomach. "When you found me, I realized that I was pregnant with Emilia."

Pain crashed into me like a wave, overtaking me, as if I'd carried the child myself. I guess, in a way, I had.

His voice was low as he spoke her name... my name. "Lucia."

"It happened again when you rescued me from Marcus' compound, only this time, I was in a bed. The walls were stone, and the room was lit with candles." As I spoke, the vision resurfaced in my mind, the pain rising up like a beast ready to devour me whole. "Emilia made it into the world. I still remember the sound of her first cry." Something fractured inside me. "But I hemorrhaged at some point during the delivery and lost too much blood..."

His arms wrapped tightly around me, holding me. "It's rare for our kind to conceive, and when we do, it rarely makes it to term. Giving birth is especially dangerous, due to blood loss... I lost you that night, and Emilia followed you in death not long after."

A pain so sharp sank into my chest, and the air halted in my lungs. Emilia hadn't survived? The room spun for a moment, and I tried so desperately to imagine a babe whose cry was the only thing I knew. I didn't even know what she looked like, but I remembered the desire to hold her, to kiss her; experiences that had been taken from me.

It was difficult to comprehend how something that had happened over a hundred years ago could affect me so freshly... but it did, and the pain was so raw, I feared I'd carry it with me for the rest of my life.

"After that, I struggled to go on. To lose a mate not once, but three times, and at the same time to lose a child? You can't verbalize that kind of pain. I lost myself in the grief."

His words took root in my mind. Mate. I was... the reincarnation of his mate. I struggled to absorb that realization. My heart raced at the thought that I was meant for him, that he... he was meant for me. At the same time, it throbbed, aching with the pain he was reliving.

"Completely incomplete, feeling as if you'll never feel whole again." He inhaled a deep, uneven breath. "I almost ended it many times."

The weight of those words was heavy, and not just because it hurt to imagine the pain he'd suffered, but because I too had found my way into that deep, dark place before. There had been times I myself had almost ended it, but there had always been something that stopped me. Had it been that part of me that was my past lives pushing me to keep going in hopes that we might be reunited again?

"I waited for you to return to me like you always did, but year after year passed with no sign of your rebirth. I began to lose hope, afraid that something might have happened to break the chain of reincarnation." A gentle smile lit his expression when he looked to me again. "You don't know how much it meant for me to see your face the night we met."

"Why didn't you tell me sooner?"

"You're human," he said, taking my hand. "You had a life before I met you. And as time passed, I began to wonder if your memories would ever resurface. When they didn't, when you didn't remember who I was, it changed everything. I didn't want to force a bond on you, especially when you'd barely learned what I was, that our world even existed. I wanted to give you the choice. You deserved that much. I'd almost hoped you would turn me down, so I could let you live your life away from this misery. When you didn't turn me down, though, it gave me such joy, to have you in my life, even if you didn't remember. It was enough for me."

He could have told me what I was to him, could have revealed that I was his mate... but he hadn't. He had allowed me to choose him on my own terms, without the weight or the knowledge that we were meant for each other. He would have denied himself the chance to be with his mate, the one he'd searched for, for so long, if that was what I had decided.

"You... gave me a choice."

He nodded.

My chest swelled at the thought that he'd wanted to allow me to carve my own path, something that I'd wanted so desperately but had always been too scared to do.

A thought crossed my mind then. Elena. Lucia. Two lives. "You mentioned I lived three past lives. I saw Elena and Lucia; who was the third?"

240

"Moira. She was the first, but Selene will tell you more about her. Come on." He kissed my hand once more before standing. "Selene will have more answers for you. She'll be able to explain it better than I can."

Damien led me down the hall to a door I hadn't been through yet. It revealed stairs leading into what looked like a basement, but as we reached the foot of the stairs, I realized it wasn't a basement at all.

Candles came to life, dark blue flames flickered atop the wicks, illuminating the room, and I gasped, grabbing onto him. An altar stood before us, runes and symbols carved into the stone walls around it. I recognized them as the same that decorated the sword... my sword, the same that marked Damien's shoulder.

"What is this?"

"The Propylaea," he explained, coming to a stop before the altar. He turned to extend his hand to me. "Come."

I frowned, hesitating a moment, but placed my hand in his, and he knelt, guiding me down with him. "It's ok. Close your eyes and clear your mind. Don't let go of my hand, though, no matter what."

My brows furrowed as he closed his eyes and turned his face forward. There was something in the air, an odd feeling that someone or something was watching us. While I knew I didn't see anyone in the room when we entered, I could feel their presence.

I took a deep breath and closed my eyes, fearful of what I might find when I opened them again.

CHAPTER 27

Cold air rushed over me, like that of the sensation I'd felt when Damien passed us through his shadow magic. As quickly as the chilled air surrounded us, it washed away, leaving warm air in its place. The delicate scent of jasmine replaced the damp smell of the underground room we'd stood in just moments before, and I couldn't shake the sense of familiarity to it.

Damien squeezed my hand. "You can open your eyes now."

I opened my eyes and froze, failing to breathe at what I found before me. Monstrous stone columns reached to high ceilings around us. Bountiful arrays of night-blooming jasmine stretched out, clinging to the walls. Between them—as if the temple was built around them—stood the most magical trees I'd ever seen in my life. There were no leaves, the branches bare, but the very bark of the trees was pale, almost white, the trees glowing like the moon, stretching higher and higher until the branches stretched out overhead, casting us in their warm pale glow.

My eyes widened at what I found amidst those high reaching branches. The ceiling was cast in darkness, and it was as if the night sky was trapped within it, the stars glowing and shimmering above us. Dim, rippling light fell from large sconces that extended out from each column, blue flames blazing around us.

I looked at Damien as he rose to his feet, my lips parting to ask him what the hell had happened, and where he'd taken me, but I halted. He was dressed differently. A black robe of delicate fabric hung from his shoulders, his chest bare, and he wore black pants that hugged his legs down to his bare feet. I sucked in air, dropping his hand as I noticed the sleeve of what I, myself, was wearing.

Gossamer chiffon in grays and blacks cascaded down my arms, falling to the floor. Delicate gold chains draped off my shoulders over the split sleeves. Exquisite fabric hugged my frame, the bodice stitched with glittering gemstones before falling into a skirt that flowed around me. The gown was so intricately detailed that no mortal hands could have possibly made it.

"Mea paios." My child.

An ethereal voice echoed out through the stone hall, a thick accent rolling off her tongue, and I froze. I didn't know the language she spoke, but the voice sounded familiar to me somehow. The moment the strange language spilled from her lips, the voice reached into my mind, speaking in words I understood.

I raised my eyes to the back of the huge chamber. The starry sky seemed to part to reveal a crescent shape moon carved out into the stone ceiling, letting the moonlight shine down, casting a glow down onto an altar. A pair of large stone horse statues, so intricately carved they could come to life at any moment, stood merged into either side of the altar's pedestal—furious energy carved into their manes and muscles, as if they were charging into battle but frozen in time. Sitting atop the altar between them was a woman, arms draped on either side of her as she watched us from on high.

She didn't look to be much older than me, her skin perfect as untouched porcelain and just as pale. Glimmering constellations danced across her nose and cheeks like freckles, and her pale, silver eyes shined like the reflecting gaze of a nocturnal animal in the darkness. A watercolor of shimmering white and silver hair cascaded over her shoulders, spilling like a waterfall over the edges of the stone pedestal where she sat. She didn't glow in the way a light did; it was as if she absorbed all the surrounding light and reflected it off her very being.

As if she were the moon itself.

She pushed herself forward off the altar, flowing gracefully down to the floor. Her white silken gown and long hair pooled at her feet as she stood before us. Damien knelt the moment her feet met the marble, lowering his head to her. However, I couldn't bring myself to move an inch. I stood there, speechless, unable to form any thoughts at the overwhelming presence of her.

243

Damien cocked his head, and panic flashed across his face when he realized I was still standing. He grabbed my hand, tugging for me to kneel beside him.

"It is all right, warrior. She knows not what she does." Her voice was soft. The languages overlapped with one another, and yet I somehow was able to understand what she said. She glided toward me, her steps leaving no sound in their wake.

Her small hand rose to brush against my face. The moment our skin touched, my knees gave way, and I fell to the floor, my body suddenly weak and unable to hold itself up. What was this? What was happening?

"You have been neglecting your feeding, warrior." Her pale brows rose as she turned her gaze down on Damien. "I will not tolerate the continuance of this weakened state. Be sure it is remedied when you return to your realm."

He responded with silence. Her eyes drifted toward me, and the heavy gaze of those opalescent eyes felt like a crushing weight. "That aside, you've done well to bring her to me, warrior."

He lowered his head. "Your praise pleases me, goddess."

The room spun, and for a moment I thought I might vomit. "Goddess?"

Her perfect face turned to me. "I am Selene. Goddess of the Moon, and mother to the immortal race."

There was no way this was happening, no way this could be real.

She crouched down before me, tucking her knees against her chest as her arms crossed atop them, her. hair tumbling over her in a curtain of silken white waves. I couldn't seem to pull myself away as our gazes met.

Her eyes burned over me as her eyes passed over me in quiet inspection. "Your powers are returning to you, but your body is too weak to contain them."

Damien seemed to tense at her words but remained silent. Her mouth didn't move, but her voice forced its way into my mind, and I recoiled at the invasion.

Why do you not tell him, mikros? Little one. A term so endearing for a creature so powerful. Why did I know that word? How was I able to understand her?

Her question processed in my mind, playing over and over, but I couldn't bring myself to respond to her. I knew what she spoke of, and the fact that she immediately knew my secret shook me.

She rose, seeming to know my thoughts, know my answer—that I didn't tell him, not because I didn't want to, but because I couldn't bring myself to. She glided along the stone floor as she walked away from us, like a ghost.

Her fingers drifted elegantly along the stone wall. "I designed the immortals to serve me, to fight my enemies when I so needed. While

244

they were unlike mortals, they were not gods, so they could not survive the immense powers of one."

She approached one of the horse statues near her altar. Her small hand rising to pet its muzzle, and the moment her hand caressed the stone surface, the horse's head moved, coming to life as it relished in her affection.

"While they were of great use to me and served me well, they needed... assistance." Those intense eyes that glowed like the moon itself shifted to me again. "So, I bore you to the purest of immortals born of the elder blood, a child of both God and immortal, born of shadow and moonlight. Moira."

My heart stopped at her words. Selene was Moira's mother? I, no, Moira, was the daughter of a goddess?

"While I bestowed unique powers to each house, no immortal alone could contain the combined powers of the gods. When you came into being, you were gifted with the best of both races. Gifted with the ability to utilize each of the house's magics and more—stronger, fiercer than they could ever be."

I looked down at my hands. That was what Damien meant when he told me that I was different. I was never meant to be born human. I was supposed to be born an immortal like him. But as I wasn't born as an immortal... what did that make me now?

She answered my thoughts. "You are a demigoddess, trapped in human form."

Silence filled the hall as my world crumbled around me.

Realization dawned on me, and I turned to look at Damien as the story he'd told me the night before echoed through my mind. "The legend..."

Damien's pained eyes lingered on mine for a moment, the pain amplified with a near guilt. "It isn't a legend... It's our story. One that our people share across every generation in hopes that your memory will never die out, that you, our hope, will always return to us."

I shook my head in disbelief, and my gaze snapped to Selene, her eyes falling back on me.

"I bound Damien Archonis, king of the immortals, to you at birth. As one who would grow to be the strongest warrior of The Order, he was to see to your training and protect you until you could fulfill your purpose."

I looked to him, but his eyes wouldn't meet mine as he stared to the ground. Silent.

"You're a... king?" I shot to my feet, my mind reeling. "You didn't think to mention that?"

"It didn't feel like the most important thing to tell you," he said, glancing up at me nervously.

"No, I guess you're right, not nearly as important as mentioning I'm the reincarnation of the daughter of a goddess!" I stumbled back as the room spun again. "I can't..."

He reached for me, but I stepped out of his reach, and his hand recoiled. The pain in his eyes hurt, but not enough, not nearly as much as the crushing reality falling down on me. "Why didn't you just tell me? Why didn't you warn me?"

"I didn't know how you would react, if you would believe me, and I wasn't sure how exactly to break the news to you," he said, remaining knelt before me. "I would have done this better, taken a bit more time to work you into it, but with your memories resurfacing the way they are..."

My lips parted, but I couldn't quite think of how to respond to that.

"You have every right to be upset with me for keeping you in the dark, but as I promised, I'm telling you everything, now."

"When were you planning on telling me about all this? If my memories never resurfaced, what were you planning to do then?" I asked.

He faltered. "I... I wasn't sure. I was still figuring out how it would all play out. If your memories never resurfaced, it was likely your magic wouldn't either."

My magic? "I don't have any magic."

"You do," Selene said calmly from where she stood, and Damien and I both looked at her. Her eyes shifted to Damien. "But this human form was not built to handle her powers at their peak. They will destroy her." Her words were casual, the thought of my body failing of no consequence to her as she spoke to Damien.

Air sucked in through Damien's teeth as the words left her lips and he rose to his feet, as if he were prepared to argue what she was saying.

Was she talking about my heart? Was that why I was dying? Because I possessed some stupid power I wasn't meant to have? Because I was born into a body I wasn't meant to exist in?

"Is there anything that can be done, Goddess?" Damien asked, desperation in his voice.

She met his gaze, her eyes narrowing at his question. "You are bold, warrior, to ask such things of me. You know, I am forbidden from meddling in the affairs of mortals."

He dropped his head again, biting his tongue. "Apologies, Goddess, I spoke out of turn."

Her gaze turned to me, the weight of it nearly too much. I wanted to run, wanted to leave this place and drown out what she was saying.

"You may yet have enough strength to serve a purpose in this life." For a moment, I thought I might have seen a flicker of remorse in her eyes, but it faded just as quickly as it appeared. "If not, your spirit will be reborn again."

Damien's eyes widened. "But—"

"I expect you to serve her as long as she draws breath," she said, turning her heavy gaze to him. "I will not have you attempt to throw your life away again, Damien. I still have further use of you. Am I clear?"

His chest heaved, his hands closing into fists at his sides, but he spoke through gritted teeth. "Transparently, Goddess."

I then heard her voice in my head. *Whilst one sleeps, the other cannot rest. There must always be one.*

Her words sank into me like a knife, and I revisited the story he'd shared with me the night before.

The Goddess passed down another blessing, but this blessing was so powerful, and balance had to be maintained, so a curse was laid down as well. The King was bound to where he resided, waiting for his queen to return.

I turned to look at Damien, my eyes widening as realization dawned on me. He'd told me he'd almost ended it after losing me, but he hadn't. Not because he didn't want to, but because he couldn't, not while I was gone. He'd been trapped in an endless circle of loss and pain, forced to endure the loss time and time again.

"Begin her training, warrior. We will see how long she lasts," Selene commanded.

I turned to her, opening my mouth to ask her more questions, to argue, but before the words could leave my lips, the room went dark. The candles of The Propylaea flickered back to light, and we sat on the cold floor in the normal clothes we'd donned just moments before.

CHAPTER 28

My knees pressed into the cold stone floor, and my hands planted firmly beneath me as I panted. I ground my fingers into the concrete, trying to hold myself in place somehow, fearful that if I were to relax my grip, I might slip away and disappear into some other strange place.

We sat in silence for a moment, both reeling from the intense meeting with the goddess, from the warning she'd spoken to us. I wanted to deny it all, but the proof of her words had already been shown to me. The mere sight of her, her overwhelming godly presence, was enough to validate everything.

Damien rose to his feet, his eyes burning into the altar before him as if he were staring down the goddess herself. I lifted my gaze to him, but he wouldn't look at me, couldn't look at me. My heart twisted at the look in his eyes, and I reached up to touch his hand. The pain he felt seared into me, and I shrunk back as if I'd been burned with ice.

He jerked at my reaction. "Sorry, *mea luna*." He crouched beside me. "I think your Nous abilities are resurfacing."

I rubbed my hand where we'd touched, looking up at him. "Nous?"

"The power to see into a person's deepest thoughts and feelings."

Was that how I'd seen Damien's memories of Marcus and Vivienne? I struggled to come to terms with everything, but it all made sense now. The failed treatments, the failing heart. I was a mistake. A failed reincarnation, born into a body I was never meant to inhabit.

I should have never existed.

Selene's voice resonated through my mind, the words she spoke to me, everything I'd heard.

"What did she mean when she said you were neglecting your feedings?"

Damien's eyes left me at those words, and I remembered what he was. Of course. How had I not realized it? He was an immortal. Their kind were similar to vampires. They required blood.

"Have you not been..." I struggled to find the right word. "Taking care of yourself?"

"I'm fine."

I gave him a withering look. "No, you're not. How long has it been?"

"I'm not talking about this with you right now, Cas," he said, trying to walk past me.

I blocked his path. "The hell you aren't. What'll happen if you don't feed? You've looked so tired and worn the last few weeks. Is this the reason?"

His snapped. "I couldn't bring myself to after I found you!"

I stopped at his words. "What? Why?"

"I... I couldn't bring myself to drink from another female once I saw you. And I refused to force myself on you until you could make that decision to receive me on your own. I was left with no choice but to feed while you were missing. I didn't have the strength to ensure your safe return on what little energy I had left, and I exhausted every bit of it searching for you. Feeding's not as simple as you think, though." He struggled with his words. "It can get... intimate."

I choked on his words. *Intimate.*

He tensed, as if realizing something. "Before you think it, no. It's only ever been you. I haven't taken another female to bed. Ever. I refuse to take from anywhere but the wrist, I just... didn't feel right doing it now that you appeared. It felt like I was betraying you."

I couldn't help but smile at the way he seemed to think I'd even considered that to be an issue... but as my mind began to wander, my skin crawled at the thought of another woman's hands on him.

"Why can't you just..." I was a little nervous asking, still fearful of what it would be like, but I wanted to give him what he needed. "Why don't you just feed from me?"

"I'd hoped we could, but when Selene said that your body was struggling under the weight of your magic—" He grimaced, his eyes falling from me. "I can't risk losing you. I don't want to risk taking from you when you may not have the ability to give."

Something crumbled within me.

"Then I'm useless to you," I muttered. I could do nothing to help him in this body.

"No, that's not—" Damien's phone went off in his pocket, and he grabbed it—his voice sharp as a knife as he answered. "What is it?"

I could faintly hear the voice on the other end of the line as they spoke, and a muscle feathered in Damien's jaw as he listened.

"I'll be there shortly." He hung up, shoving his phone in his pocket. "It's Cole. He won't talk, so we need to get up there. I guess your training begins now." I winced at the way the words left his lips, the anger lacing his voice.

I lifted my hand to his face. "I'll be ok. I've got the best teacher I could ask for."

His eyes warmed, his hand rising to overlap mine, and he turned to lay a tender kiss on my palm. "I won't lose you, not again. I'll find a way to help your body with the stress of the magic."

"I know you will," I said, stretching up to press my lips to his. I knew better than this. Knew better than to give into the hope that he might find some solution, some way to save me. It's never amounted to anything more than disappointment in the past.

I turned, but Damien grabbed hold of my hand, pulling me back to him.

"You're not useless to me, *mea luna*. I want you to know that," he said, his voice firm and yet tender as he started into my eyes. "You don't know how much you do for me simply by being. Just to look into your eyes again, to hold you again; it's more than I could ever ask for, to have you at my side."

He pulled me closer, and I melted into his embrace.

"Don't think I haven't forgotten your feeding, though. If you need to feed, you need to do it," I said, tilting my head to give him a firm look.

"We'll talk about that later." He led me toward the stairwell, passing his hand through the air before us, and as he did, the candles around us doused, casting us into darkness. The familiar cold air swirled around us, and we emerged into another room.

I recognized the room immediately as the one I'd awoken in weeks ago after I was attacked by the darklings. There wasn't much in terms of furniture, just the bare necessities, as if it were meant for someone to use as a temporary place to stay.

"This is one of two headquarters we have. This one is primarily used by The Order for interrogations, and as a formal base in the city," Damien explained as we walked out of the room and down the hall. "The Order's numbers have dwindled in the last century, so now we offer these rooms to warriors and civilians seeking refuge."

"Are there other immortals here now?" I asked.

He nodded. "A few currently reside here, some displaced families and warriors."

His pace was quick, and I struggled to keep up with him. "What exactly is The Order?"

"The Order is the main force within the immortals that Selene commands. Males and females from each house with potential are trained in combat. We as the servants of The Order not only combat the darklings but uphold our laws as well."

I followed him as we walked, absorbing every word. "Those who don't join The Order remain as civilians, meant to thrive and birth more of our kind to fight in Selene's battles. Barrett, Zephyr, and I are the acting heads."

"With you residing as king." I cracked a mischievous grin as I looked up at him. I elongated my neck, faking an accent as I spoke like a lady of the courts of old times. "*Lord Damien*, King of the Immortals, *Lord of Darkness*."

He slammed his hand against the wall, blocking my path and my back met the wall my heart launching into my throat.

I swallowed, feeling the dark rolling power he contained as he held me in place. He lowered himself to my ear, his breath brushing over my skin, and I shivered.

"You keep talking like that and I may just enjoy making you call out my title in our bed."

Our bed. I bit my lip, heat flooding my body and stemming into my cheeks at all the ways I imagined he might attempt that. His hand came to my hip, sliding up along my waist, his thumb brushing just under my breast. My breath hitched, but I forced my composure, ignoring the heat his words brought to light within me as met his gaze, and a coy grin curved my lips.

"As you wish, milord," I said, my voice delicate as I curtsied.

I ducked under his arm before he could stop me, snickering as I slipped from his reach. He smiled and followed after me.

"And to think I spent three days worrying that you'd gotten in trouble for telling me of the immortal race," I said, undeniable irritation painting the teasing words as we made our way into the stairwell. "I'll bet you got a good laugh out of that, didn't you? King Damien."

He bit back the sly grin tugging at his lips. "It was adorable to say the least. I hated that I left you in the dark like that, but I can't say I don't entirely like the idea of me occupying your mind so heavily."

I rolled my eyes at him as he turned me away from the entrance to Johnson's medical room and led me down the hall.

Zephyr was already waiting for us in the hallway. Barrett stepped into the hallway as we neared the room, his jaw clenched as he wiped his hands with a rag. My throat tightened at the sight of the blood smeared on his skin.

I turned to look through the open door.

"Wait, Cas—"

I froze, the room spinning at what I saw. Cole rested on his knees, his body hanging forward. His wrists were held up in shackles, chains reaching up to the ceiling, suspending him. Horror tore its way through me, and for a moment, I could see myself sitting where he was, his wounds similar to my own.

That had been me.

His face was busted, tawny skin dusted with bruises, and he was bleeding. His bottom lip was split, and a mixture of blood and saliva dripped down his chin, falling into small puddles on the ground. His left eye was bruised, almost swollen shut.

I stumbled back out into the hallway, pressing my back against the wall next to the door as I heaved through the panic. My hands involuntarily grabbed onto my wrists, the bruises still fresh from my own imprisonment. For a moment I could feel the cold metal of the shackles as if they bound me once more, the searing cold chill of Marcus' knife, the sting of his cigarettes, the feel of his hands as he—

Damien was in front of me in an instant, his brows furrowed as he glanced between me and the door as I crumbled against the wall. My hands shook as he cupped my face, but I couldn't meet his eyes. If I looked at him, the truth I wanted to avoid would be clear. He'd know the extent of what I'd endured, would see me in those chains instead of Cole, would see an image I never wanted him to have to suffer. Somehow, he'd know, and with his knowledge would bring back the reality of it. I wanted so badly to just forget, to never think of those damned chains, the feel of Marcus' hands tangling in my hair, the feel of air being cut off from my—

"Cas? What's wrong?"

I shook my head, unable to respond as I tried to pull my face from his hands, but he forced me to look at him as the concern bled out of his expression. I didn't want to acknowledge it. It was still too fresh.

"Please, *mea luna*. Don't shut me out."

"I—I'm sorry, Damien. Seeing him like this it's… it's too fresh."

He drew back, his eyes widening as the pieces fell together, and Zephyr and Barrett stiffened, fury flooding their faces as they stormed back into the room, their shouts echoing through the walls.

"This is what he—" Damien couldn't finish his words, couldn't seem to let the reality of the things Marcus had done leave his tongue. "I'm taking you home. I'm not putting you through this. We'll call in another Nous user to search his memories."

I stopped him as he grabbed my hand. "Is that what you were going to have me do?"

He halted, his eyes falling on me. "I didn't know if you could, but given the signs, I believe you have the ability to, but that doesn't matter. You've been through enough."

"Let me decide that for myself," I said, my fingers tightening in the fabric of his sweater. "I just… I want to help in any way I can."

Something flickered within me, as if a spark of that flame that had been smoldering within me arose at the thought of invading Cole's thoughts, as Marcus had done time and time again with his aid. I shuddered at the thought of it, at the memory of how it felt.

And a strange desire ran through me at the thought of inflicting that same pain on Cole. A part of me recoiled from the idea, and yet another part of me seemed to rise to the surface, desperate to taste that vengeance.

"I want to do this," I said, trying to smother the trembles rattling me and Damien's brows furrowed as he assessed me, the concern clear as day in his eyes. "I know I don't know how to use my magic, and it might not work, but I want to at least try. I just... I need a moment. I wasn't prepared to see him like this. I'm sorry."

"You don't have to apologize for anything. You did nothing wrong." He held me tightly, and I feared he might change his mind, take me home where I wouldn't be able to help. "Take however long you need. He isn't going anywhere. If you need to go home for tonight and try again tomorrow, you can do that, too."

I drew a deep breath, attempting to muster as much courage as I could. "Just give me a moment."

He nodded, and I eased into him, praying his presence might somehow ease the horrid feeling pumping through my body. I hated the fear that had captured me in its clutches, wanted to chase it from my system and never be its victim again.

I *would* chase it away.

Damien's heart raced in my ear, and I narrowed in on it, allowed it to sweep me away.

Focus on that, Cas. One... Two... Three... Four... Five... I coached myself through the breaths, combating the panic that gripped me. It took a moment, but when I finally gripped a sense of control over my fear, I let out a steady breath and drew back from Damien.

The moment I stepped into the room my eyes fell on Cole. He groaned before he lifted his head, breath ragged.

Cole's eyes met mine, and a cruel grin tugged at one corner of his lips. "So you've decided to join in the fun, have you? I hear talk you know the truth now. *Demigoddess, bitch.*"

He spit blood on the floor at my feet, and I fought the urge to flinch at his movement, as every moment he'd put his hands on me flooded my mind.

"So, you *do* remember how to talk." Barrett planted a firm hand on his shoulder before slamming his knee into Cole's face, and my muscles involuntarily braced at the hit he took, remembering all the times I'd taken a similar hit. Damien tensed at my side, seeming to see and he stepped forward, catching Barrett's arm before he could hit him again.

"That's enough, Barrett," Damien said, his voice firm.

Cole slumped to the side, the chains catching him before he hit the ground, and Barrett leaned in, speaking through his teeth. "Show a little respect, *traitor.*"

My eyes drifted over his wounds. No matter how terrible he looked, I held no sympathy for him. Just as he'd had none for me when they tormented me in that chamber.

He deserves it.

I winced at the words that crossed my mind, and I forced them back. I didn't want to think like that, that wasn't me¬¬—I wasn't like him and Marcus, wasn't cold and cruel.

Was I?

"Why?" I bit out. Needing to know.

He tilted his head, those black eyes rising to me. I could feel the anger, the hurt inside him. I didn't understand how I knew it, but it was all too easy to distinguish. It raked over my skin like fiery embers, the heat passing over my body in waves.

His voice was raspy, his throat parched as he said through gritted teeth, "Anything to get back at Selene for taking my parents from me, for taking everything from me."

I swallowed, remembering his stories of his mother, of how badly it had affected him when her and his father had died. They'd been killed in the war Selene waged with the darklings, one that his parents had been swept into. Of course, he would hate me—the reincarnation of Selene's daughter. It was stupid that he blamed her, though, the same way Marcus blamed her and Damien for Vivienne's death.

Every conversation I ever shared with the kind-hearted boy I'd come to know crossed my mind, leaving a hollow pain in my chest. The pain smoldered into bitter anger as that sweet image of him burned away, leaving the cruel creature before me, one who'd assisted in my torture. "So, none of it was ever real, was it?"

A cruel grin spread across his face, and my stomach twisted. A darkness coiled inside those eyes, unlike anything I'd ever seen. "Why? Do you miss me that much? Is it a friend to share all your woes that you want, princess? Or more? I mean, I'd warm your bed if you'd like..." His eye slid to Damien. "Oh sorry, Damien. That's what you've been wanting, so I guess you could have first dibs. Maybe we could share her after that."

"Shut up," Damien said, his hands balling into fists at his side, and my cheeks flared, anger rising in my chest.

"You'll have to tell me how she is," he continued, ignoring Zephyr's warning. His smile turned knowing as he continued to taunt Damien. "I'm curious to know what she tastes like..."

"Cole, knock it off," Zephyr growled, his body growing taut as if he were holding himself back.

Cole continued still, leaning in as his voice turned breathless. "And I don't just mean her blood, but between those sweet thi—"

Zephyr roared and Vincent grabbed hold of him as he raised his fist but missed Barrett and Damien as they launched at Cole. My heart sank at the faintest sight of Cole's hands twitching in the chains, the subtle hint of a smile curving his lips.

Oh, God. He could kill them with a single touch, burst their hearts if he wanted, and Damien and the others didn't know.

"Stop! Watch his hands! Don't let him touch you." Barrett halted his brows furrowing, and Cole froze. Damien grabbed onto the collar of Cole's shirt, fist primed to punch him, but he stopped short, eyes flickering between Cole and me.

Cole's hardened gaze shifted to me, muscles and veins straining against the skin of his neck as his teeth ground together.

I didn't let the look on Cole's face scare me. I wasn't the one bound in chains now. "He can do something to your blood if he gets his hands on you."

Damien's head snapped toward me, eyes flaring. "What did you say?"

I hesitated on the spot as they all looked to me. Cole's eyes popped as I revealed his secret, and he jerked against the chains toward me. I flinched as he thrashed, as if he could get to me before I could speak another word. "I-I can't remember what Marcus called it. It… it started with an A."

Vincent answered. "Aíma?"

I nodded.

Damien looked back at Cole, his brows furrowing. "But you're half-blooded."

Cole's jaw clenched, but he didn't speak.

"What does being half-blooded have to do with it?" I asked.

Zephyr shrugged out of Vincent's hold, and seemed to assess Cole as he answered my question. "Blood traits don't typically present themselves in half-bloods born of human crossing. In fact, Cole's the first half-human I've heard of developing an ability."

"Cole's father was the last of the Aíma," Damien explained, glancing back at me. "When he died, we thought the house had fallen with him."

Hatred burned in Cole's eyes as his gaze landed back on me. I dreaded to think what he wanted to do to me now that I'd revealed his secret, what he would do to me if he got free. My heart lurched, a new fear trickling in. Fuck, would he tell them… my secret?

I narrowed my eyes one him, wondering why he hadn't told them yet. It would be the perfect leverage to use against me. Would it try to hold over me? Or did he think they now knew?

"This is as good a time as any to practice," Damien said, pulling me from Cole's hateful stare.

"Don't doubt yourself, Cas. Just take it slow, and don't push yourself too far. Pull out if it becomes too much. Just like you did earlier at breakfast when you saw my memories, focus on that physical connection. It'll come to you." Damien's eyes flickered with uncertainty, but he quickly forced a mask of confidence for my sake. "You can do this. I know you can."

I thought back to when Damien told me about Vivienne and Marcus, of how I'd seen his memories. It happened without me realizing what I was doing, and I was still unsure how exactly the ability worked, but I would never know unless I tried. If I was going to accidentally hurt anyone in the process, I would rather it be Cole.

Damien stood at Cole's side, watching me as I knelt before him. "Ground yourself to him through touch. Reach out in your thoughts until you feel that pull. Use it to guide you."

I took a deep breath, reaching out to take hold of Cole's head.

"Don't fucking touch me, bitch!" He jerked his head back, prepped to slam his forehead into mine, but before he could, Damien pulled a dagger from its sheath, pressing it to Cole's throat.

Cole went rigid, his chest heaving.

"Hurt her again, and I'll end you." Damien's lips curled, fangs bared, and he lowered himself to Cole's level. The defiance in Cole's expression didn't fade.

A mask of anger clouded the pain I knew Damien harbored as he held that knife to his throat, knowing how deeply Cole's betrayal wounded him. Despite that, there wasn't a shred of sympathy in Damien's eyes.

"Don't think the knowledge you have will protect you. I won't hesitate to slit your throat where you kneel." Damien growled, the blade pressing into Cole's neck until a pearl of blood oozed where metal met skin. "You will regret the day you chose to cross us."

When Cole didn't respond, Damien pulled the blade back, but didn't sheath it.

Trembles rattled me to the tips of my fingers as my mind wandered through every possibility of why Cole hadn't told them. Was he waiting for something? If so, what? Fuck, this wasn't the time to be dwelling on this. Not when I could get what I needed from him. A way to get to Marcus, to make him pay. I summoned every ounce of courage remaining within me to figure out how to use this power I hadn't known existed until today. I'd done it before. Surely, I could do it again.

A flood of last-minute instructions spilled from Damien's lips. "We need to know where Marcus and his group went, what they're up to, but don't linger too long in there. Anything you can get will be good. If you can't find anything, we can try again later."

I took Cole's head in my hands, closing my eyes as I focused on where we connected. It didn't take long before I felt it, as if something were pulling me in. Reaching out to whatever it was, I allowed it to guide me.

My head fell back, muscles spasming and locking up as a wave of thoughts, emotions, and memories invaded me harder, faster than they had with Damien. So many memories, too many at once. Air caught in my throat as my mind was assaulted. Images of Cole's thoughts danced across my mind, visions of his mother taking him for ice cream, of him and his parents laughing at the dinner table.

I opened my eyes, finding myself in a strange room. No... it wasn't strange. I'd grown up here. My drawings lined the walls, my desk a mess of sketches and notes from school. The sound of the front door closing reached my ears, and I wondered if Mom had gotten off work early, but he usual cheerful greeting never echoed through the house.

Heavy footfalls echoed through the walls, and I twisted in my seat as my door swung open revealing Damien, his eyes wide, chest heaving.

"Lord Damien?" I asked, my voice not my own, but that of a young Cole. "What's wrong?"

"Hey," Damien said, his face grave, but full of relief as his shoulders sagged. "I... uh. I need to talk to you."

My brows furrowed, unease swelling in my gut as my eyes trailed over him, and my heart lurched at the black blood on his sleeves. "What're you doing here? Where's Mom and Dad?"

Damien's throat bobbed, but as fear grabbed hold of me and my lips parted to speak, I was torn from the memory, plunging into another.

Amara stood before me, her head cocked as she settled her hand on her waist.

Guilt twisted my chest as I hesitated to respond to her, but she spoke up again.

"You want to get back at the goddess responsible for your parent's deaths, don't you? Why continue to serve this goddess? She's the reason for all your misery."

"But... Damien's done so much for me," I said, eyeing her. "I don't want to hurt him."

"He failed them," she said through gritted teeth, her patience growing thin, and I shrunk back. "They would still be here if it wasn't for him—for the goddess he serves. Do you intend to follow in his footsteps and serve her as well? Allow her to send more of your brothers and sisters of The Order to their deaths?"

Amara's voice bit through my conscious, echoing through my head as she spoke to Cole, luring him to their side when he was most vulnerable.

I fell from the memory, descending deeper and deeper in search of what I needed. Cole had been young, and so vulnerable in his grief that he'd been so easy to manipulate. He'd been Marcus' tool from the beginning.

Images began to flood my mind faster, almost too quick for me to latch onto as I plummeted, slamming into another memory.

I narrowed my eyes at the way Damien froze, his eyes locked on the girl, hazel eyes full of a confused curiosity as she held his gaze.

"How—" Damien cleared his throat, the shock melted from his face, and I glanced at Zephyr's gaze just as glued to the girl, his dark brows furrowed in confusion.

The images blurred by once more until I was standing at the top of the stairway in front of the campus library.

Barrett's voice reached my ears, and I wondered what poor girl he was bothering this time. Zephyr tensed before me, and as I peered around him, I frowned at the sight of the same girl we'd met at The Galleria, the one I'd seen Damien talking to earlier that day.

She looked fucking terrified as she stared up at him, but she didn't seem to back down, didn't run away. There was a defiance in those eyes, as if despite her fear she wouldn't cower to him. Zephyr's hands curled into fists, and I couldn't understand his reactions. He never got involved with Barrett's shenanigans. What had him so on edge? And why was Damien so interested in her?

I froze. She couldn't possibly be... I'd been told stories growing up about that bitch goddess' daughter, but there was no way she could be her.

This girl was human.

If there was any chance she was Moira's reincarnation, though, I needed to find out. Fuck, I hated doing this, she seemed nice... Anger churned in my gut, though as memories resurfaced of everything I'd lost. The guilt I felt for pulling this girl into the middle of everything melted away as I ground my teeth together and stepped forward.

I stepped past Zephyr as he took a step forward, speaking up before he could do so. "Barrett, you know Damien's gonna be pissed that you're pickin' on her. You should stop."

The ground slipped from beneath me and darkness swallowed me once more.

The sneaking suspicion he'd felt about what I was to Damien coiled around me as I fell further and further into his mind. Everything he'd done was to get close to me, to get to know me. It was all so he could feed any and all information to Marcus and use me to get to Damien.

A prickling pain, like the stab of a needle, shot behind my eyes. Like my body was warning me of something, but I ignored it, pressing forward. I didn't have what I needed, couldn't stop now. Just a little longer.

What were Cole and Marcus doing? What were Marcus' plans? Where had he run off to? He spoke of the darklings. What was their connection? Did he get sick kicks out of sacrificing humans and his own kind to them? Who was this woman he spoke of that wanted me?

The images blurred together as I continued my search, memory after memory filling my head until I thought my mind might fracture, and Marcus stood before me. My mind recoiled, and I almost released Cole the moment our eyes met, but I resisted. I couldn't let my fear stop me. It wasn't me he was looking at. It was Cole, whose eyes I peered through.

The smell of oil filled my senses, a flash of high chain-link fences, scrap metal and junk cars. The faint sound of rushing water reached my ears.

I couldn't seem to latch onto it, my grip loosening before I could get a grasp on his thoughts, I was pulled off track. Gravity shifted around me, and I slammed into Cole's consciousness elsewhere. Marcus walked beside me, deep in the woods, the movements blurring and swaying. My vision flickered, as if the memory was skipping like a

259

scratched disc. There was something about this memory that was oddly different, my mind not latching onto his consciousness as it did with the others. Was I reaching my limit?

Shit. My hold was slipping, and the needle-like pain worsened behind my eyes as I dug my grip on him deeper.

This is nothing. You've suffered worse at his hand. He doesn't deserve your mercy.

Marcus stopped, turning toward me, and I ignored the familiar voice rippling through my mind, the venom of it slithering over me and leaving me nauseous. I couldn't afford to dwell on it, not when I was so close to learning something of Marcus' plans, what his connection to the darklings might be. Marcus' lips moved as he spoke, but his voice was muffled, and I couldn't understand what he was saying, my hold weakening.

Dammit. Not now. Hold on a bit longer.

We passed through the mouth of a cave, stepping into the darkness as it enveloped my vision. The light of the outside forest faded the farther we went, until it was so dark, I couldn't see inches in front of my face.

Torches came to life around us, flickering as they cast a shallow light across a cavern. Darklings crawled along the ground and walls like an infestation, and terror coiled in my gut. Or was it Cole's gut?

The creatures parted, clearing a path for us as we approached what resembled a large throne carved into the rock formations at the head of the cave. Marcus came to a stop in front of me, kneeling, and the rest of us followed suit.

Panic gripped me as our eyes lifted to the strange darkling I'd met in the alley once before. While she looked different now, I would have recognized her anywhere. She sat poised on the stone seat, legs crossed as she rested back, picking remains of her most recent meal from her teeth with her long onyx claw.

She was unlike any of the other darklings. More human-like than beast, intelligence reflecting in her bottomless black eyes. The darklings cowered in her presence, while they turned on us snarling and snapping but not attacking, as if they were compelled to resist the urge to devour us. Her eyes drifted across the group before meeting mine.

As if my grip slipped from the edge of a cliff, I fell into nothingness, before slamming into my body as if it were a brick wall.

Cole fell forward into an unconscious slump, the shackles suspending him before he hit the ground. I fell back against someone's chest, hands bracing me. The room spun, the nausea surging through me too much to bear and I couldn't think straight enough to wonder who it was that caught me. I twisted away from him, and reached for a nearby wastebasket. I threw my head over it, and the contents of my stomach emptied into the bin.

Damien and the others hovered over me, talking, but I couldn't quite hear or see them, as if every one of my senses had been stolen from me. The room was blinding, every movement blurred. A cold sweat broke out over my skin, and the air rushed into my lungs in short, uneven pants.

A hand came to my back, and Damien pulled my hair from my face as I continued to dry heave. "Easy, easy. It'll pass soon."

The heaves finally began to settle, and I spit the foul taste from my mouth into the bin one last time before sitting up. I blinked, flinching at how badly the bright lights stung and I shielded my eyes as the needle-like pain continued.

"Lights. Please. Turn them off," I panted.

Damien scooped me into his arms and left the room briskly, rounding the corner into another. The couch groaned as he eased me down onto it, and I fell against the cushions, my head resting against the back as I swallowed down the bile. A dim lamp on a nearby table, barely illuminating the room, but I couldn't so much as look in its direction.

He knelt in front of me. "Just breathe. Take your time. You don't have to tell me what you saw just yet."

This was information that couldn't wait, though, and the words flew out of my mouth. "They're working with the darklings!"

He tensed, his hand tightening on mine. "They're what?"

I lifted my head from the cushion, leaning forward to rest my face in my hands. "We—they were in a cave... There were so many darklings, Damien, hundreds of them, and there was this one darkling." The image of her was fresh in my mind, and it sent a chill down my spine.

"Slow down, *mea luna*. Breathe."

I continued, though, unable to slow down. "She-she wasn't like the others, Damien. She wasn't just some beast like they are. She was more human."

Damien cursed under his breath.

"What's wrong? Do you know who she is?"

Damien drew an uneven breath. "A little over a century ago, we fought a terrible battle, one that nearly wiped us out. The darklings had started to act similarly to the way they are now, organized and more deadly. A unique darkling had appeared among them, one who retained their consciousness. She had some sort of sway over them, an influence that bent them to her will."

"The battle I saw..."

He nodded. "We suffered a devastating blow. It's known to us as The Fall of Kingdoms. Not only did we lose countless warriors, but we also lost houses, entire bloodlines. They hunted our kind down, warrior and civilian alike. Male, female, child, it didn't matter to them. They've always wanted to erase us from existence, and with her controlling them, they were poised to do just that."

I couldn't imagine the carnage he'd witnessed. I'd only seen a fraction of what he had, could still smell it. It burned me in a way that made me wonder how he himself had dealt with it all these years.

Damien growled, his words barely slipping through his clenched teeth. "Dammit, Marcus! What would possess him to side with them?"

Barrett and the others walked into the room, hopeful expressions on their faces.

"What'd she get out of him? Did she find out where Marcus and his group are hidin'?" Barrett asked.

"We've got a bigger problem than Marcus." Damien rose to his feet, turning to them. "There's a nest. A huge one, at least ten times the size of the one that took out Vivienne's group, possibly more by now."

Their hope faded, and they looked between one another.

"Do you think they've been targeting the surrounding cities to build their numbers or something?" Vincent asked.

"I don't know…" Damien looked at Zephyr and Barrett. "It appears the darkling's leader has returned."

The color drained from their faces, and fear churned in the pit of my stomach to see the ones who didn't show fear be so shaken. What did this mean for our city? For the humans and immortals who lived here? Would the darklings attack them openly? What about my parents? Kat and Cody?

Zephyr's eyes fell to the floor as he began to pace, and he ran a hand over his face. "Fuck. We need to notify the civilians. They'll be easy targets."

"Double the patrols," Damien ordered, and the others all looked at him, their faces growing grave. "No one goes alone. Hunt in groups, three at a minimum, no exceptions."

"Do we have the numbers to do that?" Vincent asked.

"It'll be tight," Zephyr said. "We'll have to start running double shifts."

"We'll need to bring in the new recruits earlier than anticipated." Damien paused a moment. "And Barrett."

Barrett's eyes lifted to Damien, brows furrowed.

"We'll need Thalia."

He blinked, his throat bobbing as he seemed to work through his words. "But she's tied down training new recruits. Without her—"

"I know, but she's just as skilled as the three of you are. We need her. We'll figure out how to make it work. Every one of us will chip in to assist her with training if need be."

Barrett groaned, his head falling back before he turned to throw his fist into the wall. Heat flooded the room, his anger burning my skin but there was also something else, something icy… fear?

"Barrett," Damien warned.

Barrett threw his arms up. "I know, I know. I'll talk to her."

I rubbed my eyes, looking up at the others who lingered in the doorway. Who was Thalia? I shoved it down as I recalled the one piece of information I'd managed to retrieve, the information we needed.

"I saw something else in Cole's mind… There's an old building somewhere on the outskirts of town, I couldn't get a good look at it, though, only flashes. There was rusted metal, and a lot of scrap and junk metal lying around, and it smelled of oil…" I tried to remember everything I'd seen and heard. "Water. I think I could hear rushing water nearby, and there was the faint sound of cars in the city, too."

"That's a good start, Cas." Damien turned back to the others. "Zephyr, I'll leave the search to you. Gather a team. I want them found and captured."

He nodded, but as he turned to leave, Damien grabbed his forearm. Damien's voice was a near growl as he spoke. "If you find Marcus, I want him brought to me. Alive."

Zephyr nodded his head, and a part of me understood the weight and meaning of Damien's words, of how he would be the one to finish Marcus.

"Vincent, Barrett, you keep working on Cole. See if you can get any more information out of him." Damien paused a moment, taking a deep breath, his voice lowering a bit. "I don't care what you have to do. He knew what he was doing the moment he betrayed The Order."

Vincent and Barrett nodded and left the room. Damien stood in the doorway, still as stone. His eyes burned into the ground, in quiet calculation.

"What are we gonna do about the darklings' nest?" I asked as Damien returned to me.

He eased onto the couch beside me, resting his chin atop his hands. "We're going to need to build our numbers, but I'm afraid it's going to get ugly, faster than we can prepare for."

My throat went dry at the thought of it. This unique darkling, who could control the rest, could form an army powerful enough to level entire houses of Damien's race. My imagination ran wild, the thought of those creatures overtaking the city, slaughtering every human and immortal they could find. I couldn't imagine encountering that many darklings. My parents, Kat, Cody; I feared for their safety.

I knew how bad it would be when the darklings unleashed themselves on the human world from the devastation I'd witnessed through Lucia's eyes on the battlefield.

How could we stand a chance against them?

CHAPTER 29

The headache and nausea persisted for several hours after I entered Cole's mind, and it had kept me up late into the night. Damien had taken me back to the house to rest, but no matter what I did, I was unable to sleep for more than an hour, most of the night spent in the bathroom, unable to keep even water down.

Damien remained at my side the entire night, unwavering. His apologies never ceased, and the guilt he felt for asking me to dive into Cole's memories overwhelmed him, the balmy sticky feel of that emotion clinging to my skin.

What he didn't understand was that I was happy that, for once, I was able to help him. I wanted to do so much for him, for Barrett, and the others. So badly that I didn't care what happened to me.

I awoke to the sound of the door opening, and Ethel entered. "O, mah dear. How is yer head? Still hev a headache?"

I pushed myself up, forcing a weak smile as she walked over to my bedside, carrying a tray of various things. "It's pretty much gone, *Mitera*. Thank you again for the medicine you gave me."

"O, donnae push yerself darlin'." She nudged me back down to lean against the headboard and pulled the blanket back over my lap. "Take all the time ye need. I brought ye some water if ye can try tae get it down. I kno' ye had a rough night."

I glanced out the window, to the bright sunlit sky just beyond the maple trees. "How late is it?"

"It's almost noon."

Exhaustion still held me in its grasp, but I'd already slept most of the day away.

"Where's Damien?"

She took a cool damp rag, tenderly pressing it to my forehead, and I sighed at the feel of it. "He's doonstairs wi' Barrett an' the others. Terrible news aboot the darklins'."

I still wasn't sure what we were going to do. How we could face that many darklings if they decided to attack.

"Afore I ferget..." She reached into her pocket, pulling out a phone. "Damien had yer number switched o'er tae this fer ye, since ye lost yers. All yer contacts and things hev already been switched o'er."

She handed it to me, and my eyes widened, my mouth falling open. It was top of the line, much nicer than the one I'd lost. "He... how... Oh, my goodness. Please, I can't accept this... I know these aren't cheap."

"Donnae ye fret, child. It's yers noo. Ye'll need tae hev a reliable means o' contact, so it's a penny worth spendin'. Damien wonnae accept anythin' of lesser quality fer ye."

"Thank you, *Mitera*," I said sheepishly, struggling to accept him spending so much on me.

She smiled, and I quickly texted Kat and Mom to let them know.

"Damien said your family has served him for many generations?" I asked, setting the phone down as she grabbed the salve she'd started applying to my healing wounds.

"Ah've bin in servitude fer nearly seventy-two years noo," she said, turning my arm over to work the salve into the cut that spanned the length of my forearm. I feared it was going to leave a scar.

"Mah parents served afore I did, and mah grandparents afore them. There are nae many human families left 'at serve The Order these days. Many hev bin killed o'er the centuries. Cuid nae ask tae serve a better family tho'. Lord Damien has always looked after us and given us everythin' we cuid eva' need."

She chuckled, her warm smile bringing the crow's feet to light along the edges of her bright eyes. "I kno' he's the king and all, but he's become more of a son tae me."

"I can tell he admires you."

Their relationship was special, and I remembered how Damien had told me his parents had passed when he was younger. I wondered if he viewed her as more of a mother figure, just as she imagined him more of a son. It gave me hope that maybe he hadn't felt completely alone. My mind wandered then, conjuring images of a younger Damien. It was strange to think of, knowing that he was nearly a thousand years old.

"I'm gonna go downstairs to see what's going on," I said, as she finished tending to my wounds.

"Are ye sure, love?" she asked tentatively, concern flitting across her face.

"Yeah. I can't stand to sit here doing nothing."

"Ah'll give ye some privacy so ye can dress, then," she said as she headed for the door. "Just try to take it slow."

I smiled and nodded as she disappeared out the door before shoving off the bed to head for the closet.

A shipment had arrived the day before, full of all kinds of clothes. My eyes widened as I took in the row of clothing lining one side of the closet. How much clothing did he think I need? As I started looking through it all, I found that Damien had ensured I had everything I could ever need. Casual attire, sleepwear, clothes for training, and as I reached into the built in drawers, my cheeks heated at the delicate lace lingerie laying inside.

It warmed my heart as I continued looking through them to find that he'd paid such close attention to the style of clothing I liked. While a part of me was awestruck at it all, another part of me cringed to think about how much it cost him to provide them. It couldn't have been cheap, and the brands were the nicest I'd ever owned.

Today was supposed to be the first day of training, so I quickly dressed myself in some leggings and a loose tank top.

My phone rang out from the room as I finished taking my morning dose, and I quickly stashed the bottle back in place before hurrying over to where it rested on the nightstand. Mom's name flashed across the screen, and I quickly grabbed it, pressing it to my ear.

"Hey, Mom."

"Hey, sweetie. How're you feeling today?"

"I'm doing ok, focusing on resting," I said, knowing it might make her feel relief that I was taking it slow.

"That's good to hear. I was relieved to see your text as I realized you hadn't given me an address of where you were going to stay. I figured you might be resting so I was afraid to bother you."

"Sorry, I ended up crashing in Damien's spare room while we sorted out the living arrangements," I partially lied, though I knew she'd see through it. I didn't want to lie to her any more than I already knew I'd be forced to. Eventually she and Dad would want to see where I was living, and as I was staying here with Damien for the foreseeable future, there would be no hiding that from them.

"I thought you were going to be staying in an apartment."

I chewed my lip. "We're still working out the details, looking at the options."

She remained silent on the other end. "Are you being careful? Using protection?"

My cheeks heated, and my mouth fell open as the words flew out of my mouth in a harsh whisper. "Mom! That's not—"

She snickered on the other end. "I was young once, too, you know, and I know how it is to be head over heels for someone. In all honesty, I'm happy you feel safe with him after everything that's happened. I had a feeling this was going to happen, I've already talk to your father, so he'll keep his mouth shut when you talk to him."

My stomach tumbled as she went quiet for a moment. "I just want you to be careful. Don't feel like you need to rush into things. I'm not ready to be a grandma just yet."

"Did you forget they stuck a thing in my arm last year?" I grumbled. "Besides, nothing like that has even happened between us."

"I know, I know," she said, and I prayed Dad wasn't around to hear this conversation happening. "I just... Try to slow down a little. You've been through a lot. I know it's easy when you have feelings for someone to want to dive in quick. I just want you to be happy."

"I'll be careful, Mom. I promise," I groaned, desperate to talk about something else.

"Don't forget to check in every so often," she said, and the hint of pain and worry in her voice left my stomach in knots.

"I won't. Maybe I'll have you guys over for dinner soon. Just give me some time to settle in and sort everything out."

"I love you so much, sweetie. I'm happy you've found something with him."

My chest swelled at her words, and a smile curved my lips. "Me too. Tell Dad I love him and that I said hi, and... that I'm sorry for blowing up on him the other night."

"I will. We understand you need some space to figure yourself out, just... I didn't think it would be permanent."

"Sorry. There's so much that happened, and... I'm just not ready to talk about it yet," I breathed, my shoulders sagging. "But... to be honest, I don't think there will ever be a time that I'll be able to live there again after everything."

I heard her let out a sigh on the other end. "Just know you're always welcome to come home if you don't know where else to go. Even if only to visit."

"Thank you," I said, easing down onto the edge of the bed.

"I'm sure you're busy settling in, so I won't keep you. Tell Damien I said hi."

"I will. Bye, Mom."

"Bye, Sweetheart."

The line went dead, and I lowered the phone into my lap, drawing a deep breath as I tried to calm my racing heart. I hoped Dad wasn't too mad at me for my outburst the other night, but he needed to understand that I wasn't a kid anymore, that I needed to make these decisions on my own, and that I couldn't stay under their thumb for whatever bit of my life remained.

My phone vibrated in my hand, and my eyes fell to the notification of a text from Kat. I tapped the screen.

> Good morning, love! That's so sweet that he got you a phone! I hope you are settling in and have gotten the rest you need. I've got work right after classes, but if you need anything, let me know.

Another text came through.

> I miss you on campus already, but don't rush it if you're not ready to come back yet. Maybe we can get lunch sometime.

And another came through shortly after that, as if she couldn't seem to get all her words down in one message.

> I'm here if you want to talk at all. About anything.

I smiled, tapping away on my screen to respond.

> I'm settling in okay. Damien has been so amazing. He's making sure I have everything I need.

My phone dinged as she responded.

> I'm so glad he's there for you. Never expected him to be such a great person. I'm glad he's proving me wrong.

My chest swelled as I typed again.

> Me too.

She texted again.

> I've gotta get to class, but if I can, I'll call you later tonight when I've finished studying if it's not too late.

> Ok. Have fun!

I hurried to the bathroom to tame my hair and crouched to reach for my hidden bottles of medicine deep in the back of the vanity. My skin crawled as I lifted the bottle. Was I really hiding these from him? I should tell him, but... how would I even do that?

Completely incomplete, feeling as if you'll never feel whole again. I almost ended it many times.

We'd only just found each other again. What would he say if he found out that our time together would be short? He needed to know, but...

I shoved them into my mouth, unable to find a solution or a means of telling him, and stashed them again before hurrying out of the bathroom and toward the bedroom door

The rich smell of a sweet smoke, similar to how a cigar smelled, wafted into the entry as I reached the foot of the stairway. That same smell had faintly lingered on Damien since I first met him, mixed with his musky scent of cedar and leather, but I'd never smelled it so strongly as I did now. Voices echoed down the hallway, and the smell and conversations grew stronger as we approached the living room.

When I peeked in from the hall, I found Damien standing near the fireplace. Thick smoke rolled from his lips, his hand holding the roll of whatever he smoked just inches from his face.

His amber and ashen eyes lit up when he caught sight of me, and my heart fluttered. "How're you feeling, *mea luna?*"

The conversation died down at his acknowledgement of my presence.

I smiled, a teasing tone painting the words as they left my lips. "*Mitera* worked her magic. I may yet live to see another day."

269

My gaze drifted across the room. James and Vincent were kicked back on the couch, Zephyr standing next to Damien. Among them was a new face, a woman speaking lowly with Barrett across the room. Naturally, Barrett had a cocky grin on his face, and her expression led me to believe he was pushing buttons that might backfire on him.

Standing nearly as tall as him, there was no denying she was a warrior. Her body resembled that of a Greek sculpture. Where her arms were exposed from her tank top, defined muscles showed, and black ink like Damien's reached out from beneath her shirt, the shadows forming into the faces of various predators, a wolf, a hawk, a panther, and so many more. She was beautiful, and I was half tempted to ask her if I could sketch her one day.

I blinked. What the hell was I thinking? This woman didn't even know me. I couldn't just go up to her and say, 'Hi, we don't know each other but I want to draw you'. There was a strange tugging in the back of my mind, though, something familiar in the way she carried herself, the sound of her voice.

Her gaze remained fixed on Barrett as she combed her fingers through her corn silk hair, pulling it back into a ponytail, as if she were preparing to get into it with him when she noticed me. Her stormy silver eyes shifted in my direction, her pale brows rising. As her face turned to me, I noticed a long scar that stretched from above her right brow down to her cheek.

Ethel dipped her head into the room from behind me. "Lord Damien, yer gonna set off the fire alarms!"

A devious grin spread across his face as he put his lips to the roll he smoked, inhaling deeply before letting the smoke slip from his lungs. "I disabled those long ago, *Mitera*."

She rolled her eyes at him. "Never mind that. Ye need tae be more careful wi' Cas, Lord Damien. She's nae built like ye."

I stiffened, twisting to her, my lips parting. She misunderstood the situation, and I knew Damien had agonized over how things had gone the night before. I knew that if it were up to him, I would've had no part in any of this. "*Mitera*. I'm okay real—"

"I'll be more careful in the future, *Mitera*." Damien said, a somber smile on his face, and my heart squeezed at the flicker of guilt in his eyes.

"Well, I need tae get lunch started. Ye lot want a bite tae eat?" she asked, looking to the others.

They all politely declined in unison.

"All right then." She looked at Damien. "Ye behave yerself noo, Lord Damien."

"I promise, *Mitera*." And with that, she disappeared down the hall.

Barrett chuckled. "*Mitera*'s getting spicy in her old age."

Damien's eyes shifted to him, and he took a hit of the... cigar? I didn't quite know what it was. "She's not wrong, though. We can't expect Cas to keep up with us as a human. We need to keep that in mind as we move forward with her training."

The words stung, and while I hated to acknowledge my own weakness, he wasn't wrong.

"We're starting with her Nous abilities as they seem to be the first that have reawakened," Damien said.

"Will I really be able to use other magic?" I asked tentatively.

"I'm not sure," he admitted. "Normally you would gain access to the magics of every House of Power, but there's no way for us to know with you being human, so we'll have to play it by ear."

Zephyr's eyes lingered on me a moment in quiet contemplation, and I frowned at him as he leaned in and whispered something to Damien.

Damien shrugged. "I'm not sure. You'll have to test that for yourself as that's your specialty."

Specialty?

"Why didn't you tell me your mate was such a cutie, Damien?" I blinked as the woman spoke up before I could. "I would've never guessed she was Lucia's reincarnation."

My cheeks heated at her words. Hearing her say out loud that I was his mate sent my heart into a frenzy, but then the name drew my attention. Did she know Lucia?

"Have we met before?" I asked tentatively.

She smiled knowingly. "In another life."

I cocked an eyebrow at that statement but stiffened as her eyes roamed over me. "You're just as small as she was too. I've heard of the reincarnation cycle, but the resemblance is crazy."

A proud grin pulled at Damien's lips as he looked from me to her. "And she's got just as much bite. I heard she knocked Amara's ass out."

Her pale brows rose, and I frowned. How did he know about that?

"Now I'm really curious." She gave me an apologetic smile. "Sorry, that was rude of me. I'm Thalia."

So, this was Thalia, a female warrior of The Order. There was something beautiful and deadly about her, the way she carried herself, the sharpness in her eyes. We'd known each other in a past life. Was it Lucia's life? Or was it during Elena or Moira's? How was I supposed to keep track of all this?

As she drew closer, I wasn't prepared for how intimidating her presence would be. Like an Amazonian woman of Grecian times, power undulated from her very being.

She tilted her head, eyes lowered over me. "Nice to finally meet you, Cas."

"Nice to meet you, Thalia," I responded.

"So, you're really her? Lucia's reincarnation?" she asked, something flickering in her eyes. Hope? Curiosity? Excitement? A number of emotions filled the air, nearly overwhelming me as the sensations of them skittered over my skin.

I nodded, wrapping my arms around myself. "Yeah, crazy right? I heard you train recruits?"

"Yeah, honestly, I'd rather be out hunting darklings again, but I know it's important." She walked around me, throwing an arm over my shoulder and leaning in, whispering into my ear. "Between you and me, though, I think Barrett keeps me there because he doesn't want me to kick his ass in dispatching darklings like I used to when he joined The Order."

I giggled, my eyes glancing briefly at Barrett, who raised a brow at us, arms crossed tightly against his chest.

"You enjoy getting under his skin, don't you?" I whispered back.

She winked in response. "Any chance I get. If he gives you any lip, you let me know."

"What're you gonna do about it?" Barrett barked.

Her eyes shifted to him, a wicked smirk curving her lips. "Put you in your place."

I tried not to laugh, but I would honestly pay money to see Thalia kick Barrett's ass any day. It was about time someone pushed his buttons the way he did ours.

Barrett stalked toward us, his eyes falling on Thalia. "You wanna go toe to toe with me?"

Thalia stepped in front of me, rising to meet his gaze, and I could hear the smile in her voice. "Go on, pretty boy. You can have the first shot."

The air turned electric around them, and before I knew it, they were in such close proximity that I feared a fight might actually break out.

"Knock it off, you two," Damien chided. "Go wreck someone else's house. Or get a room, I don't care which."

The energy fell almost immediately, and I noticed Vincent huff a laugh, but quickly stifle it the moment Barrett's gaze shifted to him. A groan broke from Barrett's throat and he rolled his eyes before turning to return to where he was originally standing. For a moment, I noticed a faint blush decorate Thalia's cheeks as she turned her head, eyes falling.

Damien stood. "All right, we've discussed enough. Let me know if you find anything new."

Zephyr nodded and pushed off, gesturing to Vincent and James to follow.

"James, I need you to pull up the GIS Map," Zephyr said as they headed for the hall, James listening intently to ever word. "I want to know of every place in the city that might match the description Cassie gave us. Knock off any that aren't within listening distance of the river. Keep in mind an immortal's hearing. It could be upwards of a quarter of a mile away..."

His voice faded out the front door, Vincent and Barrett not far behind them.

Thalia leaned in before passing me. "See ya later, Cas. I can't wait to train with you."

"Bye," I said.

The front door shut, echoing through the walls as the house emptied.

"What exactly does James do for The Order?"

"He does a number of things, but his particular skill set resides in security and hacking," Damien said, turning his gaze to me. "Kid's a genius when it comes to computers and security systems. We've had many instances where immortals have gotten mixed up with humans, either thrown in jail or hauled off to the hospital. James ensures security feeds are wiped, records are destroyed, and any loose ends are taken care of. He's been with us for ten years now. My only regret is that he didn't show up earlier."

He tamped out the embers of whatever it was he was smoking, and my mind began calculating how old James might be. He was human, and if he'd been working with Damien on security and hacking for nearly ten years, he was most definitely older than me.

"What exactly is that?" I asked, nodding toward the cigar-like roll.

He glanced at it. "It's Brierleaf. It's... kind of like a really strong... tobacco?" He frowned, as if he weren't quite sure that was an accurate comparison.

"I've never heard of it. Is it from Selene's realm?"

"Yeah. It's a nasty habit. I really should quit." He pushed off the mantel, walking over to me. "Are you sure you're feeling up to this? We can start training tomorrow."

"No, but you said so yourself, we don't have a lot of time. If it'll help, I want to do everything I can." I needed to learn as much as I could, wanted to help them get Marcus, help them with the darklings in any way I could. Whether it was truly for them or for me, I'd yet to fully grasp. Regardless, I was useless in my current state.

He sighed, rubbing his face in frustration. "I'm sorry. We've never had to rush your training like this. There's always been time to move at a safer pace."

"I'll be fine," I said, reaching out to grip his hand tightly.

"How long have you known Thalia?" I asked, easing onto the couch.

"She joined The Order several years before Barrett, almost six hundred years ago."

I tried to force my face to remain neutral at his casual statement. As if the thought of living over six hundred years wasn't something to balk at, which, to him at nearly a thousand years of age, probably wasn't out of the norm.

"They trained and pledged their vows to Selene together. You'd think having known each other for so long, they'd be closer, but she and Barrett are obnoxious as hell when they're in the same room," he grumbled.

273

"I think she likes him," I said, unable to hide my smile at the memory of how flustered they'd gotten. "You should have seen how red her face got when you called them out."

"And to make matters worse, Barrett likes her. He won't admit it, but I'm not stupid. I see how he acts when she's around, how protective he is of her."

I raised an eyebrow. "Really? He looked more annoyed than anything."

"If I didn't know him better, I'd agree." His eyes drift away from me, as if running through memories. "He's pulled a lot of strings for her, some things you wouldn't be able to do if it wasn't for his position. It's why he's so pissed she's getting pulled back on patrol."

I frowned. "Why would he get angry about that?"

"Because he's the one who originally pulled her from them to begin with, put her in charge of training recruits as she did in the past."

Why would he do that?

"Sadly, I don't know if they'll ever act on their feelings," he said, his eyes softening as his eyes fell to our conjoined hands. "She was once bonded."

"Bonded?" I asked.

He hesitated a moment, as if trying to find the right words to explain. "I guess it would be the equivalent to what humans call marriage, but on a more powerful, spiritual scale."

"Did he…" I was afraid to ask if her… bonded might have been killed, or if they had simply separated. The way the light dimmed in his eyes, though, left my heart twisting.

"He was killed on patrol many years ago, and it was shortly after that, that Barrett pulled rank and made that call. She was pissed, but… that's not my story to share." He sighed and blinked, seeming to pull himself from the sad memory. "*Mitera* should be done making lunch soon. We'll eat, and then I'm taking you to The Outpost."

"The Outpost?"

"It's the other headquarters. It's where we'll begin your formal training."

CHAPTER 30

We'd driven far into the mountains when Damien finally parked his car. Before us stood a small building in the center of a large clearing. It was nowhere near the size of the apartment complex, only standing a single story high. The car door creaked in the cold as I opened it and stepped out, eyes drifting across the dense forest surrounding us.

Further down the road behind us, we'd passed through a gate that connected to tall chain-link fences that stretched farther than I could see. I wasn't sure how many acres of forest surrounded us. It could have easily been hundreds to keep this place so well hidden from human eyes.

I followed closely behind Damien as he approached a steel door. My eyes drifted over the grounds surrounding the building. Where grass may have once been was worn to dirt and benches, training dummies, and a covered area with an assortment of tools and weapons sat nearby. I wondered what the other warriors in The Order looked like, how many there were.

"So, this is where Thalia trains recruits?" I asked as Damien climbed out of the car.

"Yeah, I had them train elsewhere today, so you could take the time you need to adjust without an audience."

I stiffened. "You didn't have to do that. I don't want to interrupt things—"

"You're not interrupting things. It would have been a lot to show up here with me. A new human with the king, and a female at that, you'd be the center of attention. The rumors are already starting to circulate after we mobilized the teams to search for you. It's only a matter of time before people learn of your return."

My eyes drifted from his as I pondered that thought, and I swallowed as I imagined being scrutinized and assessed by so many people at once. How could I ever live up to their expectations? They were hoping for their returned goddess, someone they hoped might end the war. How disappointed would they be when they learned I was a mere shadow of what they needed? A failed reincarnation trapped in a weak human body.

"Don't worry, we'll work you in. I just didn't want to put all the pressure on you on your first day."

"Thanks for that," I said nervously, though the pressure had been steadily building since I'd met Selene.

My gaze swept up to a security camera staring down at us from the edge of the roof as we approached.

"So how exactly does a human like James find himself working on security for a secret race of magical beings?" I asked. "Was it through *Mitera*? I remember you said her family's served yours for years."

He nodded. "He was getting into trouble back home, hacking into low-level security systems, planting spyware, and stealing information to sell it for cash. She asked if there was a job I could give him, a way to get him out of the hole he was digging for himself. Once we looked into him, saw his talent, I offered him a position that paid more money than he could ever make doing what he was doing without the risk of prison. It took a while, but I think the challenge was good for him. It wasn't long before he rose to become one of our head security analysts and white hat hackers overseeing the entire division."

Damien quickly punched numbers into a keypad, and there was a click as the deadbolt released. "He was a troubled teen, divorced parents, associating with the wrong crowd. I think he just needed more of a challenge."

How lucky of him that Ethel had intervened when she had.

Automatic lights came on, illuminating the entry as Damien closed the door behind us. It was a wide-open room with various chairs, tables, and couches, and I assumed it was some sort of lounge.

"This way," Damien called, beckoning me from where he stood at a doorway, and I realized I'd fallen into such a daze that I hadn't noticed him leave my side. He opened the door, revealing a stairway leading underground.

As he descended the stairs, I found my feet plastering to the floor as if they refused to take another step. Instead of the stairwell before me, it was the stairwell in Marcus' compound that stood before me, the walls becoming my cell as they narrowed in on me, the shackles tightening around my...

Damien stopped a few steps down when he realized I wasn't following. "Are you ok, Cas?"

I flinched, his words pulling me back, and took a deep breath, shoving down the impending panic licking at the pit of my stomach.

You're safe. He no longer has you.

"Yeah, sorry."

He eyed me a moment, his lips parting, but he didn't ask, and we continued downward. The stairs led down to a hall lined with a few doors, and I hadn't missed the few security cameras watching us at this level as well.

Damien's voice broke the silence as he pointed toward each of the doors. "The armory is through that door. There's a gym over there, and through here is the training facility."

"You guys really have an armory?"

"Yeah, it doesn't get used as much as used to, not as many warriors in our ranks as we've had in the past. We changed things up and it now only houses weaponry and gear for new recruits. Most warriors keep their equipment with them at all times now as it isn't exactly convenient to have them report here before heading all the way back into the city for patrol. The Complex was never set up for that purpose, though there has been discussion of upgrades to remedy that," he explained, opening the door to the training facility and entering.

Black mats lined the concrete floors, the rubber smell filling my nose, and large mirrors stretched out across the walls on both sides. The space was huge, wide-open, and housed a few punching bags, benches, as well as a number of racks with various training weapons.

"How many warriors are there in The Order?"

He shook his head. "Not as many as I'd like. We used to have a few hundred serving in our ranks, but after The Fall of Kingdoms, our numbers were drastically reduced. There are thirty-six active warriors, including our group, and thirteen new recruits who are still in training right now. Vincent, Zephyr, and Barrett each oversee their own teams."

Those weren't good numbers. Damien wasn't kidding when he said that things may get worse before we were fully prepared. How could so few warriors face an army of darklings as large as the one I'd seen? I swallowed, fearful of what a war with the darklings could mean for us all.

Damien grabbed a chair and motioned for me to come. I took a deep breath, nervous to start but eager for it at the same time.

"It was a lot to ask of you when you searched Cole's mind. I'm sorry you had to endure that." Damien carried another chair over, the

277

two facing each other. He eased onto one of them and gestured for me to sit across from him.

"I think that's the three hundredth and twenty-sixth time you've apologized," I said, cocking a brow, and I took his hand. "It was my decision to go through with it, and I don't blame you for how I felt after. I'm the one who pushed my limit, not you."

He let out a heavy sigh, but lifted his eyes to me, determination lighting them. "We aren't going to do anything like that this time."

"I'm glad I was at least able to get the information I did." I hesitated to ask, but I needed to know. "What's gonna happen to Cole?"

"We're keeping him in case we can get any further information out of him. I won't sugarcoat it, though, Cas. He won't be leaving that building unless it's in a body bag."

The fact that I didn't have so much as an ounce of sympathy had me questioning myself. When had I become so cold? When had I lost the ability to sympathize with someone? He'd lost his parents in this war, had suffered so much more than I could ever fathom. I couldn't imagine what I'd do if I ever lost my parents... and yet. I couldn't seem to find the ability to care about what had happened to him to make him do the things he'd done.

"Maybe I can get more out of him," I said, ready to search his memories again, regardless of the side effects I knew he or I would likely endure again.

He leaned forward, his gaze so piercing that I thought he also found comfort in the pain Cole had felt last night. "When you're ready, yes. You will have every opportunity to wring ever bit of information you want out of him. He isn't going anywhere, though, so for now, you focus on me."

My heart lurched, and my hands recoiled before he could take hold of them. "I don't want to hurt you, Damien. What I did to Cole hurt him, I saw the state he was in when I finished, and how badly it hurt when Marcus invaded my thoughts. I don't want to do that to you."

Pain flashed across Damien's eyes. "It's okay, *mea luna*. You only hurt Cole because you went for a lot in one go, without knowing what you were doing. We're just going to start with you reading my thoughts."

I blinked, trying to combat the rising panic in my chest as my mind played through all the possibilities, seeing Damien slumping unconscious in the same way I'd left Cole just the night before.

"It won't be the same, Cas," Damien said, his voice unflinching, and I couldn't understand how he could have such faith in me when I didn't have any in myself.

"Marcus, what he did... it isn't supposed to be painful to enter someone's thoughts."

I hesitated. "Promise you'll stop me if it hurts at all."

A warm smile curved his lips, and something tugged in my chest at the sight of it. "I'll be fine."

I held out my hands, and he took hold of them, the rough callouses of his fingers and palms against my skin sending my heart fluttering in the cage of my chest.

"There's a lot you can do with a person's mind," he said, his eyes dancing over my hands as he turned them over, his fingers lithely gliding along my skin, and I resisted the urge to shrink back as he viewed the healing bruises and cuts. "You can read someone's thoughts, feel their emotions, see memories, gauge if they are lying or telling the truth. It's especially helpful in combat to aid in anticipating your opponent's moves. You used it to communicate with me in the past, though it depended on how far apart we were. It came in handy at times."

He lifted his eyes to me, something dark lingering in their depths as he seemed to recall past knowledge of the ability. "There are also darker things that you can do. You can instill thoughts and wills into a person, make them see things that aren't really there, make them forget things, or instill memories that were never truly their own."

My mind immediately sank back into what I'd seen when I'd been held by Marcus. How he manipulated me into seeing Damien. It had been so real that I'd forgotten where I was or that he had me, and my hands began to tremble.

"Cas? Are you ok?" he asked, and the worry in his eyes made me realize my anxiety reflected in my expression.

"Marcus did something like that to me... He got into my head. I—" I couldn't bring myself to tell him the things he'd tried to do to me in Damien's image. "He made me see things that weren't really there."

Damien's eyes lowered and my fingers grew hot with the fury that burned in him. "I swear, Cas. I will make him pay for what he did to you."

"I want to learn how to do what he did, to be able to tear through his mind like he did mine." My voice was painfully even, so much so that I felt sick at the lack of sympathy I harbored, but I wanted him to burn with the same agony I had.

No. What's wrong with me?

"You'll learn, *mea luna*. I'd love nothing more than to watch you crush him under the power I know you possess. He's an insect compared to you."

Was this how I really felt? Was this what I'd become? I couldn't deny that this hadn't been the first time I'd felt such an unsettling need to hurt him, they'd grown so prevalent that not a day had gone by that I didn't think about hunting him down and ending his miserable existence. It was a darker part of me that I'd been too afraid to acknowledge. There was something building with in me, a desire for more than just revenge, but the need to get even in a way that didn't seem healthy. Had Marcus succeeded in turning me into the very monster he was?

279

"Am I wrong for feeling like this?" I asked, questioning what I was becoming. "I feel so terrible, so angry at him, and yet..."

Damien was silent for a moment. "You're not like him, Cas. I can hear it in your voice. I know what you're thinking. Give yourself some grace. What he did to you was absolutely unforgivable."

"You said he was part of The Order before everything happened, what exactly did he do?" I asked.

"He dealt in secrets," he said, and seemed to hesitate a moment before continuing. "He interrogated criminals and deserters, gathering information when needed. Sometimes going as far as crossing the veil to the other side when the need arose. He was the best at what he did."

He seemed to hate admitting that, and I could understand what Damien mean, knew from experience the skills he put to use to drag whatever information he needed from his victims. Then my thoughts narrowed in on Damien's words. Marcus dealt in secrets. I remembered how obsessed he'd seemed with our secrets, asking if Damien had told me his secret, asking if my condition was my secret.

Secrets... I wondered how many he held. How many he'd gathered in his lifetime. What were *his* secrets? I wondered if I could drag them from him, drag the name of whoever was targeting me from his mind before I silenced him for good, stopping him from ever collect another secret for his collection.

I took a deep breath, pushing it from my mind smothering the desires burning inside me as I avoided the truth Damien tried to drown out. "You just want me to try to see your thoughts, right?"

I saw his eyes flicker across my face briefly, seeming to hear the avoidance in my tone, but he didn't press. I wasn't ready to face it, didn't know if I would ever be ready to.

"Yes. As I said when you entered Cole's mind, it's easier to start with touch. You're better grounded to your target that way. Once you've learned how to do it properly, you can do it to someone from a distance. Until then, we start with touch."

He gripped my hands gently. "I'm ready when you are."

I took a deep breath, closing my eyes as he gently squeezed my hand. I focused on his touch, allowing it to ground me. I could feel the connection he spoke of, feel it in my fingertips, in my palms. Every place our skin touched was almost electric, a strange energy that I'd never paid attention to, different from the connection I'd felt with Cole. I focused in on it and allowed my mind to wander through that touch.

"Just tell me what I'm thinking." His voice was soft, almost a whisper. "A single word."

Find the thread, use it to guide the way. I focused, searching in the darkness for words or images, anything. Then, out of the darkness, I saw myself, as if I were looking in a mirror, only my eyes were closed. I was sitting before me, holding my hands. It was then that I realized I was looking through Damien's eyes at myself. I shrunk back in surprise, dropping his hand.

"What did you see?" he asked, brows raised.

"I saw through your eyes just now." I shivered, chills breaking out over my skin. "It was weird."

He chuckled. "Not exactly what I wanted you to do, but that's a strong start. I'll take it. Now, we just need to practice until you can do that intentionally."

I smiled, feeling optimistic. "Ok, let's try again."

A few hours passed, the mental toll beginning to wear on me, and I braced myself on my knees, panting as I slipped from Damien's thoughts. I'd gotten to the point where I could read what he was thinking, see what he was seeing, and was beginning to see images as he imagined them. It wasn't enough, though. I needed to be able to navigate memories. I needed to be able to get more information out of Cole.

"Let's go ahead and stop there," Damien said.

My gaze snapped to him, my words coming in bursts as I breathed through the nausea. "No, I want to try one more time."

"Cas—"

"I'm so close, Damien. One more time, please. I got a glimpse of a memory this time, and you didn't have to make me stop." I'd nearly given up when I'd hurt him a few times while accessing memories, but he'd been encouraging, taking a step back and working through other things before trying again.

He sat there for a moment, sighed, and held his hands out one more time. "Last time. I don't want to push you too far. You're not immortal, ok? You're only human. You have limits."

Letting out a shaky breath, I reached forward again, taking his hands into my own as I closed my eyes. I wasn't sure when exactly this thought of diving into someone's mind had gone from terrifying to... exciting, liberating almost, as if I could do something more than I'd ever dreamt I could.

I sank into the depths of his mind, his consciousness brushing against me like the touch of his fingertips, welcoming me. From the darkness, I found myself standing in the most beautiful hall, like a ballroom in a castle. There were no walls, save the columns holding the roof high above us. The sun shined through intricately stained glass at the head of the room that reached from floor to ceiling, the colored glass swirling in beautiful designs, and casting an array of pinks, and greens, and blues onto the mosaic tile beneath my feet. A warm summer breeze drifted over my shoulder, and the smell of grass and forest filled my senses.

The air was almost misty around me as my eyes took it all in, the haze of distant memories leaving some of the background in a blur. A crowd of people congregated in the center, dressed in beautiful gowns, their bodies moving together in fluid movements as they danced and sang. There was such wonderful energy here, so much happiness that I could feel it from across the room.

I stood on the outer edges of the great hall, leaning against one of the stone columns, the warmth of the sun's rays falling on my back as I watched the festivities from afar. Music echoed throughout the area, and those who weren't dancing stood idly nearby, drinking and chatting. It was a celebration of sorts, though I didn't know what they were celebrating.

From the crowds emerged a woman, her eyes searching the room. In that moment, my heart fluttered in my chest at her presence, something tugging deep within me toward her, but it wasn't my heart that raced. It was Damien's.

She was dressed in the most intricate gown, unlike the rest, though just as beautiful if not more. Layers of flowing, dusty blue fabric pooled at her feet, her bustier splitting above her breast, stretching out into long draping sleeves before meeting again around her neck. Her delicate hands grabbed hold of the front of her gown, lifting her skirt as she hurried toward me.

Her eyes were like moonstone, near glittering in the rays of sunlight. Sections of her near silver hair were pulled back into complex braids, draping over the rest of the curls that reached past her hips. I knew her face immediately as she grew closer.

It was me… Or. it was me in a past life.

She smiled up at me, and she positively glowed. "Come on, Damien. You'll not get out of gracing me with at least one dance this night."

I heard Damien's voice as we were dragged forward, a hint of humor on his tongue as we spoke. "I think you've had a little too much to drink, Princess."

"Nonsense, you've had too little," she chuckled, dragging him into the crowd.

I wanted to stay, wanted to see more of what our life was like, of what… we were like, but I closed my eyes, satisfaction filling me as I withdrew myself from Damien's thoughts. To have been able to successfully navigate a memory without hurting him was all I'd wanted.

I opened my eyes to find myself sitting in the chair before Damien. The nausea had subsided. I was still breathing a little heavy, but aside from that, I felt fine.

"Were you successful?" Damien searched my face nervously. "What did you see?"

"You were at some party. I saw… me, I think. I wanted a… dance…" The room spun, Damien splitting into two… three… four, and I frowned, blinking as I swayed.

What…

"Cassie?" Damien jumped to his feet, hands on me as he steadied me before I could fall from the chair.

The taste of copper filled my mouth, and something warm rolled over my lips, dripping down my chin and into my lap. I lifted my hand to touch the warm liquid dripping from my nose, and my gaze fell to my fingertips, dipped in blood. My mind hazed over, thoughts struggling to form, my lips failing to form words to speak. To question what was going on.

Blood? Why was I…

"*Fuck.* You went too far!" He lifted me off the chair and ducked into the shadows of the room. We appeared in the medical bay of The Complex, the room spinning still, and I swallowed down the bile rising in my throat. Johnson stood at his desk, writing notes, and he lifted his eyes to us, before frowning in confusion.

"Is everything o—"

"I think she's suffering a recoil!" Damien yelled as he rushed me over to a bed. I gripped his shirt as he moved to pull away from me.

"I need you over here, now!" he demanded as he lifted my chin, forcing my unfocused gaze to him as he lifted a rag to my nose to staunch the bleeding. "Can you hear me, Cas?"

His voice barely registered in my head, my mind seeming to struggle to latch onto each word, and I frowned as I tried to focus on them. "S… sorry?"

"Dammit. Cas, I need you to try to talk for me," Damien said through gritted teeth as Johnson rushed to my bedside.

"What's… recoil?" I muttered, the words struggling to pass my lips, and I swayed on the bed as speaking seemed to be too much for me to focus on while trying to stay upright.

"A recoil's what happens when you use more magic than your body is prepared to. It varies between each individual," Johnson said calmly as he began examining me, flashing a light in my eye to which I flinched away from, the light burning too deeply, just as it had the night before, but I hadn't experienced this last night.

"How long were you practicing for before this happened? Did you do anything unusual that might've tripped it suddenly?" Johnson asked Damien.

"We've been practicing her Nous abilities for the last three hours. I was about to cut her off when she wanted to try one more time," his said, voice laced with worry.

"I want you to follow my finger, can you do that?" Johnson asked, and I blinked before nodding, the words coming through a bit clearer. He moved his finger from one side to the other, and then up and down. "The affects seem to be wearing off, I don't see any sign of neurological damage."

"I'm... okay, Damien." I said, the room settling, the words becoming easier to form.

"No, you're not. I knew I should have stopped you."

I couldn't stop myself from fighting him on it. "I was... successful, though. I'll stop now... I just wanted—"

"From now on, we stop when I say so."

I halted the words on my tongue and nodded, my eyes falling to the floor.

"I want her checked out fully. Make sure she's okay and there are no signs of permanent damage," Damien ordered.

Johnson nodded and began looking me over. Damien hovered nearby; knuckles pressed to his lips as he did when he was upset.

Johnson pressed his stethoscope to my back. "Can you take a deep breath for me?"

I nodded hesitantly, inhaling deeply, falling into the routine I'd endured far too many times. He moved the stethoscope to my chest, listening for far longer than I'd like. He stopped short, his eyes lifting to me, and the moment our eyes met, I knew the thoughts forming behind his pale eyes.

He knew... He knew something was off with my heart.

I stared back at him. He was going to tell Damien. Please, anything but that.

Don't say anything, please...

Johnson's eyes went distant for a moment, before he blinked, his brows knitting as if he'd awoken from some daydream.

"What did you find?" Damien asked, returning to his side.

Johnson lifted the stethoscope over his head to drape it across the back of his neck. "She sounds good. I think she did start to suffer a recoil, but it looks like she stopped just before it set in fully and caused any serious damage."

Damien glanced back at me, and I smiled weakly. "I'm okay, really."

He ran his hand over his face, taking a deep, controlled breath. "Never again. Promise me, Cas."

"I won't push myself like that again, I promise."

He stood there a moment, eyes burning into mine as if he questioned whether I'd actually hold true to that promise. Finally, he eased a little, letting out a deep breath. "Thank you, Johnson. You're dismissed."

Johnson bowed his head before returning to his work, and Damien held out his hand. "Can you stand?"

"I think so," I said, taking it, and he helped me to my feet. My knees wobbled a bit beneath me, the room shifting, but not entirely falling back into the ripple it had been moments before.

If I hadn't pulled out of his mind when I did, the recoil could have been far more severe. A part of me grew worried as Selene's warning flitted across my thoughts, and I feared the impact my powers would inevitably have on my body.

Her body will not be able to handle the powers at their peak. They will destroy her.

She was right. I didn't have much time left. I wanted to cry at the thought, that just when I'd seemed to find the will to live, that very life would be ripped from me, regardless of what I did. What would that mean for the others? She'd made it seem as if my presence was vital to their war with the darklings. Even with my limited time, if I could help Damien destroy them, that would be enough for me, just to know he would be safe when I left this world.

How much would my body be able to handle before it gave out, though? Sooner or later, Damien was going to find out that our time was running out, and I feared it above all else, feared what he would do, feared how he would react. Would he try to hide me away like my parents had? Would he stop my training? Would he let his fear of losing me again cloud his judgement? I wasn't ready for things to change, wasn't ready for him to learn this terrible truth and suffer as I knew he would.

I wasn't ready for our time together to end.

I wasn't ready to say goodbye.

CHAPTER 31

I laid melted in the sheets, staring up at the ceiling of our bedroom. Our bedroom. It would take a while for that reality to not leave butterflies in my stomach. My cheeks heated at the memory of how Damien had pressed me against the hallway wall at the complex the night before, the memory of the things Damien said he wanted to do to me in our bed.

My heart raced in my chest, and I pulled myself from the thoughts, eager to distract myself from the heat pooling between my thighs as my mind dredged up the feel of his touch, of what I imagined it might be like to feel him that way. I checked the time on the wall clock and sighed when I found that it was only nearing one in the morning.

It had been nearly four hours since Damien and the others had gone patrolling for darklings. Vincent remained downstairs, having been put on standby to guard the house while I rested, as they still hadn't succeeded in locating Marcus. I was supposed to be sleeping and recuperating to resume training tomorrow, but I'd failed miserably at that.

The first couple of hours had been spent trying to distract myself by reading the book I'd loaned Damien, but I couldn't sit still long enough to get into it. Not while Damien was out there fighting. Was he fighting a darkling at this very moment?

No. He'll be fine. He'll be ok.

I groaned, giving up on the book as I reread the same line for the fourth time, my mind not latching onto the words. My eyes fell to the box of things Mom had given me, and I rose from the bed, grabbing it to see what all she had sent me with. There wasn't much, a few essential items, toiletries. My brows furrowed as I found a smaller box at the bottom, something about it familiar. I pulled it out, eyes falling on Mom's handwriting in the bottom corner.

Cassie 1998

1998? I would have been five. What was this? I opened the lid to find the small box filled with old artwork. Nostalgia flooded my chest as my eyes fell on the drawings of the monsters from my favorite childhood book, *Where The Wild Things Are*. A smile curved my lips at the memories, of all the times Mom had read me the story to have me up on the bed telling her I'd eat her up I loved her so. A deep ache sank into my chest. Had she meant to put this box in here? Perhaps she thought a trip down memory lane might help get my mind off things.

I gave into the temptation, allowing myself to slip away from the present troubles to fall back into the past, a time when life was easier. Drawing after drawing, I went through them, my smile widening into a grin at some of them. My eyes fell to the next piece. A poorly drawn little person stood in the center of the page, backed by an enormous shadow with a face. They were surrounded by multiple masses of black crayon on either side.

My brows knitted together. I didn't remember drawing this one.

Something tugged in the back of my mind, something familiar, and of course I found my messy signature at the bottom, the one Dad had so lovingly taken the time to help me learn. I frowned as I scrutinized the black scribbles marking the paper—the sketches becoming clearer to me with each second. The masses were human like, but hunched over, their fingers long and sharp like claws, their jaws stretched wide in a creepy grin.

My heart stuttered, and I nearly dropped the paper. This couldn't be possible... but as my eyes roamed over the black masses, there was no denying it. They weren't some monsters from a story. God, they were darklings.

I set it aside, scrambling to grab another. This drawing was of two people. It was a woman with long hair donning some sort of gown, a tall warrior holding her hand, clad in black, long dark brown hair falling around his face.

Moira and Damien.

This couldn't be real, but as I continued going through them, there was no denying what I was seeing. I'd dreamt of darklings when I was a child, had dreamed memories of our past lives.

I scrambled to pull the drawings out, laying them out before me until I could see each and every one of them, sorting out ones I knew to be from books to leave only drawings of what might memories that I'd only thought to be nothing but dreams just a few days prior.

No other memories had resurfaced after my vision of Elena. Perhaps there might be something in this mess that might help us in some way. My eyes drifted over the drawings scattered before me. I recognized so many of them, countless sketches with black masses that resembled darklings, even a drawing of what appeared to be Selene, alone. I couldn't help but feel as if she looked sad in the drawing, but it was a child's scribbles, the details too difficult to discern.

In my hand was a drawing of a huge hall with people dancing in gowns, the colors resembling the celebration with Moira I'd seen through Damien's eyes. I rose, eyes scanning over the mess of doodles for anything that looked like it may involve Damien, the darklings, or the immortals. In another drawing there was a girl with blonde hair cuddled up with a massive black panther under a tree as she read a book. I'd almost written it off as something from a book Mom had read to me growing up, but I didn't remember any stories like that, and Elena had blonde hair.

No matter how many drawings I went through, though, nothing stood out to me.

Frustration rose in my chest, and I flopped back onto the foot of the bed with a groan. It was hopeless. God, I felt so useless sitting here. I wanted to keep training, wanted to explore more of Damien's memories. There was so much I wanted to know. If only I could know everything Lucia, Elena, and Moira knew.

Knowledge of how to destroy the darkling leader was what I needed more than anything. It had been done before. How did they do it? How helpful it would be to have my memories back in full. I could be more useful, could deal with the fact that my entire world wasn't what I'd known it to be only a few weeks ago.

I raked my fingers through my hair, folding my legs beneath me as I sat up, and a thought crossed my mind. If I could use my abilities to tap into the memories of others, could I do the same with my past lives? Maybe it would be easier to access my own mind than others? Damien had told me it's easier when you're grounded by touch. No better grounding than yourself, right?

The darkling leader had been destroyed before, but how had they done it? Damien had called the battle The Fall of Kingdoms. That was during Lucia's time. Maybe I could get some more information from her; anything that could help at this point would be worth it.

I took one last deep breath, relaxing my body as I let the air leave my lungs. Just as we practiced. Closing my eyes, I focused on myself. It couldn't be that hard, right?

Lucia, focus on Lucia.

Like a target, I honed in on her, and nothing else, before diving deep into my own consciousness. Voices whispered around me, the echoes of that unknown ancient language echoing in the darkness, beckoning me. I'd heard it before, when Marcus had used his abilities on me, and a few times when I was entering Damien's mind. What were they?

The air around me grew warmer, the humidity thick against my skin. The smell of damp earth filled my nose, and I opened my eyes as the voices receded, leaving only the sound of the forest.

It must have been a new moon, for the darkness surrounding me was thick. Dirt and rocks pressed into my knees as I crouched low against the ground, hidden from something. Adrenaline pumped through me in fear and anticipation, and I didn't know what I was doing or where I was.

"Don't be a hero, Lucia. You can't push yourself like you used to. You have to pace yourself now," Damien whispered, hidden at my side. His eyes briefly drifted to me, unable to mask the worry. "Take it slow and stay with us."

"If I see the daughter of Matthias, I'm taking her down." I whispered, eyes scanning the dark forest ahead of us, wary of the sounds of animals quieting to an unusual silence.

Who was the daughter of Matthias?

"We'll do it together, *mea luna*," he whispered, taking my hand. "I understand how you feel."

I paused, feeling the life growing inside me. Our child, our daughter, so small that I couldn't yet feel her movements, but I felt her presence, her energy within me.

"I'm sorry," I whispered back to him, unease settling into my gut as I turned my gaze to him. "I just want to be done with it already. I can't sleep thinking about trying to bring Emilia into a world where these creatures roam freely, mutilating our—"

A branch snapped behind us and we twisted around, eyes darting around in the darkness. I stopped breathing, hand going to the hilt of my short sword. Was it her? Had she come?

The tree groaned, leaves scattering to the ground, and my eyes shot up. From within the pitch darkness, I could just barely make out a terrifying beast. It was perched on a large branch, and it leapt down to the ground. Terror flooded me, terror and... sorrow?

The beast stood up to its full height of nearly eight feet as its lips curled back, baring long, serrated teeth at us. A low, feral growl rippled from its throat as its head dropped low.

My heart leapt in my throat, and I shifted, my hand rising, but Damien's arm shot out in front of me, stopping me. His voice was painful as he whispered through his teeth. "It's not her in there."

We froze, watching as its six glowing red eyes drifted over us. Its shoulders hunched high, shifting with each step. Three pairs of legs held up the large frame, massive paws crushing the grass beneath it. The body almost seemed as if it weren't entirely physical, its thick black fur fading out into black billows of smoke and mist, the same way Damien's shadow magic did, the same way his shadow wolves' bodies manifested. Its long claws sank into the damp soil and it lurched forward, jaws opened wide.

"Cas?"

The sound of someone at the door pulled me from the memory and I gasped as I opened my eyes, chest heaving. I was myself again, sitting on our bed. A cold sweat had broken out across my skin, and my hands quivered, the sheets clenched in a tight grip between my fingers. I blinked as my eyes adjusted to the jolt of the light that replaced the darkness of the forest.

God, how did it feel so real every time? There had been times where I would find myself so entangled with the consciousness of a memory that I almost couldn't separate myself from them.

I rubbed my eyes, and rose from the bed, rushing to clean up the mess of drawings occupying the bed. "Come in."

The door opened, revealing a woman. She was beautiful, her heart-shaped face glowing, her sepia-brown skin lit with rosy cheeks and full lips that curved into a warm smile. Her dark brown hair was pulled back into a loose low bun, and full, side swept bangs dusted across her delicate pale gray eyes. She carried a tray with two teacups, steam rising from them as she entered.

"Hi, Cas. I hope I'm not disturbing anything. I'm Anna, Vincent's mate. He asked me to come check on you. Thought I'd bring you some tea."

"Oh! Hi, come on in. Thank you so much." I smiled, pushing myself up, the stack of drawings tucked together in my hands. "I'd actually thought of coming down. I just can't seem to fall asleep, no matter what I do."

"I had a feeling you were having trouble sleeping up here." Her expression was one of understanding as she nudged the door closed with her hip. "Worried about Damien?"

I nodded, setting the papers back into the box before placing the lid in place. My shoulders sagged as the fear resurfaced, my chest swelling until I feared it might burst. "I can't stop thinking about him."

"I understand your fears. They're ones I struggle with as well."

I blinked as she approached, realizing how rude I must seem, and I grabbed the chair at my bedside, pulling it over for her to sit. "Please, take a seat. Make yourself at home. I'd introduce myself, but it sounds like you already know my name."

She snickered. "Thank you. I brought some chamomile to help ease your nerves."

Everything about her was delicate, yet refined, from the way she lowered the tray on the bedside to how she eased herself into the seat, her feet sliding to the side as she smoothed the skirt of her emerald dress.

"Thank you. Maybe this'll help knock me out finally." I reached for one of the cups. "You mentioned you're Vincent's mate? Do the others have mates?"

She tucked a lock of her dark brown hair behind her ear before taking a sip from her cup, and the scent of her mint tea overpowered my chamomile. "Vincent is the only one right now. Barrett's charm kind of drives the females away, it seems. Thalia is probably the closest thing to a female friend he has, but they can't seem to be in each other's company without getting under each other's skin."

I stifled a laugh at her jab at Barrett. "Awe, not Barrett. He's such a teddy bear. I was sure he had the ladies falling at his feet."

She laughed, the warmth of it nurturing something deep within me. "He isn't being a jerk to you still, is he?"

I shook my head. "He was a right asshole when we first met, and I was honestly a little scared of him, but I know how to deal with him now. He's also chilled out a bit since he learned I'm Moira's reincarnation. I guess he's more afraid of Damien kicking his ass in protection of his mate than anything."

Anna smiled, but it didn't reach her pale eyes, and for the briefest moment something flitted across her eyes, a sort of sadness, but I wasn't sure what she could be sad for.

"How are you settling in? I'm sure it's been a lot to take in."

The smile faded from my face, and the inner corners of her eyebrows curved upward. My lips parted, and for a moment, I failed to find words to describe how I was feeling. I'd managed to compartmentalize most of it up to this point, but I'd be lying if I said it wasn't weighing on me. So much had happened, and I feared that if I started to think too deeply into it, it might burst free, the weight of everything I'd carefully piled upon one another toppling over until I broke down.

"It's... been an adjustment," I admitted, and took a sip of the chamomile tea, letting the warmth pool in my stomach before continuing. "I'm still trying to understand how you've all remained hidden from everything. How I've managed to live all this time and avoid becoming another one of the darklings' victims. What things mean between Damien and I and what our relationship means for me."

I stiffened, realizing how I'd just unloaded on her. "Sorry, I didn't mean to unload like that."

"It's ok, I asked because I care. If you ever need to talk, I'm here."

A smile curved my lips. "So do you serve in the order with Vincent and them?"

She shook her head. "No, I'm actually a nurse at Dr. Johnson's clinic. He has two, one in The Complex for The Order, and another for civilians like me."

A nurse. Something deep within me hesitated, becoming hyper aware of her observations, wondering if she might pick up on anything I did that might allude to my condition.

Why are you being so paranoid? She's just trying to be a friend.

"So, how long have you known Damien and the others?" I asked.

"Vincent and I first met when I accompanied Johnson to his clinic at The Complex in..." Her brows pinched together as she seemed to contemplate. "I think it was 1923. I was young, still fresh out of medical training. He and Barrett came in with some nasty injuries when a patrol went south. Barrett immediately started putting his foot in his mouth. I almost questioned whether he was injured badly enough to need medical care," she chuckled at the memory. "Thalia showed up and chewed him out for hitting on me."

1923. I wondered what 'young' meant for immortals. Did that mean she was born in the early 1900s, or earlier? Knowing that, though, the way she looked made more sense to me. Her bone structure, the fullness of her silhouette, the way she styled her hair, how she carried herself; she came from an era completely different from my own.

They all did.

"Vincent seemed to forget how to speak when I started working on stitching him up. It was cute really, and I found him requesting my care more often than not. It wasn't long after that the mating bond snapped into place, and of course, knowing Vincent, you know how close he and the others are, I was pulled into their circle before I realized it. Never in my life would I have thought I'd be friends with the king, let alone mated to one of his dearest friends."

"I can sympathize with how startling that might have been. I'm still not entirely sure what this whole mate thing means."

"It can be a lot sometimes." Anna eased her tea down onto the tray. "I'm sorry if Damien seems to be a little protective of you. Males can be incorrigible sometimes when they've found their mate, and he's been without you for so long. I'm not sure if you being in a new form makes it more like the mating bond being newly formed, as if you were meeting for the first time. If so, it's very intense for our kind during the first few months. It's difficult to explain to a human. The instincts aren't as strong for your kind as it is for ours."

My chest swelled at the thought of being his mate. I hadn't had the courage to discuss it with him, and I still wondered what that meant for me. "Damien told me the mating bond goes beyond... physical attraction."

She nodded. "Yes, for us females, we feel the same pull. Males, though, are on a completely different level. Some are extremely possessive and territorial when the bond is first established, and it's common for newly mated pairs to remain home for a week or two after the bond has been accepted."

My cheeks heated at the implication, and I remembered how much Damien seemed to struggle to pull himself away from me the night he had brought me here.

"Remain home as in..."

"I mean exactly what you're thinking," she said with a knowing smile. "I remember when Vincent and I first accepted our bond. I had to call out of work five nights in a row. He wouldn't let me leave our room."

I swallowed. *Holy shit.* I couldn't imagine that.

293

"Vincent can get rather possessive of me sometimes, and he's been extra protective lately," she said, her smile turning warm, and a calming warmth rippled over my skin. "I won't lie, though. I enjoy it sometimes."

"I understand what you mean. Damien threatened to end Barrett's life when he tried to erase my memories," I said with a chuckle.

I lingered on that thought, my mind wandering to all the times Damien had stepped up in my defense. How many lives had he ended to find me? I didn't understand how something like that could bring me comfort.

"It's weird. I never thought I could ever feel this way about someone."

She reached out to touch my hand tenderly. "If he gets to be too much for you, tell him to ease off. Seriously. Males will do anything for their mates. He'll understand, particularly since you're human."

"It's nice to talk about stuff like this with another woman. I can't talk to my best friend about this; she's human. So, it's been a bit... difficult to keep so much from her."

Why? It's not like you haven't lied to her before.

I internally winced at the thought, unable to deny it.

"If you have any questions at all, let me know. You can call me anytime. Maybe you can join me at my house, help me in my greenhouse."

"Greenhouse?" I asked, brows rising.

"I love to garden, and with winter approaching, it's the only way I can grow things. I'd love an extra hand if you're ever interested."

"I can't make any promises. I've never kept a plant alive in my life."

"I'm sure I can teach you a thing or two," she said, taking another sip of her tea, the mint filling my lungs. "It'sIt's nice to have another female in the group. There's not enough of us. Thalia is great to talk to, but she's often quite busy with training."

Her pale eyes went distant, the warmth in them fading. "I'm not sure what all the changes will mean for us, if we'll be able to spend as much time together in leisure like this."

Worry darkened her eyes, and a rush of something icy washed over me as her hand settled against her stomach. I swallowed, and, though I wanted to ask, I wouldn't. I averted my eyes, her fears and worries filling the air in such a heavy fog that I couldn't ignore them. Air filled my lungs as I drew a deep breath, calming my mind, attempting to shut them out.

Vincent had likely filled her in on what we discovered in Cole's memories. I didn't know if she'd been around to see the last war, but even without experiencing it firsthand, I knew that just the thought of it was terrifying enough, and I could only imagine how worried she must be.

I reached over to take her hand and prayed I wasn't making a hollow promise. "We're gonna get through this."

She smiled warmly at me, but the emotions still rolled beneath the surface. I paused a moment, my own concern for Damien bringing forth another thought. "There is one thing I wanted to know."

Her eyebrows rose. "What is it?"

"Selene mentioned that Damien was neglecting his feedings." Something stirred in me. "When your kind doesn't have mates... who do they feed from?"

She was silent a moment, and she seemed to contemplate her words. "There are civilian families who serve The Order when it comes to that. Unmated males and females present themselves to aid the cause."

"How do I get Damien to feed? How do I arrange it? He's too worried that he'll hurt me by... feeding from me, but I don't want him fighting the darklings and Marcus when he's not at his best. I get a feeling he's been pushing himself too hard, and I'm afraid of what it's doing to his body."

A sympathetic smile lit her face. "It isn't easy to allow a mate to feed from another. For you to be willing to have him do it, for his sake, is admirable." Her eyes fell for a moment. "For routine feedings, human blood does suffice. It is, however, weaker, but as you said, he seems to resist the idea, for fear of your health. If he were ever injured, he would need the blood of our kind. He only needs to summon one of the families to present a female for his use."

The words she chose made my skin crawl. A female for his use. My mind wandered, remembering that without Lucia here, he'd had to fend for himself for over a century. Did he use different women? Did he use the same woman? Neither made me feel any less sick at the thought, and I couldn't understand why. It was just blood. He was an immortal. He needed to feed. No big deal.

My eyes dropped to the caramel-colored liquid in my cup. There was a part of me that hated the thought of him touching another woman, but if it was best for him, I would have him do it in a heartbeat.

"Anna, how is everything here?" Vincent asked from outside the door. "Is Cas, okay?"

"Everything's good. She's just worried about Damien."

I set my tea down on the tray. "You can come in, Vincent."

The door creaked as he pushed it open. "Damien will be fine, Cas, I promise. He's a powerful warrior, plus he's got the best fighters with him. They've got his back."

"Thank you, Vincent." It did offer some relief that he wasn't out there alone, but I still worried.

Anna stood, lifting the tray. "It's getting late, Cas. Why don't you try to get some rest? Damien should be back within a couple of hours."

"Thank you for the tea, Anna," I said, offering her a smile.

"Anytime, love. You just let me know when you want to come work in the greenhouse with me. You're always welcome," she said, flashing me a smile before leaving the room.

I sat there a moment in silence, the room feeling too empty. Just a couple more hours and he would be here. I reached over to turn the lamp off and slid under the blankets. The bed was cold without Damien's warmth around me. How I wished he were here, holding me as he had the last two nights. I curled into myself, my arms wrapped around Damien's pillow, hugging it tightly as I inhaled his scent.

He's going to be fine. Just go to sleep.

The door creaked open, dragging me from sleep. Darkness greeted me when I opened my eyes to the faint shuffle of movement, and the light in the bathroom came on before the door quietly closed.

I climbed out of bed, tiptoeing to the bathroom with my heart in my throat. My mind raced with the possibilities of his condition just beyond that door, and I prayed Damien was okay after tonight's rounds.

Was he injured on the other side of this door? If so, how badly? Did any of his other wounds reopen? I gently knocked before quietly opening the door to find Damien removing his coat.

He was a mess, his leathers covered in what I could only make out as a mix of dirt, sweat, and blood.

His eyes widened when he noticed my presence. "Cas? Sorry, I didn't mean to wake yo—"

"Are you hurt?" My voice nearly broke as he approached me, my heart threatening to burst out of my chest.

"Just a few scratches, nothing major."

His words weren't enough to silence the worry surging within me. I reached for his chest, undoing the leather straps holding his knives across his chest and set them down on the floor.

"Cas..." he said, his tone soft and reassuring. I didn't stop, reaching for his shirt, lifting it over his head and tossing it to the side.

"Cas..."

My eyes trailed over him as I checked his chest, his shoulders.

"Cassie I'm—"

"Just... let me see that you're okay," I snapped, my hands shaking as I traced the healing wound on his chest left by Marcus' knife. The same knife I still felt burning in the healing cuts on my skin. Ones I feared might leave scars.

He took my hands, lifting them to gently kiss my knuckles. "I promise. I'm okay. The night was rather calm."

Calm? This was calm? The leathers he wore were ripped and torn, and I didn't know whose blood soaked into the black fabrics, whether it was his or the darklings.

I walked behind him, turning the shower head on. An indescribable urge to take care of him consumed me, to tend to any

296

wounds he had. I couldn't fight it… and I didn't, giving wholly into the urges.

"Pants off. In the shower."

He smiled but didn't object and began undressing. As he turned from me, I caught sight of a wound lining his shoulder blade, like claws had raked across his flesh.

"Were you able to find anything?" I asked, averting my gaze as he removed his pants.

"Unfortunately, no. Just the usual darklings out hunting. Barrett and the others went back out to see if they could possibly find the building you saw in your vision before they turn in for the night."

He stepped into the shower, letting the hot water pour over him. The blood, both red and black, blurred together as it mixed with the water, rolling down his body before pooling on the tile below. I quickly undressed, and climbed into the shower behind him, my heart racing, but I couldn't deny this unyielding need to tend to him. He glanced over his shoulder but before he could grab the bath sponge, I took it, lathering it with soap and began gently washing his back, cleaning away the grime and blood marring his beautiful olive skin.

If only I were strong enough to give him what he needed to thrive, to be there where he was, fighting alongside him, watching his back myself. I would only get in the way, though, regardless of how hard I trained. I was only human. What could I hope to do?

He turned to face me, his hooded trailing over me as I continued to wash his skin. Other than the wound on his shoulder, I didn't see any other new injuries, and my nerves eased. Anna's words wouldn't leave my mind, though. He needed to feed if he was going to heal properly. He didn't have the time to heal as slowly as he had been.

The claw wound from the darklings' attack nearly three weeks prior had yet to fully heal on his forearm, the tear on the top of his shoulder still a scabbed wound. He reached around the small of my back and leaned down, his lips brushing my brow tenderly.

"Damien. How do we arrange for you to feed?" I asked, my eyes not leaving the wound on his chest.

His body tensed. "I don't want to talk about that right now."

"Please, Damien. You're wounded," I said, tears welling in my eyes, frustration at my uselessness overwhelming. "You need to. I can't stop worrying while you're out fighting. You're not taking care of yourself because I'm here, and all I can think about is that my existence is holding you back."

He pinned me back against the wall, his forehead pressed against mine as his eyes pierced into me. "Your existence does anything but hold me back." His eyes burned as he held my gaze. "You give me something to live for, something to fight for. I feel more alive than I have in over a century with you at my side again."

I swallowed at the feel of him against me, of the power rippling beneath the surface. Water rained down on us as we sat there, chests

297

heaving, locked in each other's gazes. My eyes dipped to his lips, and Damien's grip on my arms tightened.

His jaw tightened. "Gods, you make it so hard sometimes."

"Hard?" I breathed.

His eyes dipped to my lips and my heart leapt at the embers burning in his eyes. "Fuck."

He leaned in close, and I wanted him closer, wanted to feel more of his skin against mine. My skin heated at his proximity, anticipation winding tighter in my stomach as the desires I'd shut out rushed to the surface.

"You make it hard to hold myself back," he breathed.

I met his molten gaze. "Then don't."

His eyes rose to mine, and for a moment he hesitated, as if unsure I meant it. But as I held his gaze, the tether holding him back seemed to snap, his desires taking hold of him.

And his lips crashed into mine.

CHAPTER 32

His kiss was intoxicating, the taste of him heavenly, like sweet liquid divinity on my tongue. I wanted more, wanted it so badly that I let every ounce of hesitation, of fear, die out and I snared my fingers into his hair, pulling him against me.

A wave of emotions rose off him, burning into my skin, searing me in a way that I never thought I would want, but I did. He'd worked his way through every wall I'd ever put up, and I wanted him to tear down any that remained, wanted him to take them down one after another until there was nothing separating us.

I tilted my head as he deepened the kiss, and I was completely and utterly at his mercy. I needed this as much as he did, wanted to know every part of him, every inch, wanted to feel him in ways I never had with anyone else.

His body tightened against me as I reached my fingers over his shoulders, grabbing onto him as I lost myself in his taste. He broke the kiss, and his lips burned a trail down my neck. A moan spilled from my lips when he cupped my breast, only to replace it with his mouth, and my back bowed, my head pressing back against the tile. A groan ripped from his throat as he worked his tongue against my skin and my body quivered with each stroke.

The feel of his tongue left me crumbling at his mercy, a heady sight slipping from my lips as he pulled the taut peak of my breast between his teeth, teasing the tender flesh.

Chest heaving, I tried to remember how to breathe as his hands glided down my ribs, then to my stomach, moving lower still. My body tensed, mind racing with the thoughts of what could happen next, what was going to happen next if we continued. The anticipation and nerves left me conflicted.

I needed him, wanted him in a way that was driving me insane. It was all so new, though, so foreign, and fear gripped me, fear of what it would be like, of feeling so exposed—of feeling… him.

He stopped, hands halting at my hips, as if sensing my hesitancy. Those beautiful amber and ashen eyes burned into me as he rested his forehead against mine, his breaths coming in heavy pants.

"Sorry, I'm going too fast. I—" he said, pulling away, and my body cried out at the distance between us.

Conflict marred his face. "Fuck. I can still faintly smell him on you. It's driving me insane. I want to erase it, replace it. I can't explain it… As a human, you wouldn't understand."

Was he talking about Marcus? Did I… did I smell like him? Was it not enough that he had left these marks?

He paused a moment, seeming to work things over in his mind, and a look of realization crossed his expression. "Wait, a minute. Have you ever—"

I nearly choked on the words catching in my throat. There'd never been anyone in my life that made me feel this way, made me feel so safe. My cheeks warmed as I lifted my eyes to him, unable to form words to express that he would be my first.

So, I shook my head, biting my lip.

"If you're not ready for this…" he whispered.

I could feel the hunger overwhelming him. He was on edge, pure desire and need consuming him, and I knew that he struggled to hold himself back. Yet, I knew somehow in the core of my soul that if I said I wanted to stop, he would immediately, no questions asked.

The air was thick as I filled my lungs, calming my nerves before I reached my hand up to his face. I gazed into his eyes, my fingers tracing the stubble along his jaw. His lashes lowered, hooded eyes moving across my face, searching for something, and he tilted his head into my touch.

I ran my thumb across his soft lips, wet from the shower, from our kisses, and his eyes closed as he relished in the sensation. Water droplets decorated his skin, and his chest rose and fell in. heavy rhythm. He was raw and ragged, and from within me, the urges and needs grew until I could no longer contain them. I didn't want to second guess anymore, didn't want to stop what had started.

My eyes dipped to his lips as I drew so close that I could feel his breath graze my skin, fill my lungs with his delicious scent of cedarwood and leather over the scent of lavender and rosemary. How did it nearly drown everything else out?

Our gazes met briefly, his eyes burning their way into the depths of my soul, and I gave into my desires, pressing my lips to his. The groan that rumbled from deep in his throat set something inside me on fire. He grabbed hold of my hips, pulling me tightly against him. I ignored my hesitancy at the feel of him, hot and thick, pressed against my lower stomach.

I pulled free from his lips, turning him until his back met the tile. He watched me, as if waiting to see what I would do, and as my lips found their way to his neck his head fell back against the tile. He closed his eyes, his head falling back as he let out a heavy breath. His hands molded to my skin as if he were sculpting clay, and I whimpered at the feeling.

"Gods, Cas. Make that sound for me again," Damien groaned.

He cupped my breasts, and as he rolled the tight tips between his fingers, I couldn't help but give into his request, my moan spilling out over his skin between kisses.

I nipped and kissed at his neck, moving down his throat to his shoulder as I traced my fingers over his chest, down to his stomach, across each ripple and dip of hard muscle. How could something be so solid, so hard, and yet like velvet under my touch? His body twitched beneath me with each movement I made, his length throbbing against my stomach. My hand lowered as I grew bolder, and my fingers brushed the tip of him.

He drew a sharp breath and his hands rose to my face, pulling me back up to him in a kiss so desperate I couldn't help but let him take every piece of me. In one swift movement, he scooped his hands under my thighs and lifted me up until my legs were wrapped around his waist. I grabbed onto his shoulders, gasping at the sudden movement, at the feel of his length brushing against my throbbing center. His tongue swept against mine as he stepped out of the tub, carrying me across the bathroom and to his bed, leaving a trail of water in our path.

I broke the kiss as he lowered me onto the foot of his bed. "Damien! Wait, we're going to get your bed wet."

"Like I give a fuck," he groaned as he leaned over me, the edge of the mattress sagging under us. "I want to make this special for you."

His mouth was on mine again, consuming me, his tongue dancing with my own. The blankets shifted as he planted his hand firmly onto the bed beside me, his other trailing lower over my ribs. My body throbbed for him in ways I'd never felt before, and I thought I might catch fire.

"Gods, you're beautiful, Cas," he whispered against my skin, and I moaned under him. "So, fucking beautiful."

Chill cascaded through me as his breath spilled over where he kissed. The world could have been ending around us and I wouldn't have cared. I was lost to him, and I never wanted to find my way out of this high.

He continued to distract me, his mouth leaving mine and nipping at my neck. The sharpness of his fangs grazed my skin, leaving ripples of a tingling sensation in their wake as he moved. His body tensed for a moment, pausing at my throat. He breathed deeply, muscles rippling before his tongue trailed up along my neck. I couldn't understand the urge I suddenly felt for him to bite me.

What would it feel like for him to take from me like that? It was strange how I suddenly wanted to give myself to him like that, to give him what he needed, to give him all that he needed. He didn't bite down, though, and I was almost disappointed, until his tongue slid along the shell of my ear, and I shivered.

Something hot built in me with each stroke of his lips and tongue. There was so much to focus on, and I struggled to keep up with it all. My breathing, my thoughts, where his hands were, where his lips were. I was lost in a sea of sensation, my skin coming alive at his touch. It was overwhelming and, at the same time, I somehow wanted more, needed more.

I bit my lip, stifling a moan as his hand dipped down, brushing the most sensitive of places between my thighs. Something wound tightly within me, a need I couldn't describe, and I felt the way my body was reacting to him.

He groaned into my ear as I shuddered against him. "Gods, you're right where I want you."

Heart racing, body aching, I struggled to contain myself as he spoke. I couldn't understand how simple words could make me feel this way. He slid his fingers up my center, and my body came alive, hips moving involuntarily as he did it again in gentle sweeps.

He pressed his hip into me, holding me in place. "Be still, *mea luna*. I've wanted this for so long. Let me worship you like the goddess you are."

My lips parted, another moan escaping me as he brushed his fingers down my center again. I tried to listen, tried to control myself as he continued to kiss and nuzzle my neck, then my collarbone. His fingers glided in lazy circles between my thighs, until my body was begging for more. I quivered and twitched under him, and my hips rose involuntarily as he sent me teetering on the edge of insanity.

He raised his face to me, kissing me once before he hovered above my lips, his muscles twitching as he struggled to hold himself back.

"Gods, the things I want to do to you right now," he growled.

I lifted my gaze to his, breathless and lost for words. The blankets beneath us were dampened, my wet hair splayed out around me. His eyes closed as I lifted my hand, brushing my thumb over his cheek. I wanted him, more of him, all of him.

When he slipped a finger inside me, my head fell back, a moan falling from my lips. He didn't stop there, didn't give me a moment to regain myself, and continued to stroke me deliciously as he grazed my skin with his lips.

"*Mea sol*," I moaned, the words breaking free of their own volition.

Damien froze at the words that left my lips, his eyes widening as he gazed down at me, and I blinked. I hadn't meant to say it... but the name was familiar. Special. One I'd called him in moments nearly lost to the past.

He kissed me then, as if he hadn't seen me in a lifetime, and he pulled me to the edge of the bed, sinking between my legs. He spread my thighs apart before I could question what he was doing and dipped his head to take me into his mouth.

My body surged, back arching as I cried out at the stroke of his tongue. It was all I could do to keep myself in place when he slipped a finger in with the next flick of his tongue. The mattress caved as my head knocked back, and I gasped his name.

It was torturous, the things he was doing to me, sweet torture, and I didn't want it to stop. Like crippling waves, he advanced and receded, bringing me to the edge of some abyss I wanted to fall into before pulling me back. Something coiled and wound tightly, deep and low within me until my body was begging for a release that was just out of reach.

"Relax for me. I'll go slow," he said, as he rose to brushing a tender kiss to my lips, and I felt the thickness of his arousal against my thigh. His breath was heavy, forehead pressed to mine as our gazes met, his eyes overflowing with adoration. "I'll be gentle, but it'll hurt at first."

I nodded, closing my eyes, as I breathed through the nervousness nipping at my stomach. He kissed me softly, his hands gliding over my skin, helping me to relax. I couldn't prepare fully for it, though, and I gasped at the sharp pain that overtook me as he slowly guided himself into me.

"Just breathe for me," he whispered against my lips. "Tell me if it gets to be too much."

I nodded as I clung to him, nails digging into his shoulders as he moved slowly, stretching me.

God, was this what it was like? When did it end? Did it feel like this every time? Air flooded my lungs in a sharp inhale, the pain making it nearly impossible to relax. No matter what I did, though, my body tensed, overwhelmed by the invasion.

I couldn't hold back the urge to resist, to push him back, my hands pressing against his chest. "Stop... I can't—"

"Sorry." Damien halted, breath ragged as he held himself in place. "Am I going too fast?"

I fell back on the bed, the pain easing at his pause. "I'll be ok. It's just..." I drew a deep breath, and I lifted my hands to cup his face. "Don't stop. Just... go slow."

He brushed a tender kiss to my lips before resting his forehead against me. His damp, dark waves spilled around my face, and I lost myself in those powerful eyes. The pain subsided a little, but faintly remained as my body adjusted to accommodate him. He tilted his head, as if in question, and I nodded for him to continue. When he did, though, the pain grew worse until tears dotted my eyes, and I didn't know how much more I could take.

"Almost there," he whispered in my ear in gentle reassurance. When I didn't respond, he took it upon himself to finish it once and for all, slicing through until I'd absorbed every inch of him, and I cried out, nails biting into his arms.

He brushed my hair from my face as my body trembled. "Sorry, *mea luna*. It's done now, it's done. Just breathe for me."

I smiled weakly up at him, and he kissed me. Not hungrily, not heavily, just… tenderly, in a way that touched a place deep within my soul. We laid there like that for a long while, and he didn't make any advances, simply allowing me the grace of a moment's reprieve.

The tender stroke of his fingers along the ridges of my face helped distract me from the discomfort, and his lips caressed my skin as he trailed sweet kisses along my throat until he found my lips again. His hand slid down between us, brushing right above where we were connected, and I moaned against his lips. Something replaced the discomfort as my body relaxed into it. Then he moved, sliding back until he almost left me fully.

I frowned at the empty feeling left in his absence. It was such a strange sensation, considering it had been so painful just moments before. When he returned, sliding back in, I wasn't prepared for the pleasure that spread through me despite the tenderness.

My lips fell open in a gasp as he slid forward in gentle thrusts that grew more powerful each time, his eyes fixated on me as I took him again and again. He didn't stop there, and each time I felt him fill me, I could feel something foreign building, my body tensing in response.

"Let it happen," he said, his eyes darkening as he devoured the sight of me nearly coming undone.

I couldn't explain the feeling gripping me, and I closed my eyes, my head tilting back as I began to lose touch with myself. He lifted me from the mattress and whipped us around so that we were sitting on the edge of the bed. I settled into his lap, straddling him, but despite the switching of positions, we remained connected, only it felt different. My body tightened around him as he filled me, reaching deeper than I imagined possible, and my head fell back as it nearly brought me over the edge.

"Fuck, you feel amazing," he groaned, eyes burning into me as he held my gaze.

Sweat had replaced the water on our skin, his skin glistening in the low light, and he was absolutely beautiful to behold. I brushed the hair from his face, kissing his forehead as I hung onto him. He grasped my hips, grounding me against him, and I gasped, back arching.

"Gods you're taking it so fucking good," he said through his teeth, and my head fell forward into the crook of his neck.

I fell into the rhythm he set, moving my hips in time with his thrusts. Each time I did, the pressure built, more and more until I couldn't stand it any longer.

"Damien, I don't—" I struggled to speak, desperate at this point, and I wrapped my arms around him, holding him, needing him. We fit together so beautifully, so perfectly.

"Please," I moaned into his ear. I couldn't breathe fast enough, my skin left molten in the wake of his touch.

His hands tightened on my hips, nails biting into my skin, and he began to move me faster, raising his hips to meet me with each stroke as he drove himself deeper, filling me entirely. Panted breaths left me as I begged him for the release just out of my grasp, and my head fell back, feeling the sensation peak until I couldn't stand it anymore.

I felt his gaze on me as he ground himself into me furiously, and I held onto him, as if I were afraid that I might lose myself entirely if I let him go.

"Come for me, *mea luna*," he growled.

His scent filled the room with tremendous force, the rich aroma of cedar and leather filling my lungs. On the next powerful thrust an indescribably powerful sensation tore through my body, reaching from my core out to my fingertips and I cried out. Any control I had left over my body slipped from my grasp, every muscle twitching and trembling as pleasure carved its way through me.

"Gods, yes," he groaned as he thrusted into me again, shattering the wave I rode, and I cried out his name. He cursed, his body tensing and tightening under me, within me, and he shuddered as he came.

I melted into him, my head falling against his chest, every muscle beneath my skin dancing erratically. We sat there a moment, our bodies shuddering as we struggled to remember how to function. Useless limbs wouldn't listen to my commands, and I couldn't so much as lift my head from his shoulder.

He rose, lifting me up with the tenderest of care and carried me around to the head of the bed where the sheets were dry. Waves of pleasure still rippling through me as he eased me onto the blankets. My eyes fluttered closed for a moment, when I opened them he was gone, and the sound of the faucet running reached my ears. I'd nearly dozed off when he returned with a warm, damp rag and began carefully cleaning me. My cheeks heated, but the act was so tender that warmth filled my chest. He tossed the rag into the laundry basket and kissed my forehead before climbing onto the bed beside me.

The bed groaned as he rolled onto his back, pulling me with him until I laid draped over his chest. "You're absolutely perfect, *mea luna*."

I smiled warmly at him as he settled. The adoration in his eyes reached out to the furthest depths of my soul.

He pressed his nose into my hair and inhaled deeply. "I love my scent on you, want it to always remain on your skin."

My heart swelled, and for some reason, I had to agree with him. "What was it I called you earlier?" I asked.

He smiled softly. "You said *mea sol.*"

"What does it mean?"

"My sun."

Something stirred deep in my chest as he pulled me closer to him.

His heart seemed to beat faster for a moment and he took a deep breath. "I'll arrange a feeding tomorrow, if it will help you feel better."

Unease sank into the pit of my stomach like rocks at the thought of him touching another woman, but I forced it back. I refused to let it show, refused to let that hesitation reflect in my eyes as I lifted my head to meet his gaze. "It will."

He pressed a kiss to my forehead. "Then it will be done, *mea luna.*"

I melted into him once more, his heart beating a steady rhythm in my ear. We laid there in silence for a moment, curled up in each other's arms, and my chest swelled at the feel of his fingers combing through my curls.

"I want you there when it happens," he muttered.

I hesitated a moment, unsure of how I'd feel to see him with another woman like that. Regardless of how he swore there was no intimacy for him, it stung. I wished I could be the one he used, but it was clear that it wouldn't benefit him. I curled tighter against him.

"If that's what you want, I'll be there, at your side."

CHAPTER 33

"We're training today, right?" I called from the bathroom as I brushed my teeth.

"Only if your body feels rested enough after yesterday," Damien called back from beyond the bathroom door. "You promised you wouldn't push yourself."

"I promise, I'm fine. I made a lot of progress in our first session. I don't want to fall behind."

We'd awoken tangled up in each other. It had been difficult to pull away from one another, and we had nearly picked right back up where we had left off the night before.

My legs were shaky and weak, and the particular soreness I felt made me smile for some reason. Thoughts of the night before resurfaced in my mind: the feeling of his touch, his lips against my skin leaving my skin tingling—the way he felt against me as we lost ourselves in one another. Chills spread out over my skin at the mere memory of it, and I couldn't understand how my body seemed to heat at the thought of him, of how an insatiable urge to return to him in bed rose in my chest.

How the need pooled between my thighs...

I shoved it down and quickly finished brushing my teeth, before taking my morning dose and stashing the bottles back in place. When I stepped out of the bathroom, Damien was still in bed where I'd left him, scrolling through his phone, his expression serious.

"Everything okay?" I asked as I turned for the closet.

"Just updates from the teams," he said, without lifting his gaze to me.

I slipped into the closet to change. As I stepped into my leggings I felt his presence wash over me, and I turned to see him lean into the doorway of the closet. His eyes raked down my body, and I swallowed at the sight of his loose sweats hanging around his hips, his chest still bare. He watched with hungry eyes as I pulled a tank top on, his hand sliding into his pocket as he leaned against the doorframe. A strange urge to take him back to bed flared in me at the sight of him, to lick and taste every inch of him before taking him inside me again and again—

I blinked, shaking off the urges. What was coming over me?

I blushed at the smile curving his lips, was my face red? Was it that obvious I was thinking dirty thoughts about him?

"I have something for you." His words snapped me back to reality, and I perked up.

He pulled out a black dagger from behind his back, slipping the blade free of its sheath. It resembled the sword passed down from Moira to Elena to Lucia, the same inscriptions and crescent moon etched with gold into the metal.

"I had it made for you. Keep it handy in case you ever need it for any reason."

My heart swelled as I took in every little detail.

He pointed to the inscriptions along the blade. "These runes are specially placed by Selene herself. It'll help against the darklings. The magics burn them with a simple touch."

I smiled as he handed it to me, running my fingers over the etched metal. "It's beautiful! Thank you so much."

"Anything for you, *mea luna*. There's a harness for it on the dresser. You're going to learn how to use that today."

I slid the dagger back into its sheath. "We're still practicing using Nous as well, right?"

Damien nodded. "Yes, but it'll be different this time. You won't just be reading my thoughts, you'll be reading my thoughts as I'm attacking you."

The thought was intimating, but a part of me relished in the challenge. "I look forward to it, then." I paused, remembering his promise to me last night. "Don't think I forgot about your promise. After we're done training, I want you to take care of yourself."

"I didn't forget." His hands came to rest against my hips as he pressed his lips to my forehead. "Just not looking forward to it."

Sweat rolled down my face, dripping to the rubber floor mats as I braced my hands on my knees, focusing on calm, even breaths to steady my heart rate. I had paced myself all morning, fearful that I might push myself too far and risk an attack. My heart raced, but it wasn't to the point of pain as I'd been careful throughout the last couple of hours and knew when I needed to take a break.

My eyes fell to the training dagger gripped in my hand. Damien called them wasters, and while they were made of a hardened plastic instead of the Elythian steel—the material from Selene's realm they used to forge their daggers—it still hurt to get hit with one. I'd likely have a bruise or two in the morning.

"You going to be okay?" Zephyr's concerned voice caught my attention, and I lifted my gaze to find him standing closer than he had before.

"Yeah. Just a bit winded," I said, offering him a smile.

"Not gonna die on us, are you?" Barrett teased, and Damien chucked a waster at him. His arm shot up, his own training dagger angled just right to deflect it, and it ricocheted off before falling to the floor.

"Calm down, Daddy Damien. I was only teasing," Barrett said with a smirk.

Damien rolled his eyes before turning back to me, "Ignore him, Cas. You're doing great. Keep pacing yourself. We can start back up when you're ready."

Zephyr rolled his shoulders, turning back to Barrett as he widened his stance and prepared to spar with him once more. Watching them fight was fascinating, their movements fluid and poetic. It was inspiring, and while I knew I'd never be any match for them, I couldn't help but hope I could become even a fraction as skilled as they were. Perhaps even as brave as they were.

Damien, Zephyr, and Barrett had started our session with stretches and warmups, followed by a short jog to start building stamina, which I'd only managed to handle half of. While I had started to work myself back into jogging recently, the near two weeks I'd been held prisoner had cost me every bit of work I'd put into it. Thankfully, Damien treated it as if I'd never exercised a day in my life, keeping the intensity low.

The last hour had been spent going through self-defense tactics with him, Zephyr, and Barrett. They'd shown me how to safely use a dagger, but not before I'd dropped it a few times, of course, at which

Barrett had teased me incessantly. It was annoying, but at the same time it was a relief to have him treat me as he did... before.

Kat seemed to be unsure of how to talk to me now, cautious of what she said every time we talked, as if she were afraid of saying the wrong thing and hurting me or churning up bad memories. I hated it, and I feared that through Marcus' actions, our relationship may have been permanently altered.

I prayed it didn't stay that way, that I could find what we had before, and she could find it in herself to be just as open and carefree with this broken version of me as we once were. Or had I lost that, too? Was this how I lost her? Was this how our friendship slowly died out?

No. She's my best friend. She wouldn't abandon me.

"All right, eyes on me, Cas," Damien said, and I blinked, pulling myself from the spiral of fearful thoughts.

I drew a deep breath, my heart rate leveling out and ready for our next set. "Was I good with these? You know, in my past lives?" I asked, motioning to the dagger in my hand.

A cocky grin formed on his face. "I was better, but there were times you put me on my ass." The look in his eyes told me that he enjoyed that in a way that left me a little hotter inside than I already felt.

"Well, keep it up," I said, gripping the hilt as I found my center, falling into a stance as I readied myself to defend against him. "I want to get to that level again."

He approached me and slid his feet apart as he flipped his own waster in his hand. Watching him move like this brought me back to the vision of him and Elena training. The way he fought hadn't changed, in fact looking at him in his training attire, his hair half pulled back and out of his face, it was almost as if time hadn't passed between now and then, his stance a near mirrored image. It was strange how the memories of Elena and Lucia had seemed to reawaken an almost muscle memory in using a weapon, and in an odd way it seemed to help me learn faster, our training becoming more like a refresher course.

His movements were calculated as he took a step toward me, initiating an attack. I shifted my weight to the side, pressing my palm to his forearm to drive the dagger away from me.

Damien twisted around, swinging for my ribs. I turned, flipping the dagger so my palm could rest against the side of the blade, and I blocked his attack, the force of it nearly overwhelming me. He turned his waster against mine, hooking my blade with the guard of his hilt before knocking the blade from my hand, and his foot slid around, catching my ankle before he yanked it out from under me. I yelped as my back hit the mat, and he was on me in a second, straddling my hips. His hand plastered onto my shoulder, anchoring me in place, before he pressed the blade to my throat.

I swallowed, my eyes locking with his as my chest heaved with each panted breath.

A low whistle slipped from Barrett's lips. "That's hot."

My gaze snapped to him, realizing him and Zephyr had stopped their sparring to watch, and my cheeks heated before I looked back at Damien. My thoughts immediately flew into a whirlwind as I realized just how he had me pinned—his body pressed so tightly against my own, sweat slick on his beautiful olive skin, thick veins protruding under the skin of his forearms as he gripped the dagger...

And never in my wildest dreams would I have thought it would be this much of a turn on to be held down with a dagger to my throat. Was there something wrong with me?

Damien let out a groan as he pushed himself off of me, his hardened gaze shifting to Barrett. "You just gonna sit there and watch or—"

"Shit, you're right. I should get some popcorn," Barrett said, planting a hand on his hip as he twirled his dagger. Damien's lips parted to retort, but before he could, Zephyr cut in.

"Come on, Barrett," Zephyr said, rolling his eyes at him and nudged his shoulder as he grabbed his bottle of water. "Let's let Cas train undisturbed. We've done all we can to help for now. We need to catch up with James and see if he's got any updates on the search, anyway."

Barrett sighed before turning to put his waster up. "Man, I was hoping to see the little spitfire put Damien on his ass. Now that's something I want a picture of."

I frowned. *Spitfire? What the hell was he talking about?*

"We'll catch up with you guys later," Zephyr said, waving back at us as Damien helped me back to my feet.

"See ya," I said, waving them off as they disappeared out the door.

"Here, get a drink," Damien said, and I realized he'd wandered to the nearby bench. He tossed me my water bottle, and I downed the last of its contents ravenously.

We set our bottles down and returned to the mat, ready to start over. I settled into the stance he'd shown me, the movement feeling so natural now that it was difficult to imagine I'd gone a lifetime without doing it—without holding a dagger in my hand. My gaze slid to the door where Zephyr and Barrett had left. I'd been wanting to ask Damien about Lucia's memory, and now that they were gone, I felt I could.

"Who's the daughter of Matthias?" I asked, as he took a step toward me to initiate the attack.

It caught him off guard, and he stopped, his brows furrowing. "Who told you about that?"

"I saw it in a dream I had about Lucia," I lied, not telling him I'd practiced on myself.

He eyed me for a moment and blinked as he ran his hand through his hair. "Very few know of Matthias."

"Lucia mentioned it during a hunt. She was adamant about taking her down." I didn't want to ask about the beast I'd seen. The sight of it had been terrifying enough, and I couldn't imagine facing something like that again.

"Matthias, like me, was from House Skiá. I didn't know him personally, but... Cas, what you have to understand is that Skiá magic, can be difficult to control."

I frowned, unsettled by that statement. "You can lose control?"

Damien nodded. "It's the dark magic among the blood traits. While the different magics each House of Power possesses can be influenced by your emotions, Skiá magic can and will feed on those emotions if you leave them unchecked."

He composed himself, and stepped forward to continue our practice, swinging his dagger to the side, which I blocked.

"So, what? Did Matthias get too worked up in a fight or something?" I stepped to the side as he moved toward me, readying to strike again.

"Actually no. I don't know the details of what happened or why he did it, but he wanted power, craved it so strongly that in his desire to gain it, he willingly let the darkness consume him."

I blocked another blow. "What happened to him?"

He stopped his advances, and something deep within the recesses of my soul stirred, tugging and pulling uncomfortably. "He became the first darkling."

I had to process that for a moment. "Wait, I thought the darklings were just creatures you guys have fought forever. They were once immortals?"

Damien nodded, his gaze slipping from mine, and I grew uneasy at the balmy guilt sliding over my skin. "Think of it as the family's dark secret."

"And the daughter of Matthias is..."

"A darkling born with the same power as Matthias. When he fell, he didn't just become some mindless creature like the darklings you've seen. The ones you see are those created by what once were his followers, weaker, mindless beings controlled by an insatiable hunger when Selene cursed them for their betrayal. He was different; he somehow kept hold of his mind."

I wondered what happened to make him pursue such a power. How long ago did the darklings appear? Was it before Moira? I had so many questions, but he continued before I could ask.

"The daughter of Matthias is a dangerous entity who can use Skiá magic to its full potential—can control the darklings with it. We called her that because of the similarities in their abilities, the fact that they retained the soul. There has never been a darkling like Matthias and the female darkling We still don't know the full extent of her powers, but what we witnessed was more than our army could handle. I personally believe Erebus had something to do with her reappearing like this."

"Who's Erebus?"

His advances stopped, and I felt like all my questions might be distracting him from our training, but I couldn't stop myself from asking.

"Selene isn't the only God. There are many, some foul and dangerous. Erebus is the God of Darkness." There was something in the way he said Erebus' name, as if just saying his name was enough to stir his anger. Did he know this God personally? "It would be child's play for him to give the darklings an edge in creating a reincarnation of our enemy. Probably thought it only fair to level the playing field, since we had the daughter of Selene reincarnating time and time again to face them."

It was difficult for me to wrap my mind around the fact that Greek Gods were more than a myth. My existence as a human, in a world I thought I knew barely a month ago, seemed so inconsequential now. How had humans survived so long amidst these wars between gods and monsters?

"Are they the same gods that people worship?"

"Only in name." Damien said, easing onto the bench. "In truth they are, Elythians, a race of creatures who came from the Godsrealm seeking entertainment from their boredom of their own realm. The Greeks worshipped them for their power."

"So, Selene's realm is called the Godsrealm?" I asked, and he nodded. "What exactly is the Godsrealm? Is it like our... realm?"

Surely, it couldn't be, not with gods and whatever other manner of creature existed there.

"Think of it as more of a parallel world to ours, both existing side by side, divided by the veil."

My mind wandered to our first meeting with Selene, and I wondered just what his relationship was like with her. He'd seemed so nervous in her presence.

"Do you like Selene?" I asked, taking a seat beside him.

"That's a loaded question," he said with an almost forced smile. "I respect her, serve her. She used to be very kind when I was young, but... something changed, something happened. I don't know what."

My heart twisted at the sight of the sorrow that flitted across his eyes at the mention of the person she once was.

"The thing about Elythians, is that they're a prideful, vain race," he said, turning to me, as if needing to explain, to defend her almost. "She has a difficult time seeing when she's cruel. To their kind, immortals and humans are temporary, easily replaced. I know there is a compassionate side to her, but I never know when she'll show that kindness, or when she'll punish you for speaking out of turn."

I knew what he meant by that, too. There had been moments where she'd seemed insulted by him asking a simple question.

"How do the darklings make more of their kind? You told me they're the reason for the disappearances."

"The darkness within them is infectious. The simple act of biting a person, human or immortal, will overcome the body with the evil coursing through their veins. Once the darkness overtakes the body, the darkling can continue on disguised as a human during the day, taking their place and blending seamlessly into society. The ones who disappeared, though... were likely devoured entirely."

My eyes flashed to him, fear icing over inside me. "You mean, if you're bitten, you could change into a darkling, Damien?"

"Don't do that to yourself, Cas. Stop that thought now." His gaze swept over me as he took my hand. "I'm careful. They've never gotten close to biting me. I never give them a chance."

It was too late. The fear was already taking hold, rooting its way into me until it solidified in my stomach. I would be powerless to stop it. It wasn't only death that could claim him if he fell to the darklings, but I could lose him to the darklings. What would I do then? I don't think I would have the strength to put him down like the others.

I hoped my next question would offer me some comfort if he ever did somehow get bitten fighting them. "Can you turn someone back after they've become a darkling?"

"There is a small window after a person's been bitten. Think of it like venom. You can draw it out, but it isn't always guaranteed to work, and sometimes it can backfire if you don't know what you're doing."

"What do you mean?"

"The person removing the darkness can also become infected. It's happened before." His eyes fell, and his voice sounded pained, as if he knew who it happened to, but I didn't pry.

"When Matthias and his followers turned on Selene, she cursed them to suffer an eternity of their own lust for power, endlessly hungering for flesh but unable to be satisfied by it."

That would explain why they always looked so emaciated, the sickly appearance that sank deep into their bones. Their very appearance was cursed.

"So, the darkling I saw in Cole's memory is The Daughter of Matthias, born again?" Damien nodded in response. "Why would Marcus side with them?"

He drew a deep breath, shaking his head. "He resents Selene for Vivienne's loss as much as he resents me. It isn't rational, but as I explained, things change when one of our kind loses a mate. He turned his back not only on our kind when he left, but on Selene as well. I didn't know he'd sided with the darklings, though. I thought he was simply a deserter."

"Will I learn how to use Skiá magic?"

He hesitated a moment, his eyes drifting from mine, and icy fear skittered over my skin. "You will eventually, but I want to be absolutely sure you're ready for that. Let's see how you handle the others first."

After hearing what happened to Matthias and his followers, I understood why it was such a dangerous ability. The thought of what I could do if I lost control of a power like that was enough to make me ill.

The pieces seemed to all fit together, everything making more sense. I'd always felt that there were similarities between Damien's magic and the darklings. It was because they were born of the same dark magic.

It was late in the afternoon when we got back to the house. We'd trained self-defense for another hour before moving on to learning how to predict an opponent's moves using Nous. I'd struggled severely with that. It was difficult to focus on reading Damien's mind while keeping track of my own movements. I may have fallen on my ass more times than I cared to admit, but I was satisfied with how far I'd come.

My phone vibrated, and I grabbed it from the counter to see a text from Kat. Hope danced in my chest, but then it faltered as I read through the words.

> Sorry, I've been quiet. I've been working every day after classes. I know you wanted to try to plan something tonight, but I'm gonna have to reschedule. The teachers have been assigning stupid amounts of work. So, it's been taking up my free time. Sorry! XOXO!

My shoulders sagged, and I typed my response.

> It's okay. Maybe we can plan a pizza date next Friday.

I set my phone down, palms pressing into the counter as I waited for the water to boil for my tea. Just what I needed. Another reason to feel down. She still seemed to be uneasy talking to me, our phone calls shorter than they used to be, and less frequent. She wasn't the reason I was already feeling unsettled, though.

A sense of uneasiness had swelled in the pit of my stomach from the moment we left The Outpost. The time was nearing when the female immortal would come... and Damien would feed. I hadn't been able to mentally prepare myself for it, though, all the time in the world might not have been enough to ready myself.

With each passing hour, nausea built in the pit of my stomach. Everything about this situation went against some strange instinct within me. Was this my past lives fighting what was coming? It was foolish. It wasn't like anything was going to happen between them. At least, that's what I kept telling myself. It didn't matter, though. No matter how much I didn't want to do this... it was necessary.

The tea kettle whistled, and I lifted it off the stovetop, pouring the hot water over the tea infuser in my cup. I needed to chill out; I couldn't be having these thoughts now. It wouldn't help the situation.

The sun set outside the kitchen window as I took a sip of the warming liquid, the last light leaking over the mountain tops in the distance. My drying curls hung over my shoulders, and I was dressed in fresh clothes. The weight of the dagger Damien gifted me, felt new as it sat strapped to my thigh. I needed to get used to wearing it, so it only made sense to wear it every chance I got. The sooner I could fight, the sooner I could be at Damien's side, fighting beside him, instead of staying behind and worrying until I made myself sick.

I lifted the cup to take another sip as the doorbell rang, and my spine straightened. Damien appeared in the doorway of the kitchen. "Are you ready for this?"

"No." My eyes fell, but I rose, setting my half empty teacup on the counter. "But it has to happen."

Damien grabbed hold of my arm as I tried to pass him. "Don't think I feel anything for this female, *mea luna.*"

"I know... It's just—" I couldn't say anymore, fearful I might say something I would regret. "Let's just get this over with."

Damien raked his fingers through his hair but didn't speak as he took lead toward the front door. This wasn't going to be easy for either of us.

It'll be over soon. Just shut up and deal.

My nerves heightened as I heard the door open and Damien welcomed the guest inside. Something in my chest clawed and fought what was to come. My steps slowed as I caught sight of her. She was perfectly poised as she walked through the doorway and she lowered her head, bowing to Damien before lifting herself back up.

She carried herself with a sense of elegance—her head held high, and she was breathtakingly beautiful. Her sun-kissed bronze skin blended with her golden-brown hair, and I couldn't help but notice how closely she resembled Marcus' mate, Vivienne, so closely that they could've been sisters. I wondered if she might come from the same family.

Vivienne was more of a wild soul, while this woman carried herself like a queen. Her hair was short, golden waves reaching just below her ears, bangs swept to the side out of her pale doe eyes. She was of a higher class, her clothes and jewelry the kind I would never have afforded in my lifetime.

Her gaze turned to me, and the way her eyes passed over me gave me the feeling I was beneath her, inferior. Confusion slipped through her mask of calm, her brows furrowing as she glanced between Damien and me for a moment. I knew what she was thinking, knew without diving into her thoughts.

Why would the king be with such a plain human as me? Why, indeed, when he could have someone like her? I chewed the inside of my lip as her eyes drifted away, as if I were nothing more than a passing thought.

"Thank you for coming, Calista," Damien said, offering her a welcoming smile.

"I'm honored you've called me to serve you again, Lord Damien," she said, bowing her head.

Something crawled over my skin at the sound of Damien's name on her tongue and the word again. I shook it off as best I could, remaining silent. The situation was bad enough; I didn't need to say something that would make it worse.

"Shall we move to the bedroo—"

"The couch." Damien's voice was a harsh command. "As always."

My hands clenched involuntarily at my sides at her assumption that he would feed from her in his bedroom. Our bedroom. Given her words and reaction, she wanted to serve him there, or had done so in the past. It left me nauseous, and I wanted to walk out the door and leave them to it.

She didn't argue, only obeyed as she dipped her head in subservience and followed him into the living room. "As you wish, my lord."

Wrong. This was so wrong. My chest burned, my skin growing hot, and I did my best to brush it off. I had to get over this. This was the reality I was going to have to deal with if I was going to be with Damien as a human. I could never provide for him in the way she could.

She eased onto the couch slowly, her delicate fingers unclasping the buttons of her sleeve before rolling it up to reveal her wrist.

Damien lifted his eyes to me, his hand extended out to the couch in a quiet gesture for me to sit next to her. I hesitated, my pulse roaring in my ears as I questioned myself, but obliged, easing onto the couch cushion.

She didn't even seem to take notice of me as her eyes followed Damien's movements, a light of awe within them. He knelt before her as he took hold of her wrist, but his free hand took mine and gripped it tightly.

In that brief moment, knowing what was about to happen, I found myself struggling to breathe. I should get up, should leave. There wasn't a place for me here in this room, but Damien's eyes locked with mine, as if he was trying to reassure me I was the only one he saw, not Calista. It did little to ease the upset in my gut, though.

My body tensed as his eyes fell to her wrist, his lips parting to reveal his lengthening fangs. Heart pounding, I watched as he bit down on her wrist, and I had to hold myself back, my body tensing as if it

317

wanted to move forward and stop this. I did. I wanted so badly to end this, to take her place, but I couldn't.

You'll never be enough. You'll never be what he needs.

The thoughts twisted something in my chest. Calista's chest expanded, and a deep breath filled her lungs, her eyes closing as he took from her. My eyes burned, and I tried to blink it away, my chest swelling with an agonizing feeling I'd never felt before. It was painful, air refusing to fill my lungs, so much so that I could barely handle it, and I wanted to run.

I tried to avert my eyes from her, focusing instead on Damien, whose eyes had lifted to me, watching me with such intensity. His gaze remained firm on me as he drank, his thumb rubbing over my hand, as if he were trying to ease my suffering.

There was no easing what I felt, no soothing over the agony tearing its way into my chest.

Calista's head tilted back, her breath heightening as her chest expanded and contracted in a heavy rhythm. I saw in my own mind her thoughts, her desires, her wishes. Damien's face appeared in her thoughts, the things she wanted to do for him—to him—manifesting before me. Then I heard her thoughts.

If you would only have me, Lord Damien. I could satisfy your hunger. Soothe the pain you feel. I could give you a worthy heir.

Before I knew what I was doing, I was up off the couch. My hand knotted in her hair as I jerked her head back into the cushion, my other hand tearing my dagger from its sheath, before pressing the blade to her throat. She gasped, her eyes popping open as I held her down, my face inches from hers.

Something had come over me, my body moving as if it wasn't my own. Realization dawned on me as words formed on the tip of my tongue, words that weren't my own. Moira, Elena, and Lucia spoke through me, their wills manifesting in my flesh centuries after their deaths. A strange, overwhelming possessiveness consumed me, and I had to stop myself from slicing the blade across her throat.

I didn't know what language passed through my lips, only knew what they meant as I spoke through gritted teeth.

"Touen estin emós."

He is mine.

CHAPTER 34

"Easy, Cas." Damien's voice was cautious as I froze, hand ensnared in Calista's hair as I pinned her against the couch. Her thoughts were still fresh in my own mind, the images of him she envisioned, the ways she wanted him. I blinked, trying to clear my mind of the visions of her hands against his chest, her lips brushing against his, her body pressing...

My chest heaved as I teetered on the edge, my hand trembling as I held the dagger to her throat.

All it would take is a single movement and she would never lay a finger on him again. Run that blade over that pretty skin.

No! What was I doing? This wasn't me. I wasn't a murderer, but no matter what I did, I couldn't move, couldn't will my hands to release her.

She stared up at me, eyes wide, body frozen in place. Everything in me wanted to cut her throat then and there, but I refused to give into that terrible urge. I wanted her out of our house, wanted to never see her face again.

Damien's hands cautiously glided over my shoulder, and his voice was a near whisper as he tried to talk me down from the ledge. "Release her, Cas."

"I saw her thoughts." My voice was almost a hiss, anger rising to the surface as the images of her desires drifted through my mind freely once more. The strange language formed on my tongue again as her thoughts rooted in my head... her promise of an heir. "Vou nolos gravosia miño en touen paios!"

You will carry no child of his!

She nodded slowly, and I released her hair before I pushed myself to my feet. My eyes remained on her as she wrapped her hand around her throat. Her panicked breath came in rushes as she tried to compose herself, her fear thick in the air, so sour and acidic that it burned my nose... so icy that it froze my skin.

For a moment I hated this ability to feel her emotions, to read her thoughts. Nausea rolled through me, my gut twisting as I struggled to forget the images of them together in my head. He'd said he never took another to bed after me, had remained faithful.

Damien pulled me against him. "That would never happen."

"But did it?" I asked, the words flying from my mouth before I could stop them.

He pulled back, blinking, his brows furrowing. "What?"

"Just tell me, did you ever... have you ever." My hands shook as I held onto his sleeve. "I saw you together in her mind, but I can't tell if it was just a dream of hers or if it was a memory, and I just..."

He took hold of my arms, lowering his face before me to meet my gaze, his eyes fierce. "Never have I taken another to bed. Since the beginning, it's only been you."

Truth. The warmth of the words filled my mind, soothing the doubt, and my body eased slightly, as if it believed it. How did I know it was the truth, though, how could I just accept that?

There's a lot you can do with a person's mind. You can read someone's thoughts, feel their emotions, see memories, gauge if they are lying or telling the truth.

My Nous ability. I'd forgotten that was something I could do. Relief washed over me, but I turned my gaze back to Calista.

Her wide eyes rose to me, and the anger, the possessive instinct swelled in my chest. "You need to leave. Now."

She bowed her head to me and stood to rush out of the living room without saying another word. The moment the front door closed behind her, my shoulders sagged, and I regained control of myself, my head clearing of the anger and irrational emotions.

Fuck. What had I done? She had what Damien needed, and I just chased her out. I wouldn't blame her if she never set foot in this house again, and yet a part of me seemed to relish in that possibility, but it was foolish.

Tears welled in my eyes at my own frustrations. "I'm sorry. I don't know what came over me. I just, I slipped, and I saw what she was think—"

Damien kissed me deeply before breaking away. His words were hot against my lips as he spoke, as if he enjoyed watching me attack her. "There is nothing more desirable than a female who will defend what's hers."

I pulled away. "Can't you just take from me? I know you're worried, but please. I'm sure I'll be fine."

"Cas I'm not..."

I pulled my hair to the side and his eyes fell on my throat, his fangs still exposed. He hesitated.

"I don't think I can go through that again..."

He didn't respond, his fingers trembling against my skin as I felt his resolve crumble.

"How would you feel if I took from another man?" I blinked. What was I saying? I was human. That was something that would never happen, anyway.

His eyes flashed, a feral light shining in them. The tips of his fingers dug into the flesh of my arms, but I held his gaze, unwavering.

"If any male ever tried to so much as touch you, let alone serve you—" He cut himself off before taking a deep breath. "I just don't want to take from you, when you're already so—"

"I'm weak! Yes, I know! You don't have to remind me!" The anger burned within me, my skin growing hot, and I regretted the words that flew from my mouth the moment they did, regretted the hurt reflecting in his eyes.

"I don't mean that you're weak, mea—"

"But I am! All I've done is take and take and need to be saved and rescued by you since we met!" His fingers gripped me tighter. "I want to help you for—"

He pulled me into him, his lips crashing into mine, cutting off what words I had left. His tongue swept past my lips as he tasted every bit of me, devouring me in the way I wanted him to, and I melted into him.

My heart leapt into my throat as he pushed me up against the wall, his powerful body anchoring me in place. He broke the kiss, his eyes trailing over me, as if gauging my emotions, and if I still wanted this. I did. I wanted it in a way that made no sense to me, instincts luring me past a point of no return, and I gave into them wholly, letting them sweep me away.

I settled against the wall, my heart thrumming as his tongue passed over his lips. He seemed to be forcing himself to slow down, his body rippling with need, but his movements slowed, his touches becoming gentler. His hand slid up from my arm, brushing against my collarbone, and he lifted my hair back over my shoulder. My heart hammered against my ribs at the anticipation and fear of what it would feel like.

322

Would it be painful? Calista's reaction seemed... pleasurable, and I winced at the thought that she felt pleasure feeding him. It felt wrong in every sense.

Chills rippled over my body as his fingertips glided over my neck, thumb lifting my jaw, and I let myself get lost in it, let it draw me back to him and out of my own head. He slid his knees between my legs, bracing me, and heat surged between my thighs.

I shuddered as he ground me against him, and his eyes darkened as he inhaled deeply. He leaned in closer, his lips brushing over the skin of my neck, and I shivered as his hot breath fanned out over my skin.

The tips of his fangs dragged against my throat, the sensation causing my skin to pebble with goosebumps. He froze, his body strung so tightly that I feared he might stop. I'd felt this before, this... hesitation. He'd done it when we—

When we slept together for the first time.

Had he nearly bitten me then? Did it hurt to not feed? Had he been suffering all this time?

"Damien?" I breathed, my hands coming to rest against his chest.

"I—" His breath was so hot against my skin, so ragged that it turned my blood molten. "I don't want to hurt you."

"You won't," I said tenderly, my hand sliding up over his arm to the back of his head.

He pressed a tender kiss to my neck before his lips parted and a needle-like pain pierced my throat. I tensed at the sensation before his hands came around my back, holding me against him, sustaining my weight as my muscles seemed to weaken, relaxing in a way I'd never felt.

The pain faded almost instantly, replaced with a warm pull. Air hitched in my lungs as my senses heightened, every brush of his fingertips amplified, electric, burning on my skin. A feeling so intensely pleasurable reached deep within me, like adrenaline taking hold of my body in a rush, and my thighs tightened around his leg as need surged within me. I shoved it back, fighting it as this wasn't the time. Why was my body reacting like this?

I slid my hands over his shoulders as I held him against me, encouraging him as I fought the need overwhelming me. He took another deep drink, and I tilted my head to the side, allowing him the room he needed as I felt myself flow into him. I focused on the fact that I was giving him what he needed to survive, that in some strange way, I was offering him strength. There was something oddly satisfying about it, and a strong flood of emotions crashed into me. Pride, love, adoration... There were so many I couldn't keep track of them as they rushed through me.

His free hand slid down from my arm, clasping onto my breast. I gasped, my knees buckling. He released my throat and pulled my shirt over my head impatiently before he lowered himself to take my breast into his mouth. My head fell back at the feel of his tongue against my skin, which had become so sensitive that it was almost too much.

I lost control of my body, unable to keep myself upright, my skin flushed. He rose, lips meeting mine again, before tugging me to the couch. He sat down, and before I could think or react, he spun me around, pulling me down backward to sit between his legs, my back pressed to his chest.

His fangs sank into my neck again, and my back arched, but his hands came around me, one rising to my throat, holding me in place, the other moving down my stomach. A groan of impatience escaped his lips as he fumbled with the buttons of my jeans before he finally got them free, and his hand slid into them. I cried out at the stroke of his fingertips against my heated flesh.

He moaned against my neck, and in that moment, I didn't know how much longer I might last, ever brush of our skin electric, amplified. Nothing could have prepared me for this, how intense it was, how sensitive my skin—my entire body—had become. He'd told me there was an intimacy when their kind fed, and—

"Oh God," I moaned as he ran his finger through my soaked center in a wicked, torturously slow rhythm. I could barely contain myself, and I couldn't understand how he'd held himself back all these years. Did these feelings go both ways?

"Is this—" I gasped as he dipped his finger inside me. "Is this what it's like every ti—" My moan cut my words short as he sank two fingers deep into me on the next thrust, curling them deep inside me as he took another deep drink.

"Only with you, *mea luna*," he said, breaking contact briefly, his hot breath spilling over my neck. "Gods, you taste fucking amazing."

My lips parted with a moan as he bit down again, my body tightening around his fingers as his words sent me over the edge and my back arched as the release exploded in me. He moaned, his body shuddering against my back as he held me tightly. His breath burned against my skin as his fangs slid free, and his tongue passed over my wound, an odd tingling sensation left in its wake.

His body twitched under me, as if he himself had climaxed at the same time I had. I melted back against him, the feeling continuing to ripple through me.

I could barely breathe as I tried to speak, my orgasm leaving me unable to think straight. "Oh, my God. What was that?"

"That." He kissed my temple, breath ragged. "Is what I've wanted to do since I found you."

"Did you—"

"I felt every bit of what you did, and the taste of it was divine," he whispered into my ear. He pulled his hand free from my jeans, and wrapped his arms around me as he cradled me against him. "Are you okay? I tried to not take too much, but Gods, it was difficult."

My eyelids slid shut as I breathed. "I'm blissfully exhausted, but okay. Better than okay, honestly."

324

He repositioned me so I sat sideways in his lap, and he pulled my head to rest against his chest as he held me. "Thank you."

"For what? I should be thanking you." My head rested against his shoulder, and his heart pounded beneath my ear.

"For giving me more than I could ever ask of you."

CHAPTER 35

I was awoken by the feeling of Damien's lips brushing against my neck. He drew me tighter against his chest, his hands roaming over my body.

"Damien," I groaned, a low laugh slipping from my throat at the sensation.

"I wondered how far I'd get before you woke." I could hear the sinful smile in his deep voice as it vibrated against the skin of my neck, and I shivered, my heart fluttering at the feel of his hard length against my ass. How many times had we made love? I had lost count, and I wasn't sure how late into the night we had kept each other up. How was it I could still want him—*need* him?

His lips brushed over my shoulder, and my back bowed against his chest as my skin came alive at his touch. My lips parted, as one of his hands slid beneath the hem of my nightshirt, coasting up my skin until he cupped my breast, and I bit my lip as the other descended over my stomach before slipping beneath the waistband of my shorts—my underwear, until he felt the slick heat already pooling between my thighs.

An appreciative hum reverberated from his throat, and whispered, "I love how wet you are for me."

He dragged his finger around that sensitive bundle of nerves I so desperately wanted him to touch, just barely avoiding it as he teased me until I was left panting in his grasp. He nipped at the shell of my ear and a moan slipped from my lips.

"Gods, I love the sounds you make."

He palmed my breast before rolling my nipple between his fingers with a light pinch, the twinge of pain more pleasurable than I'd imagined it could be, and I whimpered, needing more.

"I want to drown myself in the sounds that sweet mouth makes, almost as much as I want to drown myself in you."

His name broke from my lips on a moan as he ran his finger over that place I wanted him to touch, pleasure shooting up my spine. The brush of his stubble along his jaw as he kissed and nuzzled into my neck, tickled in all the right ways as he drove me toward the edge. I panted, one of my hands fisting in the sheets as the other grabbed hold of his arm.

He plunged his finger inside me, and tension coiled tighter until I thought I might explode. I gasped, body bucking against his hold, but he pulled me tighter against him, allowing me no room to slip from his grasp.

"Come for me," he growled, plunging two fingers in on the next stroke, and I couldn't have denied him his request if I wanted to. My body tightened around him, his words sending me over the edge as I cried out his name.

Pulling his hands from my shorts, he shifted, sliding his arm out from under me. His hungry eyes raked down my body as I stared up at him, my limbs nearly useless as the echoes of my orgasm rippled through me.

He peeled my shorts and underwear down my legs before tossing them aside. A chill swept over me as he ran his hands up my calves. His fingers grazed over my inner thighs, spreading them apart, before hooking them behind my knees and tugging me closer to him. I shuddered as his thick arousal, still hidden by his sweatpants, pressed up against my sensitive bare core.

My chest heaved as I lifted my eyes to him, taking in every detail of his face as he gazed down at me. God, he was beautiful. Perfection.

And he was mine.

I reached out, running my fingers over every ripple and dip of firm muscle, and I licked my lips as I imagined the way he would taste. My heart skipped a beat as he took both my wrists in his hand, planting them on the pillow above my head as his heated gaze met mine. His lips

crashed into mine and I parted for him, my tongue sweeping over his—
the taste of him so delicious that I wanted more, wanted to lose myself
in the chaotic whirlpool of feelings he brought to life within me.

He broke the kiss, the amber in his ashen eyes nearly glowing,
his fangs catching the light of the morning sun leaking in through the
curtains. The sight of it sent need pumping through me in a hot rush. His
hand slipped into his sweatpants before pulling his hard length free and
my mouth watered at the sight of it.

My thighs tightened at his sides as I remembered how amazing
it felt to have him inside me—how much I craved it despite how many
times I had taken him the night before. He tilted his hips forward, his
eyes remaining fixated on me as he ran his length through my wet heat.
My back arched, the flesh all too sensitive, and yet I wanted more, so
much more. His lips parted, his panted breaths coming in a rush as he
devoured the sight of me writhing with each touch.

"Gods, you're beautiful," he whispered, running himself against
me again and I moaned.

He released my wrists and brushed his thumb over my lower lip
before his hand descended further. His hand hooked under my knee,
lifting my leg until it was resting against his shoulder. His gaze fell to
where he fisted the base of his arousal, sliding it back and forth along my
center, coating himself in me until I was moaning and desperate for
more.

"Damien, please," I panted, my body crying out to feel him, the
need growing to a point where I couldn't bear it.

He shifted his hips back, guiding himself to my entrance and in
one smooth thrust, he seated himself in me. We moaned in unison as I
absorbed every inch, my body adjusting to accommodate the size of him,
and my head dipped back in the pillow. He fell into a heavy rhythm, his
thrusts desperate as he held my leg in place. I gasped as his other hand
hooked under my thigh to lift me, tilting my hips as he drove himself
deeper into me.

"Fuck," he breathed, his head falling forward as I grabbed onto
him, my nails biting into his skin as a second orgasm rolled through me.
He moaned my name as he slammed into me, chasing his own release,
and I shattered, crying out his name.

He shuddered, and I gasped at the feel of him deep inside of me
as he came. For a moment he lingered there, our bodies connected, his
chest heaving. I lifted my trembling hand, running my fingers through
the dark waves framing his face before tucking a lock of it behind his ear.

A smile crept across his face, so warm and sweet that it left my
heart fluttering. He leaned in to press a tender kiss to my lips before he
lowered my leg, slipping free of me, and collapsed into the blankets
beside me in a breathless mess.

He turned onto his side, pulling me into a tight hug, and I
burrowed into him—feeling the rush of air filling his lungs with each
breath, the pounding of his heart, which I'd noticed didn't beat in the
same two as mine, but in threes. I almost wondered what ways immortal

bodies differed from our own. A soft hum of content slipped from my throat, and I let myself get lost in the sounds and sensations of his body as we laid there for a while, just soaking each other up.

"Mmm. That's one hell of a way to wake up," I said, smiling against his chest as I inhaled his rich scent, that very scent coating my skin.

"I'd wake you up every morning like that if you liked," he said.

"That's quite tempting," I mused.

My eyes fell to his chest as I came down from the haze of need, and my brows furrowed as I took in the smooth, unmarred skin, astonishment flooding me at the fact that not a trace of his wound remained. I lifted my gaze to his shoulder, then to his forearm, the wounds from the darklings gone. I'd been so lost in my need that I hadn't even noticed that he had healed.

He smiled, cocking an eyebrow. "Like what you see?"

I met his smile with a coy grin of my own. "I *love* what I see." I lifted my hand, feeling my neck where he'd bitten me. The skin was smooth. I blinked, feeling up and down, but finding nothing, no scab, no puncture, just clear skin.

"Yeah, you won't find anything. It's a little trick we possess to hide our existence should we take from a human. That and the ability to erase a memory of our interaction so they have no memory of it happening. They're nothing compared to the abilities possessed by the other houses, but just enough to help us."

"That's handy."

He gave me a guilty grin. "Apologies, I... I didn't fully intend to wake you that wa—"

"I loved being woken like that," I said, silencing his apology.

A soft, low laugh reverberated from his throat. "Be that as it may, this is what I woke you for."

He gestured to a tray on my nightstand. All my favorite breakfast foods, tea, and a beautiful bouquet of lupine of every color lay atop the table at my bedside. I gaped at the display, confused, as I appreciated the floral beauty before me.

"Um…" I glanced back at Damien, unable to hold back the smile on my face. "What's the occasion?"

He bit back his smile. "Did you forget your own birthday?"

Was it really? I'd been so caught up on everything that I didn't even know what day it was. I opened my mouth to speak but stopped as I recounted the days. Nearly three weeks past Halloween... I grabbed my phone, looking at the calendar.

November 17th...

It *was* my birthday.

"How did you know?" I asked.

"You told me at dinner after we went to Stackhouse," he said with a crooked grin.

My eyes fell from his. He *had* asked me about my birthday, had asked a lot of questions about me that night that felt like ages ago. I smiled at the memory, at how normal I'd felt talking with him, and how he'd somehow managed to give me a day where I didn't think about my health, about my heart and what was to come. I felt like any other person in his presence.

"I'm surprised you remembered."

His brows rose as he looked at me incredulously. "I'm insulted you'd think I would forget."

I giggled, and that beautiful smile returned to his face. My phone rang, and I looked down to see Mom's name flash across the screen.

"Go ahead, your breakfast isn't going anywhere," Damien said with a warm smile. "I'm sure she's eager to talk to you."

Warmth blossomed in my chest, and I smiled as I pressed my finger to the screen before putting the phone to my ear. "Hey, Mom."

Mom and Dad's voices came in loud and clear over the phone. "Happy birthday to you! Happy birthday to you—"

A soft laugh escaped me as they sang to me, each line twisting something in my chest at the sound of their voices. "Thank you, guys."

"I can't believe my baby girl is twenty-one years old!" Dad exclaimed in the background.

"And yet you still call me your baby girl."

"You'll always be my baby girl," he said, and I rolled my eyes.

"How are you settling in?" Mom asked.

"He better be treating you right," Dad interjected.

"Dad," I grumbled. "I'm settling in just fine."

"Is there anything you need?" Mom asked in her usually doting tone. "Any furniture, or food—"

"I've got it, Mom. Honestly. Damien's made sure that I've got all I could need, and *Mitera* has been so amazing to me."

"*Mitera*?" Mom echoed.

My thoughts halted as I realized I hadn't told them about Ethel. I couldn't exactly tell them she was his servant. A housekeeper might be more believable, but then they might start asking questions. "Damien's... grandmother."

A sly grin formed on Damien's face, and he cocked an eyebrow as he watched me. I gave him a look, swatting him before turning to the side and pressing the phone to my ear.

I continued. "She visits often, practically lives here."

"That's so sweet. I'd love to meet her. Oh, and I guess it's pretty official with you guys moving in together. Does that mean we'll get to meet his parents soon?"

The smile slipped from Damien's face, and I winced inwardly.

Dad's voice came in the background. "Slow down there. We meet his parents, next thing you know they're gonna be talking about marriage. I'm not ready for my baby to be married. It's too soon."

"Oh, stop it, they've only been together for a short time. I highly doubt they're thinking of marriage already."

"Um... Mom, that's not possible," I said, hating that Damien was able to hear every word. "His parents passed when he was young."

"Oh God. I'm so sorry," Mom said, and Dad remained silent in the background.

"Maybe you can meet *Mitera* instead."

"I'd love that," she said.

"Are you guys busy today?" I asked, and Damien seemed to perk up at that question, but he avoided my gaze. "Maybe we could have lunch or something—er... I guess it's almost noon now, too late for lunch."

"We'll see," Mom said, and there was something strange to her tone, as if she were withholding something. "I won't keep you. We just wanted to wish you a happy birthday."

"Thanks, Mom."

"Love you, Cas!" Dad called from the background.

"Love you, Dad," I said loudly, and my voice softened before I continued. "I love you, Mom..." My chest swelled as I lingered on the fact that I hadn't seen her face in a few days. "I miss you."

"I love you, sweetheart, and I miss you too. You have fun today."

"I will."

We said our goodbyes and I hung up, realizing Kat had texted me while we were on the phone.

> Happy Birthday Beautiful! I didn't want to call and wake you. XOXO

I quickly texted back.

> Thank you! Damien just woke me up with breakfast and flowers! Maybe we could meet for dinner tonight!

My phone buzzed as she texted back, and my heart dipped.

> Sorry. I've got plans tonight.

331

My shoulders sagged, and I typed a quick '*ok*'. Perhaps this was just how things were going to be between us now.

"Sorry you had to hear that," I said, guilt swelling in my chest at the awkward explanation about his parents.

"They would've learned sooner or later," he said. "But don't worry about that. I don't want to linger on sad thoughts."

He lifted the tray of food and lowered it onto my lap as I tossed my phone on the bed. "I gave *Mitera* the day off, so I hope it's to your liking."

"You cooked all this? For me?" I asked, my heart squeezing as I realized he'd been up cooking this entire time.

A crooked grin curved his lips, a sense of pride lighting his eyes. "Eat. We're going out after this."

I took a bite of bacon, groaning at the salty heaven on my tongue. "Are we going to The Outpost?"

"No." He leaned in and pressed a kiss to my forehead. "No training today. Today is to be celebrated."

I clutched Damien's hands tightly as I took each step with care. He'd blindfolded me the moment we'd gotten into his car. The entire day had been planned out and he wouldn't tell me anything about what we would be doing.

"Watch your step," Damien warned, and I stumbled over something metal at my feet. He braced me, chuckling.

"You're supposed to keep me from falling," I grumbled, grabbing onto his hand tighter.

"Yeah, and you didn't. I caught you," he said with a laugh.

We came to a stop, his presence wrapping around me like a warm embrace. Where had he taken me? I could still hear the sounds of the city, the cars, the people talking as they passed us on the sidewalk. The cold fall winds blew against us, and I shivered.

Damien's arms wrapped around me as he leaned down to lay a kiss on my cheek. "Hold onto me."

The floor beneath us shook, and I yelped, the sound of metal grinding against metal ringing out as everything started to move. Damien barked out a laugh, but he released me and untied my blindfold. He leaned down to whisper in my ear as he released the fabric. "I hope you're not afraid of heights."

I flinched, blinking as my eyes adjusted to the light, and I gasped. The city grew distant before my eyes as we rose above it. The incline plane rattled as it rolled along the tracks on the mountainside beneath our feet. In all the years I'd lived here, I'd never ridden it, never had a chance to, and my mind wandered to our first date, and our game of ten thousand questions.

You've seriously never been on the incline plane?

Why is that so hard to believe?

Because you've lived here all your life.

The blue sky was clear of any clouds, warm sunlight spilling over us, and the city was a sight to behold nestled amidst the vast forest-covered mountains surrounding us.

"Knew this had to be one of the things we did today," Damien said.

I couldn't speak, the emotions leaving no words. As Damien's hands glided over my arms, I closed my eyes, curling into him. If only this moment could last forever, if only it could just remain the two of us.

"There's something I've been wondering. Be honest with me." Damien gave me a curious look but allowed me to continue. "Were you really attending classes? At the college, I mean."

He huffed a laugh as he rested his elbows on the railing. "No."

"So, how did you find me? Why were you at the campus when I saw you again?"

"You can thank The Fates for that," he said, his eyes drifting over the cityscape.

I frowned, seeing through the figure of speech for what it was. "You mentioned them before. They're real too?"

He nodded. "They're cruel bitches, but they come through sometimes. After I saw you at the mall, I almost didn't seek you out. I wanted to so desperately, but as a human, your memories were still dormant. It didn't feel right to pull you into all of this. You were safer in your own world."

He took my hand, his eyes lowering to them as he ran his thumb over my skin . "Usually when we meet for the first time, the memories start to resurface, its not always immediately, but there's always at least a flicker of a memory. However, when I looked into your eyes that first time, seeing all of your past lives… You weren't looking back at me. You didn't… see me."

My heart twisted at the sorrow in his eyes as I remembered the night we'd met at the Galleria. The look of shock on his face.

"It felt selfish of me to take you away from the world you knew, the safety of your reality. For all I knew you could have been involved with someone, been happy and content. How could I do that to you?"

He remained silent for a moment, as if losing himself to the memory before he drew a deep breath and continued. "Civilians who lead normal lives among humans attend UPJ. So, we routinely scope out the campus looking for any signs of darklings or deserter activity. We can better ensure their safety as well as the safety of the humans who go there. When I saw you again… I couldn't stay away any longer."

I remembered when he'd finally told me everything about himself, about their kind, how he'd asked me to tell him to wipe my memories. He only wanted to protect me and was willing to deny

333

himself the chance to be with his mate, if it meant I might live a normal life.

I shifted close to lean my head against his shoulder. "I'm glad you didn't stay away."

"Do you think you'll go back?" Damien asked. "Return to your classes?"

I didn't answer at first. There wasn't any point in returning. The time I had left was better spent training, helping Damien and the others. If dedicating my time to this could possibly ensure the safety of the ones I loved, then it was a clear choice to me.

"I don't think so," I said, looking out over the valley. "I never really saw much point in college. It was more for my parents' wishes than my own. I'd rather devote my time to helping you fight the darklings."

"I don't want you to miss out on your whole life because of me, Cas."

If only he knew the immense pain his words caused me. Miss out on my life? What life? Before him, my life had been nothing but doctor's visits, hospitalizations, and seclusion in my house. It had all become so tedious, so monotonous, that living day to day had become a chore. There was no life waiting for me out there, only death. If only he knew how much meaning he gave my life for once, if only I could bring myself to verbalize it to him.

If only I could find the words to tell him the truth.

My fingers laced between his, and I pressed my lips to the back of his hand. "My life is here, with you, *mea sol*. I wouldn't want to be anywhere else right now, regardless of what we stand to face. I will be here with you... Every step of the way."

A smile curved his lips, the amber in his ashen eyes glowing like honey in the rays of sunlight. "And I shall treasure every moment."

The lift came to a stop at the top, and he led me out onto the overlook. The view stretched out for miles. The wind whipped past me as I walked over to the edge, resting my arms atop the railing, taking in the view once again.

Damien's arms came around my waist as he pulled me back against him, and I tilted my head to look at him. "Would you believe me if I told you, you're the first person to ever take me out on a date?"

He frowned, eyes falling to mine. "Really? I find it hard to believe that at twenty-one you haven't been on a single date."

I laughed lightly. "A bit embarrassing, but yeah. Kat's tried to get me to go on dates, but every time I met the guy, something just felt... wrong."

He snickered, and I twisted around to look at him. "What?"

"Oh nothing, probably just your past lives clinging to the mating bond."

My gaze fell from him as I processed what he said. Had that been the reason why I'd never felt any interest in dating any guys?

334

Because a part of me, one that I hadn't known existed, knew Damien was out there waiting for me?

Waiting for his mate to return as a human... one whose health was deteriorating.

My smile faded as I stared into the horizon, those thoughts stirring the knowledge that resided in me of what was to come. I knew how things would eventually end for us.

"Well, I'm glad I had the honor of being your first." He tilted his head to gaze down at me, his smile like sunlight on my skin.

I pushed myself up, whispering, before I kissed him. "My only." Because there would be no other.

The afternoon sun had grown closer to the mountain ridges as Damien lead me through the woods of Stackhouse. I recognized the path leading to the clearing he'd taken me to before. I'd been a bit uneasy about entering these woods again after everything that had happened, but Damien had assured me we were safe this time, that no one would disturb us. It wasn't long after that, that I glimpsed the glowing blue eyes of one of Damien's shadow wolves watching us curiously from the nearby trees before running off to stand watch, and more passed by before disappearing into the forest.

I smiled nervously in anticipation as the trees parted ahead of us. "What are we doing out here?"

"I figured you'd enjoy a nice dinner."

I stopped at the edge of the clearing, frozen in place. Before us was a large blanket surrounded by candles. There was a basket with plates and utensils laid out for us. I frowned. Damien had been with me the entire afternoon. How had he managed to do this?

"How did you..."

He placed a finger over his lips. "I'm not the only one who set things up for your birthday."

"But you said you gave *Mitera* the day off."

"She didn't do this," he said. "She and I aren't the only ones who care about you, *mea luna*."

My heart swelled at that statement, words unable to form on my tongue. Had Barrett, Zephyr, and Vincent somehow helped in setting the day up? I didn't have a chance to linger on the thought as Damien took my hand and guided me closer.

I eased down onto the blanket as Damien did, and I surveyed the clearing, remembering the first time we'd been here, the sketch of him that no longer existed. I halted that train of thought and watched as Damien opened the basket and pulled out an assortment of warm food.

Whoever had helped him set this up had left this fresh for us as I could smell the roast chicken, still hot in its container.

"I don't know what it is about this place..." I started, allowing my gaze to drift around the tree line.

Damien's eyes lifted to me, lit with something I couldn't quite place. Hope? "Why do you say that?"

"When you first brought me here, I immediately felt... I don't know how to explain it. It just felt so familiar, but I've never been here before."

He didn't answer and left me in silence for a moment as he finished filling a plate for me.

His eyes lowered. "I..."

My brows rose as I lifted my eyes to him.

"I brought you here, hoping it might trigger something. A memory."

I blinked. "How?"

"You remember the memory you saw of Elena? Of us training?"

I nodded.

"That was Moonhaven."

"Yeah, I remember you mentioning the name."

His eyes drifted over to the remains of the houses that had deteriorated long ago, nature reclaiming them in her long ago. As my eyes settled on the moss-covered stonework, the sun set over the mountain ridge and slowly cloaked them in darkness.

Realization dawned on me, and my gaze snapped to Damien.

His saddened eyes returned to me, and he nodded. "This is all that remains of Moonhaven now."

I didn't have words for the sorrow that sank into me, but I couldn't understand why. Was it the part of me that was Elena that felt such deep pain? Then I remembered what Damien had told me, of what had befallen Moonhaven, how Elena... how I'd lost my life fighting to defend it.

"That's why you brought me here..."

He handed me my plate before plating his own food. "I'd hoped that maybe bringing you here might awaken your memories. It didn't work, or at least we weren't here long enough for it to happen."

I smiled sheepishly. "Sorry about that. My clumsiness has a way of ruining plans."

"It didn't ruin my plans entirely." A wicked grin tugged at his lips. "Your clumsiness led to other things I enjoyed."

My heart fluttered, my body tightening and loosening in various places as my mind raced with the thoughts of us on his living room floor, and I couldn't disagree with him.

"Shall I eat, or are you planning some other form of entertainment?" I asked, tilting my head lazily, letting the words leave my tongue in as sultry a manner as I could.

He inhaled. "That depends on what form of *entertainment* you're referring to."

336

I took a bite of my chicken. "I don't know. You're the one with the plans."

He laughed but proceeded to eat. "Don't worry, *mea luna*. I only planned to enjoy dinner with you under the stars, amidst candlelight. *Entertainment* can come later."

I smiled. "Well, I won't tempt you, *milord*."

His gaze flashed to me, and I bit back the urge to laugh as I ate my food, feigning innocence.

How I loved to tease him.

"Thank you."

Damien cocked an eyebrow as we pulled into the driveway, the street lamps casting the streets in a warm glow. "For what?"

"For... everything. For finding me when I didn't even know that I needed you. For showing me how fulfilling life can be. For... saving me, and not just from... Marcus." I couldn't find the right words to show him just how much he meant to me. "I wasn't in a good place in my life when you found me."

"Always, *mea luna*. I will always find you, no matter what."

We climbed out of the car, and as I reached the porch, Damien's hands came over my eyes. I jumped but giggled. "What is it now?"

"The day isn't yet over. There's one more thing I want to show you." His whisper was warm in my ear as he spoke, and he guided me into the house.

It boggled my mind how there could be more. The afternoon had been filled between the trip to the incline plane and dinner in the clearing at Stackhouse. He'd even offered to take me out for my first drink after we shared dinner, to which I politely declined.

I wasn't sure where he led me when we came to an abrupt stop. A door creaked open, and he guided me forward before he removed his hands from my face.

The smile slid from my face, and tears welled in my eyes. I couldn't speak, couldn't breathe, as my gaze swept through the room. Shelves lined the walls, filled to the brim with books. A single window was centered on the back wall, with a padded bench under it. Beside the bench stood an easel and an armoire, the doors open, proudly displaying an array of art supplies, more than I'd ever owned in my life. I hesitated. This couldn't be real.

I came to a stop before the nearest shelf, gliding my fingers over the spines—reading all the familiar titles, all of my favorite books, ones that I had in my collection that had been destroyed. I looked back over my shoulder to Damien, my lips parting, but no words came.

"I saw how extensive your collection was," Damien said as he leaned against the doorframe. "I spoke with your mom to try and get a list of the books you had. I know we didn't get them all, but we got a lot of them. *Mitera* helped gather everything and put the finishing touches in place while I had you out of the house. This room is yours now, *mea luna.*"

I couldn't speak, couldn't form thoughts as my eyes drifted across the room. He'd called my mom to ask for help. She'd known he'd planned this when we spoke on the phone that morning, seemed to have known he had a whole day of festivities planned for me. How long had he been planning this?

He nodded toward another section of the room. "You still have some shelves open if you ever want to get more, because I know you will. We can even expand and build taller shelves. I think we managed to replace most of the books you had. And..."

He handed me a book, the one I'd loaned him when he first came to my house. I knew it had only been a little over a month since that night, but it felt like ages.

"As promised, I didn't let Barrett ruin it."

My heart swelled, the matte dust jacket smooth under my fingertips. This book meant so much more to me now, the only piece of my life from before... but it was also a reminder of the beginning, of when we'd shared our first kiss—when he'd first reached out to me in the darkness and pulled me out when I couldn't do it myself.

I looked back at the shelves, seeing all the titles I'd spent years gathering, reading, loving; the countless art supplies that I could use to draw again. My voice broke as I spoke. "You did this for me?"

He approached me. "I knew how upsetting it was to lose your books, and I was furious when I saw all your beautiful drawings and sketches destroyed. It doesn't truly replace what you had, but it seemed like the perfect gift."

I couldn't find the words to express my gratitude, pressure building in the back of my throat as I my eyes began to burn. "I feel like thank you isn't enough... I can't believe you did this, Damien."

He wrapped his arms around me, pulling me into a tight embrace, and he placed a kiss to my forehead. "It's the least I can do. Happy Birthday, *mea luna.*"

It wasn't the fact that I had a library, or that I could draw again that had me on the verge of tears. It was how deeply he cared to do all this, to surprise me the way he had, to reach out to my mom.

I walked over to my new art corner. My fingers grazed over the pad of paper on the easel, the paper a subtle texture under my fingertips. I peered into the cabinet, and for the first time in years... I wanted to paint. I wanted to see the colors seep into the paper and breath live into the subject.

I grabbed the charcoal and watercolors, and glanced back at Damien.

"You said if I ever wanted to draw you, all I had to do was ask, right?"

The corner of his lips curved into a crooked grin. "Of course."

I pulled one of the chairs over, placing it near the window, and held out my hand. "Would you do me the honor?"

He obliged, walking over to sit on the stool. I situated the pad of paper against the easel and laid out the charcoal and watercolors. He'd even stocked some bottles of water to have on hand for the paints. My heart swelled at the fact that he hadn't seemed to leave any detail unnoticed.

His face settled against his knuckles as those beautiful eyes followed my movements. I wanted to capture the intensity of them. The burst of amber, like the rays of the sun peeking from the rim of his pupil, fading into warm gray. Such a contrasting color, so intense that it had burned itself into my being in a way that I couldn't escape even if I wanted to.

"Just stay like that, *mea sol*." A crooked grin barely lifted the corner of his lips. He obeyed.

And I put the charcoal to the paper.

"Times up! You've had her long enough, Damien! She's ours now!"

I squeaked, the paintbrush nearly falling from my hands before I could finish adding the last touch of amber to Damien's eyes as Barrett's voice rang throughout the house. Damien huffed a laugh and rolled his eyes.

I frowned, my heart threatening to burst from my chest. "What's going on?"

"You'll see, come on," Damien said, rising from the stool and I turned, placing my brush in the cup of water before tidying up my supplies.

"If you're naked and busy too bad, you knew we were coming!" Vincent called.

My cheeks heated. Oh God, who all was here?

"I should've known the moment you got laid you'd be tangled up with him every chance you got!"

I stiffened at Kat's voice, and dropped what I was doing to rush out the door and into the living room.

"Surprise!" Everyone shouted, and I froze, unable to take another step.

"Bout damn time you got out here, I was about to barge in," Barrett taunted.

A confused smile overtook me at the sight of everyone: Kat, Barrett, Zephyr, Vincent, Anna, Thalia, *Mitera*, James. They were all here. Damien came to a stop at my side, but I couldn't pull my gaze from them.

"What are you guys doing here?" I asked and frowned when I noted the bottles of alcohol Barrett had in tow.

"Fuckin' celebrating your birthday, what's it look like?" Barrett said with his usual cocky grin as he walked over to rustle my hair.

I shoved him off and frowned at Kat as she approached. "I thought you had plans tonight."

"I couldn't very well tell you I had plans to surprise you for your birthday, dummy," she said, wrapping her arms around my neck before heading for the hall along with everyone else.

"You sneaky bitch," I said, remembering how upset I'd felt that morning, how I'd feared that it was the beginning of the end of our friendship.

"Come now, Ah've got a surprise waitin' fer ye in the kitchen," *Mitera* said as she approached, nudging me in that direction.

I frowned. How did she have a surprise set up for me? Had she snuck into the house while we were in the library? I slid a glance toward Damien, and he gave me an apologetic grin.

"Any more secrets today?" I asked as we stepped into the hall.

"That was the last of them," he said, and I eyed him wearily.

"Happy Birthday!" Everyone said in unison as I entered the kitchen, the lights already dimmed, a soft glow emanating from candles lit atop a cake on the island.

Tears welled in my eyes.

Don't you dare cry, you freaking sap.

I couldn't stop them, though, as they rolled down my cheeks. Kat threw her arms around me, pulling me into a tight hug.

"Don't cry!" she said, tears welling in her own eyes.

"You can't tell me I can't cry when you're crying!" I said loudly, more tears falling.

I caught sight of Zephyr's warm smile as he watched us, and I quickly tried to wipe my face, tried to find some sort of composure, but I couldn't.

It was only days ago that I'd almost given up hope of getting free, of ever seeing them again. Here I was, though, surrounded by friends I'd only known for a short amount of time, but I couldn't imagine a life without them.

"Wait, we can't get started yet, we're still waiting on someone," Ethel said, waving Barrett away from the cake as he tried to swipe his finger through the icing.

I frowned, opening my mouth to ask, but then there was a knock at the door before it opened.

"Hello?"

My heart leapt at the voice, the voice that I'd known my entire live, the voice that had always carried words of affection and comfort from my earliest memory.

340

"Mom?" I breathed, whipping around to see them coming in through the front door.

She lit up, arms outstretched. "Happy Birthday!"

I ran to her, wrapping my arounds around her as tears dotted my eyes.

"Sorry we're late, ran into some traffic," Dad said, wrapping his arms around us in a tight squeeze.

I pulled back, looking between them. "I didn't... what are you..."

Mom glanced over my shoulder with a knowing smile, and I twisted around to see Damien, arms crossed as he leaned against cased opening of the kitchen. A warm smile curved his lips as he watched us.

I put my hands on my hips, and he put up a hand in surrender. "Ok, that was the last surprise."

"Get your ass over here and blow out these candles. *Mitera's* cakes are the best!" Barrett called as we returned to the kitchen, and Thalia swatted him. I snickered and hurried over before he could blow them out himself.

Because I knew the asshole would.

CHAPTER 36

I faintly felt the brush of fingertips along my skin. They glided over my thigh, up my stomach, against my neck. The tickle sent chills over me, and I let slip a soft groan from my throat.

I stifled a giggle as I opened my eyes slowly, exhausted from the late night of celebrating. "Damien."

A firm hand clamped over my mouth, and my eyes popped open, my breath hitching in my throat.

"Shhhh. We don't want to wake him." Marcus' voice, a sharp whisper, filled my ears as he leaned into me. He straddled me, pinning me in place with his body, and his hand pressed to my mouth, muffling my scream.

My eyes darted around in a panic, looking for concrete walls, but found I was still in our room. Or was I? Was this a trick?

"Did you have a fun reprieve, little songbird?"

His free hand rose, revealing the same knife he'd used to torment me when he imprisoned me. My blood ran cold, remembering the endless cycle of pain he put me through with it. I'd only just started to finally heal. Had it all been a dream? Had none of my time with Damien been real?

"That was such a lovely birthday," he mused. "To be surrounded by all your beloved friends again. You'd given up hope you'd see them again, hadn't you? You put on a brave face, but I know every thought dancing behind those pretty eyes. I hope you enjoyed it while it lasted."

The tip of the blade dragged against my skin, down the length of my cheek and over my neck. I winced as the blade nicked my flesh, my chest heaving as he watched my every reaction.

A sadistic grin curved his lips. "*Yes*, I love that fear in your eyes. You're ripe to be put back in chains."

No. Not again. You won't do this to me again!

Fury flared in my veins as I met his gaze—my skin growing hot, fingertips burning, and I fought to get out from under him.

"Cas! Wake up!"

I gasped as Damien shook me awake, and I shot up, frantically looking around in my panic. The smell of smoke burned my nose and lungs. What was burning?

"Cas, you need to calm down." Damien said frantically as he tried to smother the tiny flames struggling to spark to life on our bed. Where the blankets touched me, they smoldered, and my body felt hot, as if I'd spent too much time in the sun. I lifted my hands to find the tiniest of flames flickering at each of my fingertips.

It wasn't something that was burning. It was me. *I* was on fire, but it didn't hurt, the flames curled and swayed against my skin without burning my flesh.

"Close your eyes, Cas. You need to focus on your breathing. Calm your mind." Damien grabbed my wrists. He hissed as my skin burned his palms, but he didn't let go and pulled me off the bed. I tried my hardest, closing my eyes to focus through the panic, tears streaming down my cheeks.

Calm, Cas. Calm. In through the nose, out through the mouth.

The heat lessened, and after a few moments finally faded away entirely. I looked back down at my hands to find the little flames had doused. My palms were red, but somehow not burned.

"What happened?" Damien brought his hands to my face, his thumbs brushing the tears away.

My eyes didn't meet his, my hands trembling. "It was Marcus... I—it was just a dream about him." I rubbed my eyes, more tears threatening to spill at how real it had felt, as if he'd physically been there. "What was that? What happened to me?"

"That was Stoicheion, an elemental ability that I wasn't prepared for you to start learning quite yet. Your body seemed to have used it in defense." Damien pulled the sheets up, making sure the fire was fully out. My eyes fell over the bed, the blankets and mattress completely ruined, but thankfully, the bed frame remained undamaged.

I made a poor attempt to help him, my body still shaking. "I'm so sorry."

"Don't worry about the bed, *mea luna*. We'll get a new one." He turned to me then, his eyes falling to my shaking hands, and he took hold of them, before lifting to meet my gaze. "You said you saw Marcus?"

I nodded. "It was just very real. It scared me."

Damien's jaw tightened, his body stiffening, eyes widening as they locked on my neck. His hand rose slowly, lifting my hair away from my shoulder and I winced the moment his fingers touched what felt like a cut, the same place where Marcus' knife had just been. Our gazes met, and I saw the horror in Damien's eyes. My hand shot to my neck, feeling the cut, and as I pulled it back to examine it, my heart stuttered at the bit of blood on my palm.

No. That wasn't possible.

Damien pulled me into a tight embrace, his emotions like chaos boiling over within him. "That bastard must've tethered himself to you."

The words clicked but didn't make any sense. It had been a dream; how was I cut? "Tethered?"

Damien growled as he walked over to the closet and threw a shirt on before he grabbed his phone, dialing. "It's an old ability, long forgotten. Certain members of the House of Nous were known as Oneiroi, dream walkers. Those warriors possessed the unique ability to enter a person's dreams while they slept. They could even hurt them physically if they were good enough. It's an ability that hasn't been practiced for centuries, not since the wars fought before the darklings. I didn't think there was anyone still able to use it, let alone Marcus. It isn't something you can just do to anyone. You must mark them, through touch."

The world shifted beneath my feet, as the weight of what he could do to me while I slept tore through me. I was defenseless against him. "He had me unconscious so many times, he would have had numerous opportunities to do it without my knowledge."

"And he could have attacked you anytime while you slept at this point. No, he was waiting. *Sick fucking bastard*." He grabbed onto the post of the bed, as if he might rip it from the frame, but he steadied himself. "This won't be the last time he shows up. You can drive a person insane, tampering with their dreams, and the Oneiroi were especially useful in their ability to assassinate enemies in their sleep."

I swallowed, hands trembling.

"*Mea luna?*"

"I… I thought for a moment I'd never left that cell… that you'd never found me." The panic crawled over my skin, sinking its claws so deep into my chest that I thought I might fall apart. "I thought all of this had been a dream."

He returned to me, taking my face in his hands, forcing my gaze to him. "You are here, not in a cell. This is our room… and I'm real. This is real." I lifted my hand over his, feeling his skin against mine, feeling

344

everything that he was, using it to ground me here to this reality. "He no longer has you, and I won't rest until we find him."

I blinked back the tears before curling into him.

Damien's muscles twitched as he continued to hold me. He pushed the call button on his phone, placing it to his ear. It only rang once before a voice came up on the other end of the line. "Barrett. Marcus must have tethered Cas for dream walking when he had her... He attacked her in her sleep just now—"

Barrett's voice came in heavy on the other end, a flurry of words flying into Damien's ear, and Damien squeezed me tightly, as if he were reassuring himself I was here in his arms.

"She's okay, but I need that hideout found yesterday. Has James dug up anything on his end?" Damien went silent as Barrett told him whatever information they had. "Understood. Gather everyone. No one rests until he's found."

"What are we missing?" Damien growled, bracing his hands against the edge of the table, the veins popping under his skin as if he were holding himself back from doing something reckless. The night hours were dwindling now, and I wondered if the sun was beginning its ascent over the mountain ridges outside. Exhaustion had settled into my bones, sleep beckoning to me, but I resisted the urge to give in, to close my eyes and drift into the embrace that should be comforting. I couldn't, though, not until we located Marcus and put an end to all this and his miserable existence. Until we did that, he could attack me again, could do far worse than what he'd already done.

A map lay out across a table before us, illuminated by a single overhead lamp. Red sharpie marked up the paper in the form of circles, X's, and question marks noting potential locations where Marcus and his men might be hiding out.

James muttered something into his phone before hanging up from what I assumed was an update from one of the teams out searching. He popped the cap off a sharpie and marked a big X over one of the locations.

Damien's head dropped in defeat before he turned. "*Son of a fucking bitch!*"

I flinched as he slammed his fist into the wall, and I swallowed at the faint hairline cracks left in the concrete, at the bits of Damien's blood left behind. I resisted the urge to go to him, to tend to him as he paced, working things over in his mind. He'd been on edge all day, working every minute to try to locate Marcus. Would we succeed, though? He could be anywhere.

What if I was wrong about this place? What if he wasn't even hiding there?

Barrett had been unusually quiet, his eyes moving over the map in silent contemplation, his arms crossed over his broad chest. I looked over the map again, eyes trailing over every direction of the Conemaugh River. Perhaps I was wrong to think his hideout was in the city, maybe it was further out? Could it be in one of the surrounding cities?

A part of me was eager to find him, but another part of me was afraid to. Would I be able to face him? I knew from experience how skilled he was at manipulating a person's mind, how good he was at tearing them down. While I'd developed my own skills since beginning my training, I doubted my abilities when it came to fighting him.

I jumped, drawing in a startled breath as Thalia placed a blanket over my shoulders.

"Sorry, I didn't mean to scare you," she said, rubbing my shoulders. "I figured you could use a blanket. You're shaking like a leaf."

I looked down at myself, finding that I was, the tremors rattling my fingers and into my arms. Irritation flooded my chest, and I hugged myself, hating that Marcus had me so shaken. I offered her a weak smile, trying to mask the fear as I pulled the blanket tighter around me.

"Thank you."

Zephyr leaned over the table, eyes scanning the map. "And this is every place on the satellite that matches the descriptions Cas gave?"

James nodded. "Ah kept the search open tae commercial an' private residences, as thir are some properties that hev some junk cars an' what cuid possibly be metal buildings."

Zephyr's phone rang, and he quickly answered it, "Find anything?"

All our eyes flew to him as we waited in bated silence.

The room was quiet as he listened to the report from his team before a muscle feathered in his jaw. He grabbed the marker, slashing an X over another location. "Move to the next one, and report to me with anything you find."

Zephyr hung up, tossing his phone on the table, before bracing his hands against the edge and dropping his head in defeat with a sigh.

"We'll find them, Cas," Vincent said, running his hand over my shoulder in gentle reassurance, and I smiled, nodding.

"I know you will," I said, my voice too quiet as I began to fear that we might not, that I might have to face him in my dreams, and I swallowed the dread clawing its way up my throat. I hated this fear he'd instilled in me, hated this terror pumping through my veins with each passing hour that he remained hidden from us.

"What if I try searching Cole's mind again?" I asked, and everyone's attention turned to me. I pulled the blanket tighter around me, guilt flooding my chest that they were all here, working to hunt down Marcus because of me. Zephyr and Barrett had patrolled last night, and they'd now been up for 48 hours. They didn't seem affected, but surely they must be tired.

"We already tried that," Damien explained. "We had a Nous user search his memories this morning after you were attacked, but they ran into the same issue you did with any memories surrounding this place. It's as if his memory was altered or hazed over. Marcus probably did something to him and his men to ensure the locations of their hideouts remained hidden if any of them were captured."

My shoulders slumped.

"Has anyone been back to the compound where he kept her, to look for anything that might help?" Barrett asked, the first time I'd heard him speak up in the last thirty minutes since we'd checked in here to take a break from searching. I shifted my gaze to him to find his eyes remaining fixed on the map.

I gripped the blanket tighter in my hand to quiet the trembling at the thought of that place. I still hadn't been able to open up to Damien about what exactly had happened within those concrete walls. He was right, though, there was no telling what was housed in that building. The lead we need might just be there.

"Not since the cleanup," Damien answered, returning to Zephyr's side. He braced his hands on the edge of the table, the knuckles of his right hand bloodied, skin shredded from the concrete. I turned as they continued discussing everything and hurried to the bathroom to retrieve some paper towels.

"Has any of Marcus' men showed up since?" Vincent asked as I returned and came up to Damien's side.

Barrett shook his head. "I've had a team patrolling the woods around there, checking for any sign of activity since we extracted her, but it seems abandoned."

"We'll go check it out, see if there's anything we can use, any hint of another location they're using. Cas can stay here with Thalia," Damien said.

"I'm going where you go," I said with a strange calm as I took his battered hand and ran the damp paper towel over his knuckle. His gaze fell on me before the rest of them followed suit.

"I don't want you to have to set another foot in that cursed place again," he said, his eyes softening as I worked to tend to his wound.

"Whatever it takes to bring him down, I'll do it," I said, lifting my gaze to him, my eyes tired. "I don't know the layout as that night you guys found me was the first I'd ever been out of the cell, but..."

"She's got the best idea of what this place looks like. She might see something we won't know to look for," Vincent said, his eyes flickering to me briefly with a hint of sadness. I offered him a weak smile of gratitude.

Damien drew a deep breath, falling back into silence as he worked things over in his mind. His eyes drifted to me. "If it becomes too much, I'm getting you out of there."

I nodded, unsure if I was truly ready to go back to that place, but...

If it meant putting a dagger in Marcus' chest, I didn't care what I had to do.

CHAPTER 37

The sun was at its highest by the time we made it through the woods. We were so far from the city, and I'd been in such a sleepy daze that I hadn't paid attention to just where we'd gone.

I lifted my eyes to the small building before us, so well hidden in the trees, miles from any road. How had Damien managed to find me so far in the woods?

A brush of fur under my palm drew me back, and my eyes fell to the shadowy wolf at my side, one of the creature's Damien summoned with his shadow magic. He called them Lupai, and while they'd been terrifying to behold when I'd first encounter them, I found them to be affectionate, sweet creatures when you weren't their enemy.

The Lupai's body was so massive, his back reaching my hip. It lifted its head against me, begging for a pet, and it lifted my arm until it could snuggle closer against my side, its fur swaying and billowing out into black mist.

Damien knelt before one of the shadow creatures he'd summoned, holding its intent gaze for a moment. "Make sure we're undisturbed."

The creatures' eyes shifted from the cool blue to the murderous red I'd seen when they'd rescued me. Its body, as well as the others at its back, grew distorted, backs hunching higher, jaws stretching unnaturally wide to reveal serrated teeth that would tear a person to pieces with ease. The lupai whipped around before the pack split up, some running around to the back of the building, some taking off into the woods, and others dipped into the shadows of the wall before us, entering to scout ahead.

"Are you sure about this, *mea luna*?" he asked, taking my hand as the shadows bent and curled along the building's wall, the darkened doorway forming before us.

The single Lupai nuzzled into my touch, its presence somehow comforting, and I lifted my eyes to the shadows as Zephyr and the others entered the compound to begin their search.

I drew a deep breath, steeling my nerves and nodded. "I want to see that bastard dead."

"By my hand or yours, he will die, I swear it," he vowed.

Before I could let the fear take over and uproot my resolve, I took a step forward, the Lupai remaining firm at my side, Damien on my other. We entered the void, the shadows welcoming me into their cool embrace, and something deep within my chest stirred in their presence, that something reaching out to the darkness surrounding me, to Damien before the darkness receded, revealing the main room.

It felt as if time had stopped, as if none had passed, the room just as I remembered it. Broken furniture still littered the room from the fight, blood stains marked the concrete, and my eyes fell to the iron I'd used to knock Amara out. Damien looked around, and I drifted from his side, eyes scanning the room. Memories and emotions resurfaced, the terror and desperation to get free as I searched for an escape. Three doors. One down, and the others...

I approached the door I'd ran for in my desperate attempt at escape—the door I never reached—and twisted the knob, opening it. A hollow laugh bubbled up my throat at what I found. It was a closet, a dead end.

I'd chosen wrong.

It hadn't mattered in the end. I never reached it anyway, and if Damien and the others hadn't come, I would have been put back in those chains, would have likely been put through worse torture for my attempt at escaping.

Damien tried the other door, opening it to find another room. I approached him on unsteady feet as he lingered in the doorway. There was a desk with numerous screens showing the feed of cameras throughout the compound—views of the forest outside, the fire pit where we'd just been, the stairway, hallway... I pulled my gaze from the screens, terror crawling up my throat at the thought of seeing that room. I couldn't do it.

"I couldn't comb the place after we found you," Damien admitted, his eyes lingering on the screens, as if he were burning every detail into his memories. "I had a team clean and sweep the area in my stead for fear I'd lose it and tear the place apart; destroy anything we might gain to find Marcus."

I laced my fingers with his, seeking solitude in his touch. He squeezed my hand and turned to press his forehead to mine, his eyes falling shut.

The sound of movement caught my attention, and I opened my eyes to see Zephyr pass behind us to continue through the door which led to another hallway. Damien approached the desk, looking through what little remained, but there didn't seem to be anything of real value or importance, nothing describing any locations, or ties to the darklings. We stepped back out of the feed room and into the main room with the fire pit.

"There're stairs leading down," Vincent said, and my gaze snapped to where he stood, scanning the stairwell as he held the door open. The door I'd never wanted to set foot past again in my life, so badly that I'd gone to the lengths of planning to ensure I wasn't alive if they brought me back through it.

Damien started for it, and I hesitated, but followed as Vincent descended to the basement. I came to a halt at the top of the stairway, the length of it stretching on and on, and my heart pounded as the memories resurfaced, every memory I wished I could forget.

The Lupai hesitated at my side, its body rippling as it watched me.

I took the first step. The room was so hot all of a sudden, too hot, my heart racing to the point that I thought it might burst from my chest. The room spun, my mouth watering as my stomach churned.

"Cas?" Zephyr's voice reached my ears from behind me as I swayed, my palms growing sweaty. The Lupai whined and yipped, pacing at my legs.

Damien halted at the base of the stairs at the sound of my name leaving Zephyr's lips, at the alert of his Lupai and he twisted around to look up at me. His eyes widened before he rushed up the stairs toward me. I stumbled forward, the stairs rising to meet me before strong arms wrapped around my waist and—

Something shook me in the darkness. Where was I?
You shouldn't be here.

But why? Why wasn't I supposed to be here? Where was here?
"Cassie, wake up."
"Get her out of here!"
I didn't want to open my eyes, I just wanted to sleep, but movement jostled me, jerking me in a way that made it difficult.
You can't sleep. Can't—
"Gods dammit, Cas. Wake up, *please!*"
My eyelids cracked open to find a familiar ceiling, several figures leaning over me, their worry-stricken faces coming into focus.
"Cas?" I tilted my head to Zephyr, who was knelt beside me, his tawny skin pale.
"Hey, Zeph," I said absentmindedly, confused as to where I was but happy to see his face.
He let out a nervous laugh, and a smile curved his lips. "Shit, you had us worried."
Damien's warm hand ran over my hair, his fingers combing through my curls, and I closed my eyes, bowing into the affectionate touch.
"Are you okay?" Damien asked as I turned my face to see him.
"I think so," I said groggily, my brows furrowing. "What happened?"
"You passed out," Vincent answered.
"I did?" I asked, confused. "Why would I pass..."
It all came back to me. The stairway... the panic attack that had captured me in its grip before I'd even known it was coming.
"I guess I couldn't do it after all," I said under my breath.
"I shouldn't have brought you there," Damien muttered, gripping my hand.
I pushed myself up and turned to him, before lifting my hand to force his gaze to me. "I go where you go. We do this together. I swore I would be at your side every step of the way and I will no matter what we stand to face. Let the fires of hell come for us. I will face that fire at your side, and we will burn together. Let the darkness take us, I will fall at your side."
A warm smile graced his face, and despite everything I'd endured, I smiled back, knowing he would be there at my side just the same.
"Was Marcus there when you passed out?" Zephyr asked.
I shook my head. "I don't think so. Maybe he's preoccupied with something else."
A thought occurred to me, and I blinked for a moment before I looked back at Damien.
"You said Marcus tethered himself to me..."
Damien's brows furrowed. "Yeah, why?"
"So, we're linked."
His eyes narrowed. "You are."
"Does that mean I could access his mind the way he accessed mine?"

The room went quiet for a moment as Damien fell into quiet contemplation.

"In theory it might work, but I honestly don't know. I'm sure its happened before, but I don't know of any instances where an Oneiroi has tethered themselves to another wielder of the Nous ability."

"I wonder if I could reach out to him to find any information on where he's located."

Damien exchanged a nervous glance with Zephyr.

"Cas, we don't know what could happen. He might be waiting for you the moment you slip under," Zephyr said, fear painting his face, and his eyes flitted toward Damien. "Is it possible for him to trap her consciousness in his mind?"

Damien laced his fingers as he fell into deep thought. "It's a hairy ability, one that I only have so much knowledge of. Anything is possible. The mechanics of the mind are infinite when you're in the dreamscape. He could conjure anything he wanted to."

"But so could I," I said firmly. "If it looks like something bad is happening, wake me."

Damien remained silent, his fear—everyone's fear skittering over my skin like fractured webs of ice.

"It might not even work, but if it does..." I steeled my nerves, ready to face this. "I'll be quick. In and out. I just need to find that location."

Damien drew a deep breath and nodded his head.

"This is a bad idea," Barrett muttered, rising to his feet to pace.

Damien settled onto the cushion behind me, and I settled back against his chest as he wrapped his arms around me. He lowered his lips to my ear. "I'm with you, where I will always remain."

I smiled, finding strength in his words, in his presence.

"We'll wake you if anything seems off," Zephyr assured me, and I gave him a nod before drawing a deep breath and closing my eyes.

I dove into my own consciousness, searching through the darkness for anything that might be the link between Marcus and me. Nothing came into view, and I stiffened at the feeling of a familiar presence, one that left me entirely too uneasy. I looked over my shoulder yet I was greeted with nothing but the vast depths of my subconscious, an endless sea of pitch black that stretched for miles and miles with no end and no beginning.

Whatever this was, it wasn't Marcus, I didn't know how to explain it, but it didn't *feel* like him and I didn't have time to linger on it and risk him discovering me. As I turned back, I felt it, the tug of something so sickening that I immediately knew it was him. Before me, almost invisible in the darkness was a thread laced with such hate and malice that it sent my entire being on edge just to see it.

I reached out, grabbing onto it and let it guide me to him. I would only get one shot at this. I had to be quick. There was no telling what would happen if he discovered me.

Images flittered before me, tarnished and shredded, images of Vivienne, the memories slowly deteriorating before me.

He doesn't deserve your pity.

I winced at the voice, at the truth in those words. He didn't, and I held no pity for the monster regardless. I shoved through the reminder of the past, of who he was before he'd lost his mate, and I searched. The images around me shuddered, and something pressed in on me, as if the walls were closing in around me.

Shit.

Had he realized I was here? That something was wrong?

I halted as I came before another memory, one of a shop—*the* shop. I reached out, touching it and the expanse around me shuddered once more, some of the images dimming before winking out entirely. Not enough time. I turned back to the memory, focusing on a name, a street, a neighborhood, anything.

Then I saw it, a passing street sign. The memory flittered through my mind, as if I were driving along the river, then I turned onto another road. Main street. Through a neighborhood with houses full of families who had no idea a monster was passing through their false place of safety. My heart skipped a beat as we came upon it. An industrial complex. I recognized the rusted cars and fencing that stretched around the massive yard.

Darkness swept in as the memories winked out and I cursed. Time was up. I turned, looking for the thread to guide me back, and I rushed forward. Fear surged within me as phantom hands wrapped around my ankles, threatening to trap me here. I pulled free of them, reaching for the gateway out of Marcus' mind. A hand narrowly missed me, fingers slipping through my hair as I grabbed onto the thread tethering us together and was guided back to my mind.

I shot awake, my body shaking, and I realized I was covered in blankets.

Zephyr let out a heavy breath and Damien slumped at my back, every bit of tension melting away as I fell back against him, panting.

"We were just about to wake you; you went cold, and I feared the worst," Damien said, and I twisted around to see him, my heart dipping at how pale he looked, the fear etched into his expression.

"I know where it is," I said, turning my gaze from him to James, who grabbed his laptop.

"Northeast of here, along the East Conemaugh. There's a neighborhood." I pushed off of Damien, hurrying to the table where the map lay. I stopped before it, eyes scanning the map until I found the East Conemaugh and ran my fingers over it, following the path of the road.

"He was driving along the river, then turned off onto Main Street." My fingers followed the curve of the road, my mind reeling as I tried to remember what I'd seen, which turns he'd taken.

"There," I said, pointing to the mass of metal buildings just on the edge of the map.

There was no circle marking the complex, because it wasn't in Johnstown. It was in the neighboring town of Franklin.

Damien came to a stop at my side, his gaze lingering on the buildings as James circled them. A cold, murderous darkness clouded those beautiful eyes as he seemed to memorize every detail of the buildings laid out on the map.

"We strike tonight."

CHAPTER 38

My eyes fluttered, and I realized I was nodding off when my head dipped to the side. The sun had fallen behind the tops of the mountains, marking nearly forty-eight hours since I'd gotten any sleep. It was becoming difficult to keep my eyes open, though, and I feared that if I sat still for too long, I would succumb to the exhaustion.

Damien nodded to Vincent, and his gaze swept back to me, his brows furrowing. "You all right?"

I nodded, blinking through the heaviness in my eyes, and turned to focus on the buildings before us as we crouched in the nearby brush. The yard was dark, the woods surrounding us shrouded in an inky darkness. The only source of light was a single lamp hanging above a door in the center building. There were numerous warehouses, but the one in the center seemed to be the only one occupied.

"James pulled the record of owners, looks like all the others were bought out a few weeks ago," Vincent said as he crouched next to me. "Is this the right place, Cas?"

I nodded, rubbing my eyes. "This is it."

A single man resided outside the door, sitting in a folding chair. I recognized him immediately, my skin growing hot. Ethan. He'd been the first of Marcus' men I saw when I awoke in the cell—had assisted with controlling the tension and release of the chains that held me. Something rose in my chest at the sight of him. I couldn't tell if it was fear or hate, and my hand tightened on the hilt of my dagger before I realized I'd even placed my hand on it.

"How many of Marcus' men have you seen?" Damien asked Vincent, who had gotten here before us with his team to secure the location.

"Just the one by the door. We haven't seen anyone come or go so, I don't know if Marcus is here or not."

"Stay here, Cas," Damien said.

"The fuck I will," I barked, looking up at him. There was no way in hell I wasn't going to just watch from afar. I was no longer the helpless girl Marcus had manipulated and tormented. While I wasn't as skilled as they were, surely, I could assist them in some way with my abilities now.

"You don't know what's in there, Damien," I said, grabbing his arm. "I didn't have much time to get in and out of Marcus' mind, but I could try to see if I can learn what the guard knows, maybe get an idea of the layout of the building. Whether or not Marcus is here, and how many of his men may be inside."

"She's got a point," Thalia said, as she crouched beside me. I slid her a quick smile of gratitude.

"I just..." Damien contemplated a moment, his eyes locking with mine. I saw the fear within them, fear of what might happen if he brought me in there. "Don't leave my side. Stay with me."

I cupped his face in my hands. "Together. Remember? Every step of the wa—"

"Damien, look." Zephyr's voice cut across our conversation and our gazes snapped to where he pointed.

We all looked in time to see the door open. Another one of Marcus' guys stepped out, talking with the guard. Their words were inaudible from the distance between us.

"How are we gonna get in there?" Barrett whispered, his jaw tight. I'd never seen him so serious as I had in the last forty-eight hours. He'd been quiet, only chiming in when he had a question or comment, never making any of his usual remarks.

"If I take us through the shadows, there's no telling where we might come out, or how many of his men we'll find," Damien said. "I don't want to risk it with Cas here. We go in the old-fashioned way."

Barrett rolled his neck, and he grinned as he turned his gaze to Damien and me. "Good. I've been dying to pay them back for laying a hand on one of our own."

My lips parted at his words, my heart squeezing, and my gaze shifted to him.

One of our own.

The words seemed so unlike him, and yet, something bloomed in my chest at the sound of them. To know that Barrett considered me a part of their... family.

I opened my mouth but couldn't bring myself to say anything. How could I respond to that?

Damien nodded to Zephyr before I could even try to form a response, and Zephyr backed into the dark cover of the brush, vanishing from my view. I frowned, looking into the darkness where he'd vanished. Where had he gone? I looked back as one of the men disappeared back into the door, leaving Ethan in the chair alone again.

Damien took my hand, leading me along the fence line. Barrett, Vincent, and Thalia followed closely behind us as we snuck along the fence, and I glanced over my shoulder as I caught sight of one of Vincent's men standing guard, his back turned to us as he kept watch. We came to a stop at the edge of the gate, hidden from view by overgrown brush. This place looked as if it hadn't been cared for in years, nature working to reclaim it.

Faint movement in the shadows above the guard drew my attention. Atop the metal awning overhanging the entrance, stood a large raven, its head tilted as it peered over the edge to the man below. God, it was the largest raven I'd even seen, and for a moment I frowned, a wave of déjà vu sweeping over me at that thought.

"Damien, is that—"

Ethan stood to stretch and paced away from the door a few feet, and the raven leapt from its perch, body shifting as black mist enveloped it. I gasped, my hands cupping my mouth as Zephyr appeared from the shadowy mass, tackling the guy to the ground before he could react, and knocking him out. He crouched as he looked around before throwing the guy over his shoulder and hurrying over to us.

"What the hell just happened?" I whispered to Damien, not taking my eyes off Zephyr as he ran.

"Another blood trait I was telling you about. Zephyr and Thalia come from the house of Thirion, a family of shifters. They can change, take on the form of different animals." Damien pulled me to my feet as Zephyr reached us. He tossed the guy off his shoulder, his body hitting the ground with a low thud before us, unconscious.

I eyed Zephyr as he straightened and memories of our first date at Stackhouse resurfaced, Damien's taunts to the massive raven resurfacing in my mind.

They sound like awfully nosey creatures.

Zephyr looked between me and Damien. "What did I do?"

"Were you the raven at Stackhouse?" I asked, crossing my arms.

Damien huffed a laugh before looking anywhere else but me.

Zephyr gave me a sheepish smile as he ran his hand over the back of his neck. "I was curious."

"Nosey creatures indeed," I muttered, and Damien bit back another laugh.

I turned my gaze on Ethan, laid out on the pavement before me. Now wasn't the time for this. I could scold Zephyr later for butting his nose into mine and Damien's date. I lowered to my knees, my fingers quivering as I reached my hands out to touch his head.

Damien grabbed my wrist before I reached him. "Be careful."

I smiled in reassurance. "I will. I'm just gonna get an idea of what it looks like inside and how many people there are."

He hesitated a moment but released me. I pressed my fingers to Ethan's head, diving into his mind, not caring to be gentle or slow. I would tear every bit of information I could get out of him.

The darkness receded, and I found Marcus before me, standing inside the building. He only had a few guys with him, maybe three or four. The building was huge inside, with two large bays and one small room in the back. There was nothing about it that was complicated or intricate, nothing like the compound where he kept me confined. It would be easy and straightforward to navigate.

I released Ethan's mind, opening my eyes to find myself back where I'd been, surrounded by the others. It was so strange, as if I'd physically hopped from place to place, though I'd never left the ground where I knelt.

"Did you get anything out of him?" Barrett asked, kneeling on the other side of him.

I nodded, reaching my hand out to take Damien's. He told me once before that I'd spoken through our minds in the past. I wondered if I could do that now, share my thoughts with him.

"I want to try to show you what I saw."

Damien's brows furrowed as I closed my eyes. I reached out, willing my thoughts to him, and I heard as he gasped. My hands recoiled, releasing his. "Did it work? Could you see?"

"Yes. *Fuck*." He blinked, shaking his head as he let his breath out through his teeth. "Sorry, I didn't think you'd be able to do that so early."

My heart sank at the slightest hint of pain on his face. "Oh my God, I'm so sorry. I didn't hurt you, did I? I should have given you a better warning."

"No, *mea luna*. It's more like a head rush. I'm okay, promise." He smiled, and a light of confidence lit his eyes. "This actually works out better."

"I don't know how long ago this memory was. It may have been earlier. There's still a chance more could have arrived since then, and I don't know if there are other guards who might be elsewhere," I warned. I still wasn't quite skilled enough to precisely pinpoint the exact moment I wanted to see.

He grinned. "That still gives us an edge."

"Nice job, spitfire," Barrett whispered, and my cheeks heated.

"Spitfire? Really?" Thalia said with a cocked brow.

"What?" Barrett said, feigning a look of innocence.

"Pay attention, Barrett," Damien warned, and they all focused on him, humor and joking aside.

Damien wasted no time in explaining the layout of the shop to the others. I watched the front door as he spoke, an uneasiness building in my gut. I didn't know what it was, but something was off about this whole situation. There was no way it would be this easy. It seemed too perfect.

Zephyr and Vincent split off to flank the perimeter before we entered the building, two of Vincent's men following after them, leaving Thalia, Barrett, Damien, and I stationed near the gate. My eyes locked on the door, watching intently in case one of Marcus' men came out again.

The weight of my dagger grew heavy against my thigh, and I gripped the handle, heart thrumming in my ears. I was eager to put an end to Marcus, but I feared what it might cost us.

"Maybe this isn't a good idea," I whispered, unsure of myself suddenly as I watched the door, the silence too loud.

"It's going to be fine, Cas."

"What if I was wrong? What if Marcus is messing with my mind?" The uncertainties grew with each passing second of silence. "Is it only in my dreams that he can do things to me? What if he can mess with my thoughts while I'm awake as well? What if he knew I entered his mind and gave me the information? What if nothing I'd seen was real—"

Damien pressed his finger to my lips, and I froze as his eyes softened. "Cas. I believe in you."

The cold air filled my lungs as I breathed deeply. It was a failed attempt to calm myself. I wasn't fully convinced that he should believe in my abilities... in me.

"As soon as the others return, we're going in," Damien whispered, glancing back at Barrett and Thalia, who nodded in response.

I noticed out of the corner of my eye an exchange of glances between them. Barrett mouthed something, but I couldn't understand what. His eyes were softer, though, than I'd ever seen as he looked down at her. Her gaze looked equally worried, as if they were preparing themselves for something, and an icy feeling crawled over my skin.

A loud crash of metal rang out from across the yard.

"*Shit.* Barrett, Thalia, check it out. Make sure they're okay," Damien whispered through gritted teeth. *Oh God.* Had something happened to Zephyr or Vincent? Did they encounter someone?

Barrett and Thalia glanced at each other one last time before drawing their daggers and disappearing in different directions in the shadows of the brush. Damien's hand twitched as he gripped mine.

This was a mistake. I was a fool to think I could help them, to think I could stand a chance against Marcus. This was his game, had been from the beginning. I'd fallen into his trap, and they knew we were here now.

The fear of what was to come started to claw its way into me in the agonizing quiet. "What happened, Damien? Do you think they're okay?"

"Stay low," Damien whispered, his hand coming to the top of my head to urge me to duck. "They'll be fine. We just need to stay out of sight for now." He tried to hide it, but uncertainty clouded his eyes.

We sat in silence, watching the yard for any sign of movement, any sign of the others. The distant sound of a fight broke out in the same direction as the noise we heard, shouts echoing across the yard.

"Come on." Damien pushed himself to his feet. "Stay close behind me. Ready your dagger." He looked back at me. "No matter what, you stick close to m—"

A bat swung into Damien's head from the shadows.

"*Damie*—" A sharp pain splintered across the back of my head before I could even see who attacked. The world spun, and I hit the ground.

Black dots peppered across my vision, my eyes fluttering as I stretched my hand out for Damien, who lay unconscious in front of me. No. Not like this. I couldn't let myself pass out, not now… but I couldn't fight the heaviness in my eyes as I blinked, the exhaustion that had been slowly tugging me down closing in to claim me.

Footsteps approached us as I clung to consciousness, a boot settling into the pavement in front of my face, but I couldn't fight it any longer and my eyes slid shut.

CHAPTER 39

Throbbing pain echoed through my head, and I grimaced as I awoke. My eyelids were so heavy, and it took everything in me to open them. Blinding light burned my vision, and I blinked as I tried to see through the haze. Where was I?

When I tried to lift my hands to block it out, I found them bound behind me. My spine stiffened, eyes popping open. I tugged and tugged, but my arms remained restrained over the back of the foldable metal chair I sat in, and a cold sweat broke out over my brow. Something thin and tight bound my hands together, cutting into my tender, still healing wrists, and I realized my feet were strapped to the legs of the chair as well.

Shit.

My heart hammered as I searched the room, desperate to locate Damien, and terror took hold of me as I realized where we were. We were in the small back room I'd seen through the guard's memories. Whether we were prepared for it or not, we were inside the building.

There was no sign of Barrett or the others. Had they been captured as well? Or had it just been Damien and me? How long had I been unconscious? I caught sight of Damien. He was bound in the same manner, his head hanging forward.

"Damien," I whispered loudly, but he didn't respond. Air halted in my lungs as I got a better look at him. Blood painted the side of his face where he'd been hit, crimson rolling down his cheek to drip into a shallow pool on the concrete below. The plastic cut into my wrists as I tugged and pulled to free myself, to get to him.

"Save your breath. It might be awhile before he wakes up."

I froze at the sound of Marcus' voice, the metal door closing behind him as he entered the room, and I watched him carefully from the corner of my eye as he approached.

Hurt him.

Meeting Marcus' gaze, I ignored the voice rippling through my mind. Everything I'd suppressed rose to the surface, every moment of agony, every moment of fear, and I couldn't hide the malice in my voice. "This was all a trap from the beginning, wasn't it?"

"I'm afraid I don't know what you're talkin' about, little songbird."

"I'm not stupid, Marcus. I know how your mind works." I stared at him, quietly working my wrists behind me.

He stalked toward me, and I stifled the fear creeping into my bones at his proximity. I knew better than anyone what he was capable of, the things he could do to me. The things he *would* do to me. I put on a strong face, but I couldn't shake the annoying sense of dread still clinging to me.

I gasped as he grabbed my hair, fingers tangling in the strands as he jerked my head back, and he leaned over me to meet my gaze. I didn't give him the satisfaction of a wince as I stared up at him.

"Just give it up. I won't play your stupid games anymore. Nothing you do to me will get the reaction you want." I said, glaring up at him.

"Oh? That's a shame... but you've only seen what I can do when it's just you." He released my head and stalked to the side. "You see... things get a whole lot more interesting when I have the one you love."

I froze, watching his movements as he turned to Damien. *No.*

"Poor Damien." Each cruel, calculated step of his boots echoed off the metal walls, my heart faltering with each one. "He put so much faith in your ability. What a fuckin' fool."

"Don't you fucking touch him!"

Marcus whipped around, flipping his knife open, the blade too close to my face and my traitorous body flinched. He lifted my chin with the blade, and my eyes shifted to him, burning into his. "Ah, there it is. I like that fire in your eyes. I'll love it even more when I extinguish it."

362

More time. I needed more time. If I could just keep Marcus away from Damien until he could recover, or until Barrett and the others could find us. What if they couldn't find us? What if they'd been captured as well, or... I swallowed.

"Why are you working with the darklings?"

His face soured, and he released my jaw. A sense of triumph rushed over me. He hadn't known. "I saw it in Cole's mind."

"You?" His blond brows narrowed.

He came around in front of me, lowering himself to my level. A puzzled expression painted his face, and he planted his hand on my shoulder. I gasped as he tilted my chair back, just keeping me from falling back onto the concrete. His eyes drifted over my face, as he muttered under his breath. "*Shit*. It *was* you who went poking around in my head. I didn't think someone as weak as you could possibly do it, but... you really are her."

I frowned, confused.

"*Oh, this is too good*. You're really Moira's reincarnation? I didn't believe it at first, but... that's why Melantha wants you. She wants to convert you." A disturbing grin spread across his face. "After all these years. Where the hell have you been?"

He released me, and I yelped as my chair fell forward onto its legs. He turned away, yelling out as if he spoke to someone, but we were alone. "*Eris, you dumb bitch!* You knew all this time I had Selene's daughter? I'm not playing your *fucking* games anymore! Show yourself!"

Who was he talking to? I assumed that Melantha was the name of the darkling leader, who I already knew wanted me, but who was Eris?

He continued to curse the person as if they were listening, growing more crazed by the minute and my lungs sucked in panicked breaths as his fury burned a path over my skin.

My eyes drifted to Damien, who remained unconscious. Fear curdled my stomach at the fact he still hadn't awoken, and I silently begged him to open his eyes, to show me he was okay. I was too weak to get free, but surely he could break free of these bindings.

"Are you worried about him?" My body tensed as Marcus spoke, realizing he'd caught me watching Damien. He stalked over to Damien, grabbed a handful of his hair, and lifted his head. He brought his blade up to swipe some of the loose waves from Damien's face, his hair matted with blood.

I stopped breathing. "Leave him alone!"

"He looks so peaceful, Cas." He turned his gaze to me. "Would you like to wake him, or should I?"

Tears welled in my eyes as he held his knife to Damien's throat.

"Oh, how he's suffered waiting for you to return. So many years spent searching for his lost mate." Marcus' brows rose as he tilted his head, watching my reactions. "I could end it. Put him out of his misery. Come on, Cas. It'd be kind to just end him now."

I thrashed in my bindings. "*Please! Please don't!*"

363

He groaned, shoulders slumping as he rolled his eyes and released his hold on Damien's head. "Where'd that fire in your eyes go? It's no fun if you just cave like that."

I screamed as Marcus shoved Damien to the side, still bound to the chair and unconscious, he hit the ground hard.

"Stop it!" I pleaded, jerking against the ties holding me in place. The plastic bit into my skin as I tried to pull my hands apart, but I didn't stop. Heat rose in my chest, and my eyes burned as I watched Marcus' eyes dip back to Damien, who remained still on the floor.

Burn him.

"What do you want with us?" I shouted, shoving down the fury boiling within me.

A crazed grin spread across his face. "To send a message."

I stiffened.

"This is a revolution, little songbird. A declaration that we won't be Selene's pawns any longer—won't bury any more of our kind for her mistakes."

Her mistakes? My chest heaved as he grew closer, and my lips parted to speak. "It wasn't her fault what happened to Vivienne!"

The grin slid from his face, his eyes darkening, and I gasped as his hand wrapped around my throat. His fangs slid free as he bared them, his teeth grinding together.

"Don't you dare say her name," he growled. "You know nothing."

I didn't stop, and I was foolish for it, but the words kept coming through quick gasps of air. "You're the one... who made the decision to go! It was your fault!" I gasped as his grip tightened, my mouth opening to speak, but no oxygen came, and I choked out. "You want someone to blame? Look… in the mirror!"

Marcus' fist flew into the air, and I braced myself for the hit, but he froze as the door flew open, and one of his men rushed in toward him. His grip on my throat loosened, and I coughed as I filled my lungs desperately.

He whispered something in Marcus' ear, and Marcus cursed under his breath. "Watch them. Don't let them out of your sight. I'll be right back."

The guy nodded before Marcus stomped out the door and slammed it shut behind him.

I sagged in my chair, my heart threatening to burst at the hit I'd somehow managed to avoid. My eyes darted to Damien, who lay on the ground, unmoving. I watched, desperate for any sign that he was still breathing. A rattle of metal scraping along the concrete floor echoed through the room, and I turned back to see the guard drag a chair over to sit in front of us.

Were Zephyr and the others still out there? I'd yet to see them after Barrett and Thalia left us. Maybe they were okay, fighting their way to us. Whether they were or not, I couldn't let this chance of Marcus' absence go to waste.

I closed my eyes and inhaled slowly, steadying my pounding heart, thankful it still beat, that despite everything, it somehow remained strong for my sake. I couldn't bring myself to question how right now. My eyes opened again, locking on the guy who sat with us now. He was maybe several feet away from me. I glanced at my thigh; as expected, they took my dagger. I surveyed the room, trying to see if it was here with us, but found no sign of it.

Damien groaned lowly, and a wave of relief washed over me at the sound. The guard looked over to him, leaning forward as if he were about to stand. I needed to act fast. I couldn't let him go to Damien. What if he hurt him more than he was already?

"Hey, you."

His attention drifted from Damien and back to me.

I took a deep breath as I locked my eyes with his. "Release me."

His brows narrowed, and he blinked for a moment, then shook his head as he relaxed into his seat again.

Weak. Say it like you mean it. Make him bend.

I focused everything I had on him, willing myself into his mind. My voice was firm and unwavering as I spoke once more.

A command that no one could refuse slipped through my lips. *"Release me."*

His face scrunched, but he rose to his feet unsteadily, and I maintained eye contact with him as he staggered toward me. A part of him resisted, something pounding against our connection as if he were slamming his fists against a wall, but he wasn't strong enough to ignore my order. His steps were slow, too slow, and my eyes darted to the door, praying that Marcus wouldn't reappear until I was free.

Hurry up, dammit.

He knelt before me, pulling a knife from his pocket, and flipped it open to cut the bindings from my ankles, then did the same for my hands.

I rubbed my wrists as I rose to my feet, and I met his gaze again. *"Bring my dagger."*

His hands twitched at his sides and his brows knit together. I swallowed nervously as he resisted a moment, but he obeyed, walking me to the table standing behind us. I saw it laying atop the table amongst other things. My gut churned at the sight of the knives, pliers, and other tools I knew Marcus had intended to use on us.

I would die before giving him the chance.

The guard grabbed my dagger and returned to me, but as I wrapped my fingers around the handle, his grip tightened as he resisted me again. I leaned in close to him, placing my free hand over his to strengthen the connection, a connection he wouldn't be able to resist no matter what.

"Sleep."

His eyes flickered before he collapsed to the floor, unconscious.

Faster than I could think, I dropped to my knee, dagger firm in my hand, but I froze, the blade halting before it slit his throat.

I clutched the hilt of my dagger so tightly, my knuckles went white as a pearl of blood formed where my blade pressed to his throat. My chest heaved. What was I doing? Had I become something that could take someone's life so easily?

Why do you hesitate?

The dagger slipped from my fingers, bouncing off the concrete, but no sounds of metal clanging against concrete came over the roaring in my ears. My hands shook at the realization of what I'd almost done. While the whispering voice in my mind sounded like my own, it wasn't right. The venom behind it left me ill, bile rising in my throat. This wasn't me. I didn't want this.

I clenched my fists, scrambling to my feet and hurrying over to the table before he could wake, returning with zip ties and duct tape. Time was against me as I bound his hands and feet and taped his mouth shut, my eyes flitting to the door every few seconds.

Once he'd been bound, my body wouldn't respond to me for a moment, my eyes locked on him as he breathed.

"Cas?" Damien groaned, and I grabbed my dagger before rushing to his side.

"Easy, your head's bleeding." I cut his hands and feet free and pulled the chair away before helping him sit up.

He grimaced as he steadied himself, his hand rising to his head. His eyes shifted to the guy laying unconscious and bound just several feet away from us and his brows furrowed. "How'd you get free?"

I stretched up onto my knees to inspect his injury. "I told him what to do, and he listened."

He barked a low laugh but winced, clutching his head. "You're getting good at that."

While he was relieved, I felt horrible. It was my fault we were here like this. My fault we'd ended up captured and separated from the others. This had turned into a disaster, and now we were both trapped. There was no telling if Barrett and the others were faring any better. They might be dead already, and I was the only one to blame.

"I'm so sorry, Damien. It was all a trap." My eyes fell as the frustration built within me. "This was all my fault. I should have never come—"

"Cas." Damien's hand slid to the back of my neck, pressing his forehead to mine as he met my gaze. "If you hadn't come, I would still be tied up. I'd probably be worse off than I am now if it wasn't for you."

I smiled weakly, trying to push my guilt back.

Damien grunted as he pushed himself to his feet. "Where are the others? Where's Marcus?"

"I think they're outside. Marcus stormed out when one of his men came to tell him something, and he didn't look very happy about it."

He barked a low laugh. "Leave it to Barrett to piss in someone's cheerios."

"You think they're, okay?" I asked, glancing at the door.

"I'm certain of it. They're stubborn shits."

Damien regained his bearings as he looked around for his things. I slid my dagger back into its sheath on my thigh and followed him to the table where his weapons lay. He gathered them as quickly as possible, rearming himself.

"He didn't hurt you, did he?" Damien asked as he glanced at me.

"When he figured out he couldn't get through to me, he became more interested in hurting you instead."

His body tensed and a growl slipped from his throat as he spoke. "I'm going to carve that bastard up when I see him."

"I got some information out of him on the darkling leader." Damien's eyes flashed to me. "When he lured me out to the alleys those nights, he wasn't just doing it to get under your skin. He was doing it because the darklings want me. He called the darkling's leader Melantha, said she wanted to convert me."

The color drained from Damien's face. "Of course. Why *wouldn't* they want you for that? A demigoddess, gifted with your abilities, would all but ensure our defeat. It would be so easy for them to wipe us out with you at her side."

My throat tightened at the thought. Me? Used as a tool to murder not only the human race, but the immortals as well? To murder Damien? I couldn't stomach the thought.

"Marcus wasn't happy when he realized I was Moira's reincarnation, started shouting at someone who wasn't here. I think the name was... Eris?"

Damien's head turned to me, and his hands settled on my shoulders. "You're sure he said Eris? Absolutely sure?"

I nodded.

"If Eris is involved, then things just got a hell of a lot worse."

"Who's Eris?"

He slid his dagger into its sheath, fully rearmed and ready for a fight. "Eris is the Goddess of Strife and Discord. She gets off on sowing chaos and ruining people's lives. For millennia she's turned countless families and friends against one another, just for a good laugh. It doesn't matter if you're god or mortal, no one is safe from her if she sets her sights on you. Gods damn you if you upset or offend her in the slightest. She has no sympathy and cares nothing of those affected. In fact, she relishes in their suffering."

It made my skin crawl to think about. Gods and goddesses, with powers I couldn't begin to comprehend—what stopped them from destroying us all? Just how much influence did they hold in our lives? How many terrible occurrences weren't just by chance but orchestrated at their fingertips?

Damien stalked past me toward the door. He turned to press his back against the wall as he cracked the door and peered out to check the surroundings. When he nodded to me, I approached and glanced out to find the shop empty past the doorway.

We slipped past the threshold, cautious as we hugged the wall, eyes peeled for any movement. That terrible feeling I'd been fighting to push back returned, the voice in my head whispering twisted desires I harbored deep within. My hand twitched at my side, as if it couldn't wait for the moment when I could put my dagger to use. I gave in, gripping the hilt and pulling it from the sheath. Damien did the same.

Where had Marcus gotten off to?

Hurt him. Make him bleed.

I winced at the words, at the images that flashed across my mind, of me running my dagger into his chest, and a feeling of dread crept over my skin. My fears were coming true. Marcus had succeeded. He'd turned me into the same monster he was. I'd never felt such a strong desire to hurt someone, and while it sickened me, there was a part of me that longed for it more than anything.

"Cas?" Damien's voice was soft as he spoke.

I blinked, pulled from the dark depths of my mind. "Sorry?"

"Are you okay?"

I nodded, averting my eyes from his gaze. I couldn't tell him the thoughts clouding my rationale, the sickening need that had clawed its way into me.

A strong smell caught my attention, interrupting my thoughts. I hadn't noticed at first, but it had grown unbearable, and my face scrunched.

Damien must have realized it, too. "Wait, Cas, stop. Don't move."

My eyes fell to the floor, to the iridescent oily liquid shining beneath our feet. An oily ground was to be expected for a metal shop. However, the liquid pooling on the ground beneath us wasn't oil, and I stopped breathing as the smell of gasoline filled my nose. My gaze followed the trail of liquid as it split and wound in various trails and directions all around us.

It wasn't residual. It had been put there intentionally.

Damien grabbed my hand. "Get out of here, *now*."

CHAPTER 40

Damien's hand clutched mine as he led me in a rush to escape. The splash of the gasoline beneath our feet terrified me.

My heart thrashed in my chest, my feet struggling to keep up with his pace. "Slow down Damien, I can't—"

We passed through a maze of countless shells and dismantled frames of vehicles, stacked upon each other until it opened up into a wide space in the middle of the shop. An endless supply of old oil and gasoline barrels lay stacked against a far wall, and other various tools or junk were scattered around us. My gaze landed on Damien's destination, the exit at the far end of the building.

My heart sank as two men emerged from around a junk pile, their eyes widening at the sight of us before they halted, blocking our paths. Marcus stepped into view behind them, seeming surprised at first, but then his gaze hardened as it landed on me.

Damien roared, ripping one of his knives from his leathers as he released my hand and crashed into the two closest men without hesitation.

My feet didn't stop, my body falling into step as I rushed past Damien, eyes locked on Marcus, my dagger clenched in my hand.

Sink it into his flesh.

I halted moments before I did just that, as if I'd fallen into a trance. No, this wasn't me! Marcus' fist swung through the air at me, and I gasped, narrowly ducking out of its path before he slammed his leg into my side, knocking me away. The concrete bit into my body, bruising my skin as I fell, and I groaned as I slid to a stop.

"Cas!" Damien called out as he spared a glance from the two men he fought. He tried to come to my aid, but the moment he took his eyes off them, they took advantage of it, swinging a fist, which Damien barely missed before he punched the guy in the gut.

"I'm fine!" I grimaced, pushing myself to my feet as Marcus stalked toward me.

Marcus' cruel eyes met mine, a wicked grin spreading across his face. "Now, where do you two think you're going? The fun's just getting started."

My skin heated. Fun? This was all fun to him? All the pain he caused me, all the suffering? I cried out as I lashed at him, swinging my dagger against him. The world fell into a distant haze as he captured my blade with the edge of his knife. My chest heaved as I fought against his hold, my vision a tunnel of rage and hate.

I couldn't beat him in strength, his body already beginning to overpower me... but I didn't need strength. A smile tugged at my lips and Marcus' brows furrowed as he blinked. I twisted around, allowing him to force his weight through, and he stumbled forward before I swung for him again. He recovered, blocking my blow.

"Someone's been busy," he said, but I didn't give him the chance of another retort.

He blocked my next blow and ducked away from the next. His feet slid across the floor as he deflecting or dodging each of my blow, only to strike back. I barely managed to evade or block most of them, and I winced at the bruises forming where his hits managed to connect, the cuts stinging where his blade had nicked me. I refused to back down, pushing through despite the painful warnings of my heart slamming against my rib cage.

Make him hurt.

Marcus mis stepped, his gaze falling from me to the debris he'd tripped over for the briefest of seconds, and my fist slammed into his face—everything I had left concentrated into that one blow. He crashed into the stack of cars.

370

I panted, heart throbbing with each painful beat as I drew closer to my limit, but I couldn't stop myself, my voice a near growl as I stormed toward him. *"What did you do to me?"*

He lifted his head, breathless. His brows rose, and that smile crept back across his face. "Oh? Do you hear it?"

It? I ground my teeth together as I stormed up to him, grabbing a handful of his hair and shoving his head back into the metal of the frame at his back. He grunted, and I pressed my dagger to his throat. My chest heaved as I struggled to inhale oxygen, my hand trembling as I pressed the blade closer to his throat, a bead of blood forming.

"I was wondering why it got so quiet after I had you in that cell," He whispered, smiling up at me. "It feels good, doesn't it?"

I swallowed, resisting the urge to slam my fist into his face again and again. "What are you talking about?"

"To give into the urges..." His voice was so low that only I could hear, blood dripping from his broken nose. "Put that dagger to use, little songbird. You know you want to. Give into it."

"No!" I yelled, my hand trembling as my grip tightened on the hilt of my dagger. I wanted so badly to slit his throat, though. To feel his blood coat my hands. To see the light leave his pewter eyes.

Do it.

"No! Get out of my head!" I groaned, squeezing my eyes shut as I recoiled from the terrible thoughts.

Marcus laughed lowly, the guttural sound reverberating from his throat. I gritted my teeth, as I dropped my knife, clenching my fist before slugging him across the face.

"That's right, let it out. Embrace it."

I roared, hitting him again and again, blood coating his mouth more and more with each blow, but still his crazed smile remained as he watched me. I raised my fist again, the collar of his shirt clenched firmly in my other hand, my body jerking and tensing.

"Cas!" I froze at the sound of Damien's voice behind me.

I looked over my shoulder to Damien, who stood several feet from my back. Reality hit me, and I remembered where I was, what was happening.

What was I doing? My grip on Marcus' shirt loosened, the fabric slipping from my fingertips as I stumbled back. I met Damien's gaze once more. He looked pained at the sight of me, worried. My emotions churned in the pit of my stomach, and I feared I was losing all sense of who I was.

Marcus' men laid at Damien's feet, dead. I hadn't even seen Damien's fight; had forgotten he was even there with me. I'd been so absorbed in hurting Marcus that I'd become completely oblivious to everything around us.

"She's spicy, Damien." Marcus groaned as he pushed himself up, and I jerked my gaze back in time to see him brush the blood from his face. "I'd love to get her back in my room again."

Damien roared, and before I knew what was happening, he brushed past me to lash out at him. He was slower than usual, taking more hits than I expected him to, and I tensed at the sight of blood rolling down his face.

His head injury. Not only was he wounded, but he hadn't had rest in two days, had been using his magic far more than I'd seen him use before. I rushed to his side. Marcus' fist rammed into Damien's gut before he whipped around and slammed his foot into my ribs. I hit the ground, groaning at the pain echoing through my ribcage. I opened my eyes, struggling to push myself to my knees as I clenched my side where he'd kicked me, wondering if he'd broken any ribs.

Damien grabbed Marcus in his moment of distraction and slammed him up against the wall.

"Now!" Marcus yelled, and my heart dropped into the pit of my stomach. I twisted around, scanning the room. Hidden amongst the scrapped car frames at the far end of the bay, I found one of Marcus' men. I looked back, but Damien was too lost in his rage against Marcus to notice.

My brows furrowed as the guy pulled a flip lighter from his jacket pocket, and flicked the dial, sparking it to light as he hovered in the corner. Behind him laid a pile of gas cans, the flammable fluid still dripping from the spouts onto the concrete where it pooled and joined the endless trails stretching out across the shop.

The world halted.

"Stop!" I yelled, pushing myself to my feet and jolting toward him, but I wasn't fast enough. He let the lighter slip from his fingers and ran for an escape. It fell to the ground, and the moment it touched the concrete, the liquid flamed, fire surging throughout the shop around us.

The inferno split in both directions, coming for us while stretching back to the gas cans piled nearby. They exploded, the plastics blowing apart with a sound that shook the room. Fire shot up into the air in a blaze, and I fell to the floor, arms shielding my head from the debris. After a moment, I opened my eyes.

Fear carved a path through me as I sat up. I was surrounded, the flames stretching and snaking everywhere throughout the shop as it consumed everything... and me? I was trapped, cut off from Damian as he fought with Marcus, and any means of escaping the fire as it raged out of control.

The fire alarms rang out across the building, but the sprinklers didn't activate. Had Marcus orchestrated every last detail of this?

Tears welled in my eyes, my lungs failing me, and I watched in horror as Damien glanced over his shoulder, eyes widening as he found me. Marcus didn't give him the chance to pull away as he swung his knife at him. I took a step forward, but there was no way through to them, no way to help him from this distance, and the paths of fire crossed and intertwined around me.

A crash of metal caught my attention, and I looked back as Damien knocked Marcus into a stack of barrels. His head jerked to me and for a moment, the terror in his eyes made it difficult to breathe.

"Get out of here!" he yelled.

"I can't!"

Damien's eyes darted around. There were no shadows for him to use to get to me, the flames too bright with nothing to douse them, and the others were nowhere to be seen. The smoke from the burning oil singed my throat and lungs, and I coughed, the air hot around me. His eyes met mine, and he stood helpless, unable to get to me. Shadows rippled from beneath the sleeves of his coat, but they seemed to die out before they could take form, his magic exhausted.

Marcus rose slowly from the mess of barrels that Damien had just thrown him into. His eyes met mine from across the way, and something in me rose.

Hurt him.

I winced as the voice returned.

Burn him.

"No!" I gasped, clamping my hands over my ears. "Stop it!"

Do it. He deserves it.

My eyes lifted to Damien and Marcus as they collided with one another, but Damien was faltering, missing hits and taking more than he should. He wouldn't last much longer.

It would be so easy to do it.

I found myself frozen, unable to take my eyes off them as terror and fury caught me in its grip. My feet began to slide forward of its own accord, closer to the flames. Marcus knocked Damien to the ground, and the air halted in my lungs as Damien didn't get up. He twisted over onto his hands and knees, and my eyes jerked to Marcus, who had recovered fully, grabbing a broken metal pipe from the pile of junk nearby.

Make him pay. Do it now.

My hand, no longer my own, reached out into the flames, the warmth caressing my palm, lacing between my fingers. It felt as if another's hand was atop mine, guiding and pulling it away from my body. The fire flickered and licked at my skin, yet I remained unburned. I gave into the pull, stretching my hand out, my eyes closing. I should be burning, shouldn't be able to stand the heat from the intense flames snaking around the building, but it only felt as if I were basking in the sun. I opened my eyes as Marcus attacked, but Damien kicked him before recovering and rising to his feet to defend himself.

Kill him. Kill him. Kill him.

The voice was getting stronger, louder in my head, and my resistance, my denial of it, began to crumble. I begged to whatever dark thing had risen in me, as Damien stumbled.

The faintest of whispers fell from my lips, and I gave into it, my body relaxing. "Please, just save Damien."

And I no longer fought whatever it was.

My body moved involuntarily, some invisible entity coiling around my limbs, guiding me as I stepped into the fire before me. The flames sparked, rising as a great pyre around me, the power incredible and terrifying. Instinctively, I breathed deeply, as if I were inhaling it into myself, filling my lungs with the heat, the power of it.

Damien's eyes went wild when he found me, and he howled in horror. "Cassie!"

I couldn't understand what was happening as my body moved on its own, hatred consuming me, rage filling me to the brim. The only fuel that filled me now was the need to get to Marcus, to end him once and for all.

No more. No more would he torment us. No more would he torment *me*. I didn't care what happened to me in the process.

The flames enveloped me in their embrace, as the pyre flowed into me, disappearing from the ground. Heat swarmed every inch of my body, my skin burning yet not burned. My heart raced, its warning one I should heed, but I ignored it, too lost to the fury raging out of control.

Damien remained frozen as he watched me approach, all trace of fire in the building gone. Its power now dwelled within me, waiting, wanting to be unleashed, wanting to devour everything in our path.

My eyes followed Marcus as he jumped to his feet, lifting the metal pipe above his head as he charged for Damien.

"*Stop!*" The moment the word left my lips, his body went rigid, his arm falling to the side. The metal pipe slipped from his fingertips, ringing out loudly as it hit the concrete.

Marcus' gaze drifted to me, a terrified realization of what I was doing to him in his eyes. His teeth gritted, and he growled lowly. "You little bitch."

I drew closer to him, my eyes locking with his, unwavering as an uneasy calm settled over me. My steps halted when I stood between him and Damien. Something stirred in me at the sight of the blood that had seeped into the fabric of his clothes as my eyes drifted over him— the deep cuts from Damien's knife, the broken nose and busted lip I'd given him.

He hasn't had enough.

"Not nearly enough," I mused, eyes lifting to Marcus'.

Damien stood frozen at my back.

The voice grew stronger in my head, the hate, the anger, the pain he caused me swelling in my chest. It was like a choir of malice overlapping in my mind, pushing me over the ledge.

Burn him. Burn him. Burn him. BURN HIM!

My hand slid up against his chest, and I saw my skin for the first time against his bloodied shirt. Veins of hot coals stretched out across my hands and arms, and my skin glowed white. The flames I'd absorbed writhed under my flesh, and red loomed at the fringes of my sight. I couldn't control myself, couldn't stop myself.

Do it now!

His eyes locked with mine, and all that hatred and rage melted away.

He smiled…

Thank you.

Marcus' voice slipped into my mind just as I let the flames flow into him. His chest glowed white hot, and his head fell back, as a howl of agony peeled from his lips . He burned with such an intensity that before I could pull my hand from him to stop myself, he disintegrated before my eyes, ash exploding into the air around me.

I stood there a moment, silent as the haze receded. Leaving me to stand there as the weight of it all came crashing down on me.

Oh God… What had I done?

"Cassie!" Damien grabbed me, turning me to him, the fear fresh in his expression. He looked me over, his hands searching me for any burns, but I was unharmed. The flames hadn't hurt me, only moved through me.

I stood, unable to speak, unable to meet his eyes. The voice was gone, leaving no hint or trace that it had ever been there to begin with. It was only me now. I'd stopped Marcus.

No.

I'd murdered Marcus. In the cruelest of ways.

Why had he thanked me?

The blood drained from my face, my stomach twisting as the reality of what I'd just done washed over me. The sight of him burning to ash filled my min, and the sound of his agony echoed across the room, though it had long stopped. My eyes fell on my quivering hands, stained with ash and blood.

What had Marcus created in me? What had I become? I wanted to tell myself that it was to protect Damien, but I knew better.

I was a monster.

My body shook, and I lifted my eyes to him. "Damien. Something's… wrong with me. I don't know what—"

"Easy, *mea luna*. I've got you," he said and braced me when my knees threatened to buckle under me.

A nearby door swung open, and Zephyr entered, his body a mess of blood and dirt. "Damien? Gods, I'm glad we found you! What happened? We heard the explosion and Marcus' guys took off into the woods!"

My eyes darted to Zephyr, my heart swelling and deflating all at once with relief and disgust at what I must've look like, what I'd done.

Damien's eyes were pained as he stared down at me, but he turned to Zephyr. "Marcus is gone."

Zephyr's gaze shifted to me, and I couldn't meet his eyes. My stomach turned hearing Damien say those words, and I vomited on the floor. Damien whipped around to focus his attention back on me as his hand ran over my back in tender strokes. Something inside me recoiled at the affectionate touch, as if I didn't deserve the comfort.

Vincent came running in. "Guys! There're sirens headed this way! We've got to get the hell out of here!"

The room went silent, and Thalia appeared behind him. "The fuck are you waiting for? Come on!"

"*Fuck.*" Damien breathed and scooped me into his arms before taking off after them.

I couldn't speak. I could only curl into him and wish I could disappear.

CHAPTER 41

I sat curled into myself in the library, alone.

The cold temperatures of Winter's approach had crept in. The birds that had yet to migrate south pranced and sang outside the window on the branches of the maple trees. My gaze lifted to the delicate snowflakes drifting on the breeze. The first snow. It likely wouldn't stick, would only fall to melt away into nothing.

Lost in my own thoughts, I'd remained here most of the day, and the afternoon sun began to slip behind the mountains as another day came to a close. I dreaded the night, dreaded the cold emptiness the darkness brought, when the birds would leave and I would be left in the deafening quiet, alone with my own thoughts.

I'd barely slept in the last three days. The three days that had passed since Marcus had set the trap for us at the industrial complex. The three days that had passed since Damien and I fought him.

The three days since I'd murdered him.

I kept trying to tell myself I did it to save Damien, to protect him. There was no denying the terrible things that had filled my head since he'd held me in that cell, the awful things I'd wanted to do to him. How I'd wanted to hurt him like he hurt me.

Now that I'd made good on that promise...the look on his face in his final moment haunted me. The way his body crumbled into ashes, his cries of agony as the flames crawled up his throat.

He'd thanked me. Why?

The room was dark, the only source of fading light creeping in through the window where I sat. The portrait of Damien I'd drawn stared at me—the charcoal features of his face that had burned their way into my soul, the watercolor of his eyes I couldn't bring myself to meet.

The only color in my life, and I couldn't bring myself to look at it.

My phone vibrated on the nearby table, and I wondered how many texts Kat had sent me now, how many texts Mom had sent me... how many texts I'd left unread. How many times had they tried to call? What would I say? Guilt curdled in my gut, but I didn't want to talk, didn't have the energy to don the mask.

My gaze drifted over the bookshelves surrounding me, filled with all my favorite books. Under normal circumstances, I would have found the most profound joy within this room, absorbed in these endless pages. Now I didn't find happiness, only the peace that I so desperately needed.

Who was I kidding? It wasn't peace that I needed. It was a hiding place. A place where I would be alone.

I hadn't dare set foot in our bedroom since we'd returned home, couldn't even bring myself to look Damien in the eye after how cruelly I'd killed Marcus. And I hated myself for how I knew the avoidance would make him feel.

The door creaked open slowly, and quiet footsteps entered. It was Damien's angel of a servant, Ethel. It was the tenth time she'd checked on me today.

She hovered near the small table where a plate of barely touched food sat.

"Cannae ye try tae get at least a little more food down, deary?" For once, her sweet voice wasn't enough to warm me.

I couldn't bring myself to look at her. It was enough that I felt terrible for wasting the wonderful food she worked so hard to prepare. No matter how hard I tried, the second I put any food to my tongue I felt sick to my stomach. It was a feat just to get the few bites I could manage down.

"Sorry, *Mitera*. I just—" I pulled the blanket tightly around me. "I can't get it down."

She lingered a moment, but I continued to watch the birds outside the window as one by one they began to fly off for the night, leaving me in the silence... in the darkness.

Alone.

She pulled a chair from the desk over to sit down next to me. "Hev ye talked tae Lord Damien at all?"

I hesitated to speak, eyes lowering. "I can't bring myself to face him."

"Lord Damien donnae think any less o' ye." She lifted my chin to look into my eyes. "Ye shuid go tae him. He's more worried than anythin'."

"I'm... I'm such a mess. I can't stand for him to see me like this. He saw it all, saw what I did..."

"He donnae blame ye fer that, child." I sat there, silent as she took my hand, holding it tenderly. I closed my eyes, focusing on that touch, praying it could draw me out of this pit. "Ye hev tae fergive yerself. Marcus was a cruel soul. It's never easy takin' a life, but wit ye did... It 'ad tae be done."

"I know. It's just—" I couldn't find the words to express the emotions that gripped me.

She sat quietly, allowing me the room to gather myself.

My lips trembled, swollen eyes burning as tears threatened to fall again. "I wish it hadn't happened the way it did. I wish I hadn't been the one to do it."

"I kno' deary. I kno'." She leaned in and wrapped her arm around my neck. I relaxed into her embrace. The emotions I'd bottled up inside began to overflow.

And I cried into her blouse.

After an hour of coaxing and comfort, Ethel managed to convince me to come out of the library. It wasn't until after she left for the night that I summoned the courage to take her advice.

A deafening silence filled the house as I opened the door, the hinges creaking and I cringed at the noise. The house felt empty, and I wondered if Damien was here, or if he'd left to patrol with the others. I couldn't blame him for leaving, for seeking a distraction from my avoidance.

What had he thought of me the last few days? Would he be upset with me?

380

Ethel told me he hadn't left the house once since we'd returned. I wanted so desperately to hold him, to kiss him, to tend to his wounds, but I couldn't bring myself to. The thought of how he might look at me terrified me. How could I tend to and heal him when I'd done what I had? After he'd seen me in such a terrifying state.

How had I looked when I'd burned Marcus alive? Had I smiled as I did it? Would he see me differently? Would he see the monster Marcus had created?

The wood floor groaned softly despite my careful steps as I walked through the hall, and the faint crackling of the fireplace reached my ears as I neared the living room. I froze in the doorway, my heart lodging itself in my throat. It had nearly given out on me in the industrial complex, and at one point I hadn't cared, had been willing to let it stop beating if it meant killing Marcus.

How had I let myself become so consumed by my hate for him? How had I gotten to this point?

Damien sat on the couch before the fireplace, his back turned to me, and oxygen evaded me, my feet unable to take another step. My hand reached out, but I hesitated. I wanted so badly to touch him, to hold him, to kiss him. How deeply I'd longed to see those beautiful eyes I'd so desperately avoided.

Despite everything, Marcus was once his best friend. I knew he was furious with him, had wanted to end him himself for the things he'd done, but... did a part of him mourn his loss? Would he regret everything? Would he have reconsiderations that there may have been a way to reason with him? Get him help? I took a step back as the thoughts spiraled, fear and unease clouding my mind until I felt the urgency to turn and run.

His body tensed, his head lifting suddenly. He turned his head to the side, hesitating a moment, as if afraid to look over his shoulder.

What would I see in his face? His eyes? Would I see remorse? Would I see regret?

He twisted around to look at me, his eyes locking with mine, and for a moment, I couldn't breathe as a whirlpool of emotions flooded the room, too much for me to grasp onto, icy, hot, balmy, warm, cooling. What was he thinking? Everything in me screamed from the depths of my soul to go to him, to embrace him, to kiss him and soothe all his pain and sorrow, but...

I couldn't move my feet, couldn't pull myself in either direction, caught in a battle of running away and going to him.

He rose slowly, staring at me as if I were a dream, a ghost. Those beautiful amber and ashen eyes of his burned into me, as if he were afraid that if he looked away, I might vanish into thin air. I couldn't bring myself to take another step. I'd caused him so much misery over the last few days. No, over the last month. I was the source of his pain, of every ounce of misery he'd experienced since we met... since before we'd met.

I should have had him erase my memory that night, should have spared him the agony that followed, the misery that had yet to come.

As he grew closer, his eyes drifted over me, seeming to take in every detail, every bruise, every cut, scrape, and burn that still lingered on my skin... every reminder of the man I'd murdered. Faster than I was prepared, he was within reach of me, his hands coming up, stopping before he touched me.

"*Mea luna*?" Those simple words set loose a sob in my throat, my lips quivering as tears dotted my eyes, and I crumbled.

He pulled me into a deep embrace, as if I were a breath of fresh air and he'd been suffocating. I held onto him as I failed to hold the tears at bay, and he pressed his face into my hair, breathing deeply.

"I'm so sor—" He covered my mouth with his.

I grasped onto his shirt, pulling him closer to me. He only broke the kiss to cup my face, pressing his forehead against my own.

"No apologies. None," he said, his gaze darting back and forth between my eyes, and he kissed me again.

Warmth poured into me wherever our skin met, the feeling like sunlight and the feather light brush of a summer breeze. I let the sensation flood me, allowing it to drown out the sorrow that had plagued me for days. Tears rolled down my cheeks, and he only broke our kiss to hold me.

"I was afraid you would reject me if I tried to comfort you."

I lifted my eyes to him, my heart twisting at his words. His skin was pale, dark shadows looming under his eyes, and I wondered if he'd suffered as little sleep as I had. My fingers glided along the side of his face, sliding down over the overgrown stubble along his jaw.

"I was so terrified I'd lose you again, that you wouldn't want anything to do with me after everything that's happened." He lowered his head to rest his forehead atop my shoulder. His arms stretched around my waist, holding me to him.

"*Mea sol*," I said. The nickname I'd called him countless times across so many lives stirred something deep in my chest, as if it were calling to the very core of my being, the ancient soul dwelling within me.

I lifted his face to gaze into those beautiful eyes of his, seeing completion in them, my completion, a part of myself I'd longed to find but feared I never would. I'd found it... and despite everything, it was beautiful, and I longed to cherish it for whatever time I had.

"I am yours for the rest of my life," I said, tears welling in my eyes as my chest swelled. "Knowing you as I do now, there is no life I could ever live without you. I love you, so much—"

The words left my lips of their own volition and I blinked, shocked I'd said it... but I did. I loved him so much, in a way that I never thought possible.

I couldn't stop the words from coming as I said it again. "I love you, and that's probably foolish of me, and you probably think I'm naïve for saying it."

His mouth fell open as he stared down at me, shock and profound adoration filling his eyes. "You don't know how badly I've longed to hear those words. How much I've missed them... Say it again."

"I love you," I breathed.

"Again," He said, pulling me tighter against him, and I smiled, laughing as I said it again and again.

"I love you."

He kissed my cheek, the stubble of his jaw tickling me, and I wriggled in his grasp as he pulled me from the depths as he cast me in the light for which I'd named him *mea sol*. My sun.

"I love you. I love you. I love you!"

"No matter what comes our way, no matter what dangers we face, or what terrible things either of us may have to do." He took my hands, the intensity in his gaze lifting me up. "I love you. Until the end of everything. Until the sun burns up and the moon crumbles to dust. I will always love you. I will always remain at your side."

Tears spilled over my cheeks, and he kissed me deeply. I wanted to lose myself in the sensation, let it sweep me away and take me to a far-off place, far from the miseries of this world. He hooked his hands behind my knees as he lifted me and I held onto him, pulling myself so tightly against him, desperate to feel his skin. He carried me over to the couch, and my back met the cushions as he laid me down. His rich musky scent flooded the room, filling my lungs as his lips met mine once more.

His hands snaked up my shirt, and he groaned in frustration at the snugness of it caught under me. He ripped it open in his impatience, and I gasped as he lowered himself to kiss my collarbone.

A moan slipped through my lips as his hands molded against my skin, and his kisses moved up to my neck, his fangs gliding over my skin. He bit down, and my body bucked as he drank, pulling me into him. His knee slid up between my legs, and he pressed his lower half into me, grinding against me as he drank. He stopped a moment later, as if the bite was more than just taking my blood, and he kissed me once more. I could taste the faint hint of my blood on his tongue, and it sent my heart into a frenzy.

God, I wanted to feel his skin on mine, feel him inside me, and I pulled at his pants, desperate to touch him.

The front door banged open, and we both froze. Heavy footsteps came down the hall and Barrett's voice rang out. "Damien!"

Damien shot up, and I squeaked as I covered myself against the couch before Barrett came through the doorway. He froze the moment he saw us, eyes wide.

He turned away. "Fuck. Sorry, man."

"This better be fucking important," Damien growled, pushing himself up. He pulled his shirt over his head and handed it to me to

383

cover myself. I quickly took it, turning away as I slid it over my head. Just in time too, as Vincent and Zephyr entered the room.

"Shit, sorry!" Zephyr barked, and they both immediately averted their eyes.

"Well, don't just fucking stand there! What is it?" Damien barked.

Silence hung in the air, and the moment the words left Barrett's lips, my heart sank.

"Cole escaped…"

TO BE CONTINUED…

Thank you so much for taking a chance on Of Shadow and Moonlight. I hope you've enjoyed Damien and Cassie's story because book 1 only scratched the surface of everything this world and series have to offer.

I would love for you to join my reader group on discord so we can all chat about your thoughts and feelings on the Shadow and Moonlight Series. This group is the first to find out about cover reveals, books news, new releases, sneak peeks, ARC opportunities, and a way to meet other like-minded readers.

Once again, thank you so much for taking the time to read my book.

XOXO,
Luna Laurier
www.lunalaurier.com

If you enjoyed the book, please consider leaving an honest review on Goodreads & Amazon

https://www.goodreads.com/book/show/60626092-of-shadow-and-moonlight

Luna Laurier's
Taste of Darkness

Can't get enough of the Shadow and Moonlight Universe and it's characters? Join the Patreon to gain access to bonus scenes and content not in the books, bonus spicy scenes between characters (both canon and non-canon *eyes the spicy scene between Cassie, Damien, and Marcus*), NSFW artwork, ARC Team access, discounts on merch and signed books, and more!

---

www.patreon.com/lunalaurier

SHOP THE OFFICIAL MERCH STORE

LUNALAURIER.COM

Acknowledgement

A book is so much more than words on paper. Its countless hours spent planning, world building, and pouring thoughts and emotions into a physical form. It's the support and encouragement of loved ones and supporters when the imposter syndrome makes you want to quit. It's the beta readers who read through your mess of a first manuscript before it's been edited to shift through the chaos of potential plot holes, typos, and grammatical errors, to uncover the true potential of the story. It's the editors who take the time to prime and polish the story into something that is so much more magical than originally thought possible. It's the artists who craft and create the most spectacular pieces for the covers and interior that help bring the story to life. It's the ARC readers who eagerly await their copies and hype up the author, giving them that much needed boost of confidence in their work, and sharing their love of the book with others.

It's the readers who needed the story more than the author could have ever imagined.

Words cannot describe how much I appreciate all of the wonderful support and love from everyone who has had a hand in the development of this book. At 16 years, I started writing it, and when I learned how difficult it was to get a book picked up by a publishing company, I gave up. It was by some strange twist of fate that I revisited the book again when it gained a whole new life and transformed from a standalone to a more complex and intricate four-part series.

To my husband, you are my rock. You push me to pursue my dreams, and I couldn't have done with without you. You inspired the love in this story. I truly believe soulmates do exist because of you. I don't know how to explain it, but I always knew it was you, from the moment you asked me out in high school, but was patiently waiting for an answer, till someone asked if we were together, and I took your hand and said yes. I knew. I knew that you were the one I would spend my life with, even though our paths went different ways for a short time, we were brought back together by the craziest twist of fate, and I couldn't imagine having a better person at my side through this crazy journey called life. I love you.

To my son, I know how badly you wanted to read my books, I know it will be many years before you are old enough. But when you do read this, I want you to know that you are my biggest little hype man, and you fill my heart more than you realize. I love you more, sugarplum.

To my mom, you've always encouraged me to pursue my artistic passions whether its art, theatre, writing, etc. Thank you. Thank

389

you so much for doing that for me in a world where others say that art isn't a "career". I am who I am today because of you.

To my other mother, thank you for encouraging me and pushing me forward. Thank you for taking the time to read my book and always be there for me to ask any questions about your hometown. You helped bring this book to life by showing me the rich history in Johnstown, Pennsylvania. I couldn't imagine a better place for this story to take place.

To Rachel Parker, who spend so many hours on the phone and was there with me every world building step of the way even though you live clear across the country. Thank you for the spectacularly beautiful hourglasses in my story and brainstorming all the fun little Easter eggs we can fit into the story. Thank you for letting me through all sorts of crazy ideas your way as I trudged my way through the pits of book planning and design. Thank you.

To Fey, who has read this book as many times as I have and is probably just as sick of it. I'm kidding. You were there for me when I needed it most. You helped my story grow more than you probably realize. I know it wouldn't be what it is today if it wasn't for your feedback. Thank you.

To Nicole, who has been the most amazing Beta reader I could have ever asked for, who peeled back the layers and pushed me to explore my characters on such a deeper level. You helped breathe life into this story, and I cannot thank you enough for everything you have done.

To Mary Brigham, my other wonderful beta reader who inhaled my manuscript that took me years to make in one night. You crack me up, and your feedback helped me tremendously. Thank you.

To my amazing developmental editor and fellow author Natalie Cammaratta, thank you so much for all your wonderful feedback on my manuscript. I knew we were meant to be when we would cackle at book humor, and when you caught me slacking off in the comments on a random TikTok video. You've made me a much stronger writer, and I am now unable to overlook hygiene thanks to you. Your reactions as you read through my manuscript during the editing process made me cackle out loud countless times. Thank you so much for all your meticulous work on my manuscript. I cannot wait to continue through this series with you.

To my wonderful proofreader and copy editor, Alexa, you're amazing and I'm so thrilled to have had the pleasure of meeting and working you! You put the cherry on top and helped tighten the net to catch those pesky typos and grammatical errors!

To my amazing artist, Huangja. While Oceans separate us, I feel like we really connected working on the art for this project. You're so talented and amazing to work with. You really brought my characters to life, and I squealed like a fangirl every time I got an update from you. Thank you so much, I am so honored to have met you and have your beautiful work in my book and I cannot wait to work with you as the story continues!

To my fellow authors, C.J. Khemi and Kristen M. Long. Thank you so much for your encouragement and for always being there to help me if I run into an issue or have a question. You're so wonderful and I am so happy to call you friends! Thank you.

To my amazing ARC Readers! Thank you so much for all of your support and encouragement! I truly feel like I found my tribe in you all. This release would not have been possible without your support, and I cannot thank you enough.

To my amazing followers and supporters on TikTok, Instagram, and Facebook. I'm where I am now because of you. You're kind words, your encouragement, your excitement. It's propelled me forward and given me the courage and motivation to push forward and write this series.

And lastly, to my readers. Thank you for taking a chance on me. I could not have done this without you. Thank you for all your support. I am forever grateful.